Karel Čapek (Chop'-ek) (1  story writer, novelist, playwi and children's writer in C 1920s and 30s. He is best k ...u. ior his novels *War with the Newts* and *Three Novels*, and his play *R.U.R.: Rossum's Universal Robots*, which introduced the literary robot to the world back in 1921. *Tales from Two Pockets* is the fourth volume of his works to be published by Catbird Press. Please see the translator's introduction for more information about Čapek and *Tales from Two Pockets*.

Praise for *Tales from Two Pockets*

One of the Best Books of 1994. *Čapek... was able to take his mysteries to philosophical heights few in the genre aspire to.... These haunting, parable-like works reconfirm Čapek's standing as one of Czechoslovakia's most intellectually piercing literary voices.*
—Publishers Weekly

Philosophical parables about crime, guilt and justice, lightened by a sense of humor that makes them go down like candy, they constitute practically a genre of their own: Kafka meets Ellery Queen.
—Jonathan Dee, New York Newsday Fanfare

The tales are light and fresh, often funny and brimming with good will. You can't go wrong with them.
—Bettina Drew, Chicago Tribune Books

Čapek's delightfully inventive tales ... stretch the detective story to its limits and, in the process, tell us much about the mysteries of human existence.
—Katherine Ramsland, New York Times Book Review

OTHER CZECH LITERATURE IN TRANSLATION
FROM CATBIRD PRESS

TALES FROM
TWO POCKETS

by Karel Čapek

Translated from the Czech and with an introduction
by Norma Comrada

CATBIRD PRESS
A Garrigue Book

CATBIRD PRESS
16 Windsor Road, North Haven, CT 06473
800-360-2391; catbird@pipeline.com
www.catbirdpress.com

Our books are distributed to the trade by
Independent Publishers Group.

With one exception (see p. 202), all the illustrations in this
book are by Karel Čapek and his brother, Josef. None of
the illustrations were done for these stories; rather, we have
collected related drawings from a variety of their works.

See page 367 for the translator's acknowledgments.

Library of Congress Cataloging-in-Publication Data

Čapek, Karel, 1890-1938.
[Povídky z druhé kapsy. English]
Tales from two pockets / by Karel Čapek ; translated from the Czech
and with an introduction by Norma Comrada. -- 1st ed.
"Originally collected in the volumes Povídky z jedné kapsy and
Povídky z druhé kapsy in 1929"--CIP verso t.p.
"A Garrigue book."   ISBN 0-945774-25-7 : $14.95
1. Čapek, Karel, 1890-1938--Translations into English.
I. Čapek, Karel, 1890-1938. Povídky z jedné kapsy. English. 1994.
II. Comrada, Norma.   III. Title.

CONTENTS

Tales from the Other Pocket

Introduction

The Czech writer Karel Čapek (1890-1938) is best known in the English-speaking world for his plays and novels, especially for his 1920 play *R.U.R.: Rossum's Universal Robots*, which introduced the word "robot" to the world. He was also a master of the short story and a newspaper columnist, writing about literature, politics, and everything else that captured his interest.

In 1928, Čapek began publishing a new type of story in *Lidové noviny*, the widely-read newspaper for which he wrote a regular column. These tales about mysteries of all kinds surprised Čapek's friends: they knew him as a mystery reader, not as a mystery writer. He had read all the classics and contemporaries in their original languages: Chesterton, Christie, Conan Doyle, the French authors, and American authors, too — although he didn't care for the "hardboiled, blood-and-gore" American style. On his 1924 trip to England, he made a point of visiting not only Baker Street but also Dartmoor, haunt of the Baskerville hound. In 1929, Čapek's own "detective stories" were collected in two volumes: *Tales from One Pocket* and *Tales from the Other Pocket*, referred to together as "the Pocket Tales."

The late 1920s were a good time for experimenting with detective fiction. That era is now termed the Golden Age of Mystery Stories, and there was already a large body of fiction in the genre for Čapek to respond to. It was also a period of relative stability in Čapek's personal and professional life and in the life of his beloved country. Czechoslovakia had begun to move beyond the devastation wrought by World War I and the first-phase difficulties of establishing a new nation, and neither the effects of the Depression nor the rise of fascism could be foreseen. A graphoholic under any circumstances, Čapek could now indulge in writing for the pure pleasure of it.

Always interested in presenting various points of view, he found the short story a perfect form for exploring, from many sides, such themes as the nature of truth and justice, the value and the mystery of ordinary life, and the potential within each of us for a multitude of widely different but nonetheless possible lives. And alone among Čapek's enormous output of books, the Pocket Tales reflect the wide range of his personal interests, experiences, and concerns.

Crime and its causes and detection absorbed much of Čapek's attention while writing the Pocket Tales. And, as always when something captured his interest, be it crime, cacti, or Oriental carpets, he devoured all available resources on the topic. His response to an inquiry on the most interesting books he had read in 1928 was, "I don't know; but the study that most interested me this year: criminology and criminal psychology."

He was also intrigued by the idea of writing mystery stories in Czech, there being no homegrown detective-story tradition at the time. Nor, despite Jaroslav Hašek's *The Good Soldier Švejk*, was there a tradition of using everyday, conversational Czech in literature. With the Pocket Tales, Čapek broke the barrier both in his use of colloquialisms and in his style of punctuating speech. His earlier translations of modern French poets had opened doors for all subsequent generations of Czech poets; the Pocket Tales introduced a turnabout in Czech prose.

Čapek was equally intrigued by the idea of creating a different type of mystery story, one which depicted ordinary human beings caught up in highly un-ordinary, often extraordinary situations and circumstances. And, as in much of his writing, the Pocket Tales were an attempt to identify the "various roads that lead to the knowledge of truth."

Each person has a certain truth, he wrote, but it is a partial truth. We can never know the truth in its entirety, because human knowledge is limited. Even a crime, when seen from another point of view, might not be perceived as a crime at all. And even if a criminal is caught, the whole truth may never be known.

The Pocket Tales remind us that a poet's truth can be quite different from a scholar's truth; similarly, a detective's truth differs from that of a doctor, lawyer, or fortuneteller. Only relative truth is accessible to us, Čapek was saying, not absolute truth; it's just that we often tend to confuse the one with the other.

It was a horribly hot summer in Prague when Čapek began to write the Pocket Tales. He had hoped to write at the rate of one tale per day, thinking up the plots as he walked to the newspaper office and writing them down that same evening. "But thinking is hard work when you're gasping for breath like a carp," he wrote to his future wife; he would "much rather lie somewhere in the shade and groan over — no, rather than groan over, actually write the tales." In one of his letters, he remarks that he would write as long as the supply of ideas lasted; probably he would do a dozen and a half, two dozen, perhaps.

Two dozen it was, at least for *Tales from One Pocket*. But something happened halfway through their writing. "As soon as I began to occupy myself with the world of crime," Čapek said in an interview, "I became captivated almost involuntarily by the problem of justice. You will probably find the turning point in the first half of these Tales. In place of the question of how to identify and portray reality, the question of how to punish prevails." What is justice? How just is it? Who should judge? How should we punish? In an imperfect world, we are not likely to have developed perfect ways of judging and punishing. The relativity of truth is matched by the relativity of human justice.

Another switch occurs at exactly midpoint in the forty-eight tales: suddenly all the stories are being told by people other than the author. Furthermore, each storyteller's offering reminds someone else, someone apparently in the same room if not at the very same table, of yet another story. This is where *Tales from the Other Pocket* begins, and readers likely will wonder what brings such disparate types as a lawyer, a priest, a gardener, a doctor, an orchestra conductor, and an old jailbird together for a round of storytelling.

Čapek seems to have envisioned a truly pluralist mix of people who live in a pluralist, democratically-oriented society — the ideal that fueled the Czech and Slovak founders of the interwar republic. This same ideal, and the themes mentioned earlier, form the philosophical center of the trilogy of novels considered to be the high point of Čapek's literary creation, *Three Novels (Hordubal, Meteor, and An Ordinary Life)* (Catbird Press, 1990). The Pocket Tales served as a critical way station between his earlier works and his trilogy of 1933 and 1934.

Are the Pocket Tales really detective stories or are they not? In some of them, no crime has been committed at all. In others, the crime itself, or perhaps even the criminal — assuming there *is* an actual criminal — has nothing whatsoever to do with the point of the story. Sometimes there is no solution, or the solution is revealed at the very beginning, or else the solution is accidental or even irrelevant to the plot. Even the Tales which do focus on an investigation and solution to a crime are missing one or more of the principal elements of the mystery story.

The fact of the matter is that the Pocket Tales tell us much less about crime, criminals, and detection in the traditional sense than about human nature, human motivation, and the human heart and soul. Certainly techniques of detection make their appearance, but intuition, common sense, and sometimes even luck tend to prevail over more conventional methodology.

Rather, the Pocket Tales are astute psychological probes of ordinary human beings caught up in odd, or unfortunate, or funny, or moving, or improbable, or mysterious (and often criminal) goings-on. The ultimate mystery, the ultimate wonder, is that of ordinary human existence in all its variety. As Jacques Barzun wrote of the genre as a whole, "Crime is attractive but incidental." And as Flannery O'Connor wrote, "The task of the writer is to deepen the mystery rather than to resolve it."

Keep in mind, however, that Čapek not only knew everybody else's "rules" for detective fiction, but wrote a few of his own. These, along with other musings on the genre, can be found in his entertaining 1924 essay, "Holmesiana, or About Detective Stories." As to why we like such stories, he thought that reading about crime "satisfies not only our preoccupation with a suppressed, latent criminality, but also our latent and fierce proclivities for justice." Then, too, "A crime is something of a personal attack by an individual on society, and at the bottom of our hearts we are all dreadful anarchists."

Čapek also points out in "Holmesiana" that hunting is one of the oldest human instincts, and that criminals are hunted and tracked like wild animals, the very way in which Holmes stalks a herd of bank robbers. For that matter, detective stories told around the campfire are our most ancient literature, older even than cave paintings — which are themselves tales of tracking-down. The only difference, he writes, is that international hotels are our wild forests today, and banks now represent the romantic gorges through which merchants convey their treasures.

Time to go back (and forward) to the Pocket Tales, those reminders — and celebrations — of our humanity. The basic concerns informing them may well be of interest to literary researchers and critics, but everybody else simply read them when they first appeared in the newspaper, loved them, and asked for more. In a personal letter from 1928, upon learning how popular the Pocket Tales had become, Čapek said he was glad that people found them to their taste; he wasn't vain, but this time he had cooked up something people truly enjoyed, and he would be content if they gobbled them up with pleasure.

TALES FROM
ONE POCKET

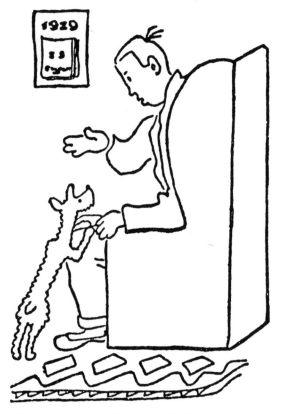

The author, drawn by his brother, Josef, the year of this
book's original publication

Dr. Mejzlik's Case

"Listen, Mr. Dastych," Detective Captain Mejzlik said pensively to the police department's shrewd old pro, "the truth of the matter is that I've come to you for advice. I have a certain case I don't know what on earth to do about."

"Out with it then," said Mr. Dastych. "Whom does the case concern?"

"Me," sighed Dr. Mejzlik. "The more I think about it, the less I understand it. You know, a person could go crazy just thinking about it."

"So who did what to you?" Mr. Dastych asked in a soothing voice.

"Nobody," Dr. Mejzlik burst out. "That's the worst part of it. I myself did something that I don't understand."

"Perhaps it's not all that bad," old Dastych consoled him. "Just what did you do, young man?"

"I caught a safecracker," Dr. Mejzlik answered gloomily.

"And that's all?"

"That's all."

"And perhaps he wasn't the right safecracker," Mr. Dastych said helpfully.

"But he was; in fact he's already confessed. He broke into the safe at the Jewish Benevolent Association; did you hear about it? His name was Rozanowski or Rosenbaum or something, from Lvov," grumbled Dr. Mejzlik. "They found the safecracking tools on him and everything."

"Well then, what would you like to know?" old Dastych encouraged him.

"I would like to know," the police captain began thoughtfully, "how it was I caught him. Wait, I'll tell you just what happened. A month ago, it was March third, I was on duty till midnight. I don't know if you remember, but it had been raining for three days straight. So I stopped in at a coffee shop for a moment, and after that I meant to go right home, to Vinohrady. But instead of that I headed in the opposite direction, toward Dlazdena Street. Tell me, please, do you have any idea why I went straight to that part of town?"

"Perhaps it was merely by chance," Mr. Dastych ventured.

"Listen, in *that* kind of weather a person doesn't drag his feet through the streets merely by chance. I'd like to know what, by all that's holy, I was doing there. What do you think, could it have been some kind of premonition? You know, something like telepathy?"

"Aha," said Mr. Dastych. "It's entirely possible."

"So you see," Dr. Mejzlik said worriedly. "There we have it. But it could also have been some kind of subconscious notion that made me drop by to see what was happening at The Three Maidens."

"That's that cheap dive on Dlazdena Street," Mr. Dastych recalled.

"Precisely. All the safecrackers and pickpockets from Pest and Halic bed down there when they come to Prague on business. We keep an eye on that place. What do you think, couldn't it have simply been ordinary police routine for me to go there and take a look around?"

"It could," declared Mr. Dastych. "Sometimes people do things like that quite automatically, especially when they feel a sense of obligation, you might say. There isn't anything strange about that."

"So I go to Dlazdena Street," Dr. Mejzlik continued, "and while I'm in the neighborhood I check the room register at The Three Maidens, and then I go on down the street. At the end of Dlazdena Street I come to a stop and I turn back again; kindly tell me, why would I have turned back again?"

"Habit," offered Mr. Dastych. "The routine habit of a patrol officer."

"Might be," the police captain agreed. "But I wasn't on duty and I wanted to go home. Maybe it was a hunch."

"There've been such cases," Mr. Dastych acknowledged. "But there's nothing mysterious about a hunch like that. After all, it's well known that people have higher powers of one kind or another . . . "

"My God," bellowed Dr. Mejzlik, "was it routine habit then, or some kind of higher power? That's what I'd like to know! — But wait: While I'm trudging along, there's some man coming toward me from the opposite direction. You'll say, why on earth shouldn't somebody be walking along Dlazdena Street at one o'clock at night, in whatever direction? There's nothing suspicious about that. I myself didn't think anything of it; but I stopped directly under the streetlight and lit a cigarette. That's what we do, you know, when we want to check out somebody at night. What do you think: was it chance, or habit, or . . . or some sort of subconscious warning?"

"I don't know," said Mr. Dastych.

"I don't either," Dr. Mejzlik shouted angrily. "Damn it all! So I'm lighting a cigarette under the streetlight and this man is coming along towards me. I wasn't even checking him out, just standing there staring at the ground. But as this fellow passed by, something started bothering me. Damn, I said to myself, there's something wrong here — but what exactly? I mean, I hadn't paid any real attention to his lordship at all. So I'm standing in the rain under the streetlight and thinking things over; and all at once it hit me: his shoes! That man had something odd on his shoes. And I'll tell you right now what it was: powder."

"What kind of powder?" asked Mr. Dastych.

"Well, *powder*. In that instant I remembered that the man had some dusty powder between the soles and the uppers of his shoes."

"And why wouldn't he have dusty powder on his shoes?" Mr. Dastych wanted to know.

"It's obvious," Dr. Mejzlik cried out. "I'm telling you, sir, in that split second I *saw*, yes, *saw* the insulating material they use in safes that gets scattered all over the floor. You know, the powder between the steel plates. And I *saw* those shoes tramping through that powder."

"That was intuition," Mr. Dastych decided. "Ingenious, but pure intuition."

"Baloney," said Dr. Mejzlik. "Man, if it hadn't been raining I wouldn't even have noticed the powder. But when it's raining, people don't usually have powder on their shoes, understand?"

"That was empirical deduction," Mr. Dastych said with certainty. "It was a brilliant inference based on experience. So what happened next?"

"Well, naturally I followed the man; he went into The Three Maidens, of course. And I telephoned for two plain-clothesmen and we raided the place; we found Mr. Rosenbaum there along with his powder and his safecracking tools and twenty thousand from the Jewish Benevolent Association's safe. The rest of it doesn't matter. But you know, the newspapers said that this time our police demonstrated considerable preparedness — what a lot of baloney! Believe me, if I hadn't by chance gone to Dlazdena Street and by chance noticed the shoes on that crook . . . What I mean is," Dr. Mejzlik said dispiritedly, "if it really was only by chance. That's the problem."

"It makes no difference whatsoever," stated Mr. Dastych. "Young man, it was an achievement for which you should be congratulated."

"Congratulated!" Dr. Mejzlik exploded. "Why should I be congratulated when I don't know what for? For my incredible shrewdness as a detective? For automatic, routine police work? For pure luck? For some sort of intuition or telepathy? Look, this was my first big case; a person has to have something to build on, right? Say that tomorrow they assign me some sort of murder; Mr. Dastych, what will I do? Am I supposed to run around the streets peering shrewdly at people's shoes? Or just go about my business and wait for some hunch or inner voice to lead me straight to the murderer? That's it, you see, that's my situation. Now the whole police force is saying: that Mejzlik, he's got a real flair; that young fellow with the glasses is going to go places with his talents as a detective. It's an awful situation, no doubt about it," Dr. Mejzlik muttered. "A person's got to have *some* kind of method. Until I had my first case, I believed in all manner of exact methods; you know, like careful observation, expertise, systematic investigation, and similar nonsense. But after dealing with this case, I see that — Listen," he blurted out with relief, "I think it was nothing but chance."

"It looks that way," said Mr. Dastych prudently. "But there was also a bit of solid observation involved and a certain amount of logic."

"And mechanical routine," the young policeman added despondently.

"And intuition. And also something of a talent for hunches. And instinct."

"Jesus Christ," moaned Dr. Mejzlik. "See what I mean? So what am I supposed to do now, Mr. Dastych?"

" — Dr. Mejzlik, you're wanted on the telephone," the waiter announced. "Police headquarters."

"Here we go," Dr. Mejzlik murmured in alarm; and when he returned to the table, he looked pale and tense. "*Check*, please," he called out irritably. "It's already started. They found some foreigner murdered in a hotel. *Damn*, if only — " and he left. It seemed that the resolute young man had a bad case of butterflies.

The Blue Chrysanthemum

"Well, I'll tell you," said old Fulinus, "how Klara comes into this story. I was in charge of the gardens on Prince Lichtenberg's estate in Lubenic in those days — that old prince, mister, he was a real connoisseur; he had Veitsche send whole trees from England, and he brought in seventeen thousand bulbs specially from Holland — but that's beside the point. One Sunday, then, I'm going down the street in Lubenic and I meet up with Klara; that was the village idiot, you know, deaf and dumb, a crazy, simple-minded fool of a girl who wandered all over, braying as cheerful as can be — can you tell me, mister, why these idiots are so blessed cheerful? Anyway, I was trying to dodge her, so she wouldn't slobber me with a kiss, when all of a sudden I caught sight of a bunch of flowers in her paws. She had some dillweed and other such stuff from the fields, but in amongst them, mister — I've seen a lot of things, but this one really bowled me over. I tell you, that crazy girl had one pompon chrysanthemum in her nosegay that was *blue*! Blue, sir! It was just as blue as *Phlox laphami;* a little slate tinge to it, with satiny, rosy edges and a center like *Campanula turbinata*, beautifully full, but all that's the least of it: mister, that blue color was then and is still to this very day absolutely unknown in chrysanthemums! Two years ago I was with old Veitsche, you know, and Sir James was bragging to me about how, the year before, one of their chrysanthemums, this import straight from China, had bloomed a speck lilac in color, but unfortunately it died on them over the winter. And here in the claws of that cackling rattlebrain was a chrysanthemum as blue as you could ever hope to see. Right.

"So here was this Klara, mooing cheerfully and shoving her

bunch of flowers at me. I gave her a little coin from my change, pointed to the chrysanthemum, and said, 'Klara, where'd you get this?' Klara cackled and snorted, just as pleased as could be, but I didn't get anything more out of her. I hollered at her, pointed with my hands, but it was no use; no matter what, she was going to throw her arms around me. I took that blue chrysanthemum and went straight to the old prince: 'Your Highness, here's what's growing somewhere nearby; let's go find it.' The old prince immediately ordered a coach so we could take Klara with us. But in the meantime Klara had gone off somewhere and couldn't be found. We stood there by the rig, swearing for a good hour — His Highness used to be with the dragoons. We were still at it when Klara dashed up with her tongue lolling out and jammed a whole bunch of fresh blue chrysanthemums at me, torn right off the bush. The prince whipped out a bill for her then and there, but Klara started boohooing with disappointment; poor thing, she didn't know about paper money. I had to give her a coin to quiet her down. Then she started dancing around and shrieking, but we set her up on the driver's box, pointed to the blue chrysanthemums, and said, 'Klara, take us there!'

"Klara whooped with glee up there on the box; you can't imagine how his High and Mightiness the coachman was horrified at having to sit next to her. Besides which, the horses would skitter every time she squealed and cock-a-doodled, oh, I'll tell you, it was the devil's own ride. After we'd been going for an hour and a half I said, 'Your Highness, we've already covered at least eight miles.'

" 'No matter,' muttered the prince, 'a hundred miles if need be.'

" 'All right,' I said, 'I'm all for it, but Klara brought back that second bouquet inside of an hour. That place can't be more than two miles from Lubenic.'

" 'Klara,' cries the prince, pointing to the blue chrysanthemums, 'where do these grow? Where did you find them?'

"Klara croaked and gurgled and pointed still further ahead; probably she liked riding up there on the coach. You know, I thought the prince was going to kill her; dear Jesus, that man could carry on! Lather was dripping off the horses, Klara was cackling, the prince was cursing, the driver only by some miracle kept from sobbing in shame, and I was working out a strategy for tracking down that blue chrysanthemum. 'Your Highness,' says I, 'this isn't going to work. We'll have to look without Klara. We've got to mark out a two-mile area on the map, divide it up into sections, and have a house-to-house search.'

" 'My God,' says the prince, 'there isn't a single park within two miles of Lubenic!'

" 'That's all right,' says I. 'The devil of a lot you'll find in a park, unless you're looking for ageratum or canna. Look, down here on the stalk is a bit of soil; that's not humus, it's a greasy, yellowish clay, most likely fertilized by human whatchamacallit. We've got to look for a place where there's plenty of pigeons; there's lots of pigeon droppings on these leaves. And most likely this grows by a fence made from peeled stakes, because here at the leafstalk is a chip of fir bark. That's our clue, right there.'

" 'What do you mean?' says the prince.

" 'What I mean,' says I, 'is that we have to look around every shed and shanty within an area of two miles. We'll break up into four search parties: you, me, your gardener, and my helper, Vencl, and that's that.'

"Well then, next morning the first thing that happened was that Klara brought me another bouquet of blue chrysanthemums. I searched all over my section after that: I drank warm beer at every local pub, ate homemade cheeses, and asked people about blue chrysanthemums. Mister, don't ask me what kind of diarrhea I got from those cheeses; it was hot, the way it some-times gets at the end of September, and I made it into every little farmhouse and had to put up with every kind of rudeness, because people thought that I was either crazy, or a salesman, or somebody from the government. But one thing was clear by nighttime: there was no blue chrysanthemum growing in my section. There wasn't any in the other three, either. Yet Klara

brought me one more broken-off branch of blue chrysanthemums.

"You know, a prince is an important person, however you
look at it. He called in detectives, put blue chrysanthemums in
their hands, and promised them I-don't-know-what if they could
show him where they grew. Detectives, mister, are educated
people; they read newspapers and the like; besides, they know
every trick and stick and they have enormous influence. Think of
it, mister: on that day there were six detectives plus ordinary
policemen, the city council, school kids with their teachers, and
even a band of gypsies prowling over that whole patch of land
inside the two-mile circle, and they tore up everything in bloom
and brought it to the manor. Great heavens, it was like Corpus
Christi Day; but as to blue chrysanthemums, there wasn't a one.
We had to keep an eye on Klara all day long; she took off in the
evening, though, and then after midnight she brought me a
whole armful of blue chrysanthemums. Straightaway we shut her
up in jail so she wouldn't yank them all up, but we'd come to a
dead end. I must say, it was mystifying; just imagine, an area no
bigger than the palm of your hand —

"Listen, a man has a right to get nasty when he's in terrible
need or when he meets up with failure; I know that. But when
His Highness told me in a fury that I was as big an idiot as
Klara, I told him straight out that I wasn't going to let an old
cretin like him talk to me that way, and I left right then and
there for the train station, and I haven't been back to Lubenic
since. But after I was seated in the carriage and the train began
to move, I tell you, mister, I broke down and cried like a child,
because I wouldn't see that blue chrysanthemum and I was leaving it behind for good. And then, while I was blubbering and
looking out the window, right there by the tracks I see something blue. Mister, it was stronger than I was: it tossed me up
out of my seat and made me pull the emergency brake — I didn't
have a thing to do with it. The train jolted when it braked, and
I got thrown down on the seat opposite — I broke this finger,
too. And when the conductor came running, I stammered about

how I'd forgotten something in Lubenic, and I had to pay a hell of a fine. Mister, I swore like a sergeant all the time I was limping back along the tracks to where that blue was. You block-head, I told myself, it's probably nothing but an autumn aster or some other worthless trash, and you've just thrown away a heathenish sum of money! I'd gone maybe fifteen hundred feet; already I was thinking that that blue couldn't have been so far back, that I must have gone past it, or at least so it seemed to me, when up on this small bank I spy a little railway guard's house, and there, peeking through the stake fence around the garden plot, is that blue. It was two clumps of blue chrysanthe-mums.

"Mister, even a child knows what those railway guards grow in their garden plots. Besides cabbages and cucumbers, there's usually sunflowers, a couple of red rosebushes, hollyhocks, tropaeolum, and some of those dahlias. But this fellow, he didn't even have that; only potatoes, beans, one black elderberry and, there in the corner, those two blue chrysanthemums.

" 'Say, mister,' says I across the fence, 'where'd you get those posies?'

" 'Those blue ones?' the watchman says. 'Why, those were left here after Cermak died; that was the guard here before me. But you can't walk on the tracks, mister. There's the sign: Walking on the Tracks is Forbidden. What are you doing here?'

" 'Friend,' I tell him, 'I thank you, and how do I get to where you are?'

" 'By way of the tracks,' he says to that. 'But nobody's allowed to walk on the tracks. What do you want? Get out of here, you damned tramp, but keep your feet off of those tracks!'

" 'How then,' says I, 'do I get out of here?'

" 'Who cares,' yells the guard, 'but not on the tracks, and that's that!'

"So I sit down by the edge of the track and I say, 'Listen, grandpa, sell me those blue posies.'

" 'I'm not selling,' grumped the guard. 'And get out of here now! You aren't supposed to sit there.'

" 'Why not?' says I. 'Where does it say I can't sit here? Walking's forbidden, but I'm not walking.'

"The guard pulled up short at that and had to be content with cussing at me over the fence. But he must have been a hermit; after a minute he quit and began talking to himself. Then half an hour later, he stepped out to have a look at the rails again.

" 'Well then,' he says as he stops beside me, 'are you getting out of here now or not?'

" 'I can't,' says I. 'Walking on the tracks is forbidden, and there's no other way to get out of here.'

"The guard thought it over for a while. Then he said, 'I'll tell you what. When I go down behind this bank, you take off along the tracks and I won't see you.'

"I thanked him heartily, and when he was gone I crept over the fence to his little garden and with his own spade I dug up both those blue chrystanthemums. I stole them, mister. I'm an honest man and I've only stolen seven times in my life; and always it was flowers.

"One hour later I was seated in the train taking those stolen blue chrysanthemums home. As I was riding past the guard's house, there he stood with his little flag, looking sour as the devil. I waved my hat at him, but I don't think he recognized me.

"There you have it, mister: there was that sign with Walking on the Tracks Is Forbidden written on it, and nobody, not us, not the policemen, not the gypsies, not even the kids figured they could go there looking for blue chrysanthemums. What power there is in a warning sign, mister! For all I know, there may be blue primroses growing in some railway guard's little garden, or the tree of knowledge or pure gold ferns; but nobody ever discovers them because walking on the tracks is strictly forbidden and that's that. Only crazy Klara went there, because she was an idiot and didn't know how to read.

"That's why I gave those blue chrysanthemums the name of Klara. I've been babying them for fifteen years now. But most likely I'm too fussy about proper soil and moisture — for sure that barbarian of a guard never watered them, he had clay hard as iron there in his garden. Well, in short, they come up for me in the spring, they develop a fungus in the summer, and they peter out by August. Think about it: I'm the only one in the world with a blue chrysanthemum, but I can't prove it. Oh, Bretagne and Anastasia, sure, they're a bit purplish; but Klara, mister, once Klara blooms for me, the whole world will talk of nothing else."

The Fortuneteller

Anyone who is knowledgeable about such things will agree that this story could never have taken place in Czechoslovakia nor in France nor in Germany, for in those countries, as is well known, judges are obliged to try sinners and punish them in accordance with the letter of the law, rather than in accordance with their own discretion and conscience. Because in this story a judge pronounces his verdict not on the basis of statutes, but on the basis of common sense, the following incident could not have taken place anywhere but in England; in fact, it took place in London, more precisely in Kensington; or, wait a moment, it was in Brompton or Bayswater; in short, there somewhere. The judge was Mr. Justice Kelley, and the woman's name was, quite simply, Myers. Mrs. Edith Myers.

The next thing you should know is that this otherwise quite respectable lady caught the attention of Police Superintendent MacLeary. "My dear," Mr. MacLeary said to his wife one evening, "I cannot get that Mrs. Myers out of my mind. I'd certainly like to know how the woman makes her living. Imagine, she's just sent her maid out, in February, for asparagus! Further- more, I've discovered that she has from twelve to twenty visitors every day, from pushcart vendors to duchesses. I know, dear girl, you'll say she's probably a fortuneteller. Well and good, but that could just be a cover for something else, for procuring, say, or espionage. Do go have a look, because I'd like to know."

"Well and good, Bob," said the excellent Mrs. MacLeary, "leave it to me."

And so it was that the next day Mrs. MacLeary, without her wedding ring of course and, on the contrary, very girlishly dressed and curled like a young woman who ought to have left such foolishness behind her long ago, with a nervous look on her baby face, rang the bell at Mrs. Myers' door in Bayswater or Marylebone. She had to wait for several moments before Mrs. Myers admitted her.

"Be seated, dear child," the old lady said once she had thoroughly scrutinized her shy visitor. "What is it you wish of me?"

"I," Mrs. MacLeary stammered, "I . . . I'd like . . . tomorrow is my twentieth birthday . . . I'd like awfully much to know my future."

"But, Miss . . . er, your name, please?" asked Mrs. Myers, and she seized a pack of cards, which she began shuffling briskly.

"Jones," Mrs. MacLeary gasped.

"Dear Miss Jones," Mrs. Myers continued, "there has been a mistake; I don't practice fortunetelling, except of course now and then, out of friendship, as every old woman does. Take the cards in your left hand and divide them into five piles. That's right. Sometimes I read the cards for amusement, but apart from that — Look!" she exclaimed, turning over the first pile. "Diamonds. That means money. And the jack of hearts. This is a beautiful spread."

"Ah," said Mrs. MacLeary. "And what else?"

"Jack of diamonds," announced Mrs. Myers, uncovering the second pile. "Ten of spades, those are journeys. But here," she cried, "we have clubs. Clubs are always challenges, but the queen of hearts is on the bottom."

"What does that mean?" Mrs. MacLeary asked, opening her eyes as wide as she could.

"Diamonds again," Mrs. Myers mused over the third pile. "Dear child, much money awaits you; but I still don't know whether it is you who will go on a longish journey or someone close to you."

"I have to go see my auntie in Southampton," Mrs. MacLeary offered.

"That will be a fairly long journey," Mrs. Myers said, turning over the fourth pile. "Someone will stand in your way, some older man — "

"Probably Daddy," exclaimed Mrs. MacLeary.

"Well then, there we have it," Mrs. Myers stated ceremoniously over the fifth pile. "Dear Miss Jones, that was the most beautiful hand I have ever seen. Within the year you will be married; a very, very rich young man will marry you, probably a millionaire or a wealthy businessman, because he travels a great deal; but before this can happen, you must overcome great obstacles; an older man will stand in your way, but you must persevere. After you marry, you will move very far away from here, probably overseas. I charge one guinea, for the Christian mission among the unfortunate blacks."

"I'm so grateful to you," Mrs. MacLeary said, taking a pound note and a shilling from her purse, "so awfully grateful! Please, Mrs. Myers, how much would it cost without all those challenges?"

"The cards cannot be bought off," the old lady remarked with dignity. "What does your daddy do?"

"He's with the police," the young lady lied with an innocent face. "He's in the detective division."

"Aha," said the old lady, and she extracted three cards from the piles. "This looks very nasty, very nasty. Tell him, dear child, that great danger threatens him. He should come to me to find out more about it. Many people from Scotland Yard come to me, you know, to read the cards for them; and they tell me everything that is in their hearts. Yes indeed, just send him along to me. You say that he's with the detective division? Mr. Jones? Tell him I'll be expecting him. Goodbye, dear Miss Jones. Next, please!"

*   *   *

"I don't like the looks of this," Mr. MacLeary declared, rubbing the back of his neck reflectively. "I don't like the looks of this, Katie. That woman was much too interested in your dear departed father. Besides that, her name isn't Myers but Meierhofer, and she's from Lubeck. Damned German," growled Mr. MacLeary, "I wonder how we can get our hands on her. I'd lay five-to-one odds she worms things out of people that are none of her business. Tell you what, I'm going to talk to the head office about this."

Mr. MacLeary did indeed talk to the head office about this; oddly enough, the head office gave the matter its serious attention, and so it happened that the worthy Mrs. Myers was summoned before Mr. Justice Kelley.

"Well, Mrs. Myers," the judge said to her, "what in God's name is all this about your telling fortunes with cards?"

"Good heavens, sir," the old lady said, "surely one must earn one's living somehow. At my age I'm not going to dance in the follies."

"Hm," said Mr. Justice Kelley. "But the charge against you is that you read the cards improperly. My dear Mrs. Myers, that is the same as if you had packaged mud bars and sold them as chocolate. For the price of one guinea, people have a right to accurate predictions. Tell me, please, how can you predict the future when you don't know the proper way to do it?"

"Not everyone complains," the old lady replied defensively. "You see, I predict things that people like to hear. That pleasure, sir, is well worth a shilling or two. And sometimes you actually hit it right on the button. 'Mrs. Myers,' this one woman said to me the other day, 'nobody, but nobody reads the cards and counsels me as well as you do.' She lives in St. John's Wood and is divorcing her husband."

"Wait," the judge cut in. "We have a witness for the prosecution here. Mrs. MacLeary, tell us what happened."

"Mrs. Myers explained," Mrs. MacLeary began glibly, "that the cards said I would be married within the year, that a very rich young man would marry me, and that I would go live with him overseas — "

"Why overseas, exactly?" asked the judge.

"Because there was a ten of spades in the second pile; that means journeys," Mrs. Myers said."

"Rubbish," rumbled the judge. "The ten of spades means expectations. Journeys are the jack of clubs; when the seven of diamonds turns up with it, it means a great deal of travel resulting in profit. Don't try to hoodwink me, Mrs. Myers. You told the witness that within the year she would marry a rich young man, but Mrs. MacLeary has already been married for three years to the excellent Police Superintendent MacLeary. Mrs. Myers, how do you account for this rubbish?"

"Oh, dear," the old lady said placidly, "this does happen from time to time. This young creature came to me all decked out in frills and flounces, but her left glove was torn; so she doesn't have any money to spare, but she does like to be stylish. She said she was twenty years old, but now it turns out she's twenty-five — "

"Twenty-four," Mrs. MacLeary burst out.

"That makes no difference; at any rate, she wanted to get married — that is, she passed herself off as a Miss. That's why I read the cards for a wedding and a rich husband; it seemed to me that fit the circumstances best."

"What about those challenges, that older man, and the trip overseas?" asked Mrs. MacLeary.

"So there would be more to it," Mrs. Myers replied candidly. "For one guinea a person should include the whole works."

"That's enough," the judge said. "It's no use, Mrs. Myers, your fortunetelling is sheer humbug. One must understand the cards. There are various theories, it's true, but never, and bear this in mind, never does the ten of spades mean journeys. You will pay a fine of fifty pounds, just as do those who adulterate food or sell worthless merchandise. You are also suspected, Mrs. Myers, of engaging in espionage; but I doubt you'll confess to that."

"As God is my witness," Mrs. Myers cried out, but Mr. Justice Kelley interrupted her: "Come, come, we'll disregard that; but because you are an alien without regular employment, the authorities will exercise their rights and order you to leave the country. Godspeed, Mrs. Myers; thank you, Mrs. MacLeary. But let me tell you, this fraudulent telling of fortunes is a cynical and unscrupulous business. Remember that, Mrs. Myers."

"What will I do?" the old lady sighed. "Just when business was starting to pick up — "

A year later or so, Judge Kelley ran into Police Superintendent MacLeary. "Lovely weather," the judge said pleasantly. "And how is Mrs. MacLeary?"

Mr. MacLeary glanced up with a sour expression. "The thing is . . . you know, Mr. Kelley," he said with some embarrassment, "Mrs. MacLeary . . . the thing is, we're divorced."

"Go on," the judge said in astonishment. "Such a nice young lady!"

"Quite so," Mr. MacLeary grumbled, "but some young good-for-nothing suddenly lost his head over her . . . some millionaire businessman from Melbourne . . . I tried to stop her, but . . . " Mr. MacLeary threw out his hands in despair. "Last week the two of them sailed for Australia."

The Clairvoyant

"You know, Mr. DA," Mr. Janowitz pontificated, "I'm not an easy person to fool; after all, I'm not a Jew for nothing, right? But what this fellow does is simply beyond belief. It isn't just graphology, it's — I don't know what. Here's how it works: you give him someone's handwriting in an unsealed envelope; he never even looks at the writing, just pokes his fingers inside the envelope and feels the handwriting all over; and all the while his face is twisting as if he were in pain. And before very long he starts telling you about the nature of the writer, but he does it in such a way that — well, you'd be dumbfounded. He pegs the writer perfectly, down to the last detail. I gave him an envelope with a letter from old Weinberg in it; he had Weinberg figured out in no time, even that he has diabetes and that he had to file for bankruptcy. What do you say to that?"

"Nothing," the district attorney said drily. "Maybe he knows old Weinberg."

"But he never even once looked at the handwriting," Mr. Janowitz protested. "He says every person's handwriting has its own aura, and he says that you can feel it, clearly and precisely. He says it's purely a physical phenomenon, like radio. This isn't some kind of swindle, Mr. DA; this Prince Karadagh doesn't make a penny from it. He's supposed to be from a very old family in Baku, according to what this Russian told me. But I'll tell you what, come see for yourself; he'll be in town this evening. You must come."

"Listen, Mr. Janowitz," the DA said, "this is all very nice, but I only believe fifty percent of what foreigners say, especially when I don't know how they make their living; I believe Russians even less, and fakirs less than that; but when on top of everything else the man's a prince, then I don't believe one word of it. Where did you say he learned this? Ah yes, in Persia. Forget it, Mr. Janowitz; the whole Orient's a fraud."

"But Mr. DA," Mr. Janowitz said defensively, "this young fellow explains it all scientifically; no magic tricks, no mysterious powers, I'm telling you, strictly scientific method."

"Then he's an even bigger phony," the DA admonished him. "Mr. Janowitz, I'm surprised at you; you've managed to live your entire life without strictly scientific methods, and here you are embracing them wholesale. Look, if there were something to it, it would have been known long ago, right?"

"Well," Mr. Janowitz replied, a little shaken, "but when I saw with my own eyes how he figured out everything about old Weinberg! Now, there's genius for you. I'll tell you what, Mr. DA, come and have a look for yourself; if it's a hoax you'll know it, that's your speciality, sir; nobody can put one over on you, Mr. DA."

"Hardly," the DA said modestly. "All right, I'll come, Mr. Janowitz, but only to keep an eye on your phenomenon's fingers. It's a shame that people are so gullible. But you mustn't tell him who I am; wait, I'll bring along some handwriting in an envelope for him, something special. Count on it, friend; I'll prove he's a phony."

You should understand that the district attorney (or, more accurately: chief public prosecutor Dr. Klapka) would, in his next court proceeding, be trying the case against Hugo Müller, who was charged with premeditated murder. Mr. Hugo Müller, millionaire industrialist, had been accused of insuring his younger brother Ota for a large sum of money and then drowning him in the lake at a summer resort; in addition to this, he had also, during the previous year, been under suspicion of dispatching his lover, but of course that had not been proven. In short, it was a major trial, which the district attorney wanted to be the making of his career; and he had labored over the trial documents with all the persistence and acumen that had made him a most formidable prosecutor. It was not an open-and-shut case; the district attorney would have given God-knows-what for one particle of direct evidence; but as things stood, he would have to rely more on his winning way with words to get the jury to award him a rope for Mr. Müller; you must understand that, for prosecutors, this is a point of honor.

Mr. Janowitz was a bit flustered that evening. "Dr. Klapka," he announced in muffled tones, "this is Prince Karadagh; well, let's get started."

The DA cast probing eyes on the exotic creature; he was a young and slender man with eyeglasses, the face of a Tibetan monk, and delicate, thievish hands. Fancy-pants quack, the district attorney decided.

"Mr. Karadagh," Mr. Janowitz jabbered, "over here by this little table. There's already some mineral water here. Please, switch on that little floor lamp; we'll turn off the overhead light so it won't disturb you. There. Please, gentlemen, there should be silence. Mr. — eh, Mr. Klapka here brought some handwriting of some sort; if Mr. Karadagh would be so good as to — "

The district attorney cleared his throat briefly and seated himself so as best to observe the clairvoyant. "Here is the handwriting sample," he said, and he took an unsealed envelope from his breast pocket. "If I may — "

"Thank you," the clairvoyant said impassively. He took hold of the envelope and, with his eyes closed, turned it over in his fingers. Suddenly he shuddered, twisting his head. "Curious," he muttered, and he took a gulp of water. He then inserted his slim fingers into the envelope and suddenly stopped; his pale yellow face seemed to turn paler still.

There was such a silence in the room that a slight rattling could be heard from Mr. Janowitz, for Mr. Janowitz suffered from goiter.

The thin lips of Prince Karadagh trembled and contorted as if his fingers were clenching a red-hot iron, and sweat broke out on his forehead. "I cannot endure this," he hissed in a constricted voice; he extracted his fingers from the envelope, rubbed them with a handkerchief, and quickly moved them back and forth over the tablecloth, as one sharpens a knife, after which he sipped agitatedly from his glass of water and then cautiously took the envelope between his fingers again.

"The man who wrote this," he began in a parched voice, "the man who wrote this . . . There is great strength here, but a — (obviously he was searching for a word) a strength that lies in wait. This lying in wait is terrible," he cried out, and dropped the envelope on the table. "I would not want this man as my enemy!"

"Why?" the district attorney could not refrain from asking. "Is he guilty of something?"

"Don't question me," the clairvoyant said. "Every question gives a hint. I only know that he could be guilty of anything at all, of great and terrible deeds. There is astonishing determination here . . . for success . . . for money . . . This man would not scruple over the life of a fellow creature. No, this is not an ordinary criminal; a tiger also is not a criminal, a tiger is a great lord. This man would not be capable of low trickery, but thinks of himself as ruling over human lives. When he is on the prowl, he sees people only as prey. And kills them."

"Beyond good and evil," the district attorney murmured with unmistakable approval.

"Those are only words," Prince Karadagh said. "No one is beyond good and evil. This man has his own strict concept of morality; he is in debt to no one, he does not steal, he does not lie; if he kills, it is as if he checkmated in a game of chess. It is his game, but he plays it squarely." The clairvoyant wrinkled his brow in concentration. "I don't know what it is. I see a large lake and a motor boat on it."

"And what else?" the district attorney burst out, scarcely breathing.

"There is nothing else to see; it is extremely hazy. It is so strangely hazy compared with that brutal and ruthless determination to bring down his prey. But there is no passion in it, only reason. A thoroughly rational contemplation of every detail. As if he were solving some technical problem or mental exercise. No, this man feels no remorse. He is so confident of himself, so self-assured; he has no fear even of his own conscience. I have the impression of a man who looks down on all from above; he is conceited in the extreme and self-congratulatory; it pleases him that people fear him." The clairvoyant sipped his water. "But he is also a hypocrite. At heart, an opportunist who would like to astound the world with his actions — Enough. I am tired. I do not like this man."

"Listen, Janowitz," the district attorney flung out excitedly, "he is truly astonishing, this clairvoyant of yours. What he described is a perfect likeness. A strong and ruthless man who views people only as prey; the perfect player of his own game; a brain who plans his moves with pure rationality and no remorse; a gentleman yet also a hypocrite. Mr. Janowitz, this Karadagh did him one-hundred percent justice!"

"You don't say," said the flattered Mr. Janowitz. "Didn't I tell you? That letter was from Schliefen, the textile man from Liberec, right?"

"It most certainly was not," exclaimed the district attorney. "Mr. Janowitz, it was a letter from a murderer."

"Imagine that," Mr. Janowitz marveled. "And I thought it was Schliefen; he's a real crook, that Schliefen."

"No. It was a letter from Hugo Müller, the fratricide. Do you remember how that clairvoyant talked about a boat on a lake? Müller threw his brother off that boat into the water."

"Imagine that," said Mr. Janowitz, astonished. "You see? That is a fabulous talent, Mr. DA!"

"Unquestionably," the district attorney declared. "The way he grasped Müller's true nature and the motives behind his actions, Mr. Janowitz, is simply phenomenal. Not even I could have hit the mark with Müller so precisely. And this clairvoyant found it out by feeling a few lines of Müller's handwriting — Mr. Janowitz, there's something to this; there must be some sort of special aura or something around people's handwriting."

"What did I tell you?" Mr. Janowitz said triumphantly. "If you would be so kind, Mr. District Attorney, I've never seen the handwriting of a murderer."

"With pleasure," said the district attorney, and he took the envelope from his pocket. "It's an interesting letter, besides," he added, removing the paper from the envelope, and suddenly his face changed color. "I . . . Mr. Janowitz," he blurted out, somewhat uncertainly, "this letter is a court document; it is . . . I'm not allowed to show it to you. Please forgive me."

A moment later the district attorney was hurrying homeward, not even noticing that it was raining. I'm an ass, he told himself bitterly, I'm a fool, how could that have happened to me? I'm an idiot! That in my haste I grabbed not Müller's letter but my own handwriting, my notes for the trial, and shoved them in that envelope! I'm an imbecile! So that was *my* handwriting! Thanks very much! Watch out, you swindler, I'll be lying in wait for you!

But all in all, the district attorney reflected, to be sure, what the clairvoyant had said wasn't so bad, for the most part. Great strength; astonishing determination, if you please; I'm not capable of low trickery; I have my own strict concept of morality — As a matter of fact it's quite flattering. That I feel no remorse? Thank God, I have no reason to: I merely discharge my obligations. And as for the rational contemplation, that's also true. But as for being a hypocrite, he's mistaken. It's still nothing but a hoax.

Suddenly he paused. It stands to reason, he told himself, what that clairvoyant said can be applied to anyone at all! These are only generalities, nothing more. Everyone's a bit of a hypocrite and opportunist. That's the whole trick: to speak in such a way that anyone could be identified. That's it, the district attorney decided, and opening his umbrella he proceeded home at his usual energetic pace.

"My God!" groaned the presiding judge, stripping off his gown, "seven o'clock already; it did drag on again! When the district attorney spoke for two hours — but, dear colleague, he won it; to get the rope on such weak evidence, I'd call that success. Well, you never know with a jury. But he spoke skillfully," the presiding judge granted, washing his hands. "Mainly in the way he dealt with Müller's character, that was a fullfledged portrait; you know, the monstrous, inhuman nature of a murderer — it left you positively shaken. Remember how he said, 'This is no ordinary criminal; he isn't capable of low trickery, he neither lies nor steals; and if he murders a man, he does it as calmly as checkmating in a game of chess. He does not kill from passion, but from cold, rational contemplation, as if he were solving some technical problem or mental exercise.' It was very well spoken, my friend. And something else: 'When he is on the prowl, he sees his fellow creatures only as prey' — you know, that business about the tiger was perhaps a bit theatrical, but the jury liked it."

"Or," the associate judge added, "the way he said, 'Clearly this murderer has no remorse; he is so confident of himself, so self-assured — he has no fear even of his own conscience.'"

"Or then again," the presiding judge continued, wiping his hands with a towel, "the psychological observation that the murderer is a hypocrite and an opportunist who would like to astound the world with his actions — "

"That Klapka," the associate judge said appreciatively. "He's a dangerous adversary."

"Hugo Müller found guilty by twelve votes," the presiding judge marveled. "Who would have thought it! Klapka got him after all. For him it's like a hunt or a game of chess. He is totally consumed by his cases — My friend, I wouldn't want to have him as my enemy."

"He likes it," the associate judge replied, "when people fear him."

"A touch complacent, that's him," the presiding judge said thoughtfully. "But he has astonishing determination . . . chiefly for success. A great strength, friend, but — " The appropriate words failed him. "Well, let's go have dinner."

The Mystery of Handwriting

"Rubner," said the editor-in-chief, "go have a look at that graphologist, Jensen. He's giving a performance for the press crowd tonight; they say he's really something phenomenal, this Jensen. Then write me fifteen lines about it."

"Right," muttered Rubner, with the reluctance appropriate to his calling.

"And make sure it isn't some kind of swindle," the editor stressed emphatically. "As far as possible, I want it checked personally. That's why I'm sending you, an old hand — "

" — — and so, gentlemen, these are the basic principles of the science properly called psychometric graphology." Thus Jensen concluded his theoretical explanation to the press that evening. "As you see, the entire system is built upon purely empirical conclusions; although, to be sure, the practical application of the precise method is so immensely complex that I can't give a more detailed demonstration in this one lecture. I shall limit myself to a practical analysis of two or three handwriting samples, rather than expound on the theoretical aspects of my step-by-step procedure; we haven't time for that tonight, I'm sorry to say. May I please have a handwriting sample of some sort from one of you gentlemen?"

Rubner, who had been waiting for this moment, immediately handed the great Jensen a sheet of paper filled with writing. Jensen donned his wonder-working eyeglasses and inspected it.

"Aha, a woman's hand," he said wryly. "Ordinarily a man's hand is more pronounced and interesting, but then — "

Mumbling something to himself, he gazed intently at the sheet of paper. "Hm, hm," he said after a moment, twisting his head; there was a deep silence.

Suddenly the graphologist asked, "This wasn't written by someone close to you, by any chance?"

"No, of course not," Rubner protested quickly.

"So much the better," said the great Jensen. "Listen, this woman lies! That is the first impression I get from her hand-writing: lying, habitual lying, lying as her fundamental means of expression. Besides, she is basically a very low-class person; an educated man wouldn't have much to talk about with her — — She is appallingly sensual; her letters have an almost fleshy shape. And she's astoundingly sloppy; her house must look — well, you can imagine. Those are the primary traits which I discussed earlier; what you first notice about a person, the external habits, that is to say, characteristics, which are expressed instantly and instinctively. A proper psychological analysis proceeds only from those characteristics which the person in question denies or represses — as he must; otherwise he would be at the mercy of his environment.

"For example," he said, placing his finger at the tip of his nose, "this person probably would not admit her innermost thoughts to anyone. She is superficial, but superficial in two senses: on the surface it appears that she has many rather pedestrian interests, but these only mask what she is really thinking; and this secret ego is in itself terribly unimaginative. I would say lewdness dominated by mental indolence. Look at this, for instance: up to this point, the handwriting is unpleasantly sensual — this is also a sign of extravagance — and then it becomes repulsively priggish; this person is too fond of her own comfort to actually seek out any adventure of the senses; of course, when the opportunity presents itself — But that isn't our concern.

"Uncommonly self-indulgent and loquacious, too. When she actually does accomplish something, she talks about it endlessly, day and night — She's much too occupied with herself; you can see she doesn't care about anyone else; it's only for her

own convenience that she clings to someone and wants him to
believe that she loves him, that only God Himself knows how
she worries about him. A man's a weakling with a woman like
this; he simply dissolves in weakness from the boredom, the
endless chatter, all that humiliating materialism.

"Notice how the beginnings of the words and especially of
the sentences are written: rather lightly, almost slapdash. This
person wants to rule the roost and, in fact, she does; not through
any drive on her part, just a pretense of importance and lots of
talk; if necessary, she resorts to the vilest tyranny of all, the
tyranny of tears.

"This is odd: after each upward stroke you see a noticeable,
almost languid downturn; something is hindering this person,
something frightens her — most likely the fear of disclosing
something that might threaten her material comfort; it must be
something very embarrassing and concealed with care; hm, I
don't know, perhaps something from the past. But after this
reaction she regains her strength, or rather goes back to her usual
ways, and she finishes her words conventionally — though with
that customary self-satisfied, rambling sweep at the end; her
vanity is already on the increase again.

"You remember that our first impression in this analysis was
mendacity. At the same time, gentlemen, you see how a more
detailed analysis ultimately confirms that first, general, somewhat
intuitive impression; this ultimate confirmation is what I call
methodical verification. — I originally said, 'a low-class person;'
but this is not the crudeness of an uncouth person, however
inconsistent that may seem. No, this handwriting is a sham; it
pretends very prettily to be something other than it really is, but
it does so for the most trivial reasons. This woman pays great
attention to trivial details, to 'correctness': she painstakingly puts
dots over all her *i*'s, but the really important matters she disre-
gards completely; no self-discipline, no morals; in a word, a
sloven.

"Most striking of all are her commas: her handwriting has
a natural slant to the right, but her commas curve in the opposite

direction. This gives the curious impression of a knife wound in the back. There is something very deceitful and malicious about this. I could say, figuratively speaking, that this person is capable of stabbing a man in the back; but given her love of comfort — and lack of imagination — she wouldn't do it. — I think that will suffice. Does someone have another, more interesting sample?"

That night Rubner came home looking like a thundercloud.

"Home at last," Mrs. Rubner said. "Did you eat supper somewhere?"

Rubner glared at her. "Starting in again, are you?" he muttered darkly.

Mrs. Rubner raised her eyebrows in surprise. "What do you mean, am I starting in again? I only asked if you wanted supper."

"See?" Rubner replied with contempt. "That's about all you can talk about, shoveling in food. One of your pedestrian interests. It's so humiliating, so boring, the endless chatter, the materialism — " Rubner sighed and gestured hopelessly. "I know only too well how they sap a man's strength."

Mrs. Rubner placed her sewing in her lap and stared attentively at him. "Franci," she said in an anxious voice, "did something unpleasant happen to you?"

"Aha," Rubner burst out sarcastically. "There you go, always so worried about me, right? Don't think you can get me to believe that! Listen, once a man sees through all those lies, once he realizes how somebody clings to him just for her own comfort . . . and out of pure sensuality. For shame!" Rubner roared. "It's enough to make a man sick!"

Mrs. Rubner shook her head and seemed about to say something, but instead she pressed her lips together and hastily resumed her sewing.

"Just look at this," Rubner hissed after a moment, and he glanced meaningfully around the room. "Disorder, slovenliness — In trivial details like this, of course, everything looks oh-so-tidy and 'correct;' but in really important matters — What are you doing with those rags?"

"I'm mending your shirts," Mrs. Rubner got out through her constricted throat.

"You're mending shirts," Rubner sneered. "So, you're mending shirts! It's understood, isn't it, that the whole world will be hearing about this! It'll have to be talked about night and day, that somebody's mending shirts! There'll be a big fuss about how important it is! And you think because of this you rule the roost around here? Well, let me tell you, it's going to stop right now!"

"Franci," Mrs. Rubner gasped in astonishment, "have I done something wrong?"

"How should I know?" Rubner snapped. "I have no idea what you've done; I don't know what you think or what you're up to; I don't know anything about you, absolutely nothing at all, because you keep everything to yourself! God only knows about your past!"

"That's enough," Mrs. Rubner flared. "Stop right there. If you say one more — " She controlled herself with effort. "Franci," she said in horror, "what's happened to you?"

"Aha!" Rubner declared triumphantly, "now we have it! What are you so scared of? Maybe something will turn up and threaten your comfy little life, is that it? But *we* know: even with all her creature comforts she still finds opportunities for little adventures, right?"

Mrs. Rubner sat as if turned to stone. "Franci," she blurted out, swallowing tears, "if you're holding some kind of grudge against me . . . then for heaven's sake tell me what it is!"

"Absolutely nothing," Rubner intoned with overpowering irony. "I hold absolutely no grudge against you whatsoever! Why should it matter if a man's wife has no self-discipline, no morals; if she's a chronic liar; if she's slovenly, lazy, wasteful, and appallingly sensual! And on top of all that a low-class — "

Mrs. Rubner broke into sobs and stood up, shedding her sewing onto the floor.

"Put a sock in it," her husband snarled with contempt. "That's the vilest tyranny of all, the tyranny of tears!"

But Mrs. Rubner was no longer listening; choking and convulsed with tears, she had flung herself into her bedroom.

Rubner howled with tragic laughter and poked his head through the doorway. "You're even capable of knifing a man in the back," he shrieked, "but you love your creature comforts too much to do it!"

The following evening Rubner dropped in at his neighborhood tavern.

"I've just been reading in your paper here about this wonderful graphologist, Jensen," Mr. Plecka welcomed him, peering over his spectacles. "Is there anything to it, Mr. Newspaperman?"

"There is," Rubner said, "and plenty. Would it be possible to get a piece of that roast, Mr. Jancik? But not too well done. Listen, he's phenomenal, this Jensen; I saw him last night. The way he analyzes handwriting is absolutely scientific."

"Then it's a fake," stated Mr. Plecka. "Mister, I'll believe anything except science. You take vitamins, for instance: as long as there wasn't any vitamins, a man at least knew what he was eating; and now you don't even know what kind of vital factors you've got right there in your roast," Mr. Plecka said in disgust. "Ugh."

"This is different," Rubner declared. "It would take too long to explain to you all about psychometrics, automatism, primary and secondary characteristics, and things like that, Mr. Plecka. But I can tell you this: that man reads handwriting like he's reading a book. And the way he describes a man from top to bottom, you can just about see him standing in front of you; he can tell you what's he's like, all about his past, what he's thinking, what he's hiding, everything! I was right there, mister!"

"Go on," Mr. Plecka grumbled skeptically.

"Let me tell you about this one case," Rubner began. "One

man — I won't mention his name, but he's very well known —
one man gave Jensen a sheet of paper with his wife's handwriting
on it. And this Jensen took one look at it and started right in:
This woman's a liar through and through, sloppy, disgustingly
sensual and frivolous, lazy, wasteful, a non-stop talker, she gives
the orders at home, she's got a wicked past, and to top it all off
she wants to murder her husband! — You can bet that man
turned white, because it was the actual truth, word for word. Just
imagine, he'd been living with her happily for twenty years and
hadn't suspected a thing! In twenty years of marriage with this
woman he hadn't seen one-tenth of what Jensen saw at first
glance! That's quite a feat, you have to admit. Mr. Plecka, that
ought to convince even you!"

"What amazes me," Mr. Plecka said, "is that for twenty
years this idiot, this husband, didn't notice a thing."

"Please," Rubner said hurriedly, "when this woman had
play-acted so cleverly, and this man was otherwise very happy
with her — A man who's that happy is blind. And then, too, he
didn't have these exact scientific methods. So there you have it:
something may seem white to your eyes, but to a scientist it's all
the colors of the rainbow. Experience, my friend, doesn't mean a
thing; these days you've got to know exact methods. You're
amazed that this unnamed fellow didn't even suspect that he was
sharing his home with a monster; well, he simply didn't apply
scientific methods to her, that's what it is."

"And now he's getting a divorce?" Mr. Jancik, the owner,
joined in the conversation.

"I don't know," Rubner replied carelessly. "I'm not interested in such foolishness. I'm only interested in how this Jensen
figured out from her handwriting what nobody else even
suspected. You think you know someone for years on end as a
good and decent person, and then all at once, pow! you find out
from his handwriting that he's a thief or a snitch. No, a man
should never take anyone at face value; only an analysis like this
can show what's really going on inside!"

"But if that's true," Mr. Plecka wondered uneasily, "you'd be scared to write anything to anybody."

"Right," replied Rubner. "Just think of what graphological science will mean for criminology, for instance. Why, they could lock a man up before he ever stole a thing; his handwriting would show he's got a secondary trait for swiping stuff, and pow! he's off to the slammer! This has a fantastic future. Like I tell you, it's a proven science, there's not the least doubt about it." Mr. Rubner glanced at his watch. "Uh oh, ten o'clock; I really ought to be home."

"Why so early tonight?" Mr. Plecka grumbled.

"Well, you know," Rubner said sheepishly, "the wife might start complaining that I'm always leaving her by herself."

Proof Positive

"You know, Tonik," examining magistrate Mates said to his closest friend, "it's a matter of experience; I don't believe any alibis, any excuses, or any idle chatter; I don't believe the accused or the witnesses. People lie, even when they don't mean to. You get a witness swearing to you that he doesn't harbor any animosity towards the accused, and even while he's saying it he's completely unaware that, in the depths of his soul, in his subconscious, he hates him because of some repressed jealousy or resentment. Everything the accused tells you has been thought through and cleverly concocted in advance; everything a witness tells you is driven by the conscious or even unconscious intent to help or harm the accused. This I know, friend: people are flat-out mendacious bastards.

"Then what can we believe in? In chance, Tonik; in those involuntary, unwitting or, I might say, uncontrollable impulses or actions or words that people let slip every now and then. Everything can be faked or prearranged, everything is a smokescreen or a scam, everything but chance; you can spot it right off the bat. Here's my method: I simply sit there and let people babble on about whatever they've invented and organized beforehand; I pretend to believe them, I even encourage them so they'll babble more and better, and I lie there in wait until they blurt out some tiny, involuntary, unintentional word; a man has to be a psychologist, you know. Some examining magistrates employ tactics for befuddling the accused; that's why they keep interrupting and flustering him, and in the end, the poor, dazed rabbit's ready to confess, if need be, to the murder of the Empress Elizabeth. I want to be absolutely certain; that's why I wait, slowly and patiently, until this systematic lying and equivocation that the experts call testimony produces a tiny, inadvertent gleam of truth. In this vale of tears, you know, pure truth emerges only through oversight, only when a human being somehow makes a slip of the tongue or some other kind of blunder.

"Listen, Tonik, I don't have any secrets from you; we've been friends since boyhood — you'll remember, I know, how they gave you a licking when I was the one who broke that window. I wouldn't tell this to anyone else, but there's something I'm so ashamed of that I've got to get it out; there's no use denying it, people need to confess. I'm going to tell you how well this method of mine worked just recently in my . . . in my most private life; in short, in my marriage. And then you can tell me, if you wish, that I was a fool and a cad. I deserve it.

"Well, old friend, I . . . yes, I was suspicious of my wife, Marta; in fact, I was insanely jealous. I got it into my head that she was carrying on with that . . . with that young . . . I'll call him Artur; I don't think you know him. Wait, I'm not a savage; if I'd known for certain that she loved him, I'd have said, Marta, let's go our separate ways. But the worst of it was, I didn't know for certain; Tonik, you have no idea what kind of torment that is. My God, it was a nasty year! You know the kind of stupid tricks a jealous husband will pull: he shadows his wife, he spies on her, he eavesdrops, he makes scenes . . . But keep in mind that I am, as chance would have it, an examining magistrate; believe me, friend, my home life for the past year was one continuous cross-examination from morning till . . . till bedtime.

"The accused, I mean, Marta, acquitted herself splendidly. Even when she cried, even when she was offended and fell silent, even when she testified as to where she'd been all day and what she'd been doing, I watched and waited in vain for her to make some slip of the tongue, to somehow give herself away. Of course, she often lied to me, I mean, she lied from habit, but women do that routinely; a woman will never tell you candidly that she spent two hours at the dressmaker's — she'll make it seem that she was at the dentist's, or at the cemetery visiting her mother's grave. The more I hounded her — Tonda, a jealous man is worse than a rabid dog — the more I bullied her, the less certain I was. Each word she uttered, each excuse she made I picked at, poked, and probed ten times over; but I found nothing more than the usual, deliberate half-truths and half-lies that, as we're both well aware, constitute normal human relationships, and marriage in particular. I know how I felt after all that; but when I think of what poor Marta must have gone through, my friend, I wish I could bite my tongue off.

"Well, Marta went off to Frantiskovy Lazne this year — the spa there specializes in women's ailments, you know, and the fact is, she wasn't looking at all well. Needless to say, I had her watched — I paid this shady character to do it, though all he really did was make the rounds of the taverns there . . . It's odd how your entire life is tainted when only one part of it goes awry; you may only have a stain in one small spot, but your entire body feels unclean. Marta wrote to me . . . somewhat hesitantly and timidly . . . as if she couldn't understand what had gone wrong; naturally I scrutinized her letters carefully and searched between the lines . . . And then one day I got a letter from her that was addressed to 'Frantisek Mates, Examining Magistrate' and so forth, and when I opened the envelope and took out her letter, the first thing I saw was: 'Dear Artur'!

"I tell you, friend, my hands were shaking. So here it was at last. Sometimes it does indeed happen that, when you've been writing several letters, you pop some of them into the wrong envelopes. It was pure, idiotic chance, wasn't it, Marta? As for me, friend, I felt sorry for her, revealing her hand to me like that.

"Don't misunderstand me, Tonik, my first instinct was to not read the letter meant for this . . . this Artur, but to send it right back to Marta; in any other circumstance, that's exactly what I would have done. But jealousy is an ugly passion and it makes you do ugly things. I read that letter, friend, and I'll show it to you, because I carry it around with me. Take a look at it:

Dear Artur,

Please don't be angry with me for not having answered your letter until now, but I've been worried because Franci [that's her nickname for me] hadn't written for such a long time. I know he's really busy, but after having gone so long without any news from my husband, I was walking around like a lost soul. You wouldn't understand that, Artur, but it's true. Anyway, Franci's coming here next month, so perhaps you could come, too. He writes that he's working on a really interesting case right now; he didn't say which one, but I think it's the Hugo Müller murder case; I can't wait to hear about it. I'm sorry that you and Franci haven't seen much of each other lately, but that's only because he's been really busy lately. If things had been like they used to be, you could have gotten him out and about more with other people or taken him for rides in your car. You were always so kind to us and you haven't forgotten us even now, even though things have changed; Franci is so nervous now, he's just not himself. But you haven't even told me what your girlfriend is doing. Franci complains, too, that it's really hot in Prague; he ought to come here and unwind, but I'm sure he's working in his office till late at night. When are you going to the seashore? I hope you take your girlfriend with you; you have no idea what it's like for a woman to miss someone. With best wishes,

Sincerely yours,
Marta Matesova

"Well, Tonik, what do you think of that? I know it's not brilliant correspondence; it's a pretty feeble effort in terms of style and subject matter. But, my dear friend, what a light it throws on Marta and her relationship with that wretched Artur! I'd never have believed her if she had told me how she felt; but here in my hand was something so inadvertent on her part, so spontaneous . . . So you see that truth, unequivocal and irrefutable truth, is revealed only as a result of oversight. I could have cried for joy — and also shame, at having been so idiotically jealous.

"What did I do then? Why, I tied a string around the documents on the Hugo Müller murder case, locked them in a drawer, and the next day I was in Frantiskovy Lazne. When Marta saw me, her face turned pink and she stammered like a little girl; she looked as if she had done something quite outrageous. I kept a straight face. 'Franci,' she said after a moment, 'did you get my letter?'

" 'What letter?' I asked in surprise. 'God knows you hardly ever write me.'

"Marta looked at me in a startled way and sighed as if a load had lifted from her mind. 'Then I must have forgotten to mail it,' she said, and she fumbled around in her purse until she came up with a somewhat crumpled letter. Dear Franci, it began. I couldn't help laughing to myself. By now, most likely, Artur's already sent back the letter that wasn't meant for him.

"After that, not another word was said about the matter; needless to say, I began to tell her about the Hugo Müller case, which interested her so much. I think that to this very day she believes I never received that letter.

"And that's everything; since then there's at least been peace in our little family. But go ahead and say it, wasn't I a fool to be so despicably jealous? Now, of course, I'm trying to make up for how I treated Marta; it wasn't until I saw her letter that I realized how much the poor girl worries about me. At any rate, it's off my mind now. A man's more ashamed of his foolishness than he is of his sins.

"But it's a classic case of how something can be proved beyond a doubt by pure and simple chance, isn't it?"

* * *

At almost that very same moment, the young man referred to herein as Artur said to Marta: "Well, my pet, did it work?"

"What, sweetheart?"

"That letter you pretended to send by mistake."

"It worked," said Marta, and then she lapsed into thought.

"You know, darling, I'm almost ashamed at how really desperately Franci believes me now. Ever since then he's been so nice to me . . . He carries that letter around with him next to his heart." Marta shivered slightly. "It's really frightful the way I'm . . . I'm deceiving him, don't you think?"

But Artur didn't think so; at least he said that he most decidedly did not.

The Experiment of Professor Rouss

(The expatriot professor, in addressing his Czech audience, finds that he has not only lost his former command of that language, but is reduced to expressing certain thoughts in English — albeit a frequently awkward and often Czech-influenced English. His linguistic stumbles are indicated by the *italicized* words and phrases. —*Translator*)

Especially notable among those in the audience were: the Minister of the Interior, the Minister of Justice, the Chief of Police, a row of Parliament members, several other high government officials, prominent lawyers, eminent scholars and, of course, members of the press, for they must be present at everything.

"Gentlemen," began Professor C. G. Rouss of Harvard University, our famous American compatriot, "the experiment I will show you has roots on the previous work of a long line of my learned colleagues and collaborators; *indeed*, there isn't anything new in the whole thing, and, er, *really*, it's . . . it's an old hat!" he burst out cheerfully, having recalled the right words. "Only this method uses and, er, and the practical applying of some theoretical *experiences*, this was the goal for my work. I ask the best criminal experts to judge this thing according to their own practice. *Well*.

"The whole thing is this: I tell you a word, and you must tell me another word, the one that hits you that very moment, even if it is *nonsenze*, er, rubbish, I mean, nonsense. And in the end I will tell you, according to the words you tell me, what you have in your head, what you are thinking about and, er, and what you are hiding. Do you understand it? I will not explain it to you *theoretically*; these are associations, repressed notions, a little *suggesce* and things like that. I will be very short: you must — er, *well,* cut off your will power and thinking; subconscious *con-nectiony* will come loose, and I will know from this what — what — " The famous professor groped for words. "*Well, what's on the bottom of your mind.*"

"What's on the bottom of your mind," someone prompted from the audience.

"Exactly," C. G. Rouss said with satisfaction. "You must only say *automatically* what at that moment comes to your tongue, without all *control* and *rezervationy.* My *businys* will then be to *analyzovat* your notions. *That's all.* So I want to show you this on a criminal *kaze,* er, case, and then on somebody out of the audience what will volunteer. *Well,* Mr. Chief of Police will tell us what is the *kaze* of this man. Please, then."

The police chief rose and said, "Gentlemen, the man you will see in a moment is Cenek Suchanek, a farmer and journeyman locksmith from Podunk. We've had him under arrest for a week as a suspect in the murder of Josef Cepelka, a cab driver who has been missing for fourteen days. The reasons for our suspicions are that the missing Cepelka's car was found in the suspect Suchanek's garage, and traces of human blood were found on the steering wheel and under the driver's seat. The suspect, of course, denies the charge; he claims he bought the car from Cepelka for six thousand, because he himself wanted to go into the taxicab business.

"We found out that the missing Josef Cepelka had actually talked about being fed up with everything, and that he was going to sell his old car and go somewhere else as a driver; but there is no trace of him after that. Because there is no further evidence, the suspect Suchanek will be brought before an examining magistrate tomorrow. I asked permission to bring him here so that our esteemed compatriot, Professor C. G. Rouss, could conduct his experiment; if the professor will continue . . . "

"*Well,*" said the professor, who had been busily taking notes, "you please will let him come in here now."

At a sign from the police chief, an officer led in Cenek Suchanek; he was a sullen fellow whose expression indicated that they could all go to hell. As far as he was concerned, he wasn't going to yield an inch to anybody.

"Come here, you," C. G. Rouss scolded him in a severe tone of voice. "I will ask you nothing. I will only say a word to you, and you must say immediately the first word that occurs to you, understand it? So pay attention: glass."

"Shit," replied Mr. Suchanek.

"Listen, Suchanek," the police chief said quickly, "if you don't answer decently, they'll take you away for questioning right now, understand? And they'll keep you there all night. So watch it! Now, once again!"

"Glass," Professor Rouss repeated.

"Beer," muttered Suchanek.

"So you see," the renowned professor said, "how very well it is going."

Suchanek looked up suspiciously. Was there a catch to this?

"Street," said the professor.

"Cars," Suchanek answered reluctantly.

"You must be quicker. Farmhouse!"

"Field."

"Lathe!"

"Steel."

"Very good." It seemed that Mr. Suchanek no longer objected to this game. "Mama!"

"Aunt."

"Dog!"

"Doghouse."

"Soldier!"

"Gunner." So it went, blast after blast, faster and faster. Most likely Mr. Suchanek was beginning to enjoy it; it reminded him of trumping cards. God, the memories this game sent flitting through his mind!

"Travel!" C. G. Rouss threw out at a breathless pace.

"Road."

"Prague!"

"Beroun."

"Hide!"

"Bury."

"Scrub!"

"Stains."

"Rag!"

"Sack."

"Shovel!"

"Garden."

"Hole!"

"Fence."

"Corpse!"

Nothing.

"Corpse," the professor repeated insistently. "So, you buried him by the fence, did you?"

"I didn't say nothing," Mr. Suchanek burst out.

"You buried him by the fence in your garden," C. G. Rouss repeated sternly. "You killed him on the road to Beroun. You wiped off the *bloud* on the car with a gunnysack. So what did you do with the gunnysack?"

"That's not true," shouted Suchanek. "I bought that car from Cepelka! Nobody's going to trap me . . . "

"Hold it," said Rouss. "I will ask the *policemen* to please go there to see. It isn't my *businys*. Take this man out. Please, gentlemen, that only took seventeen minutes. It was too quick. It was a silly *kaze*. More often it takes an hour. So I would like, please, to take one of the gentlemen here and I will give him some words. It will take lots longer, because I don't know what that gentleman has for a *secret* — how do you say that?"

"A secret," someone from the audience prompted.

"A secret," rejoiced our eminent compatriot. "I know, just like the name of Smetana's opera. Let us take lots of time for this gentleman to leak for us his nature, his past, his most hidden *ideazy*."

"Thoughts," a voice from the audience prompted.

"*Well*. I ask you please, gentlemen, who will volunteer to be *analyzovat*?"

There was a pause; someone guffawed, but no one stirred.

"Please," C. G. Rouss repeated. "It will not hurt, you know."

"You go, my dear colleague," whispered the Minister of the Interior to the Minister of Justice.

"Go up there as a representative of your party," one parliament member said as he nudged another.

"You're a section chief, you do it," a high official prodded his colleague from another ministry.

It was already beginning to be somewhat embarrassing; no one volunteered.

"Please, gentlemen," the American scholar said for the third time, "maybe you are scared that you will let your cat out of a bag?"

At this the Minister of the Interior turned to those seated in back of him and hissed: "One of you gentlemen get on up there!"

In the rear of the auditorium someone coughed modestly and stood up; he was a gaunt, somewhat shabby-looking older man whose Adam's apple was moving up and down in agitation. "I — . . . ehm," he said hesitantly, "when nobody — so I thought I'd — more or less . . . "

"Come here," the great American authority interrupted him, "and sit down. You must say what occurs to you first. You must not think, you must spill it out *mechanically*, not even you yourself know what. Do you understand it?"

"Yes, sir," the willing guinea pig said, a bit ill at ease before such a distinguished audience; then he cleared his throat and blinked anxiously, like a student taking final exams.

"Tree," the man of letters fired at him.

"Stately," the old fellow whispered.

"What, please?" the man of letters asked, somehow not comprehending.

"Giant of the forest," the man explained bashfully.

"Ah, yes. Street!"

"Street . . . a street in ceremonial array," offered the little man.

"What do you mean?"

"A procession, sir. Or a funeral."

"*So.* So all you have to say is 'procession.' Only one word, if possible."

"Yes, sir."

"So then: business."

"Flourishing. Business crisis. Business as usual. Politics as usual. Shady business."

"Hm. Office."

"Please, sir, what kind?"

"It doesn't matter. Just tell a word, quickly!"

"Perhaps if you'd say 'agency' . . . "

"*Well.* Agency!"

"Authorized," the little man blurted out with pleasure.

"Hammer!"

"Force. They extracted a confession by force. His head was smashed in with a hammer."

"*Curious,*" the scholar muttered. "Blood!"

"Blood money. Blood innocently shed. History written in blood."

"Fire!"

"By fire and sword. The valiant fireman. A fiery speech. Mene tekel."

"This is a strange *kaze,*" the professor said perplexedly. "Once more. You must say only your first idea, do you understand? Only what *automatically* comes to mind when you hear the word. *Go on.* Hand!"

"The hand of friendship. Helping hand. Hands clutching the flag. With clenched fists. With dirty hands. He got his hands slapped."

"Eyes!"

"The watchful eye of the public. Pull the wool over their eyes. Eyewitness. Throw off the blinders. Blind to the truth. The innocent eyes of children. Cheated blind."

"Not so much! Beer!"

"Small beer. High spirits. Demon rum."

"Music!"

"Music of the spheres. They played to beat the band. A nation of musicians. Dulcet tones. The great powers acted in concert. The gentle pipes of peace. Our glorious national anthem."

"Bottle!"

"Vitriol. Unrequited love. She died in the hospital in terrible pain."

"Poison!"

"Poison pen. Poisoning the well."

C. G. Rouss scratched his head. "*Never heard that*. Again, please. I want to make it clear to you, gentlemen, that you always start from . . . er, from very *plain*, ordinary things, so you find the main *interest* and *profession* of the man. So then. Record!"

"Record time. Settle the record. Settle the score. Go down in the records of history."

"Hm. Paper!"

"Not worth the paper it's printed on," the little man proclaimed energetically. "Official papers. Get it in down on paper."

"*Bless you*," the scholar said irritably. "Stone!"

"The first to cast a stone. Tombstone. Rest in peace," the guinea pig responded warmly. "Ave, anima pia."

"Car!"

"Triumphal car. The wheel of fate. Ambulance. A long line of cars draped in black."

"Aha!" exclaimed C. G. Rouss. "*That's it!* Horizon!"

"Gloomy," the old fellow said with lively delight. "New clouds on the political horizon. His horizon is limited. Widen your horizons."

"Weapons!"

"Deadly weapons. Fully armed. They fought with flying colors. Shot in the back," the guinea pig gabbled enthusiastically.

"We won't give up the fight. The roar of battle. Battle of the ballot box."

"Elements!"

"Raging elements. Elemental resistance. Criminal elements! An element of mystery! An element of doubt! Elementary, my — "

"Enough," C. G. Rouss restrained him. "You're with a newspaper, right?"

"Yes, sir," the guinea pig replied passionately. "Have been for thirty years. I'm Vasatko, the editor."

"I thank you," our famous American compatriot said drily, and he bowed. "*Finished, gentlemen.* By *analyzovat* the notions of this man we — er, we discover that he is a journalist. I think it would be useless to do this *experiment* more. *It would only waste our time.* I think this experiment failed. *So sorry, gentlemen.*"

"Look at this," Mr. Vasatko called out from his office that evening, as he went through the papers on his desk. "The police report that they found the body of Josef Cepelka; it was buried by the fence in Suchanek's garden, and underneath it they found a bloodstained gunnysack. You know, this Rouss hit the nail on the head after all! You won't believe this, but I didn't say one word about newspapers, and he pinpointed me squarely as a newspaperman. Gentlemen, he said, you have here before you a prominent, respected journalist — — Well, I wrote up his lecture for an article: 'The deductions of our renowned compatriot were received with flattering acknowledgment in our professional circle.' Wait, I ought to put a little more style into it: 'The amazing deductions of our renowned compatriot were received, as was their due, with lively and flattering acknowledgment in our professional circle.' That's how it should read."

The Missing Letter

"Bozena," the cabinet minister said to his wife, helping himself to a substantial serving of salad, "I received a letter this afternoon that will interest you. I'll have to bring it up at the cabinet meeting. But if it ever got out, a certain political party would be in a very prickly plight. Here, see for yourself," he said, reaching first into his left vest pocket and then into the right. "Wait, now what did I do with it?" the minister muttered, poking his hand into his left vest pocket again; whereupon he put down his fork and began digging with both hands in the rest of his pockets. A careful observer would have discovered that a cabinet minister has the same surprising number of pockets, on every conceivable side and surface of his body, as do ordinary men; and that inside them he keeps pencils, notes, keys, the evening paper, official documents, toothpicks, old letters, matches, ticket stubs, his coin purse, his fountain pen, his pocket watch, pocket knife, pocket comb, and countless other indispensable everyday objects; and that in fumbling through his pockets, a cabinet minister mumbles, "Now where did I put that?" and "I must be crazy," and "Wait a minute," just as would any other human creature rummaging through his pockets. But the man's wife was not devoting a great deal of attention to this activity, for she said, as any other wife would have done, "Look, you'd better eat; your dinner's getting cold."

"Right," the minister said, putting the contents of his pockets back in their authorized places, "I probably left it on the desk in my study; that's where I was reading it. Can you imagine," he continued in great spirits, helping himself to a slice of the roast, "can you imagine somebody sending me an actual, authentic letter from — Just a second," he said uneasily, and he got up from the table. "I'll just take a look in the study. I probably left it on the desk." And he was gone.

When after ten minutes he had not yet returned, Bozena went looking for him. The minister was sitting on the floor in the middle of his study examining, page by page, the papers and letters which he had removed from his desk.

"Would you like me to reheat your dinner?" she asked, with only a trace of annoyance.

"Right away. In just a minute," the minister answered, preoccupied. "I probably mislaid it somewhere among my papers. It would be silly if I couldn't find it . . . But that's not possible. It has to be here somewhere."

"Eat first," his wife advised, "and then look for it."

"Right away, right away," the minister said peevishly. "The minute I find it. It was in a sort of yellow envelope — Well then, I *am* crazy," he fumed, starting on the next stack of papers. "I read it right here at my desk, and I didn't move from this spot until you called me to dinner — Now where could I have put it?"

"I'll send your dinner in here," his wife decided, and she left the minister still sitting there amidst his piles of papers. Then complete silence settled in, while outside trees rustled and stars fell. It was almost midnight when Bozena began to yawn and then to head cautiously for a look in the study.

The minister, minus his coat, disheveled and perspiring, was standing in the center of the disorderly room. All about him on the floor were heaps of papers, the furniture had been dragged away from the walls, the rug was piled in one corner, and on the desk sat his dinner, untouched.

"For heaven's sake, man," she exclaimed, "what are you doing here?"

"Good God, can't you leave me in peace?" the minister snapped back. "Do you have to keep interrupting me every five minutes?" Of course he immediately realized the injustice of this and he added, in gentler tones, "I've got to do this systematically, you understand. Inch by inch. It's got to be here somewhere, because no one else but me has set foot in this room. If only I didn't have so many damned documents here!"

"Don't you want me to help you?" she offered sympathetically.

"No, no, you'd just get it all mixed up," the minister fretted, gesturing towards the unspeakable disarray. "Go on to bed, I'll be there right away — "

At three in the morning the minister got into bed, sighing heavily. It just isn't possible, he told himself: I received that letter, in a yellow envelope, in the five o'clock mail; I read it at my desk, where I continued to work until eight o'clock; at eight I went into dinner, and less than five minutes later I hurried back to search through the study. Surely those five minutes couldn't have been long enough for anyone to — "

At this the minister bailed out of bed, landed on both feet, and dashed back to the study. True, the window was open, but the study was on the second floor and, in addition, the window faced the street — it's hardly likely, the minister supposed, that anyone could have entered unnoticed through the window! But, he decided, I'll need to check out that angle in the morning.

Once again the minister deposited his stately form in bed. Wait a minute, he suddenly thought, I remember reading in some book that a letter like that usually goes unnoticed when it's lying right under your nose! Once again he raced to the study, so that he might look and see what was lying right under his nose; what he saw, of course, were mounds of papers, wrenched-out drawers, and the vast, hopeless confusion resulting from his search — cursing and sighing, the minister returned, wide awake, to bed.

He held out until nearly six o'clock; at six he was already demanding urgently over the telephone that his colleague, the Minister of the Interior, be awakened immediately "in this highly important matter, do you hear me!" When at last the connection was made, he fired off frantically: "Excuse me, sir, I beg of you, please send me at once three or four of your most competent men . . . yes, detectives, of course . . . your most dependable, it goes without saying. I'm missing an extremely important document . . . my dear sir, this is the most incomprehensible . . . Yes, I'll be waiting for them — Leave everything just as it is? Do you really think that's necessary? — Right. — Theft? I don't know — Of course, this is absolutely confidential; not a word to anyone, you understand — Thank you, and forgive me for . . . I'm deeply obliged to you, sir!"

By eight o'clock it turned out that the most competent and most dependable men were seven in number, for seven men in bowler hats presented themselves at the minister's door.

"You see, gentlemen," the minister began, leading the seven most competent men into his study, "last night, right here in this room, I put down a certain . . . um, very important letter . . . in a yellow envelope . . . addressed in violet ink . . . "

One of the seven most dependable men let out a whistle. "He really tore the place up," the man said with professional admiration, "the damned swine."

The minister stopped short. "Who exactly?"

"The thief," the detective replied, scrutinizing God's own disaster in the study.

The minister turned weak pink in color. "Exactly," he said quickly. "Actually, I was a bit careless myself when I was looking for it; yes, gentlemen, I . . . er, but I can't entirely rule out the letter being here somewhere . . . misplaced or fallen behind something . . . I might even say that it couldn't be anywhere else *but* in this room. I think that . . . yes, I could state with complete certainty that this room has been examined systematically. But it is your affair now, gentlemen, to undertake with . . . whatever is within human capability."

There are many things within human capability. Consequently, three of the most competent men shut themselves up in the study so as to examine it systematically; two more questioned the maid, the cook, the housekeeper, and the chauffeur; and the remaining two left for parts unknown of the city in order to, as they put it, launch an investigation.

That evening, the first three of the most competent

announced that the letter being somewhere in the minister's study was now ruled out entirely, for they had gone so far as to extract the pictures from their frames, take the furniture apart, and catalog every sheet of paper. The next two reported that only the maid had entered the room, when, at the request of the minister's wife, she had carried in the dinner while the minister was seated on the floor; that she, in turn, had carried out the letter could not be ruled out entirely, and so an investigation had been launched as to who her boyfriend was — he was an employee of the telephone company and presently under their surveillance. The remaining two were investigating somewhere in parts unknown.

That night the minister did not and could not fall asleep, repeating incessantly to himself: at five o'clock that letter in the yellow envelope arrived; I read it at my desk in the study, and I didn't leave the study until I went to dinner; ergo, the letter must still be there — but it isn't. He was saddened and discomfited by this contradictory and altogether impossible enigma, and so he took a sleeping pill and slept like a log until morning.

In the morning he found that, inexplicably, only one of the seven most competent was poking about the house; no doubt the others were launching an investigation throughout the entire republic.

"It's moving right along," the Minister of the Interior informed him over the telephone, "and I expect to have a report in no time. According to what you told me about the contents of this letter, sir, we know only too well who would have an interest in it . . . If we could get a search warrant for a certain ministry, or better yet for a certain newspaper office, we'd know still more; but, as I say, it's moving right along."

About one o'clock that night — it was a clear, moonlit night — Bozena heard footsteps in the library and, arming herself with all the courage of a respectable woman, went there on tiptoe. The library door was ajar, one of the bookcases was open, and standing before it in his nightshirt was the minister, leafing solemnly through the pages of one of the volumes and mumbling softly all the while.

"For heaven's sake," she gasped, "what are you doing now?"

"I just wanted to look something up," the minister replied vaguely.

"In the dark?" she wondered.

"I can see," the minister insisted, and he put the book back in its place. "Goodnight," he said in a low voice, and he went slowly off to bed.

Bozena shook her head. Poor man, she said to herself, he can't sleep for that wretched letter.

The next morning the minister looked rosy and well-nigh content.

"Tell me, please," his wife said, "what on earth were you looking for in the library last night?"

The minister set down his spoon and opened his eyes wide. "I? What's got into your head? I wasn't in the library. I was sleeping like a hoopoe."

"But I talked with you there! You were thumbing through some book or other, and you said that you wanted to look something up!"

"Nonsense," the minister said in disbelief. "You must have been dreaming. I didn't budge once the entire night."

"You were standing there by the middle bookcase," she continued, "and you hadn't even turned on the lights. You were thumbing through some book in the dark, and furthermore you insisted that you could see very well."

The minister clutched his head. "Woman," he blurted through clenched teeth, "are you suggesting that I'm a sleepwalker? Never mind," he added, composing himself, "you were dreaming. I am not, I trust, a somnambulist!"

"It was one o'clock in the morning," she maintained, adding somewhat irritably, "Are you saying that maybe I've lost my mind?"

The minister twirled his spoon thoughtfully in his tea.

"Wait a minute," he said suddenly. "Show me where it happened."

His wife steered him to the library. "You were standing right here by this bookcase, and you'd taken a book down from that very shelf."

The minister turned toward the shelf in bewilderment; on it sat a complete and impressive set of the Collected Laws and Statutes. "I'm the one who's lost his mind," he muttered as he scraped his fingers along the row of books and, almost mechanically, pulled out a volume which had been replaced upside down. It fell open in his hand; tucked inside was a yellow envelope addressed in violet ink.

"You know, Bozena," the minister marveled, "I could have sworn that I didn't take one step from the study; but now I dimly recall that after reading the letter I said to myself: I've got to look up that statute from 'thirty-three. I probably took the book back to my desk to make a few notes; but because the thing kept closing up again, I must have stuck the letter in it and then later clapped the book shut and automatically put it back in place — But that I would have gone to this very book subconsciously, would have seen it in my sleep, that's — hm; best not to mention this to anyone. People might very well think — It would give the wrong impression, mysterious psychological phenomena and all that."

A moment later the minister was telephoning exuberantly to his colleague at the Ministry of the Interior: "Good morning, sir, now about that missing letter — No, of course you haven't found any traces yet; I've got it here in my hand! . . . What's that? How did I find it? My dear friend, I'm not going to tell you. There are methods, you know, that even the Ministry of the Interior is not aware of — I realize, naturally, that your people did all they could; they can't be blamed for not being on top of everything — You're quite right, it's best that we not mention it

— Not at all, you're too kind . . . and a good day to you, too, sir!"

Stolen Document 139/VII, Sect. C

At three o'clock in the morning the telephone jangled at garrison headquarters: "Colonel Hampl here, of the General Staff. Send me two men from the military police *immediately*, and tell Lieutenant Colonel Vrzal — *yes, of course* from Intelligence, *that's no business of yours* — tell him to come here *at once* — *Yes*, now, tonight — *Yes*, get him a car. And *hurry*, for God's sake!" And with that he hung up.

An hour later Lieutenant Colonel Vrzal arrived at the spot, which was God knows where in some garden suburb. He was greeted by an older, badly worried gentleman in civvies, that is, in shirt and trousers only. "Vrzal, the damnedest thing happened to me. Sit down, sit down. The damnedest, filthy, wretched, rotten, stupid thing. Vile, cursed business. Imagine this, if you can: day before yesterday, the head of General Staff hands me this document and says, 'Hampl, you'd better deal with this at home; the fewer people know about it, the better — don't say a word about it at the office. Now off with you, take a few days' leave and sit on this at home, but be on your guard!' And so I did."

"What kind of document was it?" asked Lieutenant Colonel Vrzal.

Colonel Hampl hesitated a moment. "Well," he said, "you might as well know: it was from Section C."

"Aha," Lieutenant Colonel Vrzal said meaningfully, and his manner became exceedingly grave. "Go on."

"Look," said the miserable colonel. "I had it with me all day yesterday, but what by all the sacraments was I supposed to do with it at night? Stick it in the stamp drawer? That's no good, and I haven't got a safe; and if anybody knew I had it with me, that would be amen and the end of it. So that first night I hid it under the mattress; by morning it looked like a wild boar had been rolling around on it."

"I can believe it," said Lieutenant Colonel Vrzal.

"What else would you expect?" the colonel sighed. "My wife is even fatter than I am. Well, the second night my wife gave me some advice: 'I'll tell you what,' she said, 'let's put it in the macaroni canister and hide it overnight in the pantry. I'll lock the pantry and keep the key with me,' she said — because we have this maid who's even fatter, and she'll eat anything. Nobody would think of looking for it in the pantry, right? Well, it seemed like a good idea to me."

"Does your pantry have a single or a double window?" Lieutenant Colonel Vrzal interrupted.

"By Jove!" the colonel exploded. "That never occurred to me! It's a single window! I was thinking the whole time about the Sazava case and other such foolishness, and I completely forgot to take a look at the window! Damned, wretched business!"

"What happened next?" the lieutenant colonel urged.

"Well, what didn't happen next. At two in the morning my wife hears the maid screeching downstairs. So she goes down to see what's going on, and Mary's yelling, 'There's a burglar in the pantry!' My wife dashes back for the key, and me, I rush to the pantry with my pistol and — stupid, damned business, the pantry window's jimmied, forced open, and the noodle can with the document is gone. And the burglar's gone, too. That's all," sighed the colonel.

Lieutenant Colonel Vrzal drummed his fingers on the table. "And Colonel, sir, nobody knew you had this document at home?"

The unhappy colonel threw up his hands. "I don't know. Those filthy spies snoop out everything." Just then he remembered Lieutenant Colonel Vrzal's official position and lapsed into embarrassed confusion. "What I mean to say is, they are very clever people," he corrected himself lamely. "But I didn't tell a soul about it, word of honor. However," he added triumphantly, "nobody could possibly have known that I put it in the macaroni canister."

"While we're on the subject, where were you when you put it in the canister?" the lieutenant colonel asked.

"Here, at this table."

"Where exactly was the canister?"

"Wait," the colonel reflected. "I was sitting here, and I had the canister right in front of me."

The lieutenant colonel leaned against the table and stared out the window in dreamy thought. The red-and-gray house opposite was silhouetted against the dawn. "Who lives over there?" he asked idly.

The colonel banged on the table. "Damn it, I forgot all about that! Wait, some kind of Jew lives there, a bank director or something. Damned business, now I see what happened! Vrzal, I think we're on the track of something here!"

"I'd like to see the pantry," the lieutenant colonel said evasively.

"Come on, then. This way, this way," the colonel guided him with eagerness. "Here it is. That can was on the top shelf. Mary!" the colonel bawled. "What are you gaping at? Go down in the cellar, or up in the attic!"

The lieutenant colonel put on his gloves and swung himself up to the window, which was fairly high. "Forced open with a chisel," he said, examining the frame. "Of course, the sill is made of softwood; colonel, sir, a boy could have split it easily."

"Damned business," the colonel said, truly amazed. "Damned people, making such wretched windows!"

Outside, two tin-soldier types were posted in front of the fence.

"Is that the military police?" asked Lieutenant Colonel Vrzal. "Good. I still need to take a look at the outside. But Colonel, sir, I must caution you not to leave the house until further orders."

"Certainly," the colonel agreed. "But why, exactly?"

"So that you'll be available in case — The two soldiers will remain here, of course."

The colonel snorted and then swallowed something. "I understand. Would you care for some coffee? My wife could fix it for you."

"There's no time to spare," the lieutenant colonel said drily. "Meanwhile, of course, don't say anything about the stolen document to anyone, unless . . . unless you're requested to do so. And one more thing: tell your maid that the burglar stole some canned goods, that's all."

"But listen," the colonel called after him in desperation, "you are going to find that document, aren't you?"

"I'll do my best," Lieutenant Colonel Vrzal replied, and he clicked his heels together, military style.

For the rest of the morning Colonel Hampl sat like a small mountain of woe. At times he imagined two officers arriving to arrest him; at other times he tried to visualize somehow what Lieutenant Colonel Vrzal might be doing and how he was probably setting in motion the vast and mysterious apparatus of military intelligence. He frequently pictured the alarm at general headquarters and moaned aloud.

"Karlous," his wife said to him for the twentieth time (prudently she had long before, in the early morning hours, hidden his revolver in the maid's trunk), "wouldn't you like a little something to eat?"

"Leave me alone, for God's sake!" the colonel snapped. "I think that Jew across the way must have seen me."

His wife only sighed and went back to the kitchen to cry.

At that moment the doorbell rang. The colonel stood up and straightened his clothing, so that he might with proper military dignity receive the officers coming to take him into custody. (Which ones might they be? he wondered absently.) But instead of officers, a small, ginger-haired man entered, bowler hat in hand, smiling at the colonel like a toothy squirrel. "Beg your pardon, but I'm Pistora from the police station."

"What do you want?" the colonel blurted out, inconspicuously shifting from attention to at ease.

"They tell me your pantry's been burgled," Mr. Pistora grinned in a somewhat confidential manner. "So I came on by."

"What the devil business is it of yours?" the colonel bellowed.

"Beg your pardon," Mr. Pistora beamed, "but this is our bailiwick, you know. Your maid here, she was saying this morning at the baker's that your pantry got burgled, and so I said to the captain, captain, sir, I'll just drop on by."

"It wasn't worth it," the colonel snarled in dismissal. "All they took was a . . . a box of macaroni. Kindly keep out of it."

"It's funny," Mr. Pistora remarked, "that they didn't make off with nothing more than that."

"It's very funny," the colonel remarked bitterly, "but it's no business of yours."

"Maybe somebody interrupted 'em while they was at it," Mr. Pistora beamed again, in a sudden burst of enlightenment.

"Good day to you, sir," said the colonel bluntly.

"Beg your pardon," said Mr. Pistora, his smile a touch mistrustful, "but I'll have to take a look at that pantry first."

The colonel was ready to explode, but in his misery he merely surrendered. "Come on then," he said, fed up with it all, and he led the little man to the pantry.

Mr. Pistora scanned the small, narrow closet with enthusiasm. "Yes indeedy," he said, looking quite pleased, "window forced open with a chisel. That'll be Pepek or Andrlik."

"What are you talking about?" the colonel asked sharply.

"Why, it was either Pepek or Andrlik that did it; but my guess is Pepek's still doing time. Now if it was only the glass pushed in, that would be Dundr, Lojza, Novak, Hosicka, or Kliment. But this was Andrlik."

"You're never wrong, I suppose," muttered the colonel.

"You think somebody new is doing pantries?" Mr. Pistora suddenly grew solemn. "Don't seem likely. Mertl, now, he forces windows, too, but he never goes in through pantries, never, sir;

he busts in by the toilet and he only takes linen and laundry."
Mr. Pistora displayed his squirrel's teeth anew. "Yes indeedy, I'll
just go look in on Andrlik."

"Give him my best," the colonel grumbled. It's unbelievable,
he mused, when once again he was left to his melancholy
brooding, it's unbelievable how incompetent these policemen are.
They could at least look for fingerprints or footprints — that's
how a professional would handle things; but to go about it in
such an idiotic way — Imagine the police bumbling around in
international espionage! I'd like to know what Vrzal is doing
now.

The colonel could not resist the temptation and telephoned
Lieutenant Colonel Vrzal; after a half-hour of fuming he finally
managed to get through. "Hello," his voice rang out melliflu-
ously, "Hampl here. I was just wondering how long — I know,
you can't talk about it, but I only — I know, but if you could
just tell me whether there's anything — Good God, still nothing?
— I know, it's a difficult case, but — Wait a minute, Vrzal,
please. It's occurred to me that, out of my own pocket, you
understand, I could offer ten thousand to whoever catches the
thief. That's all I've got, but you know what this means to me
— I know it isn't; but as a purely private — Yes, exactly, my own
private affair; nothing official about it — Or you could split it
with the private detectives, how's that? — I understand, you
know nothing about it; but if you could somehow let the men
know that Colonel Hampl's promising ten thousand — Right,
have your sergeant pass the word — Not at all, don't mention it!
— Sorry to have bothered you. And thanks."

Colonel Hampl felt somewhat relieved by this generous
decision; he had the impression now of having made at least
some kind of personal contribution toward tracking down the
damned thieving spy. Exhausted by the excitement, he lay down
on the sofa and began to picture a hundred, two hundred, three
hundred men (all ginger-haired and baring squirrel's teeth like
Mr. Pistora) inspecting trains, stopping cars headed full speed
toward the frontier, lying in wait for their quarry on street

corners, and then suddenly stepping forward with the words: "In the name of the law, you're under arrest. Come with me and keep your big mouth shut." Then he dreamed that he was taking an examination in ballistics at the military academy, and he groaned heavily and woke up in a sweat. Someone had rung the doorbell.

Colonel Hampl sprang to his feet and tried to collect his thoughts. Upon opening the door he found himself confronted by the squirrel teeth of Mr. Pistora. "I'm back," the teeth announced. "Beg your pardon, sir, but he's the one."

The colonel struggled to understand. "Who?"

"Well, Andrlik," said Mr. Pistora, for once failing to display his array of teeth. "Who else? Pepek's been put away, just like I thought."

"Why do you keep going on about this Andrlik?" the colonel snapped impatiently.

Mr. Pistora rolled his bright little eyes. "But he's the one that stole the noodles from the pantry," he said earnestly. "They've got him down at the station house now. Beg your pardon, but I've come to ask — Andrlik, see, he says there wasn't any noodles in that can, just a bunch of papers. So I just wanted to know if that's true."

"Where," the colonel shouted without pausing for breath, "where's that bunch of papers?"

"In my pocket," beamed Mr. Pistora, baring his teeth. "Now where did I — " He rummaged through his baggy jacket. "Aha. Is this yours?"

The colonel whipped from Pistora's hand the precious, rumpled Document 139/VII, Sect. C. His eyes flooded with tears of relief. "My dear, dear fellow," he exhaled, "I would have given — never mind what — to have this back again. Wife!" he roared, "come here! I want you to meet officer — special agent — uh — "

"Inspector Pistora," the little man said, exhibiting, in his great pleasure, his entire set of dentures.

"He's found the stolen document!" the colonel trumpeted. "Get the brandy and some glasses. Mr. Pistora, I'd . . . you have no idea . . . I mean, if you only knew . . . Here's to you, Mr. Pistora!"

"Well, it wasn't anything," Mr. Pistora grinned. "That's strong stuff, sir! Oh, and that can, ma'am, that can's down at the police station."

"Devil take the can," the colonel roared blissfully. "My dear Mr. Pistora, how did you find my papers so quickly? Your health, Mr. Pistora!"

"And yours, sir," Mr. Pistora said respectfully. "But my Lord, sir, that wasn't anything at all. If it's pranks in the pantry, we go for Andrlik or Pepek, but Pepek's sitting out two months in jail. If it's upstairs, though, that's either Pisecky, Limping Tondera, Kaner, Zima, or Houska."

"Oh my," the colonel marveled. "But tell me, what if it's a case of spying, say? Cheers, Mr. Pistora."

"Thank you kindly — As to spies, sir, we don't get that sort of thing, you know. Brass doorknobs, now, that's Cenek and Pinkus, and there's only one who does copper wire, a fellow named Tousek; and if it's tavern fittings, that's bound to be Hanousek, Buchta, or Slesinger. We go straight to the source, sir. As to safecrackers, why, we've got the name of every safe-cracker in the republic. There's — hic! there's twenty-seven of 'em now, but six of 'em's put away."

"Serves them right," the colonel declared bloodthirstily. "Drink up, Mr. Pistora!"

"Thank you kindly," said Mr. Pistora, "but I'm not much of a one for drinking. Beg your pardon, here's to you, sir. These here — hic! these here crooks aren't very smart, sir; they only know one trick, and they just keep at it till somebody retires 'em from business again. Like this Andrlik. 'Aha,' he says when he sees me coming, 'it's Mr. Pistora about that pantry. Mr. Pistora,' he says to me, 'it's not worth it no more, all I got was a bunch of papers in that can. I had to pull out before I could grab anything else' — 'On your feet, meatball,' I says to him, 'you'll get at least a year for this.'"

"A year in prison?" Colonel Hampl countered somewhat sympathetically. "Isn't that a bit much?"

"Well, it is breaking and entering, you know," Mr. Pistora grinned. "I do thank you kindly, sir; I still have a busted shop window to see to, that'll either be Klecka or Rudl. But if you need anything else, just give us a call at the station. Just ask for Mr. Pistora."

"Please, sir," the colonel said, "if perhaps — hm — for your services — That is, those papers aren't . . . That is, they're nothing special, but . . . I wouldn't have wanted to lose them, do you see? Here, if you'll accept something for your trouble," he said all at once, and he shoved a fifty into Mr. Pistora's hand.

Mr. Pistora was surprised and touched. "Now, there's no need for that," he said, quickly shoving the hand with the banknote into his pocket. "It really wasn't anything — But I thank you kindly, sir; and if you ever need anything again some-day . . . "

"The fact is, I gave him fifty," Colonel Hampl said, complacently, to his wife. "Twenty would have been plenty for that tulip, but — " The colonel waved his hand magnanimously. "At least he found the damned thing."

The Man Who Looked Just a Bit Suspicious

"Sergeant Kolda," said Mr. Pacovsky, "I've got something for you." Mr. Pacovsky had been a policeman in Austrian times, a mounted policeman actually, but after the war he couldn't get used to the new circumstances somehow, so he took his pension, went off to have a look at the world, and ended up as innkeeper of The Lookout Inn; true, it's in a somewhat remote area, but nowadays that kind of place is beginning to be fairly popular, what with the excursions, the views, swimming in the lake, and similar attractions. "Sergeant," said Mr. Pacovsky, "there's something I can't figure out. I've had this one guest for fourteen days now, name of Roedl. I don't really know what it is, because he pays up, doesn't drink, doesn't gamble, but . . . I'll tell you what," Mr. Pacovsky said suddenly, "come over and take a look at him some time."

"What's the matter with him?" asked Sergeant Kolda.

"That's just it," said Mr. Pacovsky, annoyed, "I don't know. It's nothing you can really put your finger on, but — How should I put it? The man looks just a bit suspicious to me. Yes."

"Roedl, Roedl," Sergeant Kolda pondered. "The name doesn't tell me anything. What does he do?"

"I don't know," said Mr. Pacovsky. "He's supposed to be a bank clerk, but I can't get out of him what bank he works for. It looks just a bit suspicious to me. He's polite enough, but — And he never gets any mail, either. I have the feeling he's avoiding people. And it just looks a bit suspicious to me."

"How do you mean, he avoids people?" asked Sergeant Kolda.

"He doesn't exactly avoid them," Mr. Pacovsky stated uncertainly, "but . . . who on earth goes to the country in

September? And every time a car stops in front of the place he goes up to his room, even when he's in the middle of a meal. Really, that's what happens. I'm telling you, I don't like the looks of this Roedl one bit."

Sergeant Kolda thought it over for a while. "You know what, Mr. Pacovsky," he proposed sagely, "maybe you could tell him you close The Lookout up in the fall. Let him go to Prague or some other place, that's what you should do! Why should we have to put up with him here? That's what."

The next day, Sunday, the young police officer Hurych, nicknamed Dreamboat and Angelpuss, was going off duty; on the way home it occurred to him to drop by the inn, and he went straight from the woods to the rear courtyard of The Lookout. When he reached the back gate, he stopped to blow the ashes out of his pipe. At that very moment he heard the rattle of a window on the second floor overlooking the courtyard, and something thudded to the ground behind him. Dreamboat raced into the yard and grabbed the shoulder of a man who, for no reason at all, had leaped from the window. "Sir," he said disapprovingly, "what are you doing?"

The man he was holding by the shoulder was pale and expressionless. "Why shouldn't I jump?" he replied faintly. "I live here, don't I?"

Officer Dreamboat studied the situation briefly. "Maybe you do," he said, "but your jumping from the window is just a bit suspicious."

"I didn't know it was prohibited," the expressionless man apologized. "Ask Mr. Pacovsky if I don't live here. My name's Roedl."

"Maybe it is," said Officer Dreamboat. "Show me your papers."

"Papers?" said Mr. Roedl hesitantly. "I don't have any papers with me. I'll write away for them."

"We'll write away for them ourselves," said Dreamboat obligingly. "You come along with me, Mr. Roedl."

"Where?" protested Mr. Roedl, his face ashen. "What right . . . what right do you have to take me in?"

"Because there's something just a bit suspicious about you, Mr. Roedl," Dreamboat declared. "You just hold your tongue and come along with me."

Sergeant Kolda was seated at the police station in his bedroom slippers, smoking a long, old-fashioned pipe and reading the police weekly. When he saw Dreamboat with Mr. Roedl, he launched into a tirade: "My God, Dreamboat, what are you doing to me? Can't I have a little peace even on Sunday? What are you hauling people in here for on a Sunday?"

"Sergeant, sir," announced Dreamboat, "this man looks just a bit suspicious to me. When he saw me going into The Lookout, he jumped out of a window into the courtyard and tried to run off into the woods. And he doesn't have any papers, either. So I brought him in. He says his name's Roedl."

"Well, well," Sergeant Kolda said with interest. "Mr. Roedl. So now we've got you, Mr. Roedl."

"You can't arrest me," Mr. Roedl said uneasily.

"We can't," agreed Sergeant Kolda. "But we can keep you here, can't we? Dreamboat, hop on over to the inn, go through Mr. Roedl's room, and have his things brought here. Take a seat, Mr. Roedl."

"I . . . I refuse to make any statement whatsoever," stammered Mr. Roedl. "I'll file a complaint . . . I protest — "

"My God, Mr. Roedl," Sergeant Kolda sighed, "you do look just a bit suspicious! I'm not going to get into an argument with you. Just sit over there and keep your trap shut." Whereupon he picked up his newspaper and went on reading.

"You know, Mr. Roedl," he said presently, "anybody can see just by looking at you that something's wrong. If I were in your shoes I'd tell all, and then you'd have some peace of mind. But if you don't want to, well, that's fine, too."

Mr. Roedl sat there, pale and bathed in sweat; Sergeant Kolda studied him, snorting in annoyance, and then went to turn the mushrooms that he was drying over the stove.

"Look here, Mr. Roedl," he began again after a time, "we're going to check out your identity; and meanwhile you'll be sitting in custody and you won't have anyone to talk to. Don't be pigheaded!"

Mr. Roedl persisted in stubborn silence, and Sergeant Kolda, grumbling in disgust, cleaned his pipe. "All right," he said, "look at it this way: it'll be maybe a month before we find out who you are; but that month, Mr. Roedl, won't count towards your sentence. It'd be a shame to lose a whole month of your sentence that way!"

"And if I confess," said Mr. Roedl, wavering, "then . . . "

"Then you'll be remanded into custody, that's what," Sergeant Kolda explained, "and that'll count towards your sentence. Do whatever you like. You look a bit suspicious to me, and I'll be glad when they turn you over to the district court. That's all there is to it, Mr. Roedl."

Mr. Roedl sighed; in his shifty eyes appeared an expression of sorrow and near exhaustion. "Why," he asked, wrenching out the words, "why does everyone say there's something a bit suspicious about me?"

"Because you look scared," Sergeant Kolda replied sensibly. "You're hiding something, Mr. Roedl, and people don't like that. How come you never look anyone straight in the eye? You're uneasy. That's what it is, Mr. Roedl."

"Rosner," the pale, dispirited man corrected him.

Sergeant Kolda thought it over. "Rosner, Rosner: wait a minute, which Rosner? That name sounds familiar to me somehow."

"Ferdinand Rosner, of course," the man blurted out.

"Ferdinand Rosner," Sergeant Kolda repeated, "that rings a bell. Ferdinand Rosner."

"The Vienna Depository Bank," the pale man prompted.

"Aha!" Sergeant Kolda exclaimed joyfully. "Embezzlement. Now I've got it. Of course: Rosner! My dear man, we've had a warrant out for you for the last three years! So you're Rosner," he repeated with delight. "But why didn't you say so right away?

Would you believe it, I came that close to throwing you out the door, and you're Rosner! Dreamboat," he trumpeted at Officer Hurych, who was just coming in, "would you believe it, this is Rosner, the embezzler!"

"That's me," Rosner winced rather plaintively.

"There now, Rosner," Sergeant Kolda comforted him, "you'll get used to it. Be happy that it's finally out in the open. But tell me, dear man, where in God's name have you been hiding out these past three years?"

"Hiding out," said Rosner bitterly. "Either in sleeping cars or high-priced hotels. Nobody there asks who you are or where you're from."

"Oh my," Sergeant Kolda sympathized, "your overhead must have been enormous!"

"You can't imagine how much," Rosner said, beginning to relax. "But I couldn't very well go to the sort of place that's always being raided by the cops, could I? No, sir, I had to keep on living above my means! I never stayed anywhere longer than three nights, till now — and now you've collared me."

"Why, yes," Sergeant Kolda said by way of consolation, "but your money was already beginning to run out, wasn't it, Rosner? It would've all come to the same end."

"It would have," Rosner agreed. "But I tell you, I couldn't have kept it up much longer. You know, I haven't had a real heart-to-heart talk with anyone for three years, till now! Why, I couldn't even eat my meals in peace! As soon as somebody started looking at me, I'd get out of there fast . . . Everyone stared at me so strangely," he moaned. "I used to think everyone was from the police. Just imagine, even Mr. Pacovsky!"

"Don't you worry yourself about that," Sergeant Kolda said. "What I mean is, Mr. Pacovsky really was a policeman once."

"You see?" Rosner grumbled. "And you expect somebody like me to escape notice? But why did everyone stare at me so strangely? Do I look like some kind of criminal?"

Sergeant Kolda looked him over thoughtfully. "I'll tell you something, Rosner," he said, "not now you don't; now you look just like everybody else. But you used to look a bit suspicious, dear boy; I don't know what it was that struck me as kind of odd about you . . . Well," he decided, "Dreamboat can take you to your cell. It isn't six o'clock yet, so they can count today as part of your sentence. If it wasn't Sunday, I'd take you there myself, just so you'd know that — hm, that there's no hard feelings. It was just that strangeness of yours that did it, Rosner; but now everything's fine. Lock him up, Dreamboat!"

"You know, Dreamboat," Sergeant Kolda said that evening, "I don't mind telling you, I liked that Rosner a lot. A really decent man, isn't he? I doubt if they'll give him more than a year."

"I put in a good word for him," said Officer Dreamboat, blushing, "so they'd give him two blankets. He isn't used to sleeping on a bunk . . . "

"That's right," observed Sergeant Kolda. "And I'll tell the guard to have a few words with him now and then. Just so this Rosner will know he's back among people again."

The Poet

It was a routine police matter: at four o'clock in the morning, an automobile knocked down an old, drunken woman on Zitna Street and drove off at high speed. And now Dr. Mejzlik had to determine which automobile it was. Such responsibilities weigh heavily on a young police captain.

"Hm," Dr. Mejzlik said to Officer 141, "from a distance of thirty paces, then, you saw a fast-moving car and a body lying in the street. What did you do first?"

"First, I ran over to the victim," the policeman reported, "to apply first aid."

"First, you should have identified the car," Dr. Mejzlik grumbled, "and then worried about the old lady. But perhaps," he added, scratching his head with a pencil, "I would have done the same thing. At any rate, you didn't see the number on the license plate; was there anything else about the car — ?"

"I think," Officer 141 said slowly, "that it was a dark color of some kind. Possibly dark blue or dark red. It wasn't easy to see because of the exhaust fumes."

"Oh, Christ," Dr. Mejzlik despaired, "then how am I going to find that car? Am I supposed to chase after all the drivers in the city and ask them ever so kindly to tell me whether or not they ran over an old lady? What do you expect me to do?"

The policeman shrugged his shoulders with the helplessness of a subordinate. "Sir," he said, "one witness has reported in to me, but he doesn't know anything, either. He's waiting outside, sir."

"Well, bring him in," Dr. Mejzlik said with disgust, and he searched in vain for some clue to spring forth from the meager accident report. "Name and address, please," he said mechanically, without so much as looking at the witness.

"Kralik, Jan, engineering student," the witness said stolidly.

"And you were were present, sir, when at four o'clock this morning an unknown automobile knocked down Bozena Machackova?"

"Yes, and I'd have to say it was the driver's fault. You see, Captain, the street was completely empty; if the driver had slowed down at the intersection — "

"How far away were you standing?" Dr. Mejzlik interrupted him.

"Ten paces. I was seeing a friend home from a — a coffee house, and while we were walking along Zitna Street — "

"Who is your friend?" Dr. Mejzlik interrupted again. "I don't see his name here."

"Jaroslav Nerad, the poet," the witness said with a certain amount of pride. "But I doubt if he could tell you anything — "

"Why not?" Dr. Mejzlik grumbled again, clutching at any straw.

"Because he . . . he's the sort of poet that, if something unpleasant happens, he bursts into tears like a little child and runs home to hide. Anyway, while we were on Zitna Street, suddenly there came rushing up from behind us, at an insane speed, this car — "

"License number what?"

"I don't know, sir, I didn't notice it. I was watching that insane driving, and I immediately said to myself that — "

"And what kind of car was it?" Dr. Mejzlik interrupted.

"Four-cylinder internal combustion engine," the expert witness answered. "Of course, I'm no good at makes of cars — "

"And what color was it? Who was in it? Was it a convertible or a sedan?"

"I don't know," the witness said in confusion. "I think it was a sort of black car, but I can't come any closer than that, because when the accident happened I said to Nerad: Look, those bastards knocked somebody down and didn't even stop!"

"Hm," Dr. Mejzlik commented with dissatisfaction. "That is, admittedly, a fitting and no doubt correct moral reaction, but I would rather you'd gotten the license number. I am amazed, sir, how incapable people are of simple observation. You're absolutely convinced that the driver is at fault, you're absolutely convinced that people like that are bastards, but as for systematic, practical observation — Thank you, Mr. Kralik; I won't delay you any longer."

Within the hour, Officer 141 had rung the bell at the lodgings of the poet Jaroslav Nerad. Yes, the poet Nerad was at home, but he was sleeping. Moments later, the poet himself was at the doorway, rolling small, astonished eyes at the policeman; he couldn't remember, exactly, just what wrongdoing he had committed.

At length he was able to grasp why they wanted him at the police station. "Must I go?" he asked suspiciously. "The fact is, I don't remember anything at all; that night I was a bit — "

"Smashed," the policeman said understandingly. "I've known many poets, sir. So get dressed, sir; I'll wait for you."

Whereupon the poet and the policeman began to chat about neighborhood bars, life in general, various celestial phenomena, and many other matters; only politics was alien to both. Thus, in friendly and instructive conversation, the poet arrived at the station house.

"You are Mr. Jaroslav Nerad, poet," Dr. Mejzlik said to him, "and witness. You were present when an unidentified automobile knocked down Bozena Machackova."

"Yes," the poet sighed.

"Can you tell me what kind of car it was? Whether it was a sedan or a convertible, what color, who was in it, what the license number was?"

The poet struggled with his thoughts. "I don't know," he said. "I didn't notice."

"You don't recall any details?" Dr. Mejzlik pressed.

"Not a one," the poet said candidly. "I never pay attention to details, you see."

"Thank you," Dr. Mejzlik fired off with considerable irony. "Just what, if may I ask, were you paying attention to?"

"The total mood," the poet replied vaguely. "You know, the long, deserted street . . . at dawn . . . and how that woman lay there on the ground — " Suddenly he leaped to his feet. "But I wrote something about it after I got home!" He fumbled in his pockets and began to pull out an increasing number of wrappers, bills, and other scraps of paper. "No, that's not it," he kept muttering, "that's not it, either — Wait, maybe this is it," he said, absorbed in studying the back of an envelope.

"Show it to me," Dr. Mejzlik said indulgently.

"It's nothing," the poet objected. "But if you like, I'll read it to you." Whereupon, rolling his eyes rapturously and melodiously elongating the syllables, he recited:

> march of dark houses once twice to stop to stand
> aurora plays upon a mandolin
> why girl why do you blush
> with oncoming car 120 HP to the end of the earth
> or to Singapore
> stop stop the car flies on
> our great love sprawls in dust
> a girl a broken blossom
> swan's neck bosom drum and cymbal
> why do I weep so much

"And that's all of it," Jaroslav Nerad declared.

"Excuse me," said Dr. Mejzlik, "but what does it mean?"

"Well, it's the automobile accident, of course," the poet said in astonishment. "You mean you don't understand it?"

"I don't think so," Dr. Mejzlik said with a frown. "Somehow it doesn't convey to me that on July 15, at four o'clock in the morning, on Zitna Street, an automobile with license number such-and-such knocked down a sixty-year-old drunken beggarwoman, Bozena Machackova; and that she was injured and taken to the General Hospital, and that she nearly died. Your poem, sir, insofar as I can tell, did not mention those particular facts. No."

"Sir," the poet said, rubbing his nose, "that is only raw,

surface reality. A poem is inner reality. Poems are unfettered, surreal images which reality evokes in the subconscious of the poet, you see? Visual and aural associations, you might say. And the reader must yield himself to them," Jaroslav Nerad proclaimed reprovingly. "Then he will understand."

"I beg your pardon," Dr. Mejzlik erupted. "No, wait a minute, loan me your opus. Thank you. All right then, here we have, hm: 'March of dark houses once twice to stop to stand.' Please explain to me, if you will — "

"But that's Zitna Street," the poet said serenely. "Those two rows of buildings, you see."

"And why isn't it, say, Narodni Avenue?" Dr. Mejzlik asked skeptically.

"Because it isn't as straight," came the answer with conviction.

"All right. 'Aurora plays upon a mandolin' — Well, we'll grant that one. 'Why girl why do you blush' — Please, where does this girl come into it?"

"The red sunrise," the poet said laconically.

"Aha. Excuse me. 'With oncoming car 120 HP to the end of the earth' — Well?"

"Maybe that was when the car arrived," the poet explained.

"It was 120 horsepower?"

"I don't know about that; it means that it was coming fast. As if it wanted to soar to the end of the earth."

"I see. 'Or to Singapore' — Why exactly Singapore, for heaven's sake?"

The poet shrugged his shoulders. "I don't know. I suppose it's because the Malays are there."

"And what is the relationship between the car and the Malays? Hm?"

The poet fidgeted uneasily. "Maybe the car was brown, could that be it?" he pondered. "Certainly something there was brown. Why else would it have been Singapore?"

"Look," said Dr. Mejzlik, "that car has already been red, blue, and black. What am I supposed to choose from all that?"

"Choose brown," the poet advised. "It's a nice color."

" 'Our great love sprawls in dust / a girl a broken blossom,' " Dr. Mejzlik read on. "This broken blossom, is that the drunken beggarwoman?"

"I wouldn't write about a drunken beggarwoman," the poet said, offended. "She was simply a woman, do you see?"

"Aha. And what is this: 'swan's neck bosom drum and cymbal' — is that free association?"

"Show it to me," the poet said in confusion, and he bent over the piece of paper. " 'Swan's neck bosom drum and cymbal' — What can that be?"

"I just asked that," Dr. Mejzlik grumbled somewhat touchily.

"Wait," the poet reflected, "there must have been something that reminded me — Listen, doesn't it strike you that sometimes the numeral two looks like a swan's neck? Look at this," and with Mejzlik's pencil he wrote a 2.

"Aha," Dr. Mejzlik said attentively. "And what of the bosom?"

"Surely that's a three, two curves, right?" the poet marveled.

"You still have the drum and cymbal," the police captain burst out, his voice taut with suspense.

"Drum and cymbal," the poet Nerad said thoughtfully, "drum and cymbal . . . that might just possibly be a five, mightn't it? Watch," he said, and he drew the numeral 5. "That little belly is like a drum, and the cymbal above it — "

"Wait," Dr. Mejzlik said, and he wrote down 235 on the piece of paper. "Are you certain that the car had the license number 235?"

"I paid no attention whatsoever to any numbers," Jaroslav Nerad proclaimed resolutely. "But something like that must have been there — Or why else would it be here?" he marveled, inspecting his little composition. "And, you know, this is the best part of the entire poem."

* * *

Two days later, Dr. Mejzlik called on the poet. This time the poet was not asleep, for he had a girlfriend of some sort there, and he began a futile search for a vacant chair to offer the police captain.

"I can't stay," said Dr. Mejzlik. "I only came to tell you that it really was a car with license number 235."

"What car?" the poet wondered.

"Swan's neck bosom drum and cymbal," Dr. Mejzlik poured out in a single breath. "And Singapore, too."

"Oh, of course; now I know," the poet remarked. "So you see, here you have inner reality. Would you like me to read you a couple of other poems? You'll understand them now."

"Some other time," the police captain answered without hesitation. "When I have another case."

Mr. Janik's Cases

This Mr. Janik is neither the Dr. Janik from the government ministry, nor the Janik who shot the estate-owner Jirsa, nor the stockbroker Janik who is said to have made a run of three hundred and twenty-six at billiards, but Mr. Janik the head of the firm of Janik and Holecek, wholesale dealers in pulp and paper goods; he is a respectable and rather short gentleman who once courted a Miss Severova but, in his despair at her refusal, never married; in brief, the Janik in question, to avoid all possibility of error, is known as Janik the pulp-and-paper man.

Now, Mr. Janik the pulp-and-paper man got involved in this following matter by sheer luck, somewhere along the Sazava River, where he was spending his summer vacation, when they were searching for the body of Ruzena Regnerova, who had been murdered by her fiancé, Jindrich Basta, who had soaked the poor woman's body in kerosene, burnt it, and buried it in the woods. Although Basta had been proven guilty of murdering Ruzena, no trace of her body or bones could be found. For nine days the police had been tramping through the forest guided by Basta, who kept pointing out to them that this is where it was or that is where it was; they kept digging and shoveling, but to no avail. It was clear that the exhausted Basta was either leading them on a wild goose chase or playing for time. He was a young man from a respectable and well-to-do family, this Jindrich Basta, but probably the doctor had squeezed his head too hard with the forceps when he came into the world; in brief, there was something wrong with him, he was a peculiar and perverted human being. For nine days now he had led the police all over the forest, pale as a ghost, his eyes twitching with a nystagmus of horror; it was painful and awkward to look at him. The police floundered about with him through bilberries and marshes; by now they were so furious that it's a wonder they didn't snap and bite, and they were thinking to themselves, you animal, we'll haul you around till you steer us to the right spot in spite of yourself! Basta, so spent that he could hardly drag himself along, sank to the ground yet again and rasped: "Here, here's where I buried her!"

"On your feet, Basta," a policeman bawled at him. "This isn't the place! Get moving!"

Basta stood up, tottering, and staggered on a little farther until he once again collapsed with exhaustion. The order of the procession was something like this: four uniformed officers, two plainclothesmen, a pair of gamekeepers, and some old codgers with shovels; and, convulsively shuffling along behind, a livid wreck of a human being, Jindrich Basta.

Mr. Janik knew the policemen from the local inn; consequently, he was allowed to join this tragic procession through the woods without being yanked aside and told to mind his own business. Besides, he was carrying a parcel containing canned sardines, salami, cognac, and similar commodities, which came in very handy. On the ninth day things were bad, so bad that Mr. Janik resolved: I won't tag along with them again. The policemen were very nearly barking with rage and exasperation, the gamekeepers were protesting that they'd had enough of this and had plenty of other work to do, the old codgers with the shovels were grumbling that twenty per day was damn little for a tough job like this and, crumpled on the ground, Jindrich Basta was shaking in convulsions, no longer responding to the shouts and demands of the police. At this bleak and bewildering moment Mr. Janik did something which was not, so to speak, on the agenda: he knelt down beside Basta, thrust a ham roll in his hand, and said compassionately: "Here, Mr. Basta — come now, Mr. Basta, can you hear me?" Basta uttered a howl and burst into tears. "I'll find it . . . I'll find it, sir," he sobbed, and he tried to stand up; at that moment one of the plainclothesmen came over and lifted him to his feet almost tenderly. "You can lean on me, Mr. Basta," he encouraged him. "Mr. Janik'll take hold of you from the other side; that's it. Now then, Mr. Basta, you'll show Mr. Janik where it was, won't you?"

An hour later, Jindrich Basta, smoking a cigarette, stood over a shallow pit from which a thigh bone protruded.

"Is that the body of Ruzena Regnerova?" Sergeant Trunka asked grimly.

"Yes," Jindrich Basta said calmly, and he flicked the ash from his cigarette into the open pit. "Is there anything else you want, gentlemen?" —

"You know, sir," Sergeant Trunka declared to Mr. Janik that evening at the inn, "you're a regular psychologist, that's all there is to it. To your health, sir! He softened up the minute you called him 'Mr. Basta'! He was trying to cling to his self-respect, the miserable wretch, and here we were shoving him around — But tell me, please, how did you know that being polite to him would work?"

"Oh," said the hero of the day, blushing modestly, "that's just the way I am, you know. I say 'Mr.' to everyone, you know. And then I felt sorry for him, so I thought I'd offer him a ham roll — "

"Instinct," announced Sergeant Trunka. "That's what I call a nose for it, and psychology, too. To your health, Mr. Janik! It's a waste of talent, though, you really ought to join the force — "

Some time after that, Mr. Janik took the night train to Bratislava. A Slovak paper mill was holding its annual stockholders meeting there, and since Mr. Janik was very much involved with the mill, he wanted to attend. "Wake me up before we get to Bratislava," he said to the conductor, "or else I'll sleep right on through to the Austrian border." Whereupon he crawled into his berth, pleased at having the compartment to himself, settled down comfortably as a dead man, reflected for a few minutes on various business matters, and fell fast asleep. He had no idea what time it might have been when the conductor opened the door of the compartment for some passenger, who then undressed and climbed into the upper berth. Only in a half-dream did Mr. Janik see a pair of socks and two extraordinarily hairy legs dangling down, and hear the grunts of someone burying himself in the bedcovers, followed by the click of the light switch and then clattering darkness again. Mr. Janik dreamed about a number of things, mostly that he was being pursued by hairy legs, and then he was awakened by a prolonged silence and the sound of somebody outside calling: "Until we meet again at Zilina!" At that he leaped up from his berth and looked out the window; he saw that day was breaking, that the train had come to a stop in the Bratislava station, and that the conductor had forgotten to wake him. In his panic he didn't even stop to swear, but with feverish speed tugged his trousers and the rest of his clothes over his pyjamas, shoved all his odds and ends into his pockets, and jumped onto the platform just as the signal was being given for the train to leave.

"Oof," Mr. Janik spluttered, and he shook his fist at the departing train and went into the men's room to finish dressing. When finally he got around to organizing the contents of his pockets, he was horror-struck: in his breast pocket, instead of one billfold he had two. The fatter of the two, which wasn't his, contained sixty new Czechoslovak five-hundred-crown notes. Obviously it belonged to his traveling companion of the previous night, but how it had got into his pocket Mr. Janik, still half asleep, couldn't for the life of him imagine. Very well then, the first thing to do, of course, was to get hold of somebody from the police to whom he could hand over the stranger's billfold. The police left Mr. Janik sitting on the brink of starvation while they telephoned to Galenta, so that the people there could notify the passenger in berth number 14 that his billfold, with the money, was at the police station in Bratislava. Then Mr. Janik had to give them information about himself, and then he went off to have breakfast. Then someone from the police tracked him down and asked him if there hadn't been some kind of mix-up; the fact was, the gentleman in berth number 14 claimed that he hadn't lost a billfold. Mr. Janik had to go back to the police station and explain for the second time how the billfold had come into his possession. Meanwhile, two plainclothesmen had taken the sixty bills away somewhere, and only after Mr. Janik had waited for half an hour, seated between two detectives, did they deliver him to some exalted, high-level police official.

"Mr. Janik," said the exalted, high-level police official, "we're sending a telegram at this very moment to Parkan-Nana to have the passenger in berth number 14 detained. Can you give us an exact description of him?"

About all that Mr. Janik could say was that the passenger had remarkably hairy legs. The exalted, high-level police official was not overly satisfied with this. "You see, those notes are forgeries," he said suddenly. "You'll have to remain here until we can confront you with your fellow passenger."

Inwardly Mr. Janik cursed the conductor, who had not wakened him in time and thus was to blame for Mr. Janik, in his haste, winding up with that confounded billfold in his pocket. After perhaps an hour, a message arrived from Parkan-Nana to the effect that the passenger in berth number 14 had gotten off the train at Nove Zamky; where he had gone after that, by foot or by other means, was, for the time being, unknown.

"Mr. Janik," the exalted, high-level police official said at last, "we won't keep you here any longer; we're turning this matter over to Inspector Hrusek in Prague, who's first-rate on these counterfeits. But I want to assure you that this is very serious business. You go on back to Prague as fast as you can, and they'll call you there. In the meantime, thanks for coming across those forgeries in such a lucky way. That was no mere accident, sir."

Scarcely had Mr. Janik returned to Prague than police headquarters called; he was met by a huge, heavy-set gentleman whom everyone there addressed as President, and the sallow and scrawny individual named Inspector Hruska. "Sit down, Mr. Janik," said the heavy-set gentleman as he broke the seal on a small package. "Is this the billfold that you . . . um, that you found in your pocket at the Bratislava train station?"

"Yes," sighed Mr. Janik.

The heavy-set gentleman counted the new notes inside the billfold. "Sixty," he said. "All with the serial number 27451. That's the number they telegraphed us from the frontier at Cheb."

The scrawny man picked up one of the notes, closed his eyes and rubbed it between his fingers, and then sniffed at it. "These here are from Graz," he said. "The ones from Geneva aren't so sticky."

"Graz," the heavy-set gentleman repeated, deep in thought. "That's where they make these things for Budapest, isn't it?"

The scrawny man merely blinked. "I guess I could go to Vienna," he offered. "But the Vienna police still won't hand him over to us."

"Hm," muttered the heavy-set gentleman. "Then figure out some other way for us to get hold of him. If nothing else works, tell them we'll exchange him for Leberhardt. Well, a pleasant journey, Hruska. And as for you, sir," he said, turning to Mr. Janik, "I really don't know how to thank you. You're the one who found Jindrich Basta's girl, aren't you?"

Mr. Janik turned red. "That was only a fluke," he said quickly. "I really . . . I had no idea that . . . "

"You've got a real knack for this, Mr. Janik," the heavy-set gentleman said approvingly. "It's a God-given talent. Most people couldn't track down a clue to save their souls, while others stumble right on top of them. You ought to join us, Mr. Janik."

"I really couldn't," Mr. Janik protested. "I . . . what I mean is, I've got my own business . . . doing very well actually . . . an old established firm I inherited from my grandfather . . . "

"Suit yourself," the huge man sighed, "but it's a pity all the same. It isn't everyone who has your kind of luck. We'll meet again, Mr. Janik."

About a month later, Mr. Janik was having dinner with a business friend from Leipzig. Needless to say, at a dinner of that kind, between businessmen, cost was not a consideration — the brandy in particular was exceptionally good — and by the end of the evening Mr. Janik had absolutely no intention of walking home, so he beckoned to the waiter and said: "I'll need a car and driver!" On leaving the hotel, he saw that a car was already waiting in front of the entrance. So he got inside, slammed the door, and in his cheerful mood clean forgot that he hadn't told the driver where he lived. The car started up nonetheless, and Mr. Janik, comfortably installed in a corner, fell asleep.

How long the ride lasted, he had no idea; but he was awakened by the car stopping and the driver opening the door: "Here we are, sir. You're to go upstairs, sir." Mr. Janik glanced around to see where on earth he could possibly be, but since it didn't really make that much difference to him, thanks to the brandy, he went on up the stairs and opened a door, behind which he could hear a noisy conversation. There were perhaps twenty men in the room, all of whom turned to stare anxiously at the door as he entered. Suddenly there was an odd silence. One of the men stood up and came toward Mr. Janik: "What do you want? Who are you?"

Mr. Janik looked around in astonishment. He recognized five or six of those present — they were wealthy people who, it was rumored, shared certain political interests, but Mr. Janik never meddled in politics. "Well, look who's here," he said cheerfully, "if it isn't Mr. Koubek and Mr. Heller. And you too, Ferry! Boys, I could do with a drink."

"What's he doing here?" raged one of the group. "Is he one of us?"

Two others from the group pushed Mr. Janik back into the hallway. "How'd you get here?" one of them demanded savagely. "Who told you to come here?"

Mr. Janik was sobered by this lack of friendliness. "Where am I?" he asked indignantly. "Why the devil did you bring me here?"

One of the two men raced downstairs and pounced on the driver. "You damn fool," he shouted, "where did you pick him up?"

"In front of the hotel, where else?" the driver shot back defensively. "They told me this afternoon, wait for some man in front of the hotel at ten tonight and bring him here. This man got in my car at ten on the dot and never said a word, so I drove him straight here — "

"Good God," yelled the other, "it's the wrong man! You've really blown it for us now!"

Resigned, Mr. Janik sat down on the stairs. "I get it," he said complacently, "it's some kind of secret meeting, isn't it? Now you'll have to strangle me and bury the corpse. Glass of water!"

"Look," said one of the two men, "you're just confused. That wasn't Mr. Koubek or Mr. Heller up there, understand? It's a mistake, that's all. We'll get you back to Prague. Sorry for the misunderstanding."

"Don't mention it," Mr. Janik said magnanimously. "I know the driver's going to shoot me on the way back and bury me in the woods. It doesn't matter. Idiot that I was, I forgot to give him my address. This is what I get for it."

"You're drunk, aren't you?" the man asked with unmistakable relief.

"More or less," Mr. Janik agreed. "I had dinner with Meyer, and he's from Dresden, see. I'm Janik, wholesale paper and pulp," he introduced himself from his seat on the steps. "A fine old firm founded by my grandfather."

"Go sleep it off," the man advised him. "And once you've slept it off, you won't even remember that we — hm, that we inconvenienced you like this."

"That's right," Mr. Janik said with considerable dignity. "You go sleep it off, too. Where's my bed?"

"It's back at your house," said the man. "The driver's going to take you home. Here, I'll help you stand up."

"No need for that," Mr. Janik demurred. "I'm not as drunk as you are. You go sleep it off. Driver, take me to Bubenec."

The car headed back towards Bubenec, and Mr. Janik, with a foxy glint in his eye, paid close attention to where they were starting from and which way they were going.

The next morning he telephoned police headquarters and related his adventures of the previous night. "Mr. Janik," replied the voice from headquarters after a moment's silence, "this is of *extreme* interest to us. I beg you to come down to headquarters *at once*."

When Mr. Janik arrived, four people were waiting for him, with the huge, heavy-set gentleman at their head. Mr. Janik had to tell once more what had happened and whom he had seen. "The license number of the car was NXX 705," added the heavy-set gentleman. "A private car. Of the six persons Mr. Janik recognized, three are new to me. Gentlemen, I'll leave you now. Mr. Janik, come with me."

Mr. Janik sat like a small, shy schoolboy in the large office of the heavy-set gentleman, who was now pacing to and fro, deep in thought. "Mr. Janik," he said at last, "the first thing I must ask you is: not a word to anyone about this. Reasons of state, do you understand?"

Mr. Janik nodded silently. Dear God, he thought to himself, I've let myself in for it again!

"Mr. Janik," the heavy-set gentleman said suddenly, "I'm

not trying to flatter you, but we need your services. You're lucky, that's all there is to it — People can talk all they like about method, but a detective who doesn't have plain dumb luck is worthless. We need people who are lucky. We've got more than enough brains; what we need are a few lucky breaks. What you really ought to do, you know, is join us."

"But what about my business?" Mr. Janik whispered, thoroughly miserable.

"Your partner can look after that; it would be a shame to waste a gift like yours. Well, what do you say?"

"I'll . . . I'll have to think it over," stammered the unhappy Mr. Janik. "I'll come and see you in a week; but if I really have the knack . . . and if that's what I should do . . . I just don't know; but I have to go now."

"All right," said the heavy-set gentleman, giving him a massive handshake. "But don't doubt for one minute that you have the knack. See you next week."

Less than a week had gone by when Mr. Janik turned up again. "Well, here I am," he declared, his face beaming.

"Made up your mind?" asked the heavy-set gentleman.

"Yes, thank God," Mr. Janik sighed happily. "What I mean is, I've come to tell you that it won't work, that I'm just not cut out for it."

"No? But why not?"

"Picture this," announced the jubilant Mr. Janik, "my partner's been stealing from me these past five years, and I, idiot that I am, never had the faintest idea what he was up to! Well, just ask yourself, what kind of detective would *I* make? For five years I worked side by side with that rascal, and I never once caught on! So you can see I'd be worthless, God be praised! And I was already starting to get so nervous! My goodness, I'm glad that nothing's going to come of it! I'm safely out of it now, aren't I? Thank you, sir, many, many thanks!"

The Fall of the House of Voticky

One day there arrived at the office of Detective Captain Dr. Mejzlik a smallish man with gold-rimmed glasses and a worried expression. "Archivist Divisek," he murmured. "Captain, I've come to consult you . . . as a prominent criminologist; that is, I've been told that you happen to be . . . that is to say . . . most particularly in regard to the more complex cases — That is to say, this is an unusually puzzling case," he declared emphatically.

"Just tell me what it's all about," said Dr. Mejzlik, reaching for a notepad and pencil.

"There ought to be an investigation," archivist Divisek blurted out, "as to who murdered Sir Petr Berkovec, how his brother Henricus died, and what happened to Sir Petr's wife, Katerina."

"Berkovec, Petr," Dr. Mejzlik reflected. "To my knowledge we've received no report of his death. You'd like to make a statement, is that it?"

"Oh, no," the archivist said. "That is to say, I've only come to you for advice, you see. Something terrible must have happened."

"When was it?" Dr. Mejzlik prompted. "First of all the date, please."

"In the year fourteen hundred and sixty-five, of course," said Mr. Divisek, looking reproachfully at the captain through his glasses. "You ought to know that, sir: during the blessed reign of King Jiri of Podebrady."

"I see," said Dr. Mejzlik, and he tossed the notepad and pencil aside. "In that case, my dear sir," he stated with conspicuous cordiality, "it would be better to talk with Dr. Knobloch," by which he meant the police physician. "Why don't I call him?"

The archivist frowned. "What a shame," he said, "since you were so highly recommended to me. You see, I am in the midst of preparing a historical work on the reign of Jiri of Podebrady, and when I stumbled, yes, stumbled across this matter, I didn't know where to turn for advice."

Harmless, Dr. Mejzlik decided. "My dear sir," he said quickly, "I'm afraid I can't be of much use to you. I must confess that I'm far too weak in history."

"That's a mistake," Mr. Divisek noted sternly. "You ought to know history. But since the relevant historical material is not known to you at first hand, sir, I will introduce you to all the known facts; unfortunately, there are very few of them. First and foremost, there is the letter from Sir Ladislav Pchac of Olesna to Sir Jan Borsovsky of Cercany. You are, of course, aware of this letter."

"I'm sorry to say that I'm not," Dr. Mejzlik confessed with the contrition of an ill-prepared schoolboy.

"But, my good man," Mr. Divisek burst out in astonishment, "the historian Sebek published this letter seventeen years ago in his *Regesta*! At the very least you ought to know *that*! However," he added, adjusting his glasses, "neither Sebek nor Pekar nor Novotny nor anyone else devoted proper attention to this letter. And this very letter, which of course you ought to have known about, led me to the clues in this case."

"Aha," Dr. Mejzlik said. "Go on."

"First of all, the letter," said the archivist. "Unfortunately, I don't have the text with me, but only one of its references pertains to our case. He — that is, Sir Ladislav Pchac — writes to Sir Jan Borsovsky that his uncle — that is to say, Sir Jan's uncle, Sir Jesek Skalicky of Skalice, in this Year of Our Lord 1465, is no longer in attendance at the court in Prague, in view of the fact that His Royal Highness commanded Sir Jesek, 'due to the woeful deeds at Votice Velenova,' as the writer puts it, henceforth to come no more to the royal court, to repent of the

Lord God his choleric temper, and to await divine justice. You understand by this," the archivist explained, "that we would say that His Royal Highness confined Sir Jesek to his own estates and holdings. Doesn't something about that strike you as odd, sir?"

"Not at the moment, no," Dr. Mejzlik said, drawing a remarkable spiral on his notepad.

"You see!" Mr. Divisek exclaimed triumphantly. "Sebek didn't notice it, either. It is a *very* striking circumstance, sir, that His Royal Highness did not summon Sir Jesek — whatever those woeful deeds might have been — to proper secular judgment, but committed him to divine justice instead. His Highness makes it unmistakably clear," the archivist continued, with obvious deference, "that these woeful deeds are of such a nature that the sovereign himself exempts them from worldly justice. If you knew His Highness, sir, you would realize that this is an extraordinarily unusual occurrence. King Jiri of blessed memory was most firm in his regard for the strict and proper discharge of justice."

"Perhaps the king was afraid of Sir Jesek," Dr. Mejzlik offered. "After all, in those days — "

The archivist sprang from his chair in indignation. "Sir," he stammered, "what are you saying? That King Jiri might have been afraid of someone? And of a mere knight at that?"

"Then there was some sort of favoritism involved," Dr. Mejzlik said. "You know, the way we — "

"No favoritism!" Mr. Divisek cried out, quite red in the face. "Perhaps one could speak of favoritism during the reign of King Vladislav, but during the reign of King Jiri — no indeed, sir, how could you even think of such a thing! He would have banished you for even suggesting it!" The archivist calmed himself somewhat. "No favoritism. Sir, it's obvious that there must have been something singular about those woeful deeds for His Royal Highness to have abandoned Sir Jesek to divine justice."

"And what were those deeds?" Dr. Mejzlik sighed.

Archivist Divisek looked surprised. "But that is what you

have to find out for me," he said in amazement. "What is a criminologist for? That's the reason I've come to you!"

"Oh, for heaven's sake," Dr. Mejzlik began defensively, but the archivist would not allow him to finish. "First you must know the facts," he instructed. "When I noticed those obscure references in the letter, I began to investigate those woeful deeds at Votice Velenova. Unfortunately, no records have survived; however, in the church at Votice Velenova I found the tombstone of Sir Petr Berkovec, and that stone, sir, is dated 1465! As you know, Sir Petr was the son-in-law of Sir Jesek; that is, Sir Petr married Sir Jesek's daughter, Katerina. Here is a photograph of the tombstone — now, don't you notice something peculiar about it?"

"No," Dr. Mejzlik said, examining both front and back of the photograph of the tombstone, on which was carved a knight with his hands crossed on his breast, surrounded by an inscription in gothic letters. "Wait, there's a fingerprint here in the corner."

"It's probably from my finger," the archivist said, "but notice the inscription!"

"Anno Domini MCCCCLXV," Dr. Mejzlik read with some effort. "The Year of Our Lord 1465. That's the year of this man's death, right?"

"Of course it is; don't you know anything? But take a look: some of the letters are noticeably larger than the others!" And the archivist quickly wrote with the pencil: ANNO DOMINI MCCCCLXV. "The sculptor deliberately made the letters O, C, and C larger; it's a cryptogram, do you see? Write down the letters O, C, C — doesn't anything strike you about them?"

"OCC, OCC," Dr. Mejzlik muttered, "that could be — aha, it's short for OCCISUS, right? That means 'murdered'!"

"Yes," the archivist proclaimed solemnly. "That is the manner in which the sculptor indicated to posterity that the nobly-born Sir Petr Berkovec de Wotice Welenova had been murdered. There we have it!"

"And his father-in-law, this Jesek Skalicky, murdered him,"

Dr. Mejzlik declared in an unexpected burst of historical enlightenment.

"Nonsense," Mr. Divisek said scornfully. "If Sir Jesek had murdered Sir Petr, His Royal Highness would have summoned him before the king's bench. But that's not all, sir: directly beside this tombstone is another, under which lies Henricus Berkovec de Wotice Welenova, the brother of Sir Petr; and on that stone is the very same date, 1465, only without a cryptogram! And on that same stone, Sir Henricus is shown with a sword in his hand; the sculptor obviously wanted to indicate that Sir Henricus had died in honorable battle. And now tell me, for heaven's sake, how these two deaths are connected!"

"Perhaps it's only a coincidence," Dr. Mejzlik suggested uncertainly, "that this Henricus lost his life that same year — "

"Coincidence!" the archivist shouted in exasperation. "Sir, we historians do not acknowledge coincidence! Where would we be if we admitted that something had happened by coincidence? There must be some kind of causal relationship! But I've not yet finished telling you everything. In the following year, 1466, Sir Jesek Skalicky died; and, if you please, his holdings at Skalice and Hradek fell to his cousin, Sir Jan Borsovsky of Cercany, whom I mentioned before. Do you realize what that means? It means, sir, that Sir Jesek's daughter, Katerina, who as every child knows was married in 1464 to this same Sir Petr Berkovec, was no longer living! And the Lady Katerina, if you please, has no tombstone anywhere! Would you say it is also coincidence that the Lady Katerina utterly vanishes from our sight immediately following the death of her husband? What about that? Do you call that coincidence, sir? And why is there no tombstone for her? Coincidence? Or does it have to do with those woeful deeds for which His Royal Highness committed Sir Jesek to divine justice?"

"It's altogether possible," Dr. Mejzlik supposed, with somewhat greater interest.

"It's altogether certain," Mr. Divisek proclaimed, admitting no doubts. "And now, you understand, it is a question of who killed whom and how everything is connected. The death of Sir Jesek does not interest us, because he survived those 'woeful deeds;' otherwise, King Jiri would not have bid him repent of them to the Lord God. We must establish who killed Sir Petr, how Sir Henricus died, how to account for the Lady Katerina, and what Sir Jesek Skalicky had to do with all this!"

"Wait," Dr. Mejzlik said, "let's draw up a list of the parties involved:

1. Petr Berkovec — murdered;
2. Henricus Berkovec — killed in battle, right?
3. Kate — vanished without a clue;
4. Jesek Skalicky — abandoned to divine justice. Is that it?"

"It is," said the archivist, blinking cautiously. "You might have said Sir Petr, Sir Jesek, and so forth. But go on."

"At the same time," Dr. Mejzlik reflected, "you eliminate the possibility that this Jesek could have murdered his son-in-law Petr Berkovec, because in that case he would have been brought before a jury."

"Summoned before the king's bench," the archivist amended. "Otherwise, that is correct."

"Then that leaves only Henricus, Petr's brother. Most likely Henricus murdered his brother — "

"That's not possible," grumbled the archivist. "If he had, they wouldn't have buried him in the church — at least not next to his brother."

"Aha. Then Henricus merely arranged for the murder of his brother and later himself was killed in some battle, right?"

"Why then would Sir Jesek have received a reprimand from the king for his violent temper?" retorted the archivist, fidgeting in dissatisfaction. "And where would Katerina have disappeared to?"

"That's true," Dr. Mejzlik muttered. "Listen, this is a complicated case. Let's suppose that Petr caught his wife Katerina *in flagrante* with Henricus and killed her. Her father, Jesek, found out about it and murdered his son-in-law in anger."

"That wouldn't work, either," objected Mr. Divisek. "If Sir

Petr had killed Katerina for adultery, her father would have agreed with what he'd done. Believe me, in those days they were quite strict about that sort of thing."

"Wait a minute," said Dr. Mejzlik, deep in thought. "Let's say that Petr simply killed her; maybe he got into an argument with her — "

"But then they'd have erected a tombstone for her," claimed the archivist, shaking his head. "That won't do. Sir, I have racked my brain over this for a year now, and nothing fits together."

"Hm," said Dr. Mejzlik, contemplating the rather short roster. "Confounded business. Maybe we're missing some fifth person."

"What would you do with a fifth?" asked Mr. Divisek reproachfully. "You don't even know what to do with the four we have!"

"Then it must have been one of those two who killed Petr Berkovec: either his father-in-law or his brother — I'll be damned!" Mejzlik shouted abruptly. "Listen, it's Katerina! She's the one who did it!"

"Oh, dear!" the archivist burst out in evident distress. "I didn't even want to think about that! Good Lord, could she really have done it? And what would have happened to her then?"

Dr. Mejzlik's ears grew red with concentration. "Just a minute," he said, and he leaped up, pacing the room in agitation. "Yes," he cried, "yes, I'm beginning to see it now! My God, this is quite a case! Yes, it's coming together now — and Sir Jesek has the leading role! Yes, the circle is closing! And that's why Jiri — Now I understand! Listen, he was one sharp operator, King Jiri!"

"He was," Mr. Divisek stated piously. "Let me tell you, he was a wise monarch!"

"Look," said Dr. Mejzlik, sitting down on his desktop and landing on the inkstand, "this is how it could have happened; and I'd swear on a stack of Bibles that it's exactly what did happen! Now first of all, any hypothesis we advance must take into account all of the known facts; nothing, not even the slightest circumstance, can be allowed to contradict it. In the second place, these facts must be arranged into a single, continuous action; the simpler, the more contained and connected the action, the more likely that things happened exactly that way and not otherwise. We're talking now about reconstruction of the events, see. The hypothesis that places all known facts into the most connected, most rational chain of events is without qualification the one for us, do you understand?" said Dr. Mejzlik, looking severely at the archivist. "This is our basic rule of methodology."

"Yes," the archivist said obediently.

"Now the facts which we must bear in mind probably occurred in the following order:

1. Petr Berkovec married Katerina;
2. Petr was murdered;
3. Katerina disappeared without a tombstone;
4. Henricus died in some conflict;
5. The king rebuked Jesek Skalicky for his violent temper.
6. But the king did not have Jesek brought to trial: so Jesek Skalicky was somehow or other in the right.

"Are these all the known facts? They are. To continue: it follows from the known facts that neither Henricus nor Jesek murdered Petr. Who, then, could have murdered him? Katerina, obviously. This conjecture is supported by the fact that we have no tombstone for Katerina; probably she was simply buried somewhere like a dog. And why then was she not summoned for proper trial? Because, obviously, some hot-headed avenger killed her on the spot instead. Was it Henricus? Obviously not; if Henricus had punished Katerina by killing her, old Jesek might well have approved; but why then would the king have criticized Jesek later for his violent temper? It follows from this that Jesek, her enraged father, did away with Katerina. And now the question is, who killed Henricus in combat? Who did that, sir?"

"I don't know," the archivist sighed plaintively.

"Who else but Jesek?" shouted Dr. Mejzlik. "There's no one

else who could have done it! That's the only way we come full circle in the whole affair, can't you see that? Look at it this way: Katerina, wife of Petr Berkovec, was — hm, how to put it — was burning with sinful desire for his younger brother, Henricus."

"Do you have evidence of that?" asked Mr. Divisek, enormously interested.

"It follows from a logical process," Dr. Mejzlik said decisively. "Listen, it's either money or a woman; you can take that as a given. To what extent Henricus returned that passion, I don't know; but we have to look for a motive here, a reason for Kate to have murdered her husband. And I can tell you right now," Dr. Mejzlik declared in an authoritative voice, "that she did it!"

"I suspected that," the archivist sighed gloomily.

"And now her father, Jesek Skalicky, arrives on the scene as avenger of the family honor. He kills his daughter because he doesn't want to turn her over to the hangman; and afterwards he challenges Henricus to a duel, because that unfortunate young man is more or less an accessory to the crime and to the damnation of his only daughter. Henricus falls in the duel, sword in hand. Of course there's an alternative here: Henricus shields Katerina from her enraged father with his own body and falls in the duel. But the first alternative is better. Thus you have the woeful deeds. And King Jiri, because he perceives how seldom human judgment is called upon to judge an act so savagely righteous, quite reasonably abandons this appalling father, this violent avenger, to divine justice. A decent jury might have done the same. Within the year, old Jesek dies alone and grief-stricken, probably of heart failure."

"Amen," said archivist Divisek, clasping his hands. "That's how it was. The King Jiri I know could not have acted otherwise. Listen, that Jesek was a harsh and splendid character, wasn't he? It's all perfectly clear now; you can see it right before your eyes. And the way everything fits together," the archivist marveled. "Sir, you have performed an invaluable service to historical scholarship. This casts such a dramatic light on the people of that era, and indeed — " Mr. Divisek, overcome with gratitude, threw out his hands with a flourish. "When my *History of the Reign of King Jiri of Podebrady* is published, I will take the liberty, sir, of sending you a copy, and there you will see how I deal with this case as a scholar."

Some time after that, Dr. Mejzlik really did receive the impressive volume titled *The History of the Reign of King Jiri of Podebrady*, with a warm inscription from the archivist Divisek. He read the entire book from A to Z, for — let us admit it — he was quite proud of his contribution to a scholarly work; but he found nothing there until, on page 471, among the bibliographical notes, he read the following:

Sebek, Jaroslav, *Regesta XIVth and XVth Centuries*, p. 213, letter from Sir Ladislav Pchac of Olesna to Sir Jan Borsovsky of Cercany. Of interest is the comment concerning Sir Jesek Skalicky of Skalice, which merits particular attention but has not thus far been subjected to proper scholarly methodology.

The Record

"Your Honor," Officer Hejda announced to District Judge Tucek, "I've got a serious bodily injury for you. God in heaven, it's hot out there!"

"So make yourself comfortable," the judge advised him.

Officer Hejda propped his rifle in a corner, slung his helmet to the floor, and unbuttoned his coat. "Oof," he said. "That damned scoundrel! I've never had a case like this one before, Your Honor. Take a look." So saying, he lifted up a heavy object he'd deposited earlier by the door, loosened the knot of the blue kerchief in which it was swathed, and unwrapped a stone as big as a human head. "Just take a look at this," he repeated earnestly.

"What's it supposed to be?" asked the judge, scraping at the stone with a pencil. "Piece of limestone, isn't it?"

"It is, and it's a whopper," Officer Hejda confirmed. "So here's my report, Your Honor: Vaclav Lysicky, brickmaker, age nineteen years, residence the brickyard, got that down? struck or hit with this stone, hereby attached as evidence, weight thirteen pounds, two ounces, Frantisek Pudil, farmer, residence Dolni Ujezd number 14, got that down? on the left shoulder, as a result of which said individual suffered a dislocated shoulder, fractured arm and collarbone, bleeding wound in the shoulder muscle, and a torn tendon and rotator cuff, got that down?"

"Got it," said the judge. "But what's so special about it?"

"It'll knock you for a loop, Your Honor," Officer Hejda vowed emphatically. "I'll tell it to you just the way it happened. It was three days ago when this Pudil sent for me. You know him, Your Honor."

"Yes, I know him," said the judge. "We had him in here once for usury and once — hm — "

"It was on account of that illegal card game. Anyway, it's that same Pudil. He's got that cherry orchard that goes all the way down to the river, you know; it's where the river bends back on itself and that's why it's wider there than anyplace else. Anyway, Pudil sends for me that morning on account of something's happened to him, and where do I find him but in bed, groaning and swearing something terrible. According to what he says, the night before, he's out in his orchard looking over his cherries, and he catches some kid red-handed up in a tree stuffing cherries in his pockets. Well, this Pudil's a pretty rough customer, you know; so he unstraps his belt, pulls the kid out of the tree by his leg, and gives him a good hard thrashing with his belt. And at that very moment someone calls over to him from the other bank, 'Pudil, turn loose of that kid!' This Pudil's eyesight isn't so good, I think it's on account of all his drinking; he can just barely make out somebody on the other side of the river standing there staring at him. That's why he says, just to be on the safe side, 'Mind your own business, troublemaker,' and whomps on the kid even more. 'Pudil,' hollers the man on the other bank, 'turn loose of that kid, you hear me?' Pudil's thinking to himself, what can he do to me, and that's why he shouts, 'Stick it in your ear, fathead!' No sooner does he say it than he's laying flat on the ground with this godawful pain in his left shoulder; and the man on the other bank goes, 'That'll teach you, you stupid farmer!' Listen, they had to carry this Pudil away, I mean he couldn't even stand up; and right there next to him's this stone. So they went to get the doctor that same night. The doctor wants them to take Pudil to the hospital, on account of his bones are all smashed to slivers; they say his whole left arm'll be lame from here on out. Only this Pudil doesn't want to go to the hospital on account of he's harvesting. So the next morning he sends for me and says I have to search for that moron, that rotten rat that did it to him. Fair enough.

"But listen, when they showed me that stone, I just stood

there gawking at it. I mean, it's limestone, but there's some kind of pyrite in it, so it's a lot heavier than it looks. Lift it yourself. I figured it was about thirteen pounds, three-and-a-half ounces — turns out I was only off by one-and-a-half ounces. Believe me, to throw a stone like this you'd really have to know how to throw. Then I take a look at that orchard and the river. Where the grass was all squashed was where Pudil toppled over, and from there it was over six feet to the water's edge; and that river, Your Honor, at first glance that river looked to be a good forty-five, forty-six feet wide, because that's where it bends around. Your Honor, I start yelling and jumping and I'm saying somebody get me about sixty, sixty-five feet of line right away! When they bring it I drive a stick in the spot where Pudil toppled, tie the line to it, strip down, and swim to the other bank with the end of the line in my teeth. And guess what, Your Honor: that line was barely long enough to make it to the other side, and after that comes a portion of the bank, and not until then do you have this little footpath. I measured it three times; from the stick to the footpath it's sixty-three feet, two-and-three-quarters inches on the nose."

"Hejda," said the judge, "that can't be right. Sixty-three feet, that's one long distance. Listen, wasn't this man standing in the water, like maybe in the middle of the river?"

"That's what I thought, too!" replied Officer Hejda. "Your Honor, from one side to the other it's well over six feet deep, on account of that curve in the river there. And there's still a big hole in the bank from where the stone was; the bank over there's sort of paved over, you know, so the water won't wear it away. That man for sure pulled that stone out of the embankment, but he could only of pitched it from the footpath, because he couldn't of stood in the water and he would of skidded on the embankment. What that means is, he threw it the whole sixty-three feet, two-and-three-quarters inches."

"Maybe he had a slingshot," the judge said uncertainly.

Officer Hejda looked at him reproachfully. "Your Honor, you must of never shot a slingshot before. Just try to shoot a thirteen-pound stone from a slingshot; what you'd need is a catapult. Your Honor, I sweated over this stone for two days. I tried to put some kind of noose around it and sling it; you know, like the hammerthrow. I want to tell you, it slipped out of the noose every time. Sir, it was a clean toss, just like a shot put. And you know," he burst out in his excitement, "you know what that is? It's a world record, that's what."

"You're kidding," the judge said in astonishment.

"A world record," Officer Hejda repeated solemnly. "Only the regulation shot is heavier: it weighs fifteen pounds, six-and-three-quarters ounces, and this year's record in the shotput is something like fifty-two-and-a-half feet. For nineteen years, sir, the record was fifty feet, ten-and-a-half inches, but last year some American, what was his name? Kuck or Hirschfeld or something, he threw it almost fifty-two-and-a-half feet. So something like a thirteen-pound shot would go sixty-two feet, four inches. And what we have here is seven-and-a-quarter inches more! Your Honor, this man could throw a shot a good fifty-three feet without even practicing! Sweet Jesus, fifty-three feet! Your Honor, I'm an old shot-putter. When our unit was in Siberia, the boys were always yelling, Hejda, toss one over there — actually, that was hand grenades, you know. And in Vladivostok I was throwing with these American sailors; I put the shot forty-six feet, but their chaplain put it a couple of inches more. I want to tell you, we were really in shape in Siberia! But this stone here, sir, I could only throw it fifty feet, ten-and-a-quarter inches; I couldn't get anything more out of me or it. Sixty-three feet! By God, I said to myself, I've got to get my hands on this fellow; he'll break the record for us. Think of it, swiping the record from the Americans!"

"What about Pudil?" the judge objected.

"The hell with Pudil," cried Officer Hejda. "Your Honor, I straight off launched a search for this unknown breaker of the world record; well, it's in the national interest, isn't it? But first I had to guarantee that he wouldn't get penalized for what he did to Pudil."

"Now just a moment there," the judge protested.

"Wait; I only guaranteed it if he for sure throws a thirteen pound, two-ounce stone across the river. Don't worry, I just explained about how it'd be this glorious feat and how the whole world'd read about us; and I said that whoever it was would bring in crowds by the thousands. Good grief, Your Honor, from that moment on all the young men for miles around drop their harvesting and rush to the dock so they can throw stones to the other side of the river. That embankment's already completely busted, so now they're breaking up boundary markers and knocking down stone walls for something to throw. And the boys, the whole worthless lot of them, are throwing stones all over the village — you wouldn't believe the number of dead chickens there. And I'm standing on the embankment and supervising; of course, nobody throws farther than the middle of the river — Your Honor, there'll be a rise in that riverbed for sure, what with those stones halfway blocking it up already. Then along towards evening they bring this young man over to me, and they're saying he's the one who flattened Pudil with that stone. You'll see him yourself, the damned scoundrel, he's waiting outside. 'Listen, Lysicka,' I tell him, 'you threw this stone at Pudil?' 'Sure,' he says, 'Pudil cussed me out, and I got mad, and that was the only stone around — ' 'So here's another stone just like it,' says I, 'now throw it as far as Pudil's side. But if you don't make it, you shifty rascal, you'll be sorry right down to your socks!'

"So he picks up the stone — he's got paws like shovels — and he takes a stance at the edge of the footpath, and he aims. I'm watching him, he's got no technique, no style, he isn't using his legs or his trunk, and splat! he throws the stone in the water maybe forty-six feet. That's not bad, you know, but — All right, I'll show him how to do it: 'Look, knucklehead, you have to position yourself like this, right shoulder back, and when you throw, you have to thrust with your shoulder at the same time, understand?' 'Sure,' says he, and then he twists all around like a saint at the stake and splat! he throws the stone thirty feet.

"You know, that made me mad. 'You trickster,' I yell, 'you

popped Pudil? You're lying!' 'Officer Hejda, sir,' he says, 'God's truth I popped him. You put Pudil there and I'll hit him again, the mean, no-good snake.' Your Honor, I run back to Pudil and I beg him, 'Mr. Pudil, sir, look, there's a world record on the line here. Please, go cuss him out again from your side so this brick-maker'll throw at you one more time.' And you won't believe this, Your Honor: this Pudil says no way is he going back there, not for nothing. You see how it is? These people just don't have any public spirit.

"So back I go again to Vaclav the brickmaker. 'You phony,' I yell at him, 'it's not true you clobbered Pudil. Pudil says it was somebody else.' 'That's a lie,' says Lysicky, 'I did too do it.' 'Then,' says I, 'show me if you can throw that far!' This Lysicky only scratches himself and kind of smiles. 'Officer Hejda, sir,' says he, 'I can't do it just cold like that. When I pegged Pudil, I was really burned up.' 'Vaclav,' I tell him, peaceful like, 'you throw it over there, I let you go; you don't throw it over there, you sit in prison for serious bodily injury, on account of you crippled Pudil. You scoundrel, you'll get six months for it.' 'So I'll sit it out while it's winter,' says Vaclav; so I arrested him in the name of the law.

"Now he's waiting out there in the hall. Your Honor, if you'd just get it out of him if he really threw that stone or if he's just bragging! I think he's scared and backing down. But slap him with at least a month for misleading the authorities, or anyway fraud. After all, lying's just not allowed in sports, you know; there'd be a severe penalty for that, sir. I'll bring him in."

"So you're Vaclav Lysicky," the district judge said, looking austerely at the fair-haired delinquent. "You've confessed that you threw this stone at Frantisek Pudil with intent to harm and that you inflicted serious bodily injury. Is this true?"

"Please, Your Honor, sir," began the culprit, "it was like this: this Pudil is walloping some kid there, and I holler across the river at him to leave off, and he starts cussing me out — "

"Did you throw this stone or not?" snapped the judge.

"Please, sir, I threw it," the culprit said penitently, "but he was cussing me out, so I grabbed hold of that stone — "

"Damn it, man," cried the judge, "why are you lying? Don't you know there's a grave penalty for trying to bamboozle the authorities? We know very well you didn't throw that stone!"

"I threw it, sir," stammered the young brickmaker, "but that Pudil said to me, stick it in your ear — "

The judge looked questioningly at Officer Hejda, who shrugged his shoulders helplessly. "Strip down, you," the judge thundered at the miserable offender. "I mean now — your pants, too! Do it!"

Now the young giant stood as God had created him, and he was shaking. No doubt he was terror-stricken that he would be tortured and that this was all part and parcel of being under arrest.

"Take a look at those deltoids, Hejda," said Judge Tucek. "And those biceps — what do you say to them?"

"Hm, he could have done it," Officer Hejda expertly supposed. "But his abdominals could use some work. Your Honor, you need abdominals in the shot put, you know, so you can swivel your trunk. I could show you *my* abdominals — !"

"Those are abdominals if I ever saw them," muttered the judge. "Just look at those bulges. Good grief, what a rib cage," he said, sticking a finger into the yellow down on Vaclav's chest. "But those legs are weak; these country boys tend to have bad legs."

"On account of they don't bend their knees," Officer Hejda said critically. "Those aren't any kind of legs. A thrower's got to have first-rate legs, sir!"

"Turn around," the judge barked at the young brickmaker. "What about the back?"

"That part up around the shoulders there's good," Officer Hejda ventured, "but down below, nothing; the man has no power in his trunk. Your Honor, what I think is, he didn't throw it."

"Get dressed, you," the judge fired at the brickmaker. "Listen, young man, for the last time: did you throw that stone or not?"

"I threw it," Vaclav Lysicky mumbled with mulish obstinacy.

"You jackass," sputtered the judge, "if you threw that stone, then it's serious bodily injury and you come before the district court and get several months, understand? So quit your bragging and confess that you trumped up this whole business with the stone. I'll give you three days, for misleading the authorities, and then you can go. So which is it, did you hit Pudil with that stone or not?"

"I did," Vaclav Lysicky said stubbornly. "He was cussing me out there across the river — "

"Get him out of here," roared the district judge. "Damned scoundrel!"

No more than a moment later, Officer Hejda stuck his head around the door once again. "Your Honor," he said vengefully, "you can get him for property damage, too. He pulled that stone out of the embankment, you know, and now the embankment's all broke to pieces."

The Selvin Case

"Hm, my greatest success, that is, the success which gave me the greatest pleasure — " reminisced the old master Leonard Unden, great poet, Nobel laureate, and so forth. "My young friends, at my age a man no longer gives a damn for laurels, ovations, mistresses, and similar nonsense, especially when they've long been a thing of the past. When a man's young he enjoys it all, and he'd be a fool if he didn't. The only drawback is that when he's young, he doesn't have the wherewithal to enjoy things. Actually, life ought to proceed in reverse: first a man would be old and do his fullest and most praiseworthy work, because he isn't fit for anything else; only later would he arrive at his youth, so that he could enjoy the fruits of his long life. You see how an old man rambles on. What was I going to talk about? Oh yes, my greatest success. I'll tell you, it wasn't any of my dramas or any of my books — and there truly was a time when my books were read. My greatest success was the Selvin Case.

"Of course, you can't be expected to know what it was all about; why, it must be twenty-six, no, twenty-nine years ago now. Yes, it was twenty-nine years ago, on a beautiful day, when a diminutive, white-haired woman dressed in black came to see me. And before I could ask her, with that courtesy of mine which was so greatly appreciated then, what it was she wanted, plop, she had knelt down on the floor in front of me and broken into tears. I don't know why it is, but I can't bear to see a woman cry.

" 'Sir,' the old woman said when I had calmed her somewhat, 'you are a poet. I beg you, in the name of your love for your fellow human beings, save my son! Surely you've read in the papers about the Frank Selvin case — '

"I think I must have seemed a bearded baby; although I read the papers, I hadn't noticed anything about a Frank Selvin. At any rate, so far as I could understand in the midst of her sobbing and wailing, the situation was this: Her only son, Frank Selvin, twenty-two years old, had been sentenced that very day to penal servitude for life, for the murder and attempted robbery of his Aunt Sofie. What exacerbated the circumstances in the eyes of the jury was that he refused to confess to his deed. 'But he's innocent, sir,' grieved Mrs. Selvinova, 'he's innocent, I swear it! On that terrible evening he said to me: I've got a headache, Mother, I'm going out for a stroll. Sir, that's why he can't prove his alibi! Who'd take any notice of a young man at night, even if they happened to meet up with him? My Frank was a bit of an impetuous boy, but you were young once yourself; just think of it, sir, he's only twenty-two! How can they destroy a young man's whole life like that?' And so on. I tell you, if you could have seen that broken-hearted, white-haired mother, you'd have realized what I realized at the time: that one of the worst agonies is to feel sympathy for someone when you're powerless to help. Well, I'll tell you what I did: in the end I swore to her that I would do everything I possibly could, and that I would not stop until the matter had been resolved, and that I believed in the innocence of her son. At these words she tried to kiss my hand. When the poor old thing blessed me, it was all I could do not to kneel before her in turn. You know how foolish you can look when someone is thanking you as if you were the Lord God Himself.

"And so, from that moment on, the Frank Selvin Case became my personal cause. Needless to say, I began by studying the trial record. I tell you, never in my life have I seen a trial conducted in such a slipshod manner; it was, patently, a judicial scandal. The case itself was fairly simple: One night, the maid of the Aunt Sofie in question, a certain Anna Solarova, fifty years old and mentally deficient, heard someone moving about in her mistress's, that is to say, Aunt Sofie's bedroom. She went to see why her mistress wasn't asleep, and upon entering the bedroom she saw the window wide open and a man's figure leaping from the window into the garden. She let out an ear-splitting scream; and when the neighbors arrived with a light, they found Miss Sofie lying on the floor, strangled with her own scarf. The wardrobe where she kept her money had been broken open and some of the linen scattered about; the money was still there — obviously, at that moment the maid had interrupted the murderer. This, then, was the *materia facti.*

"The next day, Frank Selvin was arrested. The maid, it appeared, had testified that she recognized the young man as he was leaping from the window. It was established that he was not home at that time: he returned home about half an hour later and went straight to bed. Further, it was brought out that the reckless young man was in debt. Further, some busybody had been found who'd testified, importantly, that Aunt Sofie had confided in her a few days prior to the murder: supposedly, her nephew Frank had come to her, cap in hand, for a loan. When she refused — she was frightfully stingy, by the way — Frank supposedly had said: Watch out, Aunt Sofie, something's going to happen that'll make people sit up and take notice! — And that was all, insofar as Frank was concerned.

"And now consider the trial itself: it lasted half a day, from start to finish. Frank Selvin simply maintained that he was innocent, that he had gone for a walk, after which he went straight home to bed. None of the witnesses was cross-examined. Frank's attorney — court-appointed, naturally, since Mrs. Selvinova had no money for a better defense — was an easy-going old fool who confined himself to directing attention to the youth of his injudicious client and, with tears in his eyes, imploring the kind-hearted jurors to be lenient. Nor did the public prosecutor take many pains over his job: he thundered at the jury for twice returning verdicts of not guilty just prior to Frank Selvin's trial; where, he demanded, was society headed if every crime was protected by the loose tolerance and leniency of juries? — It appears that the jury gave heed to this argument and wanted to make it clear that there would be no complaints about their laxness or lenience. They simply decided, eleven to one, that Frank Selvin was guilty of the crime of murder. That, then, was the entire case.

"Let me tell you, once I found all this out I felt absolutely desperate. I was boiling with rage, even though I'm not a lawyer or, perhaps, precisely because I'm not a lawyer. Just imagine: the star witness is mentally deficient; on top of that, she's nearly fifty years old and thus likely experiencing menopause, which might well lessen her reliability. It was nighttime when she saw that figure in the window; as I found out later, it had been a warm night but very dark, so she couldn't have recognized the man with any degree of certainty. You can't even determine the height of a person with any accuracy in the dark; I tested that very thoroughly for myself. And in addition to everything else, the woman hated young Frank Selvin in a manner that was nothing short of hysterical, because he used to make fun of her. It seems that he called her 'Hebe, the white-handed cup-bearer,' which for some reason she considered a mortal insult.

"Another point: Aunt Sofie hated her sister, Mrs. Selvinova, and in point of fact they never spoke. The spinster couldn't even bring herself to speak of Frank's mother by her proper name. If Aunt Sofie said that Frank had threatened her in some way, it could very well have been some spiteful, old-maidish accusation that she'd concocted for the purpose of humiliating her sister. As for Frank, he was a young man of average talents, a clerk in some office. He had a girlfriend to whom he wrote sentimental letters and bad verse, and he fell into debt, as they say, through no fault of his own. It was because of his excessive sentimentality that he became a habitual drinker. His mother, poor woman, was a paragon of goodness, afflicted with cancer, poverty, and grief. Well, that was how things looked on closer inspection.

"Of course, you couldn't possibly know what I was like in the days of my youth. Once my passions were aroused, there was

no holding me back. I wrote a series of newspaper articles titled
'The Frank Selvin Case;' point by point I demonstrated the
unreliability of the witnesses, particularly the star witness. I
analyzed discrepancies in the testimony as well as the bias in
some of the depositions; I argued the absurdity of presuming that
the state's witness could have recognized the culprit; I demonstrated the utter incompetence of the judge and the flagrant
demagoguery of the public prosecutor's summation. But that
wasn't enough for me. While I was at it, I began to attack the
entire judicial establishment, the penal code, the jury system, the
whole callous, selfish order of society. Don't even ask about the
uproar that resulted. I had already made somewhat of a name for
myself at the time, and the younger generation took my side; in
fact, there was even a demonstration in front of the courthouse.
At that point young Selvin's attorney came running to see me,
wringing his hands over what he considered the difficulties I had
caused. He said that he'd already filed an appeal and that Selvin's
sentence would undoubtedly have been commuted to a few years'
imprisonment, but that the court of appeals could not be
expected to yield to mobs in the street and would therefore
dismiss his appeal. I told the worthy counselor that I was not
concerned only with the Selvin Case, that what concerned me
were the larger questions of truth and justice.

"Selvin's attorney was right: the appeal was dismissed. But
the judge was pensioned off. That was when, my young friends,
I let myself go with a vengeance. Do you know, even today I'd
call it a holy war for justice. No question about it, many things
have changed for the better since those days, and you have to
admit that I deserve a small part of the credit. The Selvin Case
found its way into newspapers in every corner of the globe. I gave
speeches to workers in taverns and to delegates from all over the
world at international congresses. 'Reverse the Selvin Decision'
was, in its time, as much of an international rallying cry as, say,
'No More War!' or *Votes for Women!* When Selvin's mother died,
seventeen thousand people followed the coffin of that tiny,
wizened woman, and over her open grave I spoke as I had never

spoken before in my life. God knows, friends, inspiration is a strange and formidable thing.

"For seven years I waged that war, and that war was the making of me. It was not my books but the Selvin Case that gained me a worldwide reputation. — They call me the Voice of Conscience, the Knight of Truth, and things of that sort; some of them will even be on my tombstone. No doubt for some fourteen years or so after my death, the schoolbooks will relate how the poet Leonard Unden fought for truth; then that, too, will be forgotten.

"In that seventh year the star witness, Anna Solarova, died. Before her death she confessed and admitted in tears that her conscience was troubling her. She had, she said, given false evidence at the trial; in truth, she could not say that the murderer in the window was Frank Selvin. The priest, a well-meaning man, brought the information to me. By that time I had a better understanding of the ways of this world, and that's why I didn't go to the newspapers but rather sent the good priest to the courthouse. Within a week a new trial was ordered for Frank Selvin. Within a month Frank Selvin once again stood before a jury. A first-rate lawyer pulverized the prosecution's case, free of charge, whereupon the public prosecutor rose and recommended that the jury acquit Frank Selvin. And the jury decreed by unanimous vote that Frank Selvin was not guilty.

"Yes, that was the greatest triumph of my life. No other success gave me such pure satisfaction — — and, at the same time, such a feeling of emptiness. Truth be told, I began to miss the Selvin Case — it left a curious void in its wake. Then one day my maid announced that some man wanted to speak to me.

" 'I am Frank Selvin,' said the man, and he remained standing in the doorway. And I felt — I don't quite know how to tell you — I felt disappointed, somehow, that this Selvin of mine looked like . . . I have to admit it, like a lottery agent: a bit fleshy and pasty-faced, with the beginnings of baldness, somewhat sweaty and extremely commonplace; moreover, he reeked of beer.

" 'Esteemed and illustrious bard,' stammered Frank Selvin

(imagine calling me 'esteemed and illustrious bard' — I could have kicked him!). 'I have come to express my thanks to you . . . my greatest benefactor.' It sounded as if he had learned it by rote. 'I will be indebted to you for the rest of my life. Words of gratitude are too weak — '

" 'Not at all,' I said quickly, 'it was my duty. Once I was convinced that you had been wrongly condemned — '

"Frank Selvin shook his head. 'Gifted bard,' he said plaintively, 'I would never try to lie to my benefactor. The fact is, I killed the witch.'

" 'If that's the case,' I exploded, 'why didn't you say so in court?'

"Frank Selvin gazed at me reproachfully. 'Gifted bard,' he said, 'that was my right. A defendant has the right to plead innocent, does he not?'

"I must admit that I was stunned. 'What do you want from me now?' I demanded.

" 'I have come to you, gifted bard, only to thank you for your magnanimity,' Selvin said in a mournful tone which, apparently, he regarded as deeply moving. 'You gave your support to my poor old mother, too. God's blessing on you, noble poet!'

" 'Get out!' I screamed insanely. The fellow flew down the stairs like a shot. Three weeks later he stopped me in the street; he was slightly drunk. I couldn't get rid of him. For quite a while I couldn't understand what it was he wanted, until he grabbed my lapels and explained. He said I'd ruined his life: if I hadn't written about his case, the appeals court would have granted his attorney a hearing and he, Frank Selvin, wouldn't have spent seven years, blamelessly, in prison. The very least I could do now, he said, would be to show some consideration for his straitened circumstances, for which I was at fault through having interfered in his trial. In short, I had to slip some money into his hand. 'God's blessing on you, benefactor,' Mr. Selvin said in conclusion, his eyes moist.

"On the second occasion he approached me more menacingly. He said that, thanks to his case, I'd done very well for myself; but I had gained fame only because I'd taken up his cause, so why shouldn't he get something out of it? I was entirely unable to convince him that I owed him nothing in the way of a commission. I simply gave him more money.

"From that time on he confronted me at shorter and shorter intervals. He would sit on the sofa and sigh that he was suffering remorse for having done in the witch. 'I'm going to give myself up, noble bard,' he'd say gloomily, 'but for you it would be an international disgrace. Still, I don't see how else to attain peace of mind.' — I tell you, those fits of remorse must have been frightful, judging by what I paid out to that fellow so that he could continue to suffer through them. Finally I bought him a ticket to America; whether he found peace of mind there, I don't know.

"Well, that was the greatest success of my life. My young friends, when you write an obituary for Leonard Unden, say that with the Selvin Case he engraved his name on our hearts in golden characters, and so on; our thanks to him forevermore."

Footprints

That night Mr. Rybka was walking home in a particularly good mood, first because he'd won his game of chess (that was a nice checkmate with the knight, he congratulated himself as he walked along), and second because fresh snow had fallen and it crunched softly beneath his feet in the fine, pure silence. Good heavens it's beautiful, thought Mr. Rybka; a city covered with snow is all of a sudden such a small town, such an old-fashioned little place — it almost makes you believe in night watchmen and horse-drawn carriages; it's funny how snow makes everything seem timeless and rustic.

Crunch, crunch, Mr. Rybka looked around for an untrodden path, just for the joy of hearing the crunch; and because he lived on a quiet back lane, he came upon fewer and fewer footprints. Look, a man's boots and a woman's shoes turned in at this gate, probably husband and wife — I wonder if it's a young couple, Mr. Rybka said to himself softly, as if he wanted to give them his blessing. Over there a cat had run across the road and left its pawprints, like blossoms, in the snow; good night, kitty, your feet are going to be cold. And now there was only a single chain of footprints, the deep prints of a man, a clear and distinct chain of steps unfurled by a lone pedestrian. Which of the neighbors came this way? Mr. Rybka asked himself with friendly concern; so few people walk by here, there's not a single wheel tread in the snow, we're on the outskirts of life. When I reach home, the street will pull its white feather-bed up to its nose and dream that it's only a child's plaything. It's too bad the old newspaper lady will trample all over it in the morning; her footprints will criss-cross it like a rabbit's —

Suddenly Mr. Rybka stopped. Just as he was going to cross

the snow-bright street to his house, he saw that the chain of footprints in front of him turned away from the sidewalk and continued into the street in the direction of his gate. Who could have come to see me? he asked himself in surprise, and his eyes followed the clear, distinct footprints. There were five of them, and right in the middle of the street they came to an end with the sharp impression of a left foot. Beyond that there was nothing but immaculate, untouched snow.

I must be crazy, Mr. Rybka said to himself — the man must have gone back to the sidewalk! — But as far as he could see, the sidewalk was nothing but smooth, powdery snow, without a single human footprint. Well I'll be damned, Mr. Rybka marveled, I guess the rest of the footprints are over on the other sidewalk! And so he walked in a wide arc around the incomplete chain of footprints, but there was not a single mark on the other sidewalk; and farther on, the entire street was lighted by the soft, untouched snow, so pure it took his breath away. No one had passed that way since the snow had begun to fall. That's odd, Mr. Rybka muttered, the man must have walked backwards to the sidewalk, stepping in his own footsteps; but he would've had to walk backwards in his footprints all the way to the corner, because there was only *one* set of tracks in front of me there, and they were headed in the same direction I was. But why would the fellow do such a thing? Mr. Rybka asked himself in amazement. And how could he fit his own footprints *to a T* if he was going backwards?

Turning his head away, he unlocked the gate and went into his house. Although he knew it was nonsense, he wondered if there might not be some snowy footprints *inside* the house; of course not, how would they get there! Maybe I only imagined it, Mr. Rybka muttered uneasily, and he leaned out the window. By the light of the street lamp he could clearly see the five sharp, deep footprints that ended in the middle of the street, and then nothing. Dammit, thought Mr. Rybka, rubbing his eyes; once I read a story about a single footprint in the snow, but here's a whole row of them, and then suddenly nothing — where did that fellow go?

Shaking his head, he began to undress; but suddenly he stopped, went to the telephone and, his voice somewhat strained, called the police station. "Hello? Captain Bartosek? Look, there's something peculiar going on here, *very* peculiar — Maybe if you could send somebody over here or, better yet, come yourself — All right then, I'll be waiting for you at the corner — I don't *know* what's going on — No, I don't think it's dangerous; the only thing is, nobody should trample on the footprints — I don't *know* whose footprints! Fine, I'll be waiting for you."

Mr. Rybka put his clothes back on and went out again. He went carefully around the footprints and took care not to disturb them even on the sidewalk. Shivering with cold and excitement, he waited at the corner for Captain Bartosek. It was silent, and the peopled earth shone peacefully out into space.

"At least it's nice and quiet," Captain Bartosek grumbled cheerlessly. "Up to now, we've been dealing with a free-for-all and a drunk. Phooey! — So what've you got here?"

"Take a look at these footprints, Captain," Mr. Rybka said, his voice quavering. "Here's where they start."

The captain turned on his flashlight. "He was pretty lanky, almost six feet," he said, "judging by the size of the prints and the length of his stride. Pretty good boots, handmade, I'd guess. He wasn't drunk and he was moving right along. I don't know what it is you don't like about these footprints."

"That," Mr. Rybka said briefly, and he pointed to the incomplete chain of prints in the middle of the street.

"Aha," Captain Bartosek remarked, and without further ceremony he headed straight for the final footprint, squatted on his haunches, and shone his flashlight down. "Nothing wrong with it," he said comfortably. "It's a good, solid, perfectly normal footprint. His weight rested more on the heel. If the man had taken another step or jumped, his weight would have shifted to his toes, see? It's obvious."

"And that means — ?" Mr. Rybka asked in intense anticipation.

"What it means," the captain said placidly, "is that he didn't go any farther."

"Then where did he go?" Rybka burst out feverishly.

The captain shrugged his shoulders. "I don't know. Do you suspect him of something?"

"Suspect him?" Mr. Rybka said, astonished. "I only want to know where he went. Look, if he took his last step here, then where, for Christ's sake, did he take the next one? I mean, there aren't any more footprints here!"

"I can see that," the captain said drily. "So what do you care where he went? Is it someone from your family? Is somebody missing? Then what the hell difference does it make to you where he's gone?"

"But there must be some explanation," Mr. Rybka faltered. "Do you think maybe he walked backwards in his own footprints?"

"Nonsense," growled the captain. "When you walk backwards, you take shorter steps and plant your legs wider apart to get a better balance; besides, you don't lift your feet up, so this man would've dug ruts with his heels all along there in the snow. Those footprints were stepped in one time only, sir. You can see how sharp they are."

"Then if he didn't go backwards," Mr. Rybka insisted stubbornly, *"which direction did he go?"*

"That's his business," grumbled the captain. "Look, if he didn't do anything wrong, we've got no right to meddle in his affairs. We have to have some kind of charge against him. Then, of course, we'd launch a preliminary investigation . . . "

"But how can a man just disappear in the middle of a street?" cried Mr. Rybka, horrified at the thought.

"You'll just have to wait, sir," the captain advised him

patiently. "If somebody's disappeared, his family or someone will notify us in a day or two, and then we'll start searching for him. As long as nobody misses him, though, there's nothing we can do. Can't be helped."

A dark anger began rising in Mr. Rybka. "I beg your pardon," he said sharply, "but I'd have thought the police would have to be at least a *bit* interested when an ordinary, peaceful pedestrian disappears for no reason at all in the middle of the street!"

"Look, nothing's happened to him," Captain Bartosek soothed him. "There's no sign at all of a struggle — If somebody'd attacked or kidnapped him, there'd be a slew of footprints here — I'm sorry, sir, but there's just no reason for me to get involved."

"But Captain," Mr. Rybka threw up his hands, "at least explain to me . . . It's still such a mystery . . . "

"It is," the captain agreed thoughtfully. "You have no idea, sir, what a lot of mysteries there are in this world. Every house, every family is a mystery. When I was on my way here I heard a young woman sobbing in that little house over there. Sir, mysteries aren't our business. We're paid to enforce law and order. What on earth did you think, that we chase criminals out of curiosity? Sir, we chase them so we can lock them up. There has to be law and order."

"Exactly!" burst out Mr. Rybka. "But you have to admit it's not law and order when, right in the middle of the street, someone . . . well, let's say, rises straight up in the air!"

"It's all a matter of interpretation," said the captain. "There's a police regulation to the effect that if anyone's in danger of falling from a great height, we have to tie him up. First you get a warning and then you get a fine. — If the gentleman just rose up in the air of his own free will, then of course a police officer would have to warn him to strap himself in a safety belt; but probably there wasn't any police officer here," he said apologetically. "Otherwise he would have left some footprints, too.

Besides, it's possible the gentleman left by some other means, right?"

"But how?" asked Mr. Rybka.

Captain Bartosek shook his head. "Hard to say. Could be some kind of Holy Ascension or Jacob's ladder," he said vaguely. "Ascension could be considered kidnapping, especially if there was an indication of violence; but I think it usually happens with the consent of the party concerned. But maybe the man knew how to fly. Haven't you ever dreamed you were flying? All you have to do is give a little push with your feet, and up you go . . . Some people fly like balloons, but me, when I fly in my dreams, I have to kick off from the ground every so often; I think it's because of this heavy uniform and my sword. Maybe the man fell asleep and started to fly in a dream. But there's no law against that, sir. Of course, on a busy street a police officer would have to give him a warning. Or wait a minute, maybe it was levitation; these spiritualists believe in levitation, you know. But spiritualism isn't against the law, either. There was this Mr. Baudys who told me that with his own eyes he saw a medium hanging in the air. Who knows, maybe there's something to it."

"But Captain," Mr. Rybka said reproachfully, "you can't really believe that! It would be a violation of the laws of nature — "

Captain Bartosek shrugged his shoulders in resignation. "I know that, sir, but people violate all kinds of laws and regulations. If you were on the force you'd see it all the time . . . " The captain waved his hand. "I wouldn't be surprised if they even violated the laws of nature. Altogether, people are a pretty sorry bunch, sir. Well, good night to you; it's freezing out here."

"Won't you come in for a cup of tea . . . or a glass of slivovice?" Mr. Rybka suggested.

"Why not?" the captain muttered dejectedly. "You can't even go into a tavern in uniform, you know. That's why policemen don't drink much.

"Mystery," he continued, seated in an easy chair and gazing thoughtfully at the snow melting off the toes of his boots.

"Ninety-nine people out of a hundred would've passed by those footprints and never noticed a thing. And you yourself don't notice ninety-nine things out of a hundred that are damned mysterious. We're pig-ignorant about the things of this world. But some things aren't mysterious. Law and order isn't mysterious. Justice isn't mysterious. The police aren't mysterious, either. But every person walking along the street is a mystery, because we can't get at him, sir. As soon as he steals something, he stops being a mystery, because we lock him up and that's that. At least we know what he's doing, and any time we want we can watch him through his cell window, right? But I ask you, why do newspapers print headlines like 'Mysterious Discovery of Corpse!' What's mysterious about a corpse? When we find one, we measure it and we photograph it and we cut it up, we know every fiber in and on it, we know what it last ate, how it died, you name it; and besides that, we know somebody probably killed it for money. Everything's clear and straightforward . . . You can pour me some more of that black tea, sir. All crimes are clear and straightforward, sir; at least you know the motives and things like that. But what your cat is thinking, that's a mystery, or what your maid dreams about, or what's on your wife's mind when she's staring out the window. Everything's a mystery, sir, except criminal cases; a criminal case is a specified slice of reality with strict definitions, a little cross-section we can hold up to the light. If I took a look around me here, sir, I'd get to know all kinds of things about you. But what I'm doing is looking at the toes of my boots, because officially we're not interested in you. What I mean is, nobody's brought any charges against you," he added, sipping his hot tea.

"There's this strange notion," he began again after a moment, "that the police, especially detectives, are interested in mysteries. We don't give a damn about mysteries; what interests us is disorderly conduct. Sir, crime doesn't interest us because it's mysterious, but because it's against the law. We don't chase crooks out of intellectual curiosity; we chase them so we can arrest them in the name of the law. Listen, streetcleaners don't

run around the streets with brooms so they can spot people's
traces in the dust, but so they can sweep and tidy up all the filth
life leaves behind. Law and order aren't a bit mysterious. Keeping
order is dirty work, sir; and whoever wants to keep things clean
and tidy has to poke his fingers into all kinds of nasty stuff.
Well, somebody has to do it," he said despondently, "just as
somebody has to slaughter calves. But slaughtering calves out of
curiosity, that's barbaric; it should only be done as a skilled trade.
When it's someone's duty to do something, then at least he
knows he's authorized to do it. Look, justice has to be as unques-
tioned as the multiplication tables. I don't know if you could
prove that *every* theft is wrong; but I can prove to you that every
theft is against the law, because I can arrest you every time. If
you scattered pearls in the street, then a policeman could give
you a ticket for littering. But if you started performing miracles,
we couldn't stop you, unless we called it a public nuisance or
unlawful public assembly. There must be some kind of breach of
order for us to intervene."

"But Captain," Mr. Rybka objected, wriggling with dissatisfaction, "is that really enough for you? What happened
here is . . . is such a strange thing . . . is something so mysterious . . . and you . . . "

Captain Bartosek shrugged his shoulders. "And I just
brushed it aside. If you like, sir, I'll have the footprints removed
so they don't interfere with a good night's sleep for you. But I
can't do more that that. Did you hear something just now?
Footsteps? That's our night patrolman, so that means it's seven
minutes past two. Good night, sir."

Mr. Rybka accompanied the captain to his gate. In the
middle of the street there was still the incomplete and incomprehensible chain of footprints — A police officer was approaching
on the opposite sidewalk.

"Mimra," Captain Bartosek called out, "anything new?"

Officer Mimra saluted. "Not much, captain," he reported.
"A cat was meowing over there in front of number 17, and I rang
the doorbell so they'd let her in. They left the gate open at

number 9. They dug up the street at the corner and failed to leave a red lantern, and the signboard at Marsik the grocer's is loose at one end; they'll have to take it down in the morning so it doesn't fall on somebody's head."

"That's all?"

"That's all," said Officer Mimra. "They'll have to spread sand on the sidewalks in the morning, so nobody breaks a leg; we'll want to start ringing all the doorbells at six — "

"Everything's in order, then," said Captain Bartosek. "Good night!"

Mr. Rybka took one last look at the footprints which had led into the unknown. But where the last footprint had been were now two wide, sturdy imprints from Officer Mimra's workboots; and from there his wide footprints plodded on in a clear and continuous chain.

"Thank God," Mr. Rybka sighed, and he went to bed.

The Receipt

That hot August evening the out-door café on Strelecky Island was crowded, so Minka and Pepa had to seat themselves at a table that was already occupied by a gentleman with a bushy, drooping moustache. "If you don't mind," said Pepa, and the gentleman simply shook his head. (The old nuisance, Minka said to herself, he had to sit right at our table!) So the first thing that happened was that Minka, with the air of a duchess, sat down on the chair which Pepa had wiped off for her with his handkerchief. Next, without further ado, she quickly pulled out her compact and powdered her nose so that even in this heat, God forbid, it wouldn't shine a smidgen. And as she was taking out the compact, there fell from her purse a crumpled slip of paper. Immediately the gentleman with the moustache bent down and retrieved it. "You ought to hang on to that, miss," he said gloomily.

Minka turned red, first of all because a strange gentleman had spoken to her, and in the second place because she was annoyed at having turned red. "Thank you," she said, and then she promptly turned back to Pepa. "It's a receipt from the shop where I buy my stockings."

"Precisely," said the melancholy man. "You never know, miss, when it might be needed."

Pepa considered it his duty as a gentleman somehow to intervene. "What do you want to hang on to stupid bits of paper for?" he asked, not looking at the man. "You'd have your pockets stuffed full in no time."

"Makes no difference," the gentleman with the moustache said meaningfully. "Sometimes that's more valuable than I don't know what."

Minka's face acquired a strained expression. (That old nuisance is going to poke his nose right in our conversation; God, why didn't we sit somewhere else!) Pepa decided to put an end to it. "How do you mean, more valuable?" he asked coldly, and he drew his brows together in a frown. (That's so becoming to him, Minka observed admiringly.)

"As a clue," muttered the old nuisance, and in lieu of a formal introduction he added, "What I mean is, I'm Officer Soucek, Police Officer Soucek, see? We had a case like that just the other day," he said with a wave of his hand. "You never know what you're carrying around in your pockets."

"What sort of case?" Pepa couldn't help asking. (Minka intercepted a glance from a young man at the next table. Just wait, Pepa, I'll fix you for not talking to me!)

"Why, the one about that woman they found way out near Roztyly," said the man with the moustache, and he lapsed into silence.

Minka suddenly picked up interest, no doubt because a woman was involved. "What woman?" she demanded abruptly.

"Why, the one that they found out there," Officer Soucek mumbled evasively and, somewhat at a loss, he fished a cigarette from his pocket. At that point something entirely unexpected happened: Pepa hastily dug his hand into his pocket, produced his lighter, and offered the man a light.

"I thank you," said Officer Soucek, obviously touched and honored. "You know, when those harvesters found that dead woman in the cornfield there between Roztyly and Krc," he explained by way of expressing his gratitude and returning the favor.

"I never heard anything about that," said Minka, her eyes widening. "Remember, Pepa, when we were in Krc that time? — So what happened to her?"

"Strangled," Officer Soucek said matter-of-factly. "She still had the cord around her neck. I won't say anything in front of the young lady here about what she looked like; July, you know, and when she'd already been laying there for something like two months — " With disgust Officer Soucek blew out a cloud of smoke. "You wouldn't believe what somebody in that condition looks like. Why, their own mother wouldn't recognize 'em. And the flies — " Officer Soucek shook his head mournfully. "Once their skin's gone, miss, it's goodbye and amen to beauty. And it's the devil's own job to identify somebody after that, you know. As long as they've still got eyes and a nose, you can do it; but after laying there more than a month in the sun — "

"But there must have been a monogram somewhere on the corpse," offered Pepa, the expert.

"Forget monograms," grumbled Officer Soucek. "Look, single girls don't put their initials on nothing, because they tell themselves, why bother, I'll just be getting married anyway. That female didn't have a single monogram on her, so forget it!"

"And how old was she?" Minka joined in, her interest growing.

"Maybe twenty-five, the doctor said; you know, according to the teeth and so on. And going by her clothes, she looked to be a factory girl or a housemaid, but most likely she was a housemaid, because she had on this kind of petticoat that country girls wear. And besides, if she'd been a factory girl, probably there would've already been a search on for her, because factory girls generally stick to the same job or the same part of town. But these housemaids, when they switch jobs nobody knows and nobody cares. That's a funny thing about housemaids, but it's true. So we said to ourselves, since it's been two months now and nobody's come looking for her, then she's got to be a housemaid. But the main thing was that receipt."

"What sort of receipt?" Pepa asked eagerly, for he no doubt perceived within himself the heroic makings of a detective, a sea captain, a Canadian trapper or the like, and his face assumed the concentrated and resolute expression required in these situations.

"Well, it was like this," said Officer Soucek, gazing mournfully at the ground. "We didn't find nothing on her, nothing. The fellow that did her in took everything that could of been worth something. Except her left hand was still hanging on to a piece of the strap from her purse, and the purse minus the strap was found a little farther off in the cornfield. Most likely he was trying to grab her purse, too, but when the strap broke, it wasn't worth nothing anymore, so he threw it out in the field; but he took everything out of it first, you know. So all that was left in it was what had got stuck in the lining, a ticket for streetcar number 7 and this receipt from a china shop for a fifty-five-crown purchase. That's all we found."

"But that cord around her neck," said Pepa. "That should've given you something to go on!"

Officer Soucek shook his head. "It was only a piece of clothesline, it wasn't any use. We had nothing at all but the streetcar ticket and the receipt. Well, of course we told the newspapers that a female corpse had been found, about twenty-five years of age, gray skirt and striped blouse, and if a housemaid had been missing for about two months, then notify the police at once. We got over a hundred calls; May's the month, you know, when these housemaids usually switch jobs, nobody knows why; but it turned out they were all false alarms. But the amount of work you go to, checking them all out," Officer Soucek said gloomily. "You take some little pot-scrubber from a house in Dejvice, say, who turns up again somewhere in Vrsovice or Kosire, and you lose a whole day running around. And all for nothing; the silly thing's not only alive and kicking, she's laughing at you. Say, that's a nice tune they're playing now," he remarked, bobbing his head pleasurably to the beat of Wagner's Valkyrie motif, which the café band was attacking with all its strength. "Sort of sad, though, isn't it? I'm very partial to sad music. That's why I go to all the big funerals and keep an eye on the pickpockets."

"But the murderer must have left some kind of clue," Pepa supposed.

"See that Casanova-type over there?" asked Officer Soucek, suddenly alert. "Ordinarily he goes after collection boxes in churches. I'd like to know what he's up to here. No, the murderer didn't leave any clues. But I can tell you this, when you find a murdered girl, then you can bet her boyfriend did it. That's what usually happens," he said bleakly. "But don't you worry about that, young lady. We would of known who'd done her in, but first we had to find out who she was. That was the hard part, see."

"But surely," Pepa said uncertainly, "the police have their methods."

"Indeed they do," Officer Soucek agreed dolefully. "Like that method where you look for a grain of barley in a sack of rice. You need patience, man, patience. You know, I like to read those detective stories, all those microscopes and things. But why would you look at that poor girl through a microscope? Unless you wanted to see some fat, happy maggot taking his wife and kiddies for a stroll. No offense, miss, but it always vexes me when I hear somebody talk about methods. It's not like reading a book and guessing in advance how it all turns out, you know. It's more like they give you a book and say: All right, Soucek, read this word for word, and every time you come across the word 'however,' write down the page number. — That's what this job's really like, see. No method's going to help you, and no fancy gimmicks, either. What you have to do is just keep on reading, and at the end you find out there isn't one 'however' in the whole book. Or else you have to run all over Prague and track down the whereabouts of something like a hundred Annas or Markas, until you discover, detective style, that not a one of them's been murdered. That's what somebody ought to write a book about," he said disapprovingly, "and not about the Queen of Sheba's stolen pearl necklace. Because that, friends, is what real detective work is."

"Well then, how did you go about it?" asked Pepa, knowing beforehand that *he* would have gone about it in a very different way.

"How we went about it," repeated Officer Soucek, deep in thought. "First off we had to start somewhere, see. Well, to begin with we had that ticket for streetcar number 7. Now *just suppose* that this girl, if she really was a housemaid, worked in a house somewhere near that streetcar line. That didn't have to be true, maybe she just took that streetcar by chance; but you have to start somewhere, right? Except that number 7 goes from one end of Prague to the other, from Brevnov by way of Mala Strana and Nove Mesto to Zizkov; so there wasn't much we could do with that. Then there was that receipt. With that, at least we knew that some time or other she'd bought something from that china shop for fifty-five crowns. So we went to the shop."

"And they remembered her there," Minka burst out.

"Dead wrong, miss," muttered Officer Soucek. "They didn't remember her at all. But Dr. Mejzlik, he's our captain, he went there himself and asked what you could buy for fifty-five crowns. 'All kinds of things,' they told him, 'depending on how many things you buy; but for an even fifty-five crowns, there's only this English teapot, just big enough for one person.' — 'I'll take one, then,' our Dr. Mejzlik says, 'but sell it to me wholesale.'

"So then the captain calls me in and says, 'Look, Soucek, here's a job for you. Let's assume the girl was a housemaid. Girls like that are always breaking things, but when it happens the third time the mistress of the house tells her, you clumsy goose, this time you pay for it out of your own money. So the girl goes and buys only *one* item, to replace whatever it is she broke. And the only item at fifty-five crowns is this teapot.' 'That's pretty damned expensive,' I says to him. And he says, 'That's the whole point. First of all, it tells us why that housemaid kept the receipt: that was a ton of money for her, and maybe she figured that someday the mistress would pay her back. In the second place, look: this is a teapot for one person only. So either the girl worked for one person only, or else her mistress had a single person for a roomer and the girl was the one who served that person breakfast. And this single person was probably a woman, because a single man would hardly buy himself a nice, expensive teapot like this one; men hardly even notice what they're drinking out of, right? So most likely it was a single woman; because a spinster like that, who's renting a room, always likes something nice that's all her own, and so she buys herself just this sort of extravagant, high-priced thing.' "

"It's true," exclaimed Minka. "You know, Pepa, like that nice little flower vase I have!"

"There you are," said Officer Soucek. "But you don't have the receipt. Anyway, then the captain says, 'Now, Soucek, let's suppose something else; it's weak as water, but we have to start somewhere. Look, a person who throws away fifty-five crowns on a teapot isn't going to live in Zizkov. (Dr. Mejzlik was thinking about that number 7 line again, that streetcar ticket, you know.) There aren't many roomers in central Prague, and people who live in Mala Strana only drink coffee. I'd guess it would probably be that area where number 7 travels between Hradcany and Dejvice. I'd almost say,' he says, 'that a lady who drinks tea from an English teapot like this one could live nowhere but in a little house with a garden. You know the fad these days for anything English, Soucek.' — You have to understand that sometimes our Dr. Mejzlik gets these wild ideas. 'So what I want you to do, Soucek,' he says, 'is take that teapot, go to the part of town where that better class of ladies sublets rooms, and ask questions. And if somebody actually has a teapot just like this one, then find out if a housemaid didn't quit work there some time in May. It's a damned feeble clue, but we have to give it a shot. So off you go, Soucek, it's your case now.'

"Listen, I don't like all this guesswork. A real detective's not some kind of stargazer or fortuneteller. A detective doesn't go in for speculating much; oh, it's true, sometimes you come across the right thing by chance, but chance, that's not what I call honest detective work. That streetcar ticket and that teapot, now, at least that's something you can see and get your hands on. But the rest of it's only . . . a figment of the imagination," said Officer Soucek, a bit sheepish at having used such an erudite phrase. "So I set about doing it in my own way. I went from house to house in that part of town and asked if they didn't have a teapot like that one around somewhere. And would you believe it, at the forty-seventh house I came to, going right down the line, the housemaid says, 'Oh sure, that's the same kind of teapot this lady who rooms here with the missus has!' So I waited while she went to get the lady of the house. She was a general's widow, see, and she rented out rooms to two ladies. And one of the ladies, a Miss Jakoubkova, she was a teacher of English and she had just that kind of teapot for her tea. 'Ma'am,' I says, 'didn't you have a maid who left here some time in May?' 'That's right,' says the landlady, 'we called her Marka, but what her other name was, I don't remember.' 'And some time before that, didn't this girl break a teapot?' 'She did,' says the landlady, 'and she had to buy a new one out of her own pocket. But my goodness, how did you know about that?' 'Well, ma'am,' says I, 'we hear just about everything.'

"So after that it was easy; first of all I found out who the housemaid was that this Marka was best friends with — housemaids always have a girlfriend, just one, but she tells her everything — and from her I found out that the girl's name was Marka Parizkova and she came from Drevic. But most of all I wanted to know who the young man was this Marka went out with. The friend said she thought it was somebody named Franta. Who this Franta was, she didn't know, but she remembered that she went with the two of them to the Eden Dance Hall once, and that some young Casanova there had called out to this Franta, 'Hey, Ferda!' Well, then we referred the case to Officer Fryba in our division; he's the expert on these aliases, you know. And right away Fryba says, 'Franta alias Ferda, that would be this fellow from Kosire who calls himself Kroutil, but his real name is Pastyrik. Captain, sir, I'll go get him, but there needs to be two of us to do it.' So I went with him myself, although that's not really my line of work. We collared this Pastyrik at his girlfriend's; it was pretty nasty, he wanted to shoot it out. Then Captain Maticka went to work on him back at the station. Nobody knows how he does it, but in sixteen hours' time he got everything out of Pastyrik, how he did in this Marka Parizkova in the cornfield right after she got off work and then robbed her of a few crowns. Of course he'd promised to marry her — they all do that," Officer Soucek added gloomily.

Minka shuddered. "Pepa," she breathed, "that's awful!"

"Not now it isn't," Officer Soucek said solemnly. "What was awful was when we were standing there by her body in that field and all we could find was that receipt and that streetcar ticket. Two tiny, good-for-nothing bits of paper — but all the same, we evened the score for poor Marka. Like I told you, never throw nothing away, nothing. Even the least little thing can turn out to be a clue or evidence. No sir, you never know what's in your pocket that might be important."

Minka sat perfectly still, her eyes filled with tears. And suddenly, with a warm burst of affection, she turned to her Pepa and from her moist hand let fall to the ground the crumpled receipt which, the entire time, she had been nervously pressing between her fingers. Pepa didn't see it, because he was gazing up at the stars. But Officer Soucek saw it and, sadly and knowingly, he smiled.

Oplatka's End

Toward three o'clock in the morning, plainclothes officer Krejcik noticed that the shutters of a bakery at No. 17 Neklanova Street were half raised. Accordingly, he rang the bell and, although he was off duty, peered under the shutters to see if there was anyone inside. At that moment a man burst out of the bakery, fired a bullet into Krejcik's belly from half a step away, and made his escape.

Officer Bartos, who at the time was patrolling his assigned beat on Jeronymova Street, heard the shot and started running in that direction. At the corner of Neklanova Street he very nearly collided with the fleeing man, but before he could shout "Halt!" a shot burst out and Officer Bartos fell to the ground, wounded in the belly.

The street was awakened by the screech of police whistles; patrolmen from the entire area converged; three men from the police station arrived on the double, buttoning their jackets as they ran; within a few minutes a motorcycle from precinct headquarters roared up and the captain jumped off. By then Bartos was already dead and Krejcik, clutching at his belly, was dying.

By morning some twenty arrests had been made; this was done at random, because nobody had seen the murderer. On the one hand, the police had to find a way to avenge the deaths of two of their men. And on the other hand, this is ordinarily what happens, the assumption being that, by some divine stroke of luck, one of the suspects will break down and confess. At headquarters, interrogations were carried out non-stop, day and night. Pale and harried criminals, well known to the police, writhed on the rack of endless questioning; but they shook even more at the thought of what would happen when a couple of policemen took

them in hand after the questioning ended, for the city's entire
police force was seething with a dark and fearsome rage. The
murder of Officer Bartos had violated that familiar, unofficial
relationship which exists between the professional policeman and
the professional criminal. If he had simply been shot, so be it —
but you don't even shoot dumb animals in the belly.

By the next night, toward the early hours of the morning,
every policeman even on the farthest outskirts of the city knew
that Oplatka had done it. One of the suspects had squealed:
"Sure," Valta said, "Oplatka done those two on Neklanova Street,
and he'll knock off a few more; he don't care, he's got TB." All
right then, it's Oplatka.

That same night, first Valta was arrested and then
Oplatka's girlfriend and three men from Oplatka's gang; but not
one of them could or would say where Oplatka was hiding out.
How many uniformed officers and plainclothesmen were sent to
track Oplatka down is another matter. But in addition to these,
every policeman, as soon as he had gone off duty, quickly swilled
some coffee at home, muttered something to his wife, pulled
himself together, and started off on his own to look for Oplatka.
Oh yes, everybody knew Oplatka, that green-face little runt with
the skinny neck.

Towards eleven o'clock at night, Officer Vrzal, who had
completed his rounds at nine, hastily changed into street clothes
and told his wife that he was just going to have a look around
the area. He came across a small, slight man near the Rajska
Garden who seemed to be keeping well in the shadows. Officer
Vrzal, though unarmed and off duty, moved in a little closer to
see; but when he was within three yards of him, the man thrust
his hand in his pocket, shot Vrzal in the belly, and fled. Officer
Vrzal clutched at his belly and tried to run after him. After a
hundred yards he collapsed, but the police whistles had already
started shrilling and several men were chasing after the fleeing
shadow. Behind Rieger Park a few shots were heard. A quarter
of an hour later several cars, draped with policemen, were racing
towards upper Zizkov, and patrols consisting of four or five men

prowled through the new construction sites in that quarter.
Towards one o'clock, a pistol-shot was heard behind Olsansky
Pond; someone on the run had fired at a youth returning from
his girlfriend's house, but had missed him. At two o'clock, a
posse of uniformed and plainclothesmen surrounded the abandoned Zidovske kilns and, step by step, moved in closer. A cold
rain began to fall. Toward morning it was reported that, just
beyond the distant suburb of Malesice, someone had fired at a
toll-keeper who had left his booth. The toll-keeper had started
to run after him but wisely decided that it was none of his
business. It was clear that Oplatka had slipped away into the
countryside.

   Some sixty policemen returned from the abandoned kilns,
soaked to the skin and so enraged with helplessness that they
could have wept. God in heaven, it was infuriating! The bastard
had shot down three of the city's policemen — Bartos, Krejcik,
and Vrzal — and now he was running loose in the territory of
the regional police! *We* have first rights, the city's uniformed and
plainclothes officers maintained, and now we have to share this
runt, this stinking Oplatka, with *them*! Listen, we're the ones he
shot at, so it's *our* affair, right? We don't want the regionals
butting in; all we need them to do is block his way so he has to
go back to Prague.
   Throughout the day a cold rain fell. That evening, towards
twilight, Regional Officer Mrazek was on his way to Pysely from

Cercany, where he had gone to buy a battery for his radio. He was unarmed and whistling to himself. As he was going along, he saw a smallish man in front of him. There was nothing out of the ordinary about this, but the small man stopped, as if uncertain which way to go. Now who might that be, Mrazek asked himself, and at that same moment he saw a flash and toppled over, clutching his hand to his side.

That same evening, needless to say, regional police throughout the area were put on the alert. "Listen, Mrazek," Captain Honzatko said to the dying man, "I don't want you worrying about this. Word of honor, we'll get our hands on the son of a bitch. It's that Oplatka, and I'm betting he'll try to make it to Sobeslav — that's where he was born. God knows why these bastards head for home when their number's up. Give me your hand, Vaclav; I swear to you we'll find that man and finish him off, no matter what." Vaclav Mrazek made an effort to smile — he had been thinking of his three children, but now he was imagining that he saw regional police officers gathering around him on all sides . . . he thought maybe Toman from Cerny Kostel was among them . . . surely Zavada from Votice was there . . . Rousek from Sazava, too; his buddies, his buddies . . . What a beautiful sight, thought Vaclav Mrazek, all of us together! Then Mrazek smiled for the last time; after that there was nothing but inhuman agony.

That night it happened that Regional Sergeant Zavada from Votice decided to search the night train from Benesov. Who knows, maybe Oplatka's in there somewhere; would he risk taking a train? Lights flickered in the cars; passsengers dozed on the seats, hunched together like weary animals. Sergeant Zavada went from car to car, thinking, how the hell do I recognize a man I've never seen? At that instant, a yard away from him, a young man with a hat over his eyes jumped up, there was a loud report, and before the sergeant could unhitch his rifle from his shoulder the man had left the passenger car, brandishing a revolver. Sergeant Zavada only had time to shout "Stop him!" before he collapsed, face down, in the aisle.

Meanwhile, the young man had jumped from the train and was running toward the freight cars. A railwayman, Hrusa, was strolling beside the freight cars with a lantern and promising himself, well, as soon as No. 26 pulls out I'll go lie down for a while in the shed. At that same moment a man ran into him. In nothing flat, old Hrusa had blocked his path; it was pure masculine instinct. Then he saw some sort of flash, and that was all; even before No. 26 had left the station, old Hrusa was lying in the shed, but on a plank, and the railwaymen were making their way inside to take a look at him, their heads bared.

A few men ran panting after the fleeing shadow, but it was already too late. By this time, undoubtedly, he had crossed the tracks and entered the fields. And at that moment, throughout the countryside enfolded in autumn slumber, a frenzied panic began to spread out in an ever-widening circle from the railway station with its twinkling lights and its cluster of frightened people. People crowded into their cottages, scarcely daring to set foot beyond the door. It was rumored that, in such-and-such a place or other, someone had seen a wild-looking stranger; he was either a tall, thin man or else a short man in a leather coat. A postman had seen someone hiding behind a tree. Someone on the main road had signaled a coachman named Lebeda to stop, but Lebeda had lashed at his horses and driven off. It was a fact that someone sobbing with fatigue had stopped a child on her way to school and snatched her little bag with a piece of bread in it. "Give me that," the man had snarled, and he ran off with the bread. At that point the villagers bolted their doors, holding their breath in terror. At most they dared press their noses against the windowpane, looking out with suspicion on the gray and empty countryside.

At the same time another, related event was taking place. One after the other, from every direction, regional police officers began to assemble; who knows where they all came from. "My God, man," shouted Captain Honzatko at an officer from Caslav, "what are you doing here? Who sent you? Do you think I need cops from all over Bohemia to catch one thug? Do you?" The officer from Caslav shed his helmet and scratched the nape of his neck in confusion. "Well, you see, sir," he said with a beseeching glance, "Zavada was my buddy . . . and if I wasn't in on this — well, I couldn't do that to him!" "Damn it," thundered the captain, "that's what every one of them's telling me! Close to fifty officers have already showed up here without orders — what am I supposed to do with you?" Captain Honzatko gnawed his moustache savagely. "All right, take the stretch of highway from the crossroads up to the woods. Tell Voldrich from Benesov that you're relieving him." "That won't work, sir," the officer from Caslav replied sensibly, "what I mean, sir, is Voldrich, he'd never stand for it, and that's a fact. It'd be better if I was to take the woods from the edge up to that secondary road — who's on duty there?" "Semerad from Veselka," the captain growled; "now listen and remember: on my authority, if you see anyone, you're to shoot without warning. No cold feet, understand me? I'm not letting my men get shot. Now march!"

Then the stationmaster arrived. "Well, Captain," he said, "thirty more turned up." "Thirty what?" Captain Honzatko sputtered. "Why," said the stationmaster, "railwaymen, of course. You know, on account of Hrusa. He was one of our men, so they've come to offer a hand — " "Send them back," the captain shouted, "I don't need any civilians here." The stationmaster shifted uneasily from one foot to the other. "Look, Captain," he offered soothingly, "they've come here all the way from Prague and Mezimosti. It's a good thing when they stick together like that. You see, they won't take no for an answer now that Oplatka's killed one of their own. They've got a right to it, in a way. So if I were you, Captain, I'd do them a favor and take them on." The captain, his temper rising, growled that he wished to hell they'd just leave him alone.

In the course of the day, the wide circle gradually tightened. That afternoon the commander from the nearest garrison head-quarters telephoned to see if reinforcements were needed from the military. "No," Captain Honzatko snapped disrespectfully, "this is _our_ affair, understand?" Meanwhile, some city police officers had arrived by train from Prague; they argued fiercely with the regional sergeant, who was going to send them straight back again. "What?" raged Inspector Holub in a fury, "you want to send us back? He's killed three of our people and only two of your fair-haired boys! We've got more right to him than you do, you tin-star wonders!" No sooner had this conflict been settled than a fresh one broke out on the far side of the circle among the regional police and the gamekeepers from the forest. "Get out of here," the officers fumed, "this isn't a rabbit hunt!" "The hell with you," replied the gamekeepers, "these are *our* woods and we have a right to be here any time we damn well please. Understand?" "Use your heads, folks," said Rousek from Sazava, trying to get things straightened out, "this is *our* business and nobody else's barging in on us." "That's what you say," the game-keepers retorted. "That kid the man took the bread from is our man Hurka's kid. There's no way we're letting that pass, so forget it!"

That evening the circle was closed. When darkness had fallen, each man heard the hoarse breathing of the man on his right and the man on his left, and the squelch of footsteps in the viscous earth. "Stay put" were the words that sped quietly from man to man. "Don't move!" The silence was heavy and harrow-ing; now and then dry leaves rustled in the darkness of the circle's center or a drizzle of light rain hissed; now and then a man's footstep squelched in passing or something metallic clinked, perhaps a rifle or a strap. Toward midnight, someone in the darkness cried "Halt!" and fired a shot. At that same moment things somehow became oddly confused, the scattered reports of some thirty rifle-shots rang out, and everyone began to run in that direction. Suddenly another shout was heard: "Get back! Nobody move!" They fell back into some sort of order and once again the circle was closed; but only now did they all fully realize that in the darkness before them a lost, spent man was trapped in his hiding place, lying in wait for the chance to strike out in a rabid assault. Something like an uncontrollable shudder passed quickly from man to man; from time to time the heavy drip of

water plashed like a furtive step. God, if only we could see!
Christ, if only it were light!

Day began to dawn mistily. Each man discerned the outline
of the man next to him, marveling that he had been so close to
a human being. In the middle of the circle of men the contours
of a dense thicket or copse appeared (it was a covert for hares),
and it was so quiet there, so utterly quiet — Captain Honzatko
tugged feverishly at his moustache: damn, we'll have to wait it
out, or —

"I'm going in," murmured Inspector Holub. The captain
snorted. "*You're* going in," he said, turning to the nearest of his
men. Five men rushed into the thicket; a crackle of broken
branches was heard and then, suddenly, silence. "Stay where you
are," Captain Honzatko shouted to his men, and he moved
slowly toward the trees. Soon there emerged from the thicket the
broad back of a regional officer dragging something, some sort of
huddled body, the feet of which were being held by a gamekeeper with a bushy moustache. Behind them Captain Honzatko,
scowling and sallow, squeezed his way out of the thicket. "Put
him down right here," he gasped, wiping his forehead; he looked
around as if surprised at the hesitant circle of men, scowled still
more, and shouted, "What are you gawking at? Dismissed!"

In some confusion, man after man straggled forward to the
diminutive, bowed body on the ground. So this was Oplatka: the
gaunt arm sticking out of the sleeve, the small, greenish, rain-
smeared face on the thin neck — God, what a pitiful runt, this
wretch Oplatka! Look, he took a bullet in the back, and here's a
little hole in back of his jug-ear, and here, too . . . Four, five,
seven shots got him! Captain Honzatko, who was kneeling by
the body, stood up and cleared his throat dispiritedly. Then,
uneasily and almost shyly, he raised his eyes — There stood a
long, solid line of regional officers, rifles on shoulders, bayonets
shining above. God, what sturdy men, like tanks, and arrayed in
a row as if on full-dress parade, no one saying a word. — On the
other side a black cluster of city police officers, hefty men one
and all, pockets bulging with revolvers; then the blue-uniformed

railwaymen, short and stubborn; then the gamekeepers in green, lanky fellows, sinewy and bearded, their faces red as peppers. — Why, it's like a public funeral, thought the startled captain; they've formed a square, as if they were going to fire a salute! Captain Honzatko gnawed at his lip in senseless and stinging torment. — That runt on the ground, rumpled and stiff, a sick crow riddled with bullets, and there, all those hunters — "Damn it all," shouted the captain, gritting his teeth, "isn't there a sack or something here? Cover that body!"

Some two hundred men began to disperse in various directions. They did not speak to each other except to grumble about the bad roads and mutter sullenly in reply to excited questions, "Sure, he's dead, he's good and dead, now leave us alone!" The regional officer who stayed on guard over the covered body snapped angrily at the rural onlookers: "What are you hanging around for? There's nothing here to gawk at! It's no business of yours!"

At the regional boundary, Officer Rousek from Sazava spat out, "Dirty killers! It makes me sick. God, I just wish I could've had at that Oplatka on my own, man to man!"

The Last Judgment

Pursued by several warrants and a whole army of policemen and detectives, the notorious multiple-killer Kugler swore that they'd never take him, and they didn't — at least not alive. The last of his nine murderous deeds was shooting a policeman who was trying to arrest him. The policeman indeed died, but not before putting a total of seven bullets into Kugler, three of which were definitely fatal. To all appearances he had escaped earthly justice.

Kugler's death came so quickly that he had no time to feel any particular pain. When his soul left his body, it might have been surprised at the oddness of the next world, a world beyond space, gray and infinitely desolate — but it wasn't. A man who has been jailed on two continents looks upon the next life merely as new surroundings. Kugler expected to charge on through, equipped with a bit of courage, just as he'd done everywhere else.

At length the inevitable Last Judgment got around to Kugler. Heaven being eternally in a state of emergency, he was brought before a special court of three judges and not, as his previous conduct would ordinarily merit, before a jury. The courtroom was furnished simply, like courtrooms on earth, with one exception: there was no provision for swearing in witnesses. The judges were old and worthy councilors with austere, weary faces. The formalities were somewhat tedious: Kugler, Ferdinand; unemployed; born on such-and-such a date; died . . . At this point it was shown that Kugler did not know the date of his own death. Immediately he realized that his failure to remember was damaging in the eyes of the judges, and his attitude hardened.

"Of what do you consider yourself guilty?" the presiding judge asked.

"Nothing," Kugler replied obstinately.

"Bring in the witness," the judge sighed.

In front of Kugler there appeared an extraordinary gentleman, stately, bearded, and clothed in a blue robe strewn with golden stars; at his entrance the judges rose, and even Kugler stood up, reluctant but fascinated. Only when the old gentleman took a seat did the judges sit down again.

"Witness," began the presiding judge, "Omniscient God, this court has summoned You in order to hear Your testimony in the matter of Kugler, Ferdinand. As You are the Supreme Truth, You need not take the oath. We ask only that, in the interest of the proceedings, You keep to the subject at hand and not branch out into particulars that have no legal bearing on the case. And you, Kugler, don't interrupt the Witness. He knows everything, so there's no use denying anything. And now, Witness, if You would please begin."

That said, the presiding judge took off his spectacles and leaned comfortably on the bench before him, evidently in preparation for a long speech by the witness. The oldest of the three judges nestled down in sleep. The recording angel opened the Book of Life.

The Witness, God, cleared his throat and began:

"Yes, Kugler, Ferdinand. Ferdinand Kugler, son of a factory official, was a bad, unmanageable child from his earliest days. He loved his mother dearly but was ashamed to show it; that's why he was unruly and defiant. Young man, you infuriated everyone! Do you remember how you bit your father on the thumb when he tried to spank you because you'd stolen a rose from the notary's garden?"

"That rose was for Irma, the tax collector's daughter," Kugler recalled.

"I know," said God. "Irma was seven years old then. And do you know what happened to her later?"

"No, I don't."

"She got married; she married Oskar, the son of the factory

owner. But she contracted a venereal disease from him and died of a miscarriage. You remember Rudy Zaruba?"

"What happened to him?"

"Why, he joined the navy and died in Bombay. You two were the worst boys in the whole town. Kugler, Ferdinand was a thief before his tenth year and an inveterate liar. He kept bad company, the drunken beggar Dlabola, for instance, with whom he shared his food."

The presiding judge motioned with his hand, as if perhaps this was unnecessary information; but Kugler himself asked shyly, "And . . . what happened to his daughter?"

"Marka?" said God. "She lowered herself considerably. In her fourteenth year she prostituted herself; in her twentieth year she died, remembering you in the agony of her death. By your fourteenth year you were nearly a drunkard yourself, and you often ran away from home. Your father died from grief and worry, and your mother nearly cried her eyes out. You brought dishonor on your home, and your little sister, your pretty sister Marticka, never married: no young man would come calling at the home of a thief. She's still living alone and in poverty, exhausted from sewing each night and humiliated by her scant earnings from people who take pity on her."

"What's happening right now?"

"This very minute she is at Vlcak's, buying thread. Do you remember that shop? Once, when you were six years old, you bought a colored glass marble there; and that very same day you lost it and never ever found it. Do you remember how sad and angry you were then, and how you blubbered?"

"Where did it roll away to?" Kugler asked eagerly.

"Down the drain and into the gutter. As a matter of fact, it's still there, after thirty years. Right now it's raining on earth, and your marble is shivering in a gush of cold water."

Kugler bent his head, overcome. But the presiding judge fitted his spectacles back on his nose and said mildly, "Witness, we are obliged to get on with the case. Has the accused committed murder?"

The Witness nodded his head. "He murdered nine people. The first one he killed in a brawl, and while in prison for it he was completely corrupted. The second was an unfaithful sweetheart. For that he was sentenced to death, but he escaped. The third was an old man, whom he robbed. The fourth was a night watchman."

"Then he died?" Kugler shouted.

"He died after three days of terrible pain," God said, "and he left six children behind. The fifth and sixth people were an old married couple; he finished them off with an axe and found practically no money, although they had more than twenty thousand hidden away."

Kugler jumped up: "Where? Tell me!"

"In the straw mattress," God said. "In a linen sack inside the mattress. That's where they stored the money they got from usury and penny-pinching. The seventh man he killed in America; he was an immigrant, a countryman, helpless as a child."

"So it was in the mattress," Kugler whispered in amazement.

"Yes," the Witness continued. "The eighth man was a passerby who happened to be in the way when Kugler was trying to outrun the police. Kugler had periostitis then and was delirious from the pain. Young man, you were suffering terribly. The last was the policeman who killed Kugler, whom Kugler felled just as he himself was dying."

"And why did the accused commit murder?" queried the presiding judge.

"For the same reasons others do," answered God. "From anger, from greed, deliberately and by chance, sometimes with pleasure and other times from necessity. He was generous and sometimes he helped people. He was kind to women, he loved animals, and he kept his word. Should I tell about his good deeds?"

"Thank You," the presiding judge said, "it isn't necessary. Does the accused have anything to say in his defense?"

"No," Kugler replied with honest indifference; it was all the same to him.

"The court will now take this case under advisement," the presiding judge declared, and the councilors withdrew. God and Kugler remained in the courtroom.

"Who are they?" Kugler asked, inclining his head toward the three who were leaving.

"People like you," said God. "They were judges on earth, so they're judges here as well."

Kugler nibbled at his fingertips. "I thought . . . I mean, I didn't worry about it or anything, but . . . I figured that You would judge, since . . . since . . . "

"Since I'm God," finished the stately gentleman. "But that's just it, don't you see? Because I know everything, I can't possibly judge. That wouldn't do at all. By the way, do you know who turned you in this time?"

"No, I don't," said Kugler, surprised.

"Lucka, the waitress. She did it out of jealousy."

"Excuse me," Kugler ventured, feeling bolder, "but You forgot to mention that no-good Teddy I shot in Chicago."

"You're wrong there," God objected. "He recovered and is alive this very minute. I know he's an informer, but otherwise he's a good man and truly fond of children. You shouldn't think of anyone as being completely worthless."

"But really, why don't You . . . why don't You Yourself do the judging?" Kugler asked pensively.

"Because I know everything. If judges knew everything, absolutely everything, they couldn't judge, either: they would understand everything, and their hearts would ache. How could I possibly judge you? Judges know only about your crimes; but I know everything about you. Everything, Kugler. And that's why I cannot judge you."

"But why are those same people judges . . . even here in heaven?"

"Because people belong to each other. As you see, I'm only a witness; it's people who determine the verdict — even in heaven. Believe me, Kugler, this is the way it should be. The only justice people deserve is human justice."

At that moment, the judges returned from their deliberations. In stern tones the presiding judge announced: "For repeated crimes of first-degree murder, manslaughter, robbery, illegal re-entry, concealment of weapons, and the theft of a rose, Kugler, Ferdinand is sentenced to lifelong punishment in hell. The sentence begins immediately. Next case, please. Is the accused, Machat, Frantisek present in court?"

The Crime on the Farm

"Arise, defendant," the presiding judge said. "You are charged with the murder of your father-in-law, Frantisek Lebeda. During the preliminary questioning, you confessed to having struck him three times on the head with an axe, with intent to kill. Tell me: do you feel yourself to be guilty of this crime?"

The small, work-worn man trembled and swallowed something. "No," he managed to get out.

"You killed him?"

"Sure."

"Then do you feel yourself guilty?"

"No."

The presiding judge had the patience of an angel. "Look here, Vondracek," he said, "we've learned that on an earlier occasion you tried to poison him. You put rat poison in his coffee. Isn't that true?"

"Sure."

"From this it would appear that you tried to take his life once before. Do you understand me?"

The little man sniffled and shrugged his shoulders in bewilderment. "It was on account of that clover," he stammered. "He sold that clover, and I kept telling him, Dad, leave that clover alone, I'll buy me some rabbits — "

"Wait," the judge interrupted. "Was it his clover or yours?"

"Well, his," the defendant mumbled. "But what did he need clover for? So I kept telling him, Dad, at least let me have the field with the alfalfa, but he said to me, when I die Marka gets it — that's my wife — and then you can do what you want with it, you greedy grabber."

"And that's why you wanted to poison him?"

"Well, yes — "

"Because he insulted you?"

"No. It was on account of that field. He said he was selling that field."

"But, man," the judge burst out, "it was his field, wasn't it? Why shouldn't he sell it?"

The defendant Vondracek looked reproachfully at the judge. "Well, sure, but next to that field I have this strip of potatoes," he tried to explain. "That's why I bought it, to put that field together with this other one, and he said, what's it to me, that potato patch, I'm selling to Joudal."

"So you were constantly quarreling," the judge prompted.

"Well, sure, sort of," said Vondracek, frowning. "It was on account of that goat."

"What goat?"

"He milked my goat dry. I kept telling him, Dad, leave that goat alone or else give us the little pasture near the creek. But he leased out the pasture."

"And what did he do with the money?" asked one of the jurors.

"Just what he would do," the defendant said glumly. "He hid it in a strongbox. When I die, he said, you get it. But him, he didn't want to die. Even if he was already over seventy."

"Then you're saying that in these quarrels your father-in-law was at fault?"

"He was," Vondracek stated hesitantly. "He didn't want to give anything up. As long as I'm alive, he said, I run this farm and that's that. And I kept telling him, please, Dad, if you buy a cow I'll plow that field and then you won't have to sell it. But he said, after I die you can buy two cows for all I care, but I'm selling that field to Joudal."

"Listen, Vondracek," the judge said sternly, "didn't you kill him because of the money in the strongbox?"

"That money was for a cow," Vondracek replied stubbornly.

"We figured that when he died we'd get a cow. A little farm like that needs a cow. How else can I get cow dung?"

"Defendant," the public prosecutor interrupted, "we're not talking about cows, but about a human life. Why did you kill your father-in-law?"

"It was on account of that field."

"That's no kind of answer!"

"He wanted to sell that field."

"But the money would have been yours anyway, after he died!"

"Sure, but he didn't want to die," said Vondracek, offended. "Your Honor, if he'd just gone ahead and died — I never did anything bad to him, anybody around here'd tell you that. I treated him like my own father, isn't that so?" he said, turning around to the spectators. The auditorium, where half the village sat, rustled in assent.

"Yes," the judge replied gravely, over the noise, "and that's why you wanted to poison him, is that it?"

"Poison," the defendant muttered. "He didn't have to sell that clover. Your Honor, sir, anybody around here'd swear to it. You got to have clover or it's no farm at all, isn't that so?"

The audience murmured its agreement.

"Turn around and face me, defendant," the judge shouted, "or I'll clear the court. Now tell us how the murder came about."

"Well," Vondracek began hesitantly, "one Sunday I saw he was talking to Joudal again. Dad, I said to him, you can't sell that field out from under me. But he said, why should I ask you, you brickmaker? So I said to myself, that does it. Then I went out to chop wood."

"Is this the axe you used?"

"Sure."

"Continue."

"That night I said to the wife, go take the kids to your aunt's. Right off she starts crying. Turn it off, I tell her, I'm going to talk to him first. So then he comes out to the woodshed and says, that's my axe, hand it over! And I tell him, you milked my goat dry. Then he tries to grab the axe from me. So I hit him with it."

"Why?"

"On account of that field."

"And why did you hit him three times?"

Vondracek shrugged his shoulders. "Well, because — Your Honor, everybody around here's used to hard work."

"And then?"

"Then I went to bed."

"Did you sleep?"

"No. I figured up how much a cow would cost and how I'd trade that pasture for that corner field by the road. Then those fields'd be together, see."

"And your conscience didn't bother you?"

"No. What bothered me was, those fields wasn't together. And then I'd have to fix up a shed for the cow, that would cost a couple hundred. Why, my father-in-law, he didn't even have a wagon. I kept telling him, Dad, God forgive you for your sins, but this is no way to run a farm. Those two fields just belong together, they want it, you can just feel it."

"And didn't you feel anything for the old man?" the judge thundered.

"But he wanted to sell that field to Joudal," the defendant stammered.

"And so you murdered him out of greed!"

"That's not true!" Vondracek protested excitedly. "It was on account of that field! If those fields was together — "

"Don't you feel any guilt?"

"No."

"Murdering an old man means nothing to you?"

"Like I told you, it was on account of that field," Vondracek burst out, almost sobbing. "That's not murder! Jesus, Mary, and Joseph, everybody knows that! Why, Your Honor, sir, it was all in our family! I'd never do that to a stranger — I never stole nothing . . . ask anybody about Vondracek . . . and they picked me up like a thief, like some kind of thief," Vondracek moaned, choking in his sorrow.

"No, like a parricide," the judge said sadly. "Do you know, Vondracek, that the penalty for this is death?"

Vondracek blew his nose and snuffled. "It was on account of that field," he stated in resignation; after which the trial dragged on: witnesses, statements by the prosecution and the defense . . .

While the jury was out deliberating the guilt of the defendant Vondracek, the presiding judge stared out the window, lost in thought.

"On the whole, it was pretty weak," another of the judges muttered. "The prosecution never really pressed, nor did the defense have much to say . . . in short, a straightforward case any way you look at it."

The presiding judge snorted. "A straightforward case," he said, dismissing the idea with a wave of his hand. "Listen, my friend, that man feels as much in the right as you or I. It's as if I were judging a butcher for slaughtering a cow, or a mole for making molehills. At times I felt this wasn't our affair at all, if you understand me; not a question of law or of justice — Ahh," he paused to breathe and take off his robe. "I have to get away from this for a while. You know, I think the jury will acquit him. It's absurd, but I think they will acquit him because . . . I'll tell you something: I've got farming blood in me, and when that man said those fields just belonged together, well . . . suddenly I saw those fields, and I felt as if we ought to judge . . . in accordance with some sort of divine law, do you understand me? That we ought to judge those two fields. Do you know what I would rather have done? I would rather have stood up, put aside my robe, and said, 'Defendant Vondracek, in the name of God, because bloodshed cries out to heaven, sow those two fields with henbane, henbane and thorns. And until the day of your death you will have this fallow of hatred before your eyes . . . ' I'd like to know what the public prosecutor would say to that. There are times, my friend, when God alone should judge. You know, He would impose such great and terrible punishments — To judge in the name of God; but we're not equal to that. — What, has the jury reached a verdict already?" With a sigh of reluctance, the presiding judge put on his robe. "Well then, let's get on with it. Summon the jury!"

The Disappearance of an Actor

It was on September second that Jan Benda, the actor, disappeared — the Great Benda, as he had been known from the time when, at a single leap, he had soared to one of the highest rungs on the ladder of theatrical fame. In point of fact, nothing whatsoever happened on September second. The cleaning woman, who entered Benda's apartment at nine o'clock in the morning, found the bed rumpled and everything in the piggish disarray that normally characterized Benda's surroundings; but the great man himself was not at home. Inasmuch as there was nothing unusual about this, she cleaned and straightened the apartment in her slapdash fashion and went on her way again. So be it. But from that time on, not a trace of Benda was to be found.

Mrs. Maresova (that is, the cleaning woman) wasn't overly surprised at this state of affairs, either. These actors, if you please, are just like gypsies; who knows if he's off acting somewhere or off on a spree. But on September tenth a call went out for Benda; he was supposed to have been at the theater, where they were beginning to rehearse *King Lear*. When Benda still hadn't shown up by the third rehearsal, they became extremely upset and telephoned Benda's friend Dr. Goldberg, to see if he knew what had become of Benda.

This Dr. Goldberg was a surgeon and earned an atrocious amount of money from appendectomies; it's become sort of a Jewish specialty. In addition to that, he was a stout man with stout gold spectacles and a stout heart of gold; he had a passion for art, and his apartment was crammed with paintings from floor to ceiling; and he was devoted to Benda, who treated him with friendly contempt and, somewhat indulgently, always let him pick up the tab — which, just between us, was no piddling sum. Benda's tragic countenance and the beaming face of Dr. Goldberg (who drank only water) had long been a familiar sight at all those legendary sprees and wild escapades which constituted the notorious side of the great thespian's fame.

So they telephoned this Dr. Goldberg from the theater to find out what could have happened to Benda. He said that he had no idea, but that he would go out looking for him. What he didn't say was that, for an entire week, he had already been searching for Benda in all the night clubs and other pleasure spots with increasing alarm. He had an uneasy foreboding that something had indeed happened to Benda. In point of fact, it was like this: Dr. Goldberg was, so far as he could ascertain, the last person to have seen Jan Benda. Sometime towards the end of August he had accompanied Benda on a triumphant round of Prague's night life; but subsequently, Benda had failed to show up at any of their usual meeting places. Perhaps he's ill, Dr. Goldberg finally told himself, and one evening he dropped by Benda's apartment; it was on September first, to be exact. He rang the bell; nobody opened the door, but he could hear some sort of rustling inside. Dr. Goldberg therefore went on ringing the bell for a good five minutes. Suddenly he heard footsteps and the door opened. There stood Benda, wrapped in a dressing gown, and Dr. Goldberg was aghast at the sight of him, so forbidding did the famed actor appear with his hair tousled and matted and a full week's growth of stubble on his face. He looked haggard and grimy. "So it's you," he said sullenly, "what do you want?"

"Good heavens, what's the matter with you?" Dr. Goldberg burst out in astonishment.

"Nothing," Benda snarled. "I'm not going out anywhere, if that's what you want. Leave me alone!" And he'd shut the door in Goldberg's face. The day after that, he disappeared.

Now Dr. Goldberg was gazing worriedly through his thick glasses. There was something wrong here. From the caretaker of the building where Benda lived, he learned only that the other night, maybe the night of September first, a car had stopped in front of the apartment building at about three in the morning, but nobody got out. All that happened was that somebody'd honked the horn like he was giving someone inside the building a signal. Then you could hear someone leave the building and slam the front door, and after that the car drove off. As to what kind of car it was, who knows, the caretaker hadn't got up to look at it. At three o'clock in the morning, you don't get out of bed unless you have to. But that horn was honking away like those folks in the car were in one hell of a hurry and hadn't a moment to lose.

Mrs. Maresova had claimed earlier that Mr. Benda hadn't left his apartment for a whole week (except maybe at night), hadn't shaved, and probably hadn't even washed either, from the looks of him. He had sent out for food, swilled brandy, sprawled on the sofa, and that's about all. Now that others were beginning to take an interest in Benda's disappearance, too, Dr. Goldberg went back again to Mrs. Maresova.

"My good woman," he said, "listen, do you happen to know

what kind of clothes Mr. Benda was wearing when he left his apartment?"

"None," said Mrs. Maresova, "and that's what bothers me. He wasn't wearing nothing at all. I know all of his clothes, and they're all hanging right there in the closet — right down to the last pair of pants."

"But surely he wouldn't have gone out just in his underwear, would he?" asked Dr. Goldberg, very much startled.

"Not in his underwear, neither," declared Mrs. Maresova, "and not in his shoes. That's what's so funny, sir. Look, I got every piece of his laundry all written down here, because I take it to the cleaner's. Now it's all clean and back again, and I got everything sorted out and counted. He's got eighteen shirts and there's not a one of them missing, not even a handkerchief, not one single thing. The only thing that's gone is this little satchel he always carries with him. If he did go away, then the dear thing must've been wearing his birthday suit."

Dr. Goldberg looked very grave. "My good woman," he said, "when you entered the apartment on September second, did you notice any particular disorder? You know, anything knocked over or any doors broken open?"

"Disorder," pondered Mrs. Maresova. "I'd have to say the disorder was pretty much like always. Mr. Benda, you know, he lived pretty much like a pig. But outside of that, sir, there wasn't any disorder, not to speak of, no. But I ask you, where could he go when he didn't have a stitch of clothes on?"

Dr. Goldberg, to be sure, knew as little as she did. And this time, with the gloomiest of misgivings, he turned to the police.

"Right," said the police officer, after Dr. Goldberg had poured out everything he knew, "we'll search for him. But from what you said, about how he shut himself up at home for a whole week, unshaved and unwashed, sprawling on the sofa, swilling brandy, and then disappearing naked as an Ashanti, well, sir, that looks like it could be, hm, like some kind of — "

"Delirium," Dr. Goldberg blurted out.

"Right," said the officer. "We call it suicide while of unsound mind. You know, I wouldn't be surprised if that's what he did."

"But then most likely his body would've been found," Dr. Goldberg supposed uncertainly. "And besides, how far could he have gone naked? And why would he have taken his satchel with him? And the car that was waiting in front of the building — That seems more like running away, Officer."

"What about debts?" the officer had another idea. "Didn't he have debts?"

"No," said the doctor quickly. Although Benda was up to his eyeballs in debts, he never took them seriously.

"Or . . . some kind of personal problem, say . . . an unhappy love affair or syphilis or some other serious worries?"

"Nothing, so far as I know," said Dr. Goldberg hesitantly. One or two things indeed came to mind, but he kept them to himself — besides, they could hardly have anything to do with Benda's inexplicable disappearance. All the same, on his way home from the police — of course, the police would do everything in their power — he turned over in his mind all that he knew about that side of Benda. It wasn't much:

1. Benda had a wife living abroad somewhere, whom he obviously didn't care for;

2. he was keeping some girl in Holesovice, on the outskirts of Prague;

3. he was having an affair, a scandalous affair, with a woman named Greta, the wife of the big industrialist Korbel. Greta was bound and determined to be an actress, and for that reason Korbel had financed some movies in which his wife, of course, played the starring role. It was well known that Benda was Greta's lover, and that she followed him around and no longer bothered with even the appearance of discretion. For all that, Benda never talked about these things; he treated them with a contempt that was one part lofty disdain and one part cynicism, and it made Goldberg shudder. No, the doctor told himself

hopelessly, nobody knows all the ins and outs of Benda's private life. I'd bet my bottom dollar there's some sort of ugly business behind this, but it's in the hands of the police now.

Dr. Goldberg didn't know, of course, what the police were doing or what lines of investigation they were following; he waited with growing despondency to receive some kind of report. Meanwhile an entire month had elapsed since the actor's disappearance, and people were beginning to talk about Jan Benda in the past tense.

One evening Dr. Goldberg happened to run into the old actor Lebduska. As they chatted away about this and that, the conversation naturally turned to Benda. "Let me tell you, *there* was an *actor*," recalled old Lebduska. "I remember him when he was about twenty-five years old. That damned kid, he was playing Oswald! Did you know that medical students used to go watch him to study the symptoms of paresis? And when he first played King Lear — Listen, I can't even tell you how he played that role, because my eyes were on his hands the whole time. He had hands like an eighty-year-old man, scrawny, shriveled, pitiful hands — to this day I can't figure out how he did those hands. I know a thing or two about makeup myself, but I'm telling you, nobody did it like Benda. Only an actor can appreciate it."

Dr. Goldberg felt a pang of melancholy pleasure on hearing this fellow actor's obituary of Jan Benda.

"He was an actor through and through, friend," sighed Lebduska. "You wouldn't believe how he'd browbeat the wardrobe man! 'You put that nickel-and-dime lace on *my* coat,' he'd holler, 'and I'm not playing the king!' He couldn't stand the idea of wearing any of that fake theatrical stuff. Listen, when he was going to do Othello, he ran around to all the antique shops till he found this genuine Renaissance ring; and that's what he wore on his finger when he played Othello. He said he did a better job of acting when he had the real thing on him like that. It wasn't like playing a role, it was nothing less than . . . metamorphosis," said Lebduska hesitantly, not knowing if he'd used the right word. "And whenever he was in a play, every intermission he'd swear like a trooper and lock himself in his dressing room so no one could interrupt his mood. That's why he drank so much his nerves were affected," Lebduska offered reflectively. "Well, friend," he added, by way of parting, "I'm off to the movies."

"I'll come with you," proposed Dr. Goldberg, who had no particular plans for the evening. The film was some sort of seafaring adventure, but Dr. Goldberg never really knew what it was all about. The tears all but spilled from his eyes as he listened to old Lebduska rambling on about Jan Benda.

"He wasn't an actor," Lebduska continued, "he was the devil himself. What I mean is, one life wasn't enough to satisfy him. He was a louse in real life, Doctor, but on stage he was an honest-to-God king or an honest-to-God beggar, right down to his toes. I'm telling you, that man would wave his hand like he'd been ordering people around all his life; and yet his father, you know, went door to door sharpening knives. Wait, look at that: here the man's shipwrecked on a desert island, and his nails are manicured. What an idiot. And see how that beard's just glued on his face? If Benda'd been playing that part, he'd have grown a real beard, and he'd have real dirt under his nails . . . What is it, Doctor, what's come over you?"

"Excuse me," stammered Dr. Goldberg, standing up, "but I've just thought of something. Thanks very much." And he was already dashing out of the theater. Benda would have grown a real beard, he repeated to himself. Benda *did* grow a real beard! Why on earth didn't I think of that sooner?

"Police headquarters!" he shouted, flinging himself into the nearest taxi. And when he got through to see the sergeant on night duty, he demanded, with much shouting and pleading, that the sergeant for God's sake go find out immediately, yes, *immediately*, whether on September second or thereabouts they'd discovered the body of an unidentified tramp anywhere, yes, *anywhere*. Contrary to all expectation, the sergeant actually did go off somewhere to look it up or to ask, more likely from boredom than from any particular zeal or even interest. Meanwhile Dr. Goldberg was sweating with anxiety, for a horrible thought had flashed across his mind.

"Well, sir," said the sergeant when he returned, "on the morning of September second, a gamekeeper found the body of an unidentified tramp, about forty years old, in the woods at Krivoklat. On September third, the body of an unidentified man was pulled out of the Elbe near Litomerice, about thirty years of age, that had been in the water for at least two weeks. On September tenth, an unidentified man of about sixty hanged himself near Nemecky Brod . . . "

"Are there any further details about the tramp?" Dr. Goldberg asked breathlessly.

"Murder," said the sergeant, looking attentively at the agitated doctor. "According to the local police report, his skull was crushed by a blunt object. The autopsy report says: alcoholic; cause of death, injury to the brain. Here's the photograph," offered the sergeant, adding, with the air of an expert, "Man, they really walloped him."

The photograph showed the body only from the waist up. It was dressed in verminous rags, with a tattered calico shirt open at the throat. Where the forehead and eyes should have been was only a clump of matted hair and something which might have once been skin and bone. Only the bristly chin with its growth of stubble and the half-open mouth bore any resemblance to a human being. Dr. Goldberg trembled like a leaf. Is it . . . could it possibly be Benda?

"Did he . . . did he have any distinguishing characteristics?" he managed to ask, overcome with misery.

The sergeant looked through a pile of papers. "Hm. Height, five foot eight; dark hair turning gray; conspicuously decayed teeth . . . "

Dr. Goldberg heaved a loud sigh. "Then it's not him. Benda's teeth were healthy as a horse's. It's not him. Forgive me for bothering you," he jabbered happily, "but that can't be him. Absolutely impossible."

Absolutely impossible, he told himself with relief as he returned home. It may be that he's still alive. Perhaps, good heavens, perhaps he's sitting in a night club right this moment, the Olympia or the Black Duck . . .

That night Dr. Goldberg again made the rounds of Prague's night life. He drank his glass of water in all the spots where Benda had once reigned supreme, and he peered through his gold goggles into every nook and corner, but there was no sign of Benda anywhere. Then, towards morning, the doctor suddenly turned pale, cursed himself aloud for being an idiot, and raced off to his garage.

It was still early that same morning when he drove up to a certain regional police headquarters and had the police chief roused from his bed. Fortunately, it so happened that he had once, with his own hands, gutted and sewn up the gentleman and handed him, as a souvenir, his appendix pickled in alcohol. As a result of this by no means surface acquaintanceship, within two hours' time he was in possession of an exhumation order and watching, side by side with the highly disgruntled coroner, as the corpse of the unidentified tramp was disinterred.

"You can take my word for it," grumped the coroner, "the Prague police have already checked him out. It's absolutely impossible that he could have been Benda. He was nothing but a bum, an utterly filthy bum."

"Did he have lice?" Dr. Goldberg asked with interest.

"I don't know," the coroner said with disgust, "but you won't recognize anything on him now. After all, he's been in the ground for a whole month — "

When the grave was opened, Dr. Goldberg had to send for brandy; otherwise he could not have persuaded the gravediggers to haul out and carry into the mortuary the unspeakable object which had lain at the bottom of the grave, sewn up in a sack.

"Go look at it yourself," the coroner growled at Dr.

Goldberg, and he remained outside the mortuary, smoking a strong cigar.

A short time later Dr. Goldberg staggered out of the mortuary, white as death. "Come and look," he said huskily, and he returned to the body and pointed to the part that had once been a man's head. Dr. Goldberg then took a pair of tweezers and pulled back what had once been lips to reveal hideously decayed teeth or, rather, the yellow stumps of teeth, stained black with caries.

"Take a good look," muttered Goldberg as he thrust the tweezers between the teeth and removed a strip of black decay. Beneath it appeared two strong, shiny incisors. But Dr. Goldberg could stand it no longer. He rushed out of the mortuary, clutching his head in his hands.

When, somewhat later, he returned, he was pale and greatly disheartened. "So much for those conspicuously decayed teeth," he said softly. "That was only a black paste that actors put on their teeth when they play old codgers or tramps. That filthy bum was an actor," and with a despairing wave of his hand, he added, "more than that, a great actor."

That same day Dr. Goldberg called on the industrialist Korbel. He was a tall, powerful man with a chin like a galosh and a body like a stone pillar.

"Sir," said Dr. Goldberg, staring fixedly at him through his convex glasses, "I have come to see you . . . in connection with the actor Benda."

"Indeed," said the industrialist, and he sat back and clasped his hands behind his head. "Has he turned up again?"

"Partly," remarked Dr. Goldberg. "I think it will be of interest to you . . . if for no other reason than the movie that you were going to do with him . . . that you were going to finance, I mean."

"What movie?" asked the large man indifferently. "I don't know anything about it."

"I mean," said Goldberg obstinately, "the movie in which Benda was going to play a tramp . . . with your wife, Greta, as the leading lady. In fact, it was to have been made because of your wife," the doctor added innocently.

"That's none of your business," snarled Korbel. "I suppose Benda put that idea in your head . . . It was all premature talk. There may have been a plot outline of sorts . . . Benda told you that, didn't he?"

"Not at all! You yourself gave him strict orders not to breathe a word about it to anyone. You made it out to be a big secret. But you know, during the last week of his life Benda let his beard and hair grow so he'd look like a tramp. He was very thorough about details like that, wasn't he?"

"I don't know," snapped the industrialist. "Is there anything else you want?"

"So this movie was to begin shooting on September second, right? The first scene was to be played in the woods at Krivoklat at daybreak. The tramp wakes up on the edge of a clearing . . . in the morning mist . . . and shakes the leaves and pine cones off his rags . . . I can just imagine how Benda would have played that. I know he would've worn his shabbiest rags and scruffiest shoes; he had a boxful of them in the attic. That's why, after his . . . disappearance, not one item of his clothing was missing — I can't believe that never occurred to anyone! They should've known he'd rig himself up from head to toe, with his sleeves in tatters and a rope around his waist, just like a real tramp. That was a passion with him, you know, taking great pains with his costuming."

"And what happened then?" asked the large man, leaning farther back into the shadow of the living room. "Although I don't understand why you're telling me all this."

"Because on September second, at about three o'clock in the morning," continued Dr. Goldberg obstinately, "you came to pick him up . . . probably in a rental car, but certainly in a closed one. I'm guessing your brother did the driving, because he's a good sport and he knows how to keep his mouth shut. You'd arranged with Benda beforehand that you wouldn't go upstairs but just honk the horn from the street. Shortly afterward, out came Benda . . . or, to be more precise, out came a filthy, grizzled tramp. 'Get a move on,' you told him, 'the cameraman's already gone on ahead.' And you drove off to the woods at Krivoklat."

"It would appear that you don't know the car's license number," the man in the shadow said sarcastically.

"If I knew it, I'd have had you arrrested by now," Dr. Goldberg said very matter-of-factly. "By daybreak you'd arrived at the spot. It's a sort of clearing, a glade rather, surrounded by hundred-year-old oak trees — a beautiful location, sir! I think your brother stayed with the car back on the road and pretended he was working on the engine. You led Benda about four hundred feet away from the road, and that's where you said: 'Well, here we are.' 'Where's the cameraman?' asked Benda. At that moment you struck him the first blow."

"With what?" came the voice of the man in the shadow.

"With a lead pipe," said Dr. Goldberg, "because a wrench would have been too light for a skull like Benda's; and you wanted to smash it to pieces, beyond recognition. And after you'd struck the final blow, you went back to the car. 'Ready?' asked your brother. But you probably didn't say anything, because murdering someone is no trifling matter."

"You've gone mad," roared the man in the shadow.

"Not mad. I only wanted to remind you how it most likely happened. You wanted to get Benda out of the way because of the scandal involving your wife. Your wife was carrying on much too openly — "

"You stinking Jew," raged the man in the armchair, "how dare you — "

"I'm not afraid of you," said Dr. Goldberg, adjusting his spectacles so that he looked even more uncompromising. "There's no way you can get at me, sir, no matter how rich you are. What harm could you possibly do to me? Unless you refuse to let me take out your appendix; which, sir, I wouldn't advise you to do."

The man in the shadow gave way to quiet laughter.

"Listen," he said, his tone unmistakably gleeful, "if you knew for certain only a tenth of what you've been babbling to me just now, you'd have gone to the police instead of me, right?"

"That's just it," said Dr. Goldberg gravely. "If I could prove even a tenth of it, sir, I wouldn't be here. I don't think it could ever be proved. It couldn't even be proved that that filthy tramp was Benda. That's precisely why I came here."

"To threaten me, is that it?" the man in the armchair shot back, and his hand reached for the bell.

"No, to scare you. It's not likely you're burdened with an overly sensitive conscience; you're too rich for that. But the fact that someone else knows about the whole horrible affair, that someone else knows you're a murderer, that your brother is a murderer, that the two of you murdered Benda the actor, the knife-grinder's son, the Great Benda — that, sir, will shake your lordly composure till your dying day. And as long as I'm alive, the two of you will have no peace of mind. In truth, I'd like to see you on the gallows. But at least, as long as I live, my very existence will unnerve you . . . Benda was a malicious brute; I know better than anyone how malicious he was, how conceited, cynical, insolent, and anything else you want to call him; but he was an artist. All your millions are worthless compared to that drunken clown. With all your millions you'll never accomplish what he could do with one regal gesture of his hand — a fabricated greatness but, for all that, the astonishing greatness of the man — " Dr. Goldberg threw up his hands in despair. "How could you have done it? You'll never know peace of mind again, because I'll never let you forget! Till my dying day I'll keep reminding you: Remember Benda the actor? He was an *artist*, sir, do you hear me?"

An Attempt at Murder

That evening Mr. Tomsa, chief clerk in a government office, had just settled down with his earphones and, with a gratified smile, was listening to a pleasant performance of some Dvorak dances on the radio — now that's what I call music, he said to himself contentedly — when suddenly two sharp reports sounded outside, and the glass from the window above his head shattered with a crash. Mr. Tomsa's apartment, it should be said, was on the ground floor.

And then he did what no doubt each of us would do. First of all, he waited for a moment to see what might happen next, then he snatched off his earphones and looked around rather sternly to see what had happened, and only then did he become frightened: for he saw that somebody had fired two shots at him through the window next to which he was sitting. Right over there, in the door he was facing, a splinter of wood had been ripped away and beneath it a bullet was embedded. His first impulse was to rush out into the street and seize the villain by the collar with his bare hands. But when a man is getting on in years and has a certain dignity to maintain, he generally lets his first impulse pass and opts instead for the second. And that is why Mr. Tomsa raced for the telephone and called the police. "Hello? Send somebody here at once; someone's just tried to murder me."

"Send somebody where?" said a sleepy and indifferent voice.

"Here, to my apartment," Mr. Tomsa flared in sudden anger, as if the police should have known. "It's perfectly outrageous that someone, for no reason at all, would shoot at a law-abiding citizen sitting quietly at home! This calls for a most thorough and immediate investigation, sir! It's a fine state of affairs when . . . "

"Right," the sleepy voice interrupted him. "I'll send someone over."

Mr. Tomsa fumed with impatience. It seemed to him that an *eternity* passed before the someone came trudging along, but in reality it was only twenty minutes before an even-tempered police inspector had arrived and was examining the bullet holes in the window with interest.

"Someone's been shooting at you, sir," he said matter-of-factly.

"I could have told you that," Mr. Tomsa burst out. "I was sitting right here by the window!"

"Thirty-two caliber," announced the inspector, extricating a bullet from the door with his knife. "Looks as if it's been fired from an old army revolver. See? Whoever it is must have been standing on the fence. If he'd been standing on the sidewalk, the bullet would have gone in higher up. That means he must have been aiming right at you, sir."

"That's odd," Mr. Tomsa observed caustically. "And here I thought he was aiming at the door."

"And who did it?" asked the inspector, ignoring the interruption.

"I'm sorry I can't give you his address," said Mr. Tomsa. "I didn't see the gentleman and I didn't think to invite him in."

"That makes things difficult," remarked the inspector, unperturbed. "So who do you suspect?"

Mr. Tomsa's patience was close to an end. "What do you mean, suspect?" he launched out irritably. "Look, Officer, I never saw the scoundrel, and even if he'd kindly waited until I could blow him a kiss through the window, I couldn't have recognized him in the dark. My dear sir, if I knew who it was, do you think I'd have put you to all this trouble?"

"Well, yes, there's something to that, sir," the inspector consoled him. "But maybe you can think of someone who'd profit from your death, or who might want to get back at you for something . . . . You see, sir, this wasn't an attempt at burglary; a burglar won't shoot unless he has to. But maybe somebody's got a grudge against you. You tell us who, sir, and we'll look into it."

Mr. Tomsa was taken aback: until that moment he hadn't thought about the matter in that light. "I haven't the faintest idea," he said slowly, thinking back over the peaceful life he had led as a government clerk and a bachelor. "But who, for heaven's sake, would have that kind of a grudge against me?" he said in bewilderment. "As far as I know, I haven't a single enemy in the world! It's completely out of the question," he added, shaking his head. "I simply don't have anything to do with other people. I keep almost entirely to myself, I never go anywhere, I don't meddle in anyone's affairs . . . What, for heaven's sake, would somebody want to get back at me for?"

The inspector shrugged his shoulders. "I don't know, sir, but maybe you'll think of something by tomorrow. You won't be worried staying here by yourself?"

"No," Mr. Tomsa said reflectively. That's odd, he said to himself uneasily when he was alone, why, yes *why* would somebody want to shoot at me, of all people? I'm practically a hermit, for heaven's sake. I do my work at the office and I go home — why, I hardly have anything to do with anyone else! Then why would they want to shoot me? he wondered with growing bitterness at such ingratitude; little by little he began to feel sorry for himself. I slave away like a horse, he said to himself, I even take work home with me, I'm never extravagant, I never take time out for little pleasures, I live like a snail in his shell, and bang! somebody comes along and fires a bullet at me. My Lord, what incredible hatred there is in people, marveled Mr. Tomsa, aghast. What have *I* ever done to anyone? How could someone have such an appalling, such an insane hatred for *me*?

Perhaps there's some mistake, he reassured himself, sitting on the bed and holding the boot he had just removed. Of course! It's a case of mistaken identity! The man simply thought that I was someone else, someone he had a grudge against! That must be it, he said to himself with relief, because why, why would anyone hate *me* like that?

The boot fell from Mr. Tomsa's hand. But of course, he suddenly recalled with some embarrassment, it was a silly thing for me to do, but it was really nothing more than a slip of the tongue. I was talking with Roubal and, without meaning to, I made an awkward remark about his wife. Of course, everyone knows that woman's cheating on him right and left, and he knows it, too, but he doesn't want people to know that he does. And I, ass that I am, went and stupidly let the cat out of the bag . . . . Mr. Tomsa remembered how Roubal had merely swallowed hard and dug his nails into his hands. Good heavens, he said to himself in horror, the man was crushed! Obviously he's madly in love with that woman! Naturally, I tried to smooth things over afterwards, but the man was biting his lips in anger! He's got good reason to hate me, Mr. Tomsa reflected sadly. I know he wasn't the one who shot at me, that's nonsense; but I certainly wouldn't be surprised if . . .

Mr. Tomsa stared at the floor in confusion. Or what about that tailor, he reminded himself uncomfortably. For fifteen years I ordered my clothes from him, and then one day I was told that he had a bad case of consumption. Of course, a man's apprehensive about wearing clothes that a consumptive tailor has been coughing on, so I stopped getting my suits from him . . . And then he came to see me and pleaded that he hadn't a stitch of work, his wife was sick and he needed to send his children away, and could he have the honor of my confidence in him again — Good heavens, how pale the poor man looked, and from the way he was sweating I could see how ill he was! "Mr. Kolinsky," I said to him, "look, it's no use, I need a better tailor; I've not been satisfied with your work." "I do my very best, sir," he stammered, sweating with fear and bewilderment, and it's a wonder he didn't burst out crying. And I, Mr. Tomsa reminded himself, I just sent him away saying, "I'll see," the sort of remark poor wretches like that hear only too often. The man might well hate me, Mr. Tomsa shuddered; it's horrible to go and beg someone for your very life and be sent away with such indifference. But what could I have done for him? I know he couldn't have been the one who did it, but . . .

Mr. Tomsa began to feel more and more distressed. But what's just as painful, he remembered, is the way I bawled out our file clerk. I couldn't find a certain file, so I sent for the old fellow and and yelled at him as if he'd been a schoolboy, and in front of other people, too! "I suppose this is what you call keeping things in order, you idiot, the place looks like a pigsty; I ought to throw you out on your ear — " And then I found the file in my own drawer! And the old man never said a word, only stood there trembling and blinking his eyes — Mr. Tomsa felt a hot surge of shame welling over him. A man can't very well apologize to a subordinate, he told himself without conviction, even if he has been a little hard on him. But how those subordinates must hate their supervisors! Wait, I'll give the poor devil some of my old clothes; on second thought, that would be humiliating for him, too —

Mr. Tomsa now found it unbearable to go on lying in bed; the blankets were stifling him. He sat up, wrapped his arms around his knees, and stared into the darkness. Or that business with young Moravek at the office, he thought, sick at heart. He's such a sensitive young man, writes poems and all. And when he blundered so badly in dealing with those papers, I told him, "Young man, you'll have to do these all over again," and I meant to throw the papers down on the table; but they landed at his feet, and when he bent down to pick them up his face grew red, his ears were red — I could have bitten off my tongue, Mr. Tomsa muttered. I really like that lad, and to humiliate him like that, however unintended —

Another face floated before Mr. Tomsa's eyes: the pale and swollen face of his colleague Wankl. Poor Wankl, he said to himself, he wanted to be chief clerk, and I got the promotion instead. It would have meant a few hundred more a year, and he's got six children — I've heard he'd like to have his eldest daughter trained as a singer, but he can't afford it; and I was promoted over him because he's such a slow-witted plodder, a real drudge — His wife has a terrible temper, but the reason she's so scraggy and bad-tempered is that she's always having to pinch pennies; he chews away on dry rolls for lunch — Mr. Tomsa lapsed into gloomy thought. Poor Wankl, he must have all kinds of bad feelings when he sees me, with no family at all, making more than he does; but I can't help that, can I? It makes me uneasy, though, when he looks at me in that injured, reproachful way . . .

Mr. Tomsa rubbed his forehead, which had broken out in an agonizing sweat. Yes, he said to himself, and then there's that waiter who cheated me on my bill; and I called for the owner, and he fired the waiter on the spot. "You thief," he snarled at him, "I'll see that you don't find another job anywhere in Prague!" And the man never said a word, just left . . . I could see his shoulder blades sticking out under his jacket.

Mr. Tomsa now found it unbearable to stay on the bed; he sat down by his radio and slipped on his earphones, but the radio was mute in the still, mute hours of the night. Mr. Tomsa covered his face with his hands and recalled all the people he had ever met, the odd and inconsequential people with whom he had never really gotten along and to whom he had never really given a second thought.

In the morning he stopped by the police station; he was somewhat pale and distracted. "So," the inspector asked, "have you thought of anyone who might have a grudge against you?"

Mr. Tomsa shook his head. "I don't know," he said hesitantly. "What I mean is, the people who might hold a grudge against me, there are so many that . . . " He waved his hand, baffled. "The fact of the matter is, a man never knows how many people he's wronged. You know, I'm just not going to sit by that window anymore. And I've come to ask you to forget the whole thing."

Released on Parole

"How about it, Zaruba, do you understand?" the prison warden asked when he had finished reading, almost ceremoniously, the official document from the Ministry of Justice. "It means that you have been paroled from the remainder of your life sentence. You have served twelve-and-a-half years, and throughout that time your conduct has been . . . well, simply put, exemplary. We've given you the best of references, and . . . ah . . . in a word, you can go home now, do you understand? But remember, Zaruba, if you get into any trouble, your parole will be revoked and you will have to serve out your life sentence for the murder of your wife, Marie, and then not even God can help you. So watch your step, Zaruba; next time will be for the rest of your life." The warden was so moved that he blew his nose. "You've been a favorite of ours, Zaruba, but I don't want to see you here again. So Godspeed, and the disbursements officer will pay you your money. You may go."

Zaruba, a lanky fellow nearly six foot six, shuffled his feet and stammered something or other; he was so happy that it almost hurt, and inside he was shaken by something very much like sobbing.

"Come, come," the warden said gruffly. "Don't start crying here. We've arranged for some clothes for you, and Mr. Malek, the builder, promised me he'd give you a job — What's that, you want to go see your home first? Oh, to see your wife's grave. Well, that's very decent of you. Then have a safe journey, Mr. Zaruba," the warden said hastily, and he shook Zaruba's hand. "And for goodness' sake, be careful what you do; remember that you're only on the outside conditionally."

"He's a good man," the warden said, as soon as the door

had shut behind Zaruba. "I'll tell you, Formanek, these murderers tend to be pretty decent folks. The worst of the lot are the embezzlers; nothing in jail's ever good enough for them. But my heart goes out to Zaruba."

Once Zaruba had the iron gates and courtyard of Pankrac Prison behind him, he had the uneasy and abject feeling that the nearest guard would grab him and steer him back again; he dawdled a bit, so that he wouldn't appear to be making a break for it. When he reached the street, his head reeled, all those people out there, children running around, two drivers quarreling with each other, God in heaven, there didn't used to be so many people, which way do I go? Makes no difference; nothing but cars, and all those women, is anybody following me? no, but look at all the cars! Zaruba dashed off, heading down the street towards Prague, to get as far away as he could. A tempting smell from a smoked-meats shop drifted by, but not now, not yet; then a more powerful smell tempted him: a construction site. Zaruba the bricklayer stopped and sniffed the fine aroma of mortar and beams. He watched the way an old codger was mixing lime; he longed for a bit of friendly conversation, but somehow he couldn't manage it, his voice wouldn't crawl out, in solitary you lose the habit of talking. Lengthening his stride, Zaruba continued down the middle of the street towards Prague. God in heaven, all kinds of buildings! They're making them all out of concrete, it wasn't like that twelve years ago, no, it wasn't like that in my time, thought Zaruba, but they'll fall down for sure, thin uprights like that! "Watch out, man, are you blind or what?" He was nearly run over by a car, he nearly stumbled under a clanking streetcar; after twelve years, you're no longer accustomed to streets. He would have liked to ask somebody what that big building was; he would have liked to ask how to get to the Northwest train station; as a truck filled with iron rumbled past, he tried saying to himself out loud: "Excuse me, how do I get to the Northwest train station?" No, it's no good; somehow his voice must have dried up inside him or something, you get rusty, go dumb, back in that place; the first three years he could still ask somebody a question every now and again, but after that he'd just quit. "Excuse me, how do I — ?" a rattling sound issued from his throat, but it was not a human voice.

Zaruba ran on down the street, his stride increasing. He felt as if he were drunk or walking in his sleep. It was all quite different from twelve years ago, bigger, noisier, more confusing. What a lot of people! The sight only made Zaruba sad, it seemed to him that he was in a foreign country somewhere and that he could not even talk with these people. If only he could get to the train station and go home, home . . . His brother had a cottage and children there . . . "Excuse me, how do I — ?" Zaruba tried to utter the words, but his lips moved soundlessly. Never mind, it'll wear off once I'm home, I'll be able to talk once I'm home; if I could only get to the train station!

Suddenly there was a shout from behind him, and someone shoved him onto the sidewalk. "Why don't you walk where you're supposed to?" a driver bawled. Zaruba would have liked to answer, but it was no use; he could only make a croaking sound before running on. On the sidewalk? he thought to himself, but the sidewalk's too small for me. Oh, people, I'm in such a hurry, I want to go home, excuse me, how do I get to the Northwest train station? That must be the street, he decided, it's the biggest, it's got a whole line of streetcars. But look at all the people on it, where did they all come from? Why, there's crowds and crowds, all headed the same direction, it has to be to the train station, that's why they're in such a hurry, so they don't miss the train. The lanky Zaruba strode at a faster pace, so as not to be left behind. But look, even these sidewalks aren't big enough to hold all these people, they're spreading out all across the street, a dense and clamorous throng; and new people continue to join them, moving along swiftly and shouting something; and now they've all begun to shout in an immense, unrelenting roar.

Zaruba's head was in a rapturous whirl from the din. God in heaven, how beautiful it was, all these people! At the front of the crowd they've begun to sing a marching song. Zaruba gets into step with the others and tramps forward in exhilaration;

look, now all the people around him are singing. Something thaws and wells up in Zaruba's throat, as if pressing against him, it forces itself out and it is a song, left right, left right, Zaruba is singing a song without words, he drones and growls to himself in a deep bass noise, what song is this? no matter, I'm going home, I'm going home! The long-legged Zaruba is tramping along in the front row now and singing. There are no words to his song, but it's so beautiful, left right, left right, with upraised hands Zaruba trumpets like an elephant, he feels as if his whole body is ringing with sound, his belly vibrates like a drum, his chest rumbles loudly, and in his throat is a feeling so good, so fine, like when you're drinking or crying. Thousands of people are shouting: "Down with the government!" but Zaruba cannot grasp their words and goes on blaring in exultation, "A-ah! A-ah!" Waving his long arms, Zaruba marches at the head of them all, braying and bellowing, singing and roaring, drumming on his chest with his fists and bursting out in a vast howl that swells above the heads of all like a soaring banner. "Oo-a-vah, oo-a-vah!" Zaruba trumpets, his voice, his lungs, his heart filled to the utmost, and he closes his eyes and crows like a cock. "A-oo-vah! Aaah! Hurraah!" Now for some reason the crowd halts, it cannot move forward, it swerves back in a confused surge, panting and scuffling, shrieking in agitation. "Oo-a-vah! Hurraah!" Zaruba, eyes shut, surrenders to this great and liberated voice that arises from within. Suddenly someone's hands clutch him and a winded voice rasps in his ear: "I arrest you in the name of the law!"

Zaruba opens his eyes in alarm. A policeman is clinging to one of his arms and dragging him out of the crowd, which is swaying convulsively. Zaruba moans with terror and tries to wrench his arm away from the policeman, who is twisting it. Zaruba roars in pain and, using his other hand like a mallet, clouts the policeman on the head. The policeman's face flushes and he lets go; but then he strikes Zaruba on the head with a truncheon, and again, again, again! The two huge arms begin spinning like the arms of a windmill, descending on several heads. Then two helmeted forms fasten onto him like bulldogs, Zaruba is choking with fear and trying to shake them off, striking out around him, shuddering like a madman. He is shoved and hauled off somewhere, two policemen leading him, his arms jerked behind his back, along the empty street, left right, left right. Zaruba accompanies them like a lamb; excuse me, how do I get to the Northwest train station? I have to go home.

The two policemen practically flung him head first into the station.

"What's your name?" a cold, harsh voice bawled at him.

Zaruba wanted to speak, but only his lips moved.

"Out with it, what's your name?" the harsh voice bellowed.

"Antonin Zaruba," the lanky man whispered hoarsely.

"Where do you live?"

Zaruba shrugged his shoulders helplessly. "In Pankrac," he forced out. "In solitary."

No doubt it shouldn't have happened, but it did; three lawyers — the judge, the public prosecutor, and the court-appointed counsel for the defense — discussed how they could get Zaruba off.

"Well, you could just have Zaruba deny everything," offered the public prosecutor.

"Won't work," grumbled the judge. "He already confessed under questioning that he battled it out with the police. Since the tomfool's already confessed — "

"If the policemen," suggested the defense counsel, "were to testify that they couldn't identify Zaruba with absolute certainty, that it might have been someone else — "

"Wait a minute," the public prosecutor objected, "we can't very well instruct the police to lie! Besides, they've already identified him beyond any doubt — I'd go for a plea of temporary insanity. Propose an inquiry into the state of his mind, and I'll back you up."

"No problem," said the defense counsel. "I'll propose it, but suppose the doctors say he was sane?"

"I'll talk to them," the judge volunteered. "I shouldn't, of course, but — Damn it all, I'd hate to see this Zaruba sitting out the rest of his life in solitary just for being such a tomfool. I'd rather see him anywhere but there. Good God, I'd give him six months without batting an eye. But if he has to serve out his life sentence in prison, gentlemen, it would make me damned unhappy, damned sick."

"If temporary insanity doesn't do the trick," remarked the public prosecutor, "it'll be pretty nasty for him. The confounded thing is, I've got to prosecute this as a criminal offense. What other choice do I have? If only that idiot had stopped by a tavern somewhere, we could back up the insanity plea, show that he wasn't accountable for his actions or something — "

"Please, gentlemen, work it out somehow," urged the judge, "so that I can discharge him. I'm an old man, and I don't want the responsibility of — I'm sure you understand what I mean."

"Difficult case," sighed the public prosecutor. "Well, we'll see. At any rate, the psychiatrists will keep things going for a while. The trial's tomorrow, right?"

But the case never came to trial. That night Antonin Zaruba hanged himself, evidently from fear of the punishment that lay in store for him. Because he was so very tall, he was found hanging in a curious posture, as if he were sitting on the ground.

"Rotten business," muttered the public prosecutor. "My God, what a stupid business. But at any rate there's nothing we could have done about it."

The Crime at the Post Office

"Talk about Justice," said Police Sergeant Brejcha. "I'd like to know why the pictures always show some female with a bandage on her eyes and the sort of scales they use to weigh peppers. What I mean is, Justice seems more like a policeman, to me. You wouldn't believe the things us policemen pass judgment on, without any judge, without any scales, and without all the fuss and feathers. In a few cases we tap a few jaws, and in most cases we undo our belts, but in ninety cases out of a hundred that's all justice is. But I'll tell you right now, mister, I proved two people guilty of murder all by myself, and I was the one what sentenced them to just punishment and even decided what that punishment was to be, and I've never said a word about it to nobody. But I'm going to tell it to you right now.

"You'll recall, mister, that little miss what worked here two years ago in our village post office? Sure, Helenka, that was her name. She was such a good, kind girl, pretty as a picture. Not likely you'd forget her. Well, this Helenka, mister, last summer she drowned herself; she jumped in that big pond near here and went out maybe fifty-five yards until she got to the deep part, and she didn't wash up for two days. And you know why she did it? On that same day when she drowned herself, there was this auditor from Prague who suddenly turned up at our post office and found out Helenka was short a couple hundred crowns from the cash drawer. A miserable couple hundred, mister. That bone-head of an auditor said he was going to report it and there'd be an investigation, like for embezzlement. But that evening, mister, Helenka drowned herself — from shame.

"When they pulled her out, over by the dike, I had to stay

with her till the coroner came. There wasn't anything pretty about her then, poor girl, but the whole time I kept seeing her the way she used to be, smiling behind the window at the post office — well, we all hung around there because of her, you know; everybody liked that girl. Damn it, I said to myself, that girl never stole no two hundred crowns. In the first place, I just didn't believe it; and in the second place, she sure didn't need to steal: her daddy was the miller over on the other side of town, and she was only there at the post office because of some female urge to make her own living for herself. I knew her daddy well, mister; he was sort of a literary type and a Protestant, too; and let me tell you, mister, these Protestant religious scribblers around here, they never steal nothing. Mister, I promised that dead girl right there on the dike that I wasn't going to let this business drop.

"All right then, the next thing that happens is they send some smart young man from Prague down here to the post office, name of Filipek; a very pleasant, toothy sort of fellow. Well, I went over to the post office to see this Filipek, because I wanted to check something out. It's just like all these other small-town post offices, you know: a counter with a little window, and on the clerk's side a little cash drawer for stamps and money, and right in back of the clerk is this sort of shelf, with a bunch of ratebooks and notices and papers and a scale for weighing packages and things like that. 'Mr. Filipek,' I says to him, 'please take a look in those ratebooks and tell me how much it costs to send a cable to Buenos Aires, say.'

" 'Three crowns a word,' says Filipek, without batting an eyelash.

" 'Then how much for a telegram to Hong Kong?' I ask him again.

" 'I'd have to look it up,' says Filipek, and he gets up and turns around to look at the ratebook. And while he's going through the book with his back to the counter, I squeeze my shoulders through the little window and reach my hand over to the cash drawer and pull it out. And it opens very nice and quiet.

" 'Thanks, I've got it,' says I; and that's how it could have happened. Suppose Helenka was looking something up in the ratebook. Right then, somebody could have swiped the two hundred from the cash drawer. 'Take a look, Mr. Filipek, and see if you can tell me who sent a telegram or a package from here in the last few days.'

"Mr. Filipek scratches his head and says, 'Sergeant, it can't be done. You see, that amounts to something like confidentiality of the mail — unless you do your looking in the name of the law. But I would have to notify the head office that a search has taken place.'

" 'Hold on,' I says to him, 'I don't care to do that for the present. But look, if you was to more or less . . . just for lack of something better to do . . . sort of poke through those papers and see if maybe somebody did send something from here, so that maybe Helenka had to turn her back away from the counter — '

" 'Sergeant,' says Mr. Filipek, 'what if she did? Telegram forms'll be here, but for registered letters and packages we only have a record of who something was sent to — not who sent it. I'll make a list for you of all the names I find here. Actually, I'm not even supposed to do that, but for you I will. But I don't think you'll learn beans from it.'

"Filipek was right about that. He handed me maybe thirty names — you know, not much goes on in a village post office, only a parcel now and then for some lad in the service — and there wasn't a pin in the pickings. Mister, I went out and walked and talked that case to myself from seven sides, but to no use. And it plagued me that I wasn't keeping my promise to poor Helenka.

"Then one day, it must have been about a week later, I went back to the post office again. This Filipek looks me over and says, 'Say goodbye to your bowling partner, Sergeant; I'm moving out. A new girl's coming tomorrow, from the post office in Pardubice.'

" 'Aha,' says I to that. 'Some kind of demotion, no doubt,

transferring this girl from the big city to such a crummy little village post office.'

" 'Not at all,' says Filipek, and he gives me a kind of peculiar look. 'Sergeant, this girl's being transferred here at her own request.'

" 'That's odd,' says I, 'but then you know how women are.'

" 'Odd it is,' says Filipek, but he goes on looking at me. 'And odder still is that the anonymous letter which brought about that flash-flood postal audit also came from Pardubice.'

"I whistled, and then I realized that Filipek and I were staring at each other in the very same way. And then suddenly old Uher, the postman, who was sorting the mail for delivery, he speaks up and says, 'Yeah, sure, Pardubice. That's where the supervisor over at the big estate writes to, almost every day; some young lady there at the post office. Yeah, sure, she's his sweetie.'

" 'Listen, grandpa,' says Filipek, 'do you know what her name is?'

" 'Something like Julie Touf— Toufar— '

" 'Tauferova,' says Filipek. 'That's her. That's the one who's coming here.'

" 'That Houdek,' says old Uher, 'that Houdek what's the supervisor there, he gets a letter back from Pardubice, too, almost every day. Mr. Supervisor, I tell him, here's a letter from your sweetie again. He always walks down the road to meet me. I've got this here little parcel for him today; it got sent back to him from Prague. See how it's stamped: Recipient Unknown. He got the address wrong, Mr. Supervisor did. So I'm taking it back to him.'

" 'Show it to me,' says Filipek, and he looks it over. 'It's addressed to somebody named Novak, Spalena Street, Prague. Contents: four pounds of butter. Postmark: July 14.'

" 'That's when Miss Helenka was still here,' says old Uher.

" 'Show it to me,' I says to Filipek, and I take a sniff at it. 'Mr. Filipek,' I says, 'that's odd, but this here butter was ten days on the road and it don't even stink. Grandpa, you just leave this package here and go off on your rounds.'

"Old Uher was hardly gone when Filipek says to me, 'Sergeant, this is against all the rules, but here's a penknife.' And then he left so's he wouldn't have to watch.

"Mister, I tore open that package, and inside there wasn't nothing but four pounds of dirt. So I go find Filipek right away and I tell him, 'Don't say anything about this to anyone, understand? I'm going to take care of this business myself.'

"You can bet I pulled myself together and set right out after this Houdek over at the estate. He was sitting there on a pile of planks, just staring at the ground. 'Mr. Supervisor,' says I, 'there's some kind of mix-up over there at our post office. You recall what address it was on that little package you sent to Prague ten or twelve days ago?'

"Houdek looks a little funny and then he says, 'It doesn't matter; and anyway, I don't remember now what it was.'

" 'Mr. Supervisor,' I says to him, 'it's this way. You killed our Helenka from the post office. You sent a package from there with a fake address so she'd have to weigh it on the scales. And while she was doing that, you snuck inside the cash drawer and stole two hundred crowns. Because of those two hundred crowns, Mr. Supervisor, Helenka drowned herself. That's how it is.'

"I tell you, mister, that Houdek was shaking like a leaf. 'That's a lie,' he cries, 'why would I steal two hundred crowns?'

" 'Because you wanted to have your sweetheart, Julie Tauferova, here at our post office. That girlfriend of yours sent an anonymous letter saying Helenka was missing money from the cash drawer. It's just like the two of you pushed Helenka in the pond. It's just like the two of you killed her. You have murder on your conscience, Mr. Houdek.'

"That Houdek, he tumbled down on the planks and he covered up his face, and never, never did I ever see a man cry like that. 'Jesus Christ,' he was wailing, 'Jesus Christ, I couldn't know she'd drown herself! I only thought she'd be let go . . . that she'd just go back home! Officer, all I wanted to do was marry Julie! But one of us would have had to give up our jobs if we were going to be together . . . and we can't live on one salary

. . . that's why I wanted so much for Julie to get the job here at the post office! We've already been waiting five years . . . Sergeant, we love each other so much, so much!'

"Mister, I'm not going to tell you the rest. It was almost nighttime, and here was this fellow Houdek down on his knees in front of me, and me blubbering over the whole business — I was blubbering like a ninety-year-old bride, over Helenka and over everybody else, too.

" 'That's enough,' I finally says to him, 'that's enough. I've already had it up to here. Now hand over those two hundred crowns. Right. And now listen: if it occurs to you to marry Miss Tauferova before I set this whole business straight, then I'll charge you with theft — understand? But if you shoot yourself or do anything else like that, I'll go ahead and tell why you did it. And that's that.'

"That night, mister, I sat in judgment on those two, there under the stars. I asked God how I should punish them, and I truly understood the joy and the bitterness of justice. If I did bring charges against them, this Houdek would get a couple of weeks in jail and then go on probation; and still it would be hard to prove. Houdek killed that girl — but he wasn't a common thief. To me, every punishment was either too big or too small. So that's why I was judging and punishing them myself.

"The next morning, I went back to the post office. Sitting there behind the window was this tall, pale girl with fierce, burning eyes. 'Miss Tauferova,' says I, 'I have a registered letter here,' and I gave her a letter addressed: Director of Postal Communications, Prague. She looked at me and she stuck the label on.

" 'Just a minute, miss,' I said. 'Inside this letter is a charge against the person who stole two hundred crowns from your predecessor. What's the postage?'

"Mister, there was a terrible strength in that woman; all the same, she turned ashy pale and stiff as a stone. 'Three crowns fifty,' she said, hardly breathing.

"I counted out the money and said, 'Here you are, miss. But

if those two hundred crowns should happen to turn up here —
fallen down or misplaced somewhere, you understand? — so that
everyone will know that poor, dead Helenka didn't steal them,
well then, miss, then I could take back my letter. Now what
about it?'

"She didn't say a word; she just sat there, fierce and burning
and stiff like I've never seen anybody before, anywhere.

" 'The postman will be here in five minutes, miss,' I said.
'What about it, then. Shall I mail the letter?'

"She shook her head right away. So I picked up the letter
and walked out in front of the post office. Mister, I've never
marked time in such suspense. And then, twenty minutes later,
old Uher ran out crying, "Officer, it's been found! The two
hundred crowns Miss Helenka was missing! They're found! That
new girl found them in one of the ratebooks! It was all a
mistake!'

" 'Grandpa,' I told him, 'go run and tell everybody that the
two hundred crowns have been found. You know, so that everybody will know that Helenka didn't steal them, thank God!'

"So then, that was the first thing. The second thing was to
go see the owner of the big estate. You probably don't know him;
he's a count — a little crazy, but a very nice man. 'Sir,' I tell him,
'don't ask me any questions, but there's a little matter here we
have to hang together on. Call your supervisor, Houdek, and tell
him he has to leave today for your place in Moravia. If he doesn't
want to go, tell him you're giving him an hour's notice.'

"The old count raised his eyebrows and stared at me for a
while. Mister, there's no way I could have forced myself to look
more serious than I did, more so than anyone can imagine. 'Very
well,' says the count, 'I won't ask you any questions. And furthermore, I'll summon Houdek now.'

"Houdek came, and when he saw me with the count he
turned pale, but he stood straight as a stick. 'Houdek,' says the
count, 'harness the horses and get down to the train station. You
begin service this evening at my estate in Hulin. I'll send a
telegram so they'll be expecting you. Do you understand?'

" 'Yes,' Houdek said quietly, and he fixed his eyes on me, like the eyes of the damned in hell.

" 'Have you any objections?' the count asked.

" 'No,' said Houdek hoarsely, and he never let his eyes drop from me. Mister, those eyes were agony to me.

" 'Then you must go,' says the count, and that was that. After a minute or so I saw them taking Houdek away in the coach. He sat there like a wooden puppet.

"And that's the whole story, mister. But if you go to the post office, you'll see this pale, pale woman there. She's mean and angry at everyone, and she's getting old, mean lines in her face. I don't know if she ever sees her supervisor; maybe she does go visit him sometimes, but then she comes back again meaner and angrier than before. And I see this happen and I say to myself: There must be Justice.

"I'm only a policeman, mister, but I'm telling you from my own experience: Whether there's some kind of all-knowing, all-powerful God, I don't know; even if there is, it's no use to us. But I tell you, Somebody has to be greater and more just than we are. That's the certain truth, mister. We can only punish, but there has to be a somebody, somewhere, who can forgive. I tell you, mister, truth and the highest justice are just as strange as love."

TALES FROM THE OTHER POCKET

The author, drawn by F. Bidlo

The Stolen Cactus

"Let me tell you," said Mr. Kubat, "about what happened to me last summer.

"I was at my summer place, which is like most summer places: no water, no woods, no fish, no nothing. On the other hand, it's heavily populist, politically, and there's a residents association with an active secretary, a button-and-bead factory, and a post office with a nosy old postmistress. In a word, just the way it is everywhere else. Well, after perhaps two weeks of indulging in the wholesome and hygienic effects of uninterrupted boredom, I began to sense that the local rumormongers and, for that matter, public opinion in general were viewing me somehow or other in a very unflattering light. And because my mail arrived conspicuously well-glued, so that the whole back of the envelope was gleaming with gum arabic, I said to myself: Obviously, someone is opening my mail. Damn that old witch of a postmistress! Postal workers are supposed to be clever at unsealing envelopes, you know. I'll fix that, I told myself, and I sat down immediately and began to write in my finest penmanship: 'You loathsome ghoul of a postmistress, you old snoop, you peeping busybody, you meddling frump, you viper, you fossilized old hag, you harpy, and so on, Sincerely yours, Jan Kubat.' Listen, Czech is a rich and precise language. In the space of a single breath I'd dashed off thirty-four expressions which a forthright and respectable man may apply to any lady without becoming personal or intrusive. Then I cheerfully sealed it, addressed the envelope to myself, and went off to the nearest town to put it in a mailbox. The next day I hurried to the post office and with the sweetest of smiles stuck my head through the window opening. 'Madame Postmistress,' said I, 'is there any mail for me today?' 'I'm pressing charges, you rotter,' the postmistress glared back, with the most horrible look I'd ever seen. 'Why, Madame Postmistress,' I said sympathetically, 'you haven't been reading something unpleasant, I hope.' And then I got out of there, fast."

"That's nothing," Mr. Holan said disapprovingly — he was the head gardener at the Holben greenhouses. "That strategy was too simple. I should tell you how I set a trap for a cactus thief. Old Mr. Holben is a phenomenal cactus-fancier, you know, and his cactus collection, I'm not kidding, must be worth three hundred thousand, not even counting the one-of-a-kind specimens. The old gentleman is very particular about making the collection open to the public. 'Holan,' he says, 'it's a noble hobby, it has to be nurtured in people.' But I'm thinking to myself instead that when some young cactus-lover sees the golden Gruson, let's say, which is easily worth twelve hundred, it'll only break his heart because it isn't his. But what the old gentleman wants, he gets. Then, this past year, we began to notice that some cacti were disappearing on us; and it wasn't just some of those everybody and his brother wants to own, but ones that were special. One day it was a Echinocactus Wislizenii, the next time it was a Graessnerii, then a Wittia imported right out of Costa Rica, then a species nova that Fric sent, after that a Melocactus Leopoldii, that's a unique specimen no one in Europe's seen for over fifty years, and finally a *Pilocereus fimbriatus* from San Domingo, the first one that ever came to Europe. Listen, that thief must have been some kind of connoisseur!

"You wouldn't believe how the old man raged. 'Mr. Holben,' I told him, 'just close down your greenhouses, and that'll put an end to it.' 'You're wrong there,' the old man cried, 'a cultivated taste like this is for everyone. You must catch that scurvy thief; sack the gatekeeper, hire a new one, alert the police, and all that. This is a serious matter. With thirty-six thousand pots, we can't post a guard over every single one.' So at least I hired two retired police detectives to be on the lookout; and what should happen but we lose that *Pilocereus fimbriatus*, and the only thing left behind is a dimple in the dirt. By that time I was so mad I started keeping on the lookout for the cactus thief myself.

"What you need to understand is that real cactus-lovers are something like a sect of dervishes. I think that instead of whiskers they grow bristles and prickles, that's how crazy they are about them. We've got two of those sects around here, the Association of Cactus Fanciers and the Federation of Cactus Fanciers. How they're different from each other, I don't know — I think that one believes cacti have immortal souls, while the other makes sacrifices to them; at any rate, these two sects mutually hate and persecute each other with fire and sword here on earth and probably in heaven as well. Anyway, I went around to the presidents of these two sects and in all confidentiality asked each of them if they had any opinion as to who — maybe someone from the other sect — might have pilfered the Holben cacti. When I told them which rare cacti we'd lost, they swore with absolute certainty that no member of the rival cult could have pilfered them because they were such a bunch of botchers, bunglers, and ignoramuses, they didn't have the faintest idea what a Wislizen or a Graessner was, let alone a *Pilocereus fimbriatus*. As for their own members, they'd vouch for their honesty and high-mindedness; they weren't capable of pilfering anything, except for certain kinds of cactus, of course; but if any one of them did have one of those Wislizenas, then he would surely have pilfered the rest as well for worship and religious orgies — but they, the presidents, wouldn't know anything about that. After which both honorable gentlemen told me that, besides those two publicly recognized and tolerated sects, there are also rogue cactus-lovers, and they're supposed to be the worst of all. They're the ones those two moderate sects can't stomach, and nobody else can, either, because they're fanatics and they indulge in all kinds of heresies and violence. And it's said these rogue cactus-fanciers are capable of anything.

"Since I didn't get anywhere with these two gentlemen, I

climbed up in this nice maple in our park and thought things
over. Let me tell you, it's best to think things over in the crown
of a tree. Up there, you're more or less detached from everything.
You sway back and forth with it a bit, and all the while you're
contemplating things from a loftier point of view. I think
philosophers ought to live in trees, just like orioles. And up in
that maple I worked out a plan. First I made the rounds of my
gardener friends and asked them, 'Boys, do you have any cacti
that are rotting on you? Old Mr. Holben needs them for his
experiments.' That way I picked up a couple of hundred sick
ones, and during the night I stuck them in with Holben's collection. I didn't say a word for two days, and the third day I gave
out this statement to the newspapers:

World-famous Holben Collection Menaced

We have learned that a large portion of the peerless Holben
Collection was stricken by a new and hitherto unknown disease,
most likely imported from Bolivia. The malady attacks cacti in
particular, progresses latently for some time, and then manifests
itself as rot in the roots, neck and body. Inasmuch as it appears
that this disease is highly infectious and is spread rapidly by
heretofore unidentified microspores, the Holben Collection is
closed to the public.

"After maybe ten days — during those ten days we had to
hide out so that cactus-lovers didn't deluge us with questions —
I sent the newspapers another bulletin:

Can the Holben Collection Be Saved?

We have learned that Professor Mackenzie of Kew Gardens has
diagnosed the disease that broke out in the world-famous
Holben Collection as a strange tropical mildew (*Malacorrhiza
paraguayensis* Wild.) and recommends spraying afflicted specimens with the Harvard-Lotsen tincture. To date, experiments
with this remedy, which is being applied on a grand scale in the
Holben Collection, have been highly successful. The Harvard-
Lotsen solution is carried here by the such-and-such shop.

"By the time this came out, an undercover policeman was already seated in the shop, and I had settled down by the telephone. Two hours later the policeman telephoned me, 'Mr. Holan, we've got him.' Ten minutes later I was holding a young man by the collar and shaking him.

" 'But, sir,' the young man protested, 'what are you shaking me for? I only came here to buy some of that famous Harvard-Lotsen tincture — '

" 'I know,' I told him, 'but there isn't any, just like there isn't any new disease. But you're the one who went pilfering cacti from the Holben Collection, you little devil!'

" 'So there isn't any new disease?' the young man burst out. 'Thank God! I haven't slept for ten nights for fear that the rest of my cacti would catch it!'

"Well, I hauled him to the car by the collar and went with him and the policeman to his apartment. Listen, I never saw a collection like that in all my life. This young man had a cubby-hole up in an attic in Vysocany that couldn't have been more than twelve feet square, with a blanket and a little table and chair in the corner, and the rest of it was nothing but cacti. But as to the kinds of specimens he had and the shape they were in, the man had no match.

" 'So which of these did you pilfer,' says the policeman; and I'm looking at this young hooligan, how he's shaking and gulping down tears. 'Listen,' I told the policeman, 'this isn't worth as much as we thought. Go tell your boss that this young man's fined fifty crowns and that I'll cover for it myself.'

"When the policeman had left, I said, 'Well, young friend, pack up everything of ours you took.' He's blinking hard because he's so close to tears, and he asks, 'Please, sir, couldn't I just serve time instead?'

" 'Nothing doing,' I yell at him. 'First you have to return everything you took.' So he started picking up one little pot after another and setting them to one side. There were probably eighty of them — we didn't have any idea we were missing so many, but my guess is he'd been collecting them all summer long. Just to be on the safe side, I shouted, 'What, that's all you took?'

"At that point the tears burst out. Then he picks up still one more nice little white De Laitii and a corniger, puts them with the rest, and sobs, 'Sir, none of the rest are yours, I swear it.'

" 'That remains to be seen,' I stormed, 'but right now you're going to tell me how you carted them away.'

" 'It was like this,' he gabbled, and meanwhile his Adam's apple was jumping up and down. 'I . . . what I mean is, I put on these clothes . . . '

" 'What kind of clothes?' I shout. At that he turns red in total embarrassment and stammers, 'Women's clothes, sir.'

" 'Young man,' I said in amazement, 'why women's clothes?'

" 'Because,' he choked out, 'because, sir, nobody pays any attention to old ladies, and, well,' he added, almost in triumph, 'it stands to reason that nobody'd ever be *suspicious* of an old lady! Sir, women have every known passion, but they don't have a passion for collecting! Did you ever know a woman who had a collection of stamps or beetles or incunabula or anything like that? Never, sir! Women don't have that kind of meticulousness or — or — zeal. Women are so terribly down-to-earth, sir! You know, that's the biggest difference between us and them: we're the only ones who go in for collections. What I think is, the universe is only a collection of stars. There's some kind of male god, and he has this collection of worlds, and that's why there's such a vast number of them. Darn it, if only I had as much room and resources as he does! You know that I think up new kinds of cacti? And in the night I dream about them: a cactus with golden hair and deep blue flowers, maybe — I'd name it *Cephalocereus nympha aurea* Racek — that's my name, Racek, you'll be pleased to know. Or *Mamillaria colubrina* Racek, or *Astrophytum caespitosum* Racek — oh, sir, there are such wonderful possibilities! If you only knew — '

    " 'Hold it,' I interrupted him, 'just where did you hide those cacti?'

    " 'In my bosom, sir,' he said bashfully. 'They prickle so deliciously.'

    "Listen, I didn't have the heart to take those cacti from him. 'You know what,' I told him, 'I'm taking you to see old Mr. Holben and he'll give your ears a twist.' Well, let me tell you, friends, when those two got together they stayed out there in the greenhouses all night long, walking around those thirty-six thousand little pots. 'Holan,' the old gentleman told me, 'this is the first man I've met who really knows the value of cacti.' And before the month was out, old Mr. Holben, with tears and his blessing, sent Racek off to Mexico so he could collect cacti there. Both of them believed by all that was holy that somewhere in Mexico there was a *Cephalocereus nympha aurea* Racek. About a year later we heard a strange rumor that Racek had died a beautiful death, a martyr's death. He'd gone to see some Indians there in connection with their sacred cactus Chikuli — which, in case you didn't know, is the natural brother of God the Father — and either he didn't bow down to him or he just plain stole it. To make a long story short, the dear old Indians simply trussed up Mr. Racek and sat him down on an *Echinocactus visnaga*

Hooker, which is as big as an elephant and dotted with spikes as long as Russian bayonets, in consequence of which our countryman, surrendering to his destiny, breathed his last. And that's how the cactus thief came to his end."

The Old Jailbird's Tale

"That's nothing," said Mr. Jandera, the writer. "Hunting down a thief, that we know. What's strange is when a thief is trying to track down whomever it is he stole from. That's what happened to me, you know. The other day I wrote a story and sent it off to the printer. And after it came out and I read it over, an unpleasant feeling came over me that I'd read something like it before somewhere. Damn and double damn, Jandera, I said to myself, who did you steal this material from? For three days I wandered around like a sheep with the staggers, but I simply couldn't figure out from whom I had, as the saying goes, borrowed my material. Finally I ran across an old friend and said, 'You know, I have the sense that everything about my last story was stolen from somebody else.' 'But I knew that at first glance,' said my friend, 'you stole it from Chekhov.' That took a load off my mind at once, and when later I was talking with a critic friend of mine, I said to him, 'You won't believe this, but sometimes a person can commit plagiarism and not even realize it. For instance, I stole my latest story.' 'I know,' the critic replied, 'it's from Maupassant.' So I made the circuit of all my close friends; listen, once you step on the downward path of crime, you don't know when to turn back. Just imagine, I'd stolen that very same story from Gottfried Keller, Dickens, d'Annunzio, *A Thousand and One Nights*, Charles-Louis Philippe, Hamsun, Storm, Hardy, Andrejev, Bandello, Rosegger, Reymont, and a whole string of others. It just goes to show how a person falls deeper and deeper into the ways of wickedness."

*   *   *

"That's nothing," said Mr. Bobek, the old jailbird, clearing his throat. "It reminds me of this one case where they had a murderer but couldn't find a murder to match him up with. I don't want you thinking I was the one who did it; it's just that I was lodged for half a year in the same jail where the murderer used to be. It was in Palermo," Mr. Bobek explained, and he added modestly, "I was only there on account of this suitcase that fell into my hands when I was coming by ship from Naples. It was the head guard in that place who told me about this case with the murderer. What I mean is, I taught him how to play some of our card games like francefus, cruciform-marias, and godbless, what you might call friendly games of chance. What I mean is, he was a very religious man, that guard.

"Anyway, one night these two cops — they always patrol by twos in Italy — these two cops see this fellow racing full speed down the via Butera, which runs right into the stinking harbor. So they nab him, and *porco dio*, he has this dagger in his hand, dripping blood. Of course they take him to the station, and then it's, all right, tell us who you sliced up. The boy breaks into tears and says, 'I murdered a man, but I can't tell you any more. If I told you any more, some other people would be in big trouble.' And they didn't get any more out of him.

"Of course, right away they start looking for a corpse, but they can't find one. So they order an inspection of all the dear departed who'd been reported dead at the time; but it turns out they'd all died like Christians, of malaria and things like that. So they go to work on the boy again. He says his name is Marco Biagio from Castrogiovanni and he's a journeyman cabinet-maker. He also says he slashed some Christian maybe twenty times and killed him. But who he did it to, he's not telling, because he's not making any trouble for those other people. And that was that. The only other thing he did was call down God's punishment on himself and bang his head on the floor. Never in all their born days, said the guard, had they ever seen such remorse.

"You know, cops never believe anybody or anything they

say. They figured this Marco probably didn't butcher anybody
and was lying through his teeth. So they sent the dagger off to
the university, and there they said that the blood on the blade
came from a human being and that this person had to have been
stabbed in the heart. Don't ask how they could tell, because I
don't know. But anyway, what were the police supposed to do
now? They had a murderer but no murder. And that's no good,
hauling somebody into court for an unknown murder; you have
to have a *corpus delicti*, you know. Meanwhile this Marco just
kept on praying and muttering to himself and begging them to
turn him over to the court so he could pay for his mortal sin.
'You *porco*,' they told him, 'if you want to be sentenced you have
to confess who it was you butchered. At least give us the name of
a witness, you goddamn mule.' 'I myself am the witness,' bawled
Marco, 'and I swear I murdered a man!' Well, that's how it was.

"That guard told me how this Marco was truly a fine and
worthy person and how they'd never had such a high-principled
murderer there. He couldn't read, but he always had a Bible in
his hands, even if it was upside-down sometimes, and he was
always blubbering into it. So they sent him to this kindhearted
soul of a priest so he could shore him up spiritually and, while he
was at it, question him on the sly about the who and why of the
murder. The priest came away from Marco wiping his eyes. He
said that even if Marco had gone bad somehow, he had surely
attained a state of grace and his soul thirsted for justice. But
apart from all the talk and tears, they didn't get any more out of
the priest, either. 'Let them hang me and get it over with,' said
Marco, 'then I'll have paid for my terrible crime. There must be
justice.' Well, it went on that way for more than half a year, and
they never found a suitable corpse.

"Since it was already making him look pretty silly, the chief
of police said, '*Mordiano*, if this Marco wants to hang come hell
or high water, let's give him this murder that took place in
Arenello three days after he was brought in, where they found
the old lady who was all slashed up. It's a disgrace that here we
have a murderer with no murder and no corpse, and there we've

got a nice, verifiable murder with no perpetrator. Work it out somehow. Since Marco wants to be convicted for a murder, this one can be his. We can compensate him for any number of sins if he confesses to the old lady.' So they proposed the idea to Marco and promised him he'd get the rope in no time and finally be at peace. Marco wavered for a minute and then declared, 'No, since my soul is already damned for the crime of murder, then I'm not burdening myself with still more mortal sins like lying, deception, and bearing false witness.' That's what he was like, gentlemen, a fair and just man.

"Well, it didn't go on much longer. At the jail, all they could think of now was how to get that damned Marco off their hands. 'Tell you what,' they said to his guard, 'do something, anything, so he can make a run for it. We can't send him to court because we'd only lose our credibility, and to release him when he's already confessed to murder won't do, either. Look, be discreet, but see to it that this *dio cane maledetto* somehow disappears.' Listen, from then on they sent Marco out all by himself to get pepper and thread and so on. His cell was left wide open night and day, and Marco ran around to churches and holy shrines all day long. And in the evening, if you can believe it, he'd rush back again with his tongue hanging out, to make sure they wouldn't shut the prison gate in his face at eight o'clock. Once they locked up early on purpose, and he kicked up such a racket and pounded so hard on the gate, they had to open it for him and let him go back to his cell.

"Finally, one evening, the guard said to Marco, 'You *porca madonna*, you better believe this is your last night here. Since you won't confess who you butchered, you tricky *bandito*, we're throwing you out. You can go to hell and let the devil punish you.' That night Marco hanged himself from the window in his cell.

"Listen, no doubt the priest had told him that when somebody commits suicide out of remorse he can be saved in spite of this mortal sin, because he died in a state of active repentance. My guess is the priest didn't know this for sure, or maybe it's still open to question. But what you can believe is that Marco haunted that cell. What I mean is, it was like this: whenever they locked somebody up in that cell, his conscience would begin to trouble him and he'd start regretting his criminal deeds, make penance, and get one-hundred percent converted. Of course, it took different periods of time for different kinds of crimes: for a misdemeanor it would be overnight, for a felony two or three days, and for a capital crime it would take maybe three weeks before the prisoner was converted. The ones who held out the longest were safecrackers, embezzlers and, on the whole, anybody else who made off with really big money; I'm telling you, big money hardens the heart more than anything else, somehow, or at least it clogs up the conscience. It was always most effective of all on the anniversary of Marco's death. Well, they transformed that cell in Palermo into something like a reformatory, if you get my meaning. They locked prisoners in there so they'd repent of their crimes and get religion. You know, some criminals have a lot of pull with the police, and the cops in turn make good use of some of those chiselers, so needless to say, they didn't lock everybody in there, and every now and then there'd be somebody they wouldn't even try to save. I also think that sometimes they let some of those big crooks grease a few palms so as not to get thrown into that wonder-working cell. There's not a lot of honesty even in miracles.

"That's what the head guard in Palermo told me, gentlemen, and his buddies there swore it was true. There was an English sailor in there once on account of some free-for-all, Briggs by name, and he went straight from that cell to Formosa to be a missionary. I heard later he met a true martyr's death there. It was strange how no guard would even stick a finger in Marco's cell; probably they were afraid they'd fall into a state of grace and start repenting of their own deeds.

"So anyway, like I told you, I was teaching this head guard how to play some of our more religious-type card games. You wouldn't believe how angry that man got when he lost! But once, when a few too many bad cards happened to fall his way, he shut me up in Marco's cell. '*Per Bacco*,' he yelled, 'I'll learn you!' I just lay down and went to sleep, of course. Next morning he calls me in and says, 'How about it, are you saved?' 'Damned if I know, *signore comandante*,' says I, 'I slept like a stork.' 'Then you can march right back in there,' he yells. — But what I meant to tell you a while back is, I spent three weeks in that cell and nothing came over me at all: no remorse, no nothing. And at that point the guard begins shaking his head in amazement and says, 'You Czechs must be terrible heathens or heretics, if it doesn't have any effect on you!' And then he swore at me something awful.

"And you know, from that time on Marco's cell stopped having any effect at all. No matter who they shoved in there, nobody ever again got converted or turned over a new leaf or even repented — flat-out nothing at all. The long and the short of it is, that cell went out of business. My God, they raised a stink about it! They complained to the board of directors that I'd interfered with procedure and what have you. I just shrugged my shoulders. There wasn't anything I could do about it, right? Well, they gave me three days in the black hole anyway, because, they said, I'd wrecked their cell."

The Disappearance of Mr. Hirsch

"That was a pretty good case," said Mr Taussig, "but it has one great fault: it didn't take place in Prague. You know, even in criminal matters a man should have a little consideration for his hometown. What do we care about some crime in Palermo or some damned place like that? What good is it to us? But when one of your better crimes gets pulled off in Prague, well, to me that's downright flattering. I tell myself that everybody in the whole world's talking about us now; it's kind of, you know, gratifying. Then, too, it stands to reason that wherever a really first-rate crime takes place, business goes up. It's thought to be a sign of very favorable prospects, you see, and it inspires confidence. But the culprit has to be caught.

"I don't know if you remember that case in Dlouha Street that had to do with old Hirsch. He had a shop there dealing in hides, but he also sold Persian carpets, too, and other things from the Orient. You know, for many years he had some kind of racket in Constantinople — but he picked up some sort of liver trouble there; that's why he was scrawny as a dead cat, and brown like he'd been dragged out of a tanning vat. And these rug-dealers from Armenia or Smyrna used to come see him here because he knew how to talk with them in their thieves' lingo. They're a bunch of crooks, those Armenians; even a Jew needs to keep a sharp eye on them. Anyway, this Hirsch had the hides on the ground floor, and from there a stairway wound up to his office. Directly behind the office was his apartment, and that's where Mrs. Hirsch sat; she was so fat she couldn't even walk.

"Well, one day towards noon one of the shop assistants came up to the office looking for Mr. Hirsch, to see if they were to send some hides on credit to a man named Weil in Brno; but

Mr. Hirsch wasn't in the office. True, this was kind of unusual, but the assistant told himself that Mr. Hirsch must have just popped over to see Mrs. Hirsch in their apartment next door. But pretty soon the maid came downstairs and said that Mr. Hirsch was supposed to come up for lunch. 'What do you mean, come up for lunch?' the assistant said. 'Mr. Hirsch's already in the apartment, isn't he?' 'How could he be?' the maid answered, 'Mrs. Hirsch's been sitting there all day right next to the office and she hasn't seen him since this morning.' 'And we,' said the assistant, 'haven't seen him either, have we, Vaclav?' — That was the errand-boy's name. 'I took the mail up to him at ten,' the assistant went on, 'and Mr. Hirsch chewed me out because we were supposed to have written Lemberger about those calfskins, and from that time on he never stuck his nose outside the office.' 'My stars,' said the maid, 'he's not in the office now. Maybe he had to go somewhere in town?' 'Well, he didn't go out through the shop,' the assistant said, 'or we would have seen him for sure. Maybe he went out through the apartment.' 'That's not possible,' said the maid, 'because Mrs. Hirsch would of seen him.' 'Wait a minute,' the assistant said, 'when I saw him, he had his robe and slippers on. Go see if he took his shoes, galoshes, and overcoat' — it was November, you know, and it had been raining a lot. 'If he got dressed,' the assistant added, 'then he went into town somewhere. If not, then he has to be somewhere here, doesn't he?'

"So the maid scooted back upstairs, but in a few minutes she was back again, all upset. 'Oh my stars, Mr. Hugo,' she said to the assistant, 'Mr. Hirsch didn't take his shoes or anything; and Mrs. Hirsch says that he couldn't of gone through the apartment, because he would of had to go through her room!' 'He didn't go out through the shop, either,' said the assistant. 'He wasn't in the shop at all today, he only called me into the office because of the mail. Vaclav, go look for him!' So first they dashed up to the office. Everything was in place there, except for a couple of carpets rolled up in a corner and a letter to Lemberger, still unsigned, on the desk; and the gas lamp over the desk was still glowing. 'Well, it's clear that Mr. Hirsch didn't go anywhere,' said Hugo, 'because if he'd gone anywhere, he'd have turned off the lamp, right? He must be somewhere in the apartment.' So they searched the whole apartment, but to no avail. At this, Mrs. Hirsch began crying her heart out in her armchair; it looked, this Hugo said later, like a huge mountain of jelly quivering there. 'Mrs. Hirsch,' this Hugo said — it's remarkable how a young Jew suddenly comes to his senses when he needs to — 'don't cry, Mrs. Hirsch; Mr. Hirsch didn't run off anywhere. Hides are selling well now, and besides, he doesn't have any debts. The boss must be here somewhere. If we don't find him by evening, we'll tell the police about it, but not until then; because as you know, Mrs. Hirsch, something conspicuous like this isn't good for business.'

"Well, they searched and waited until evening, but there was no trace of Mr. Hirsch. So after Mr. Hugo closed the shop at the usual hour, he went to notify the police that Mr. Hirsch was missing, and detectives were sent over from headquarters. As you can imagine, they rummaged through everything, but they didn't find even the littlest clue. They even looked for blood on the floor, but to no avail; so for the time being they sealed up the office. On top of that, they cross-examined Mrs. Hirsch and the staff about what had happened that morning. But nobody had seen anything unusual, except that Mr. Hugo remembered that shortly after ten o'clock Mr. Lebeda, a traveling salesman, had dropped in to see Mr. Hirsch and talked with him for about ten minutes. So then they went looking for Mr. Lebeda, and needless to say they found him playing poker at the Bristol Café. Well, this Lebeda straightaway hid the stakes, but the detective says to him, 'Mr. Lebeda, we're not here about gambling today, we're here about Mr. Hirsch: he's missing, and you were the last one to see him.' But it turns out that this Lebeda didn't really know anything, either; he'd been to see Mr. Hirsch about some leather harness and he hadn't noticed anything out of the ordinary, except it seemed to him that Mr. Hirsch looked even more poorly than usual. 'You look more or less like you're wasting away, Mr. Hirsch,' he'd told him. 'But Mr. Lebeda,' the detective said, 'even if Mr. Hirsch had dried up even more, he couldn't have vanished into thin air. He'd still have left some bones or dentures behind, right? And you couldn't have carried him out of there in your briefcase.'

"But wait, here's where the case takes another turn. You know how they have checkrooms at train stations where travelers can leave their suitcases and things. Well, about two days after Mr. Hirsch disappeared, the checkroom attendant told the porter that there was a trunk in there that looked just a bit suspicious to her. 'I don't know why,' she said, 'but that trunk just plain scares me.' So the porter goes over and sniffs at the trunk and says, 'You know, ma, maybe you'd better report this to the railway police.' So the railway police fetched a police dog, and when the dog sniffed at the suitcase he began to snarl and his coat bristled up. It was all pretty strange by now, and so they broke into the trunk; and squeezed up inside it was the corpse of Mr. Hirsch in his robe and slippers. And because he had that liver ailment, the poor man, he was already smelling something awful. And there was a heavy cord cutting right into his neck; he'd been strangled. But strangest of all was how he could've got out of his office in his robe and slippers and into a trunk at the railway station.

"It was Captain Mejzlik who got the case. He looks over the corpse pretty carefully, and right away he sees these tiny green, blue, and red specks on the face and hands. What made it so odd, see, is that Mr. Hirsch himself was so brown. This is a strange form of decomposition, Mejzlik said to himself, and he began to rub at one of the specks with his handkerchief; and the speck came right off. 'Take a look at this,' he said to the other detectives. 'It seems to be some sort of aniline dye. I'll want to take another look at that office.'

"To begin with, he looked around the office for any kinds of dyes, but there weren't any. Then suddenly his eyes lit on the rolls of Persian carpets. He unrolled one of them, spit on his handkerchief, and rubbed at the blue in the pattern; and this blue stain appeared on his handkerchief. 'Damned shoddy goods, these carpets,' Mejzlik said, and then he went on looking. On Mr. Hirsch's desk, in the inkstand, he found the butts of two or three Turkish cigarettes. 'Keep in mind,' he said to one of the detectives, 'that in this Persian carpet racket they invariably smoke one cigarette after another. It's one of their Oriental customs.' And then he sent for Mr. Hugo. 'Mr. Hugo,' he said, 'there was somebody else here after Mr. Lebeda, wasn't there?'

" 'There was,' said Mr. Hugo, 'but Mr. Hirsch never wanted us to talk about it. You look after the hides, he'd tell us, but stay away from the carpets; that's my concern, not yours.'

" 'I can believe it,' said Mejzlik, 'because these are contraband carpets. Look, not one of them has a customs stamp. If Mr. Hirsch wasn't with his maker now, he'd be in big trouble with the customs office. He'd be paying fines until he was blue in the face. Out with it, quick: who was here?'

" 'Well,' said Mr. Hugo, 'about ten-thirty this Armenian, or maybe he was a Jew, drove up in a big open car, he was fat and kind of yellowish, and he asked in Turkish or something for Mr. Hirsch. So I showed him the way up to the office. And right behind him came this tall, lanky fellow, a servant or something, thin as a rail and black as a black cat, and he was carrying these five big carpets rolled up on his shoulder; Vaclav and I were trying to figure out how he did it. Anyway, the two of them went into the office and were there for maybe fifteen minutes. We didn't think anything about it, but you could hear that swindler talking to Mr. Hirsch the whole time. Then the servant came back downstairs again, but this time he was only carrying four carpets rolled up on his shoulder. Aha, I said to myself, Mr. Hirsch's bought himself another carpet. Oh yes, and this Armenian turned back at the office door and said something else to Mr. Hirsch, who was still in the office, but I couldn't understand what he was saying. And then the lanky fellow threw the carpets in the car, and off they went. The only reason I didn't mention it is because it wasn't anything out of the ordinary, that's all,' said Mr. Hugo. 'We get these rug dealers in here all the time, and they're all a bunch of thieves.'

" 'Mr. Hugo,' said Mejzlik, 'you might as well know that there was indeed something odd going on. What that lanky fellow was carrying out in one of those rolled-up carpets was Mr. Hirsch's corpse. Damn it, man, you might have noticed that that fellow came down with a heavier load than he took up!'

" 'True,' said Mr. Hugo, turning pale, 'he was all stooped over! But sir, that can't be right; that fat Armenian was right in back of him and still talking to Mr. Hirsch through the doorway!'

" 'Sure,' said Mejzlik, 'he was talking to an empty office. And earlier, while the lanky fellow was strangling Mr. Hirsch, that other man kept right on jabbering. Mr. Hugo, that Armenian Jew is cleverer than you. Afterwards, then, they took Mr. Hirsch's body in the rolled-up carpet to their hotel; but because it was raining, the cheap carpet dye rubbed off on Mr. Hirsch. It's clear as crystal, no doubt about it. And at the hotel they put Mr. Hirsch's bodily remains in a trunk and sent the trunk to the train station. There you have it, Mr. Hugo!'

"Well, while Mejzlik was doing all this, his detectives had already found a clue to the Armenian's identity. What I mean is, there was a luggage sticker from a Berlin hotel on the trunk — which proved that the Armenian was a big tipper. Hotel porters all over the world, you know, use those stickers as a sign that the owner's pretty free with his money. And because this Armenian paid well, the porter in Berlin probably remembered him well. His name was Mazanian, and he was probably on his way through Prague to Vienna; but they didn't nail him until he reached Bucharest, and that's where he hanged himself when they took him into custody. Why he murdered Mr. Hirsch, nobody knows. Most likely they had some quarrel from the time when Mr. Hirsch had his business in Constantinople.

"But what this story just goes to show," Mr. Taussig ended thoughtfully, "is that the chief thing in business is quality. If that Armenian had been smuggling quality carpets instead of ones made with cheap dye, they couldn't have figured out so soon how he'd finished off Mr. Hirsch, and that's a fact. Sell shoddy goods, though, and sooner or later you pay for it."

Chintamani and Birds

"Hm," said Dr. Vitasek, "as a matter of fact I happen to know a bit about Persian carpets myself. But I also have to tell you, Mr. Taussig, that things nowadays aren't at all the way they used to be. Nowadays those rascals in the Orient won't take the trouble to dye the wool with cochineal, indigo, saffron, camel's urine, oak-gall, or the rest of those fine old organic dyes. The wool isn't what it used to be, either, and when it comes to patterns — I could weep! I suppose Persian carpets are one of the lost arts now. That's why only the old pieces that were made before 1870 have any value today; but the only way you can buy them is when some old family sells its heirlooms 'for family reasons,' as the better families say when they mean debts. Listen, once I came across a genuine Transylvanian carpet in the Rozmberk castle — one of those small prayer-rugs that the Turks turned out in the seventeenth century when they were living in Transylvania. The tourists visiting the castle stomp back and forth on it in their hob-nailed boots, and nobody has any idea of its value — it's enough to break your heart. And one of the rarest carpets in the world is right here in Prague, and nobody knows about it.

"What I mean is this: I've come to know all the carpet dealers in the city, and every so often I make the rounds to see what they've got in stock. You see, sometimes the agents in Anatolia and Persia still come across an old specimen that's been stolen from a mosque or someplace, and they wrap it up with a lot of other dry goods; then the whole bundle, regardless of what's inside, is sold by weight. And I think to myself, just suppose they were to wrap up a Ladik or a Bergama that way! That's why I drop in on this or that rug dealer from time to time, sit down on a pile of carpets, puff on my pipe, and watch them selling Bukhara, Saruk, and Tabriz carpets to half-wits; and occasionally I'll say, 'What's that one you've got underneath, that yellow one?' And what do you know, it's a Hamadan. Well, every once in a while I stop by to see Mrs. Severynova — she has a little shop in a courtyard in the Old Town, and sometimes you can find some nice Karamans and Kilims there. She's a plump, jolly lady who can talk your ear off, and she has a poodle who's so fat that it almost makes you sick to look at it. It's one of those fat, bad-tempered dogs with an irritating, asthmatic bark; I don't like them. Listen, has any of you ever seen a *young* poodle? I haven't. If you ask me, all poodles are old, just like inspectors, auditors, and tax collectors; I suppose it's the nature of the breed. But because I wanted to keep on good terms with Mrs. Severynova, I would always sit in the corner where the bitch Amina snored and wheezed away on a large carpet that had been folded in a square, and I would scratch her back. Amina liked that no end.

" 'Mrs. Severynova,' I said to her one day, 'business must be bad. This carpet I'm sitting on has been here for three years now.'

" 'It's been here longer than that,' said Mrs. Severynova; 'it's been folded up in that corner for a good ten years, but it isn't my carpet.'

" 'Aha,' said I, 'it's Amina's.'

" 'Not at all,' said Mrs. Severynova, laughing. 'It belongs to a certain lady who says she doesn't have enough room for it at home, so she leaves it here. It gets in my way, but at least Amina can sleep on it, can't you, Amina?'

"Although I pulled aside only a tiny corner of the carpet, Amina started to growl ferociously. 'Why, this is quite an old carpet,' I said, 'may I take a look at it?'

" 'Why not?' said Mrs. Severynova, and she took Amina onto her lap. 'Come now, Amina, the gentleman's only going to have a look, and then he'll fold it up again for you. Now shush, Amina, there's no need to growl! That's enough, you silly dog!'

"Meanwhile I had spread out the carpet and, let me tell you, my heart nearly stopped. It was a seventeenth-century Anatolian, a bit threadbare in places, but just so you'll know, it was what they call a bird carpet, in a Chintamani pattern with birds; in other words, a sacred and forbidden pattern. You can take my word for it, it's extremely rare; and this particular specimen measured at least five by six yards, in a beautiful white with turquoise blue and cherry pink . . . I turned to the window so that Mrs. Severynova couldn't see the expression on my face and said, 'It's certainly seen better days, Mrs. Severynova, but it'll fall to pieces altogether just lying here in your shop. Look, tell the lady I'll buy it, since she doesn't have room for it herself.'

" 'Easier said than done,' said Mrs. Severynova. 'That carpet isn't for sale, and the lady herself is always off in spa towns like Merano and Nice. I don't even know when she's back in town. But I'll try to ask her.'

" 'Yes, please do,' I said with as much indifference as I could, and I went on my way. You need to understand that, for a collector, it's a matter of honor to pick up some rarity for a song. I know a very rich and important man who collects books. He doesn't mind in the least paying a couple of thousand, if need be, for some old second-hand book; but when he picks up a first edition of Josef Krasoslav Chmelensky's poems for a few cents at a flea market, he nearly jumps for joy. It's a kind of sport, like hunting chamois. So I had made up my mind that I was going to get this carpet on the cheap and then present it to the museum, because a museum's the only place for something like that. Only there'd have to be a label on it saying: Gift of Dr. Vitasek. Well, we all have our own private fantasies, don't we? But I must confess that my brain was on fire.

"It was all I could do not to run back the very next day for that specimen with the Chintamani and birds. I could think of nothing else. Every day I told myself to hold off just one day longer; I did it to spite myself. Sometimes we enjoy tormenting ourselves. After a couple of weeks, however, it struck me that somebody else might come across that bird carpet, so I raced to Mrs. Severynova's. 'What about it?' I gasped from the doorway.

" 'What about what?' Mrs. Severynova asked in astonishment, and I tried to pull myself together. 'Why,' I said, 'I was just walking along the street here and suddenly remembered that white carpet. Will the lady sell it?'

"Mrs. Severynova shook her head. 'It can't be done,' she said, 'she's at Biarritz now and nobody knows when she's coming back.' So I looked to see if the carpet was there. Amina was lying on it, of course, fatter and mangier than ever and waiting for me to scratch her back.

"A few days later I had to go to London, and while I was there I took the opportunity to call on Sir Douglas Keith — he's the greatest living authority on Oriental carpets, you know. 'Could you by any chance tell me, sir,' I asked him, 'the value of a white Anatolian with Chintamani and birds, more than thirty yards square?'

"Sir Douglas stared at me over his glasses and snapped almost savagely, 'None at all!'

" 'What do you mean, none at all?' I said, taken aback. 'Why wouldn't it have any value?'

" 'Because no carpet of that size and pattern exists,' Sir Douglas shouted at me. 'You ought to realize that the largest carpet with Chintamani and birds that I have ever known barely measures fifteen square yards.'

"My face flushed red with joy. 'But supposing,' I said to him, 'that there were a specimen as big as that. What value would it have?'

" 'Just what I've told you, none at all!' shouted Sir Douglas. 'A specimen like that would be unique, and how in heaven's name do you determine the value of a unique specimen? If a specimen's unique, it could just as easily be worth a thousand pounds as ten thousand pounds. How the dickens would I know? Anyway, no such carpet exists, sir. Good day, sir.'

"Well, you can imagine my state of mind when I returned: My God, I've got to get my hands on that specimen with the

Chintamani and birds! What a windfall for the museum! But keep in mind, please, that I couldn't express any interest whatsoever in the carpet, because that's not how a collector goes about it. And don't forget that Mrs. Severynova had no particular interest in selling that tattered old rag that her Amina lolled around on, while that cursed woman who owned the carpet was gadding about from Merano to Ostend and from Baden to Vichy — that woman must have had a medical encyclopedia at home, she had so many disorders. At any rate, she was forever in one spa town or another. So every couple of weeks I would drop in on Mrs. Severynova to see whether the rug with all its birds was still sitting there in the corner. I would scratch the repulsive Amina till she squealed with delight and, so as not to make it too obvious, I would invariably buy a carpet of some sort. Listen, I've got so many Shiraz, Shirvan, Mosul, Kabistan, and other garden-variety carpets at home, piles and piles of them — but among them is a classic Derbent, friends, you don't see those every day, and an old blue Khorasan. But what I went through for two whole years, only a collector could understand. Talk about the torments of love, why, that's nothing compared to the torments of collecting. Still and all, no collector's yet been known to commit suicide. On the contrary, they usually live to a ripe old age. It must be a healthy passion.

"One day Mrs. Severynova suddenly said, 'Well, Mrs. Zanelli, the woman that carpet belongs to, was here. I told her I could find a buyer for that white carpet of hers, and anyway it's getting worn to threads just lying around here. But she said it was a family heirloom and she didn't want to sell it and I'm to leave it where it is.'

"Needless to say, I set out after this Mrs. Zanelli on my own. I thought she'd be some kind of society fashion-plate, but it turned out she was an ugly old witch with a purple nose and a wig and a peculiar tic that kept jumping all the way from her mouth to her left ear.

" 'Madame,' I said, and I couldn't help noticing how her mouth danced around on her face, 'I'd very much like to buy that white carpet of yours. True, it's a bit threadbare, but it just might do for my . . . my entrance hall.' And as I waited for her answer, I felt as if my own mouth were beginning to prance and twitch to the left. I don't know whether her tic was contagious or whether it was just nervous excitement, but I couldn't keep it under control.

" 'How dare you?' the dreadful woman screeched at me. 'Get out of here now, now, now," she shrieked. "That's the heirloom rug mein Grosspapa left to me! If you don't get out, I'm calling the Polizei! I'm not selling any carpets, I'm a von Zanelli, sir! Mary, see this man out of the house!'

"Believe me, I scrambled down those stairs like a schoolboy. I could have wept with fury and regret, but what good would that have done? After a year I dropped by Mrs. Severynova's again; in the meantime, Amina had become so fat and bald that she'd acquired a grunt, just like a pig. During that year Mrs. Zanelli had come back to town once more, and this time I gave in and did something which, as a collector, I'll be ashamed of to my dying day: I sent a friend of mine to her, Bimbal, the lawyer — he's a refined fellow and he has a beard, which of course gives women boundless confidence in him — and I told him to offer the worthy lady a reasonable sum for that bird carpet. Meanwhile, I waited outside, jittery as a suitor who's waiting for an answer. Three hours later, Bimbal staggered out of the house wiping the sweat from his face. 'You scoundrel,' he hissed at me, 'I ought to wring your neck. Why in God's name should I for your sake alone have to sit and listen for three whole hours to the history of the Zanelli family? And let me tell you,' he added vindictively, 'you're not going to get that rug. Seventeen Zanellis would turn in their graves if their family relic ended up in a museum! Jesus, you sure pulled a fast one on me!' And with that he left.

"But you know, once a man gets an idea into his head, he doesn't let go in a hurry; and if he's a collector, he won't stop at murder. Believe me, collecting is no job for sissies. So I made up my mind to simply steal that carpet with the Chintamani and birds. First I scouted out the lay of the land. Mrs. Severynova's shop is in a courtyard, and at nine o'clock in the evening the outer gate to the passageway is locked; but I didn't want to use a skeleton key, because that's something I know nothing about. There are some cellar stairs down from the passageway where a person could hide before the gate is locked, and there's also a small shed in the courtyard. If you got up on the roof of the shed, you could climb over into the next yard, which belongs to a tavern — and you can always get out of a tavern. So it was simple enough, and all that was left was to find a way to open the shop window. I bought a glazier's diamond for that job and practiced on my own windows till I knew how to remove a pane of glass.

"Please don't think that burglary's all that simple, however; it's much harder than operating on the prostate or yanking out a kidney. In the first place, it's hard to avoid being seen. In the second place, there's no end of waiting around and other inconveniences involved. And in the third place, there's all this uncertainty beforehand; you never know what you're going to run up against. Let me tell you, it's a tough, badly-paid line of work. If I found a burglar in my house, I'd take him by the hand and gently say, 'My dear fellow, why do you want to put yourself to so much trouble? Look, couldn't you rob people in some more convenient way?'

"I don't know how other people steal, of course, but my own experiences aren't exactly encouraging. On the evening in question, as they say, I snuck into the passageway and hid on the stairs leading down to the cellar. That's how a police report would describe it; what really happened was that I hung around for half an hour in the rain in front of the passageway, which made me more or less conspicuous to one and all. Finally, in desperation, I came to a decision, just as you finally decide to have a tooth pulled, and I stepped into the passageway. Needless to say, I collided with a servant girl who'd gone to fetch beer from the tavern next door. In order to calm her down, I muttered something to the effect that she was a sweet thing or a darling girl or whatever; it terrified her so, she took to her heels at once. For the time being, I hid on those steps leading down to the cellar. Some bastards had left a trash can standing there, full of ashes and other slop, which fell over with a huge clatter while I was engaged in my so-called sneaking around, and it spilled over, mostly on me. Then the servant girl returned with the beer and, still flustered, informed the caretaker that a suspicious character was creeping around the place. But that excellent man refused to trouble himself and declared that it was probably some drunk who'd lost his way to the tavern. A quarter of an hour later, yawning and clearing his throat, he locked the gate and things quieted down. All I could hear was the servant girl sobbing loudly and forlornly somewhere upstairs — it's odd how noisy servant girls are when they cry; must be homesickness. I began to feel cold and, besides that, the place smelled sour and musty. I groped around, but everything I touched felt slimy. My God, what a lot of prints must have been planted there by the fingers of Dr. Vitasek, our distinguished specialist in diseases of the urinary tract! When I thought it must surely be midnight, it was only ten o'clock. I'd wanted to start my burgling at midnight, but by eleven I couldn't stand it any longer. So off I went to steal. You wouldn't believe the kind of racket a person can make when trying to slink around in the dark, but the building was blessed with sound sleepers. At last I got to the window and, with a horrible screaking sound, began to cut the glass. From inside came a muffled bark. Jesus, Amina was in there!

"'Amina,' I whispered, 'shut up, you ugly beast. I've come to scratch your back.' But in the dark, you know, it was incredibly difficult to coax that diamond into the same little slit I'd just made; so I scraped the diamond back and forth over the pane, until I finally pressed just a bit harder and the entire pane popped out with a crash. That does it, now everybody will come running out, I said to myself, and I peeked around for someplace to hide; but nothing happened. Then, with an almost perverse calm, I pushed out a few more panes of glass and opened the window. Inside, Amina barked from time to time, but only halfheartedly and as a matter of form, just to show that she was doing her job. So I crawled through the window and headed straight for that loathsome bitch. 'Amina,' I whispered feverishly, 'for heaven's sake, where's your back? There we go, precious pooch, this gentleman's your friend — you slut, you like that, don't you?' Amina writhed with bliss, if a giant gunnysack can be said to writhe. So I said, in a very friendly way, 'That's right, now let go, doggie!' and I started to drag that priceless bird carpet out from under her. At this point, Amina evidently told herself that *her* property was at stake, and she began to howl. It wasn't just a bark, it was a howl. 'Jesus, Amina,' I quickly scolded her, 'quiet, you bitch! Wait, I'll get you something even nicer to lie on!' And whap! I jerked a hideous, shiny Kerman off the wall that Mrs. Severynova regarded as the best thing in her shop. 'Look, Amina,' I whispered, 'that's where you're going to go night-night!' Amina gazed at me with interest, but scarcely had I stretched out my hand for *her* carpet than she started howling again. I thought they must have heard her all the way to Kobylisi. So once again I worked the monster up to a state of ecstasy with an especially sensuous round of back-scratching, and I took her in my arms. But the instant I reached for that unique white specimen with the Chintamani and birds, she gave an asthmatic rattle and began to swear. 'Godammit, beast,' I said, at wits' end, 'I'll have to kill you!'

"Listen, I have to admit that I myself don't understand it. I looked at that fat, vile, repulsive bitch with the most savage hatred I have ever known, but I couldn't bring myself to kill the creature. I had a good knife, I had a belt holding up my pants; I could have slit her throat or strangled her, but I just didn't have the heart to do it. I sat down beside her on that divine carpet and scratched her behind the ears. 'You coward,' I whispered to myself, 'one or two quick movements is all it would take. You've operated on plenty of people in your time, and you've seen them die in terror and pain. *Why can't you kill a dog?*' I actually gritted my teeth to try and pluck up the courage, but I couldn't do it.

And at that point, I have to tell you, I broke down and cried — I suppose it must have been because I felt so ashamed of myself. And then Amina began to whine and lick my face.

"'You lousy, miserable, good-for-nothing beast,' I grumbled, and then I patted her mangy back and crawled through the window back into the courtyard. It was simply defeat and retreat. Well, what I intended to do next was jump onto the shed and go across the roof to the other courtyard and out through the tavern, but either I'd used up every last smidgen of strength or the roof was higher than I'd estimated. In any event, I couldn't get up there. So I climbed back down the cellar stairs again and stayed there till morning, half-dead with exhaustion. Idiot that I was, I might have slept on one of those carpets, but it never occurred to me. In the morning I heard the caretaker unlocking the gate. I waited for a moment and then headed straight outside. The caretaker was standing by the gate, and when he saw a stranger coming through the passageway, he was so startled that he forgot to make a fuss.

"A couple of days later I went to see Mrs. Severynova. Grates had been installed in front of the windows and, sure enough, rolling around on the sacred Chintamani pattern was that disgusting toad of a dog. When Amina saw me, she joyfully wagged that stumpy sausage which, on other dogs, would be called a tail. Mrs. Severynova beamed at me. 'There's our darling Amina, sir, our treasure, our dear little doggie. Did you know that a burglar broke in through the window the other day and our Amina chased him away? Why, I wouldn't give her up for anything in the world,' she declared proudly. 'But she's fond of you, sir. She knows an honest person when she sees one, don't you, Amina?'

"Well, that's it. That unique bird carpet is lying there to this very day — I believe it's one of the rarest carpet specimens in the world. And to this very day, that obese, mangy, stinking Amina is lying on top of it, grunting with bliss. It wouldn't surprise me if some day she smothers in her own fat, and then perhaps I'll try again. But first I have to learn how to file through a grate."

A Safecracker and an Arsonist

"The thing is," said Mr. Jilek, "if you're going to steal, you have to know what you're doing. That's what Mr. Balaban always used to say. He's the safecracker who pulled his last job at Scholle and Co. This Balaban was a very knowledgeable and prudent safecracker. Of course he was older by then, and it stands to reason that not everybody has the benefit of so much experience; a young man's more likely to take a gamble. Well, you can succeed in a lot of things with courage alone, you know, but when a person begins to think things through, chances are he loses his courage, and that's why he goes about his business with prudence. It pays off in politics and everything else.

"What Balaban used to say is that every kind of work has its own rules. And when it comes to safes, one of them is that a safecracker always has to work alone, because he can't rely on anybody else. The second thing is that he never works long in any one place, because they'll begin to recognize his work. And the third thing is that he has to keep up with the times and on top of everything new in his field. Still and all, he has to stick with tradition and probabilities, too, because the more people there are working in the same way, the harder it is for the police. That's why Balaban kept a wrench with him, even though he had an electric drill and had even learned how to handle explosives. He used to say it's pointless, nothing but vain ambition, to take on these modern armor-plated safes. He preferred working the old reliable establishments, the ones that have old-style steel safes with honest money inside, not these checks. He had it all thought out and nailed down, did Balaban. On top of that, he had a shop dealing in old brass, a real estate business, a racket in horses and, all things considered, he did pretty well for himself. Now, Balaban had gone around saying that he was only going to do one more safe, but it would be such a clean piece of work that the younger generation would be knocked for a loop. They say that the main thing isn't to make big money, but Balaban used to say that the main thing is not to get caught.

"Well, the last safe Balaban cleaned out was at Scholle and Co., of course, that factory in Bubenec, you know. But what he did there was truly a solid piece of work; that's what I was told by this police detective, a man named Pistora. Balaban climbed in through a window looking out on the courtyard, just like Dr. Vitasek, except that he had to pry some bars loose. It was a real pleasure, said Pistora, to see how neatly he took out those bars: he didn't leave one scrap of trash lying around, that's how beautifully the man worked. And at the same spot where he first drilled into the safe, that's where he opened it, too. There wasn't a single unnecessary hole or gouge, not a nick or a dent. In fact he didn't even scratch the paint on the safe any more than he had to. It was really something, said Pistora, to see the kind of love that man put into what he did. The fact is, that safe is in the police museum now, on account of it's a masterful piece of work. After scooping out the money, maybe sixty thousand, he ate a bit of bread and bacon he'd brought with him and left by the same window. Balaban used to say that the main thing generals and safecrackers have to worry about is retreating. Then he took the money to his cousin's, hid his tools with somebody named Lizner, went home, cleaned his clothes and boots, washed up, and climbed into bed like any regular citizen.

"It wasn't even eight o'clock in the morning when somebody knocked on the door and called, 'Open up, Mr. Balaban!' Balaban wondered who on earth it could be, but he opened the door with an easy conscience; and in rushed two police officers along with Inspector Pistora. I don't know if you know Pistora — he's a short little fellow with teeth like a squirrel and he's always grinning. He worked for a funeral parlor once, but he had to find another way to earn his living, because people couldn't help but smile when he'd step out in front of the coffin grinning in that funny way. What I think is, a lot of people grin only because they're embarrassed that they don't know what to do with their mouths, just like other people don't know what to do with their hands. That's why people smile in that silly, over-eager way when they talk with a great man, a king or a president, say; it isn't from pleasure so much as from embarrassment. But I wanted to tell you about Balaban.

"When Balaban saw Pistora and those two policemen, he fired off in righteous anger, 'What are you fellowth doing here? You don't have any bithness buthting in on me.' — He himself was taken aback by the way he was lisping.

" 'But Mr. Balaban,' this Pistora smiled, 'we're only here to take a look at your teeth.' And he went straight over to this hand-painted mug where Balaban kept his dentures at night — the fact is, he'd lost most of his teeth that time he leaped from a window. 'Yes indeedy, Mr. Balaban,' this Pistora says with great satisfaction, 'they wouldn't stay put, these here false teeth of yours. These teeth just come to life whenever you start to drill, and so you took them out and put them on the desk at Scholle and Co. My, but there was a lot of dust there — Mr. Balaban, you should of known that from the amount of dust on those account books, too. When we found your toothprints there, Mr. Balaban, we just had to come after you; there's no use getting mad at us. You should of wiped that dust off first.'

" 'Thon of a gun,' Mr. Balaban marveled. 'You know, Pithtora, they thay that even the cleveretht crook can make *one* mithtake.'

" 'Except you made two,' Mr. Pistora grinned. 'All we had to do was take one look and already you were our suspect, and you know why? Every regular safecracker pisses on the spot to keep from getting caught; it's kind of a superstition. Except you're such a infidel and thinker, you just turn up your nose at superstition. You think brains and reason is all you need. That's a big mistake. Yes indeedy, Mr. Balaban: if you're going to steal, you have to know what you're doing.' "

*   *   *

" 'Some people are so skillful,' said Mr. Maly, expanding on
the theme, 'that you have to give them credit. I read somewhere
about a case like that, and it may be that some of you don't know
about it. It happened in Austria somewhere. There was this
master saddler and strap-maker there, his Christian name was
Anton, and his last name was Huber or Vogt or Meyer or one
of those names Germans usually have. Anyway, this saddler was
celebrating his nameday and he was sitting at his big nameday
lunch — except they don't set that good a table in that part of
Austria, not even on namedays, not like we do. I've heard they
even eat chestnuts there. Anyway, this saddler is sitting there in
the circle of his family, and suddenly there's someone banging on
the window, 'Jesus and Mary, neighbors, your roof's burning
right over your heads!' The saddler dashed out, and sure enough,
the rafters were going up in flames. The children start yelling, of
course, the wife runs out in tears carrying the clock — well, I've
seen a whole bunch of fires, and it's my observation that people
usually lose their heads and start running out with something
completely useless, clocks or coffee-grinders or canaries in cages.
And only when it's too late do they remember that they left
grandma back inside and all their clothes and a whole bunch of
other things. Meanwhile people crowd around and start getting
in each other's way trying to put out the fire. Then the firemen
come — you know, firemen have to change into uniform before
they can start putting out a fire; but meanwhile it's already set
the next building on fire, and by evening there's fifteen of them
burnt to ashes. Anyone who wants to see a real fire has to go out
to the countryside or a small town. They don't have them in big
cities anymore; you're more likely to find yourself watching the
firemen's techniques than the fire. It's best when you can help
put out the fire yourself or, even better, advise everybody else on
how to extinguish it. Extinguishing a fire is wonderful work, the
way it sizzles and snaps; but hauling water from the river, a
person's not too happy doing that — There's something very
peculiar about people: whenever they see some disaster, they

almost wish it wouldn't stop. A great fire or flood stimulates them, somehow. You might say it gives them a sense of coming alive. Or maybe it's pure pagan wonderment, I don't know.

"The day after the fire, of course, the place was like — well, it was dead. A fire is a beautiful thing, but the aftermath of the fire afterwards is devastating; it's the same with love. All you can do is look on with this helpless feeling, thinking that you'll never pull yourself together again. Well, anyway, there was a young police sergeant investigating the cause of the fire. 'Sergeant,' the saddler Anton said, 'I'm betting that somebody lit it. Why else would it have broken out on my nameday while I was sitting there at lunch? But it beats me why somebody'd want to take revenge on me, because for sure I haven't done anything bad to anybody, not to mention my lack of interest in politics. I just don't know of anyone who'd hate me that much.'

"It was noontime and the sun was scorching hot. The police sergeant walked through the aftermath of the fire and thought that not even the devil himself could figure out how it started. 'Mr. Anton,' he said suddenly, 'what's that shining up there on that beam?' 'There used to be a dormer window there,' said the saddler. 'Must be some kind of nail.' 'Doesn't look much like a nail,' said the sergeant, 'looks more like a mirror.' 'What would a mirror be doing up there?' said the saddler. 'The only thing up in that gable was straw.' 'No, it's a mirror,' said the sergeant, 'and I'll show it to you.'

"So he propped the firemen's ladder against the charred beam, crawled up it, and said, 'You know, Mr. Anton, it's not a nail or a mirror, either one. It's the crystal from a watch that's been set right into the beam. What it's there for?' 'Beats me,' said the saddler. 'Maybe the kids were playing with it.' And suddenly the sergeant, who had been peering at the crystal this way and that, roared in pain: 'Ow! that burns like the devil! What was it?' And he touched himself gingerly on the nose. 'Dammit,' he roared a second time, 'now it's burned me on the hand! Quick, Mr. Anton, hand me up some paper!' So the saddler tore off a page from his notepad, and the sergeant stuck the paper under the crystal. 'That's it,' he said a moment later; 'seems to me, Mr. Anton, we've got it.' He was already crawling back down the ladder and holding the piece of paper in front of the saddler's eyes; a tiny hole had been burned in it and was still smoldering. 'Mr. Anton,' said the sergeant, 'this crystal is a lens, I'd like you to know. In other words, it's a magnifying glass. And now I'd like to know who set it into that beam under the pile of straw. But I'll tell you, Mr. Anton, whoever did it's leaving here in handcuffs.'

" 'I'll be jiggered,' said the saddler. 'We never had any magnifying glass or anything in the house — wait,' he suddenly cried, 'wait just a minute! I had this apprentice, a boy named Sepp, and that kid was always fooling around with the darndest things! That's why I kicked him out: he never did anything useful, because his head was always full of doing experiments and crazy things like that! To think it could have been that darn boy — But that's impossible, Sergeant. See, I kicked him out way back in the beginning of February. Who knows where he is now, but he's never showed up around here since.'

" 'If the lens is his, I think we've got it,' said the sergeant. 'Mr. Anton, telegraph the city and tell them to send me two more officers. I'm not letting anyone touch this lens. First thing we do is find that boy.'

"Of course, they found him. He was apprenticing with some trunk-maker in an entirely different town, and the sergeant barely stepped into the workshop before the boy began shaking like a leaf. 'Sepp,' the sergeant shouted at him, 'where were you on the thirtieth of June?'

" 'Here, sir,' the boy jerked out. 'I've been here since February fifteenth and I haven't been gone even half a day, I swear it.' 'That's right,' said the trunk-maker, 'I can swear to that myself, because he lives with me and has to stay here the whole time.'

" 'That's our bad luck, then,' said the sergeant. 'Looks like it can't be him.'

" 'So what did you want him for, anyway?' asked the trunk-maker.

" 'The thing is,' the sergeant replied, 'he was under suspicion that on June thirtieth, the devil take it now, he set fire to Anton the saddler's place and half the district with it.'

" 'June thirtieth?' said the trunk-maker, puzzled. 'Listen, that's odd. On June thirtieth this boy asked me: What day is today? Is it June thirtieth? Then it's St. Anton's Day, isn't it? Let me tell you, something's going to happen somewhere today.'

"At that instant the boy Sepp jumped up and tried to make a run for it, but the sergeant grabbed him by the collar. Later, on the way back, the boy confessed that he'd been furious with Mr. Anton, because the saddler, on account of his experiments, had beat him like a dog; that he wanted to get revenge on him, and that's why he'd calculated precisely where the sun would be at noon on June thirtieth, Mr. Anton's nameday, and according to that had placed the lens so that it would ignite the beam, while he himself would be God-knows-where. He'd set it all up in February and then left his apprenticeship.

"Listen, what they did next was call some astronomer in Vienna about that business with the lens, and the man was astounded at how the exact position of the sun at its zenith on June thirtieth had been calculated so precisely. He said it's nothing short of a miracle for a fifteen-year-old boy to discover that with no astronomical instruments for measuring angles.

"What happened later to this Sepp, I don't know; but I keep thinking how that young hooligan could have been an astronomer some day, or a physicist. Why, he could have been a second Newton or something, that damned kid! But the world lets so much special know-how and beautiful talent go to waste — You know, people have such patience when they're searching for diamonds in the earth or pearls in the sea; they ought to search like that in people for rare and wondrous gifts from God. Then people wouldn't go to waste, no doubt about it. And that's a great mistake."

The Stolen Murder

"That reminds me of a case," said Mr. Houdek, "which was also very carefully thought out and prepared for. But I'm afraid you won't like it, because it doesn't have an ending or solution. If it bores you, just say so and I'll stop.

"As you probably know, I live on Krucembursky Street, in Prague's Vinohrady district. It's one of those short side-streets with no neighborhood pub, not even a laundry or a grocery shop, where everybody's in bed by ten o'clock, except for those debauchees who stay up listening to the radio and consequently don't get to bed till eleven. As for those of us who live there, for the most part we're harmless taxpayers and low-level office workers, a few aquarium enthusiasts, one zitherist, two stamp-collectors, one vegetarian, one spiritualist, and one traveling salesman who, as a matter of fact, also goes in for theosophy. Apart from that, all you'll find there are landladies from whom the aforementioned persons rent clean, nicely-furnished rooms with breakfast, as they say in the classifieds. Once a week, always on Thursdays, the theosophist doesn't get home till around midnight, because that's when he does his spiritualist exercises. On Tuesdays, two of the goldfish-buffs don't get home till around midnight either, because they go to Aquarium Society meetings and then stand under the streetlight arguing about viviparous varieties and bug-eyed carp. Three years ago a drunk actually wandered down our street, but presumably he was from some other neighborhood and had simply lost his way. And then there was this Russian named Kovalenko or Kopytenko who used to come home every night at a quarter past eleven, a smallish man with sparse whiskers who lived at Mrs. Janska's, No. 7.

What this Russian did for a living, nobody knew; but he used to lounge around the house till five in the afternoon, and then go off to the nearest streetcar stop, briefcase in hand, and ride into town. At exactly a quarter past eleven he'd get off at the same stop and turn the corner into Krucembursky Street. Somebody afterwards claimed that the Russian used to go sit in a certain coffeehouse the whole time, quarreling with other Russians. But other people said he couldn't have been a Russian, because Russians never go home that early.

"One night, it was last February, I was already snoozing when suddenly I heard five shots ring out. At first I dreamed I was a little boy again, cracking a whip in our backyard, and I was terribly pleased by the sound of the sharp cracks. But then I woke up all of a sudden and realized that someone was firing a gun out in the street. So I flew to the window and opened it, and I saw a man with a briefcase in his hand lying face down on the sidewalk right in front of No. 7. — But at that same moment I heard the pounding of footsteps, and a policeman rounded the corner, ran up to the man, and tried to lift him. Then he let him go again, said Damn it! and blew his whistle. A moment later, another policeman appeared at the corner and ran over to the first one.

"Needless to say, I immediately threw on my slippers and overcoat and rushed downstairs. The vegetarian, the zitherist, one of the goldfish-buffs, two landladies, and one stamp-collector also came running out of their houses; the rest just watched from their windows, looking scared to death and telling themselves: The hell with it, I could get in trouble myself if I went out there. Meanwhile the two policemen had turned the man over onto his back.

" 'Why, it's the Russian, Kopytenko or Kovalenko, who lives at Mrs. Janska's,' I said, my teeth chattering. 'Is he dead?'

" 'I don't know,' said one of the policemen, looking baffled. 'We need to call a doctor.'

" 'W-Why are you just letting him lie there?' the frightened zitherist stuttered in protest. 'You should t-t-take him to the hospital!'

"By this time about a dozen of us had collected there, and we were shivering with cold and horror, while the policemen knelt down by the man who'd been shot and, for some reason, loosened his collar. At that moment a taxi pulled up at the corner, and the driver came over to see what was going on; probably he hoped it was some drunk he could drive back home.

" 'What's up, men?' he asked affably.

" 'A man's been sh-sh-shot,' stuttered the vegetarian. 'Put him in your t-t-taxi and t-t-take him to the hospital! Maybe he's still alive!'

" 'God,' said the cab driver, 'I hate fares like this. Well, wait here and I'll bring the cab over.' Then he walked slowly back to his cab and drove up to where we were standing. 'All right, put him in,' he said.

"The two policemen lifted the Russian and, with great effort, managed to get him into the taxi; true, he was pretty much on the small side, but maneuvering corpses around is no easy job.

" 'Look, old buddy, you go with him,' said the first policeman to the other one, 'and I'll get the names of the witnesses. Take him to the hospital, cabbie, and step on it.'

" 'Sure, step on it,' grumbled the cab driver, 'and me with lousy brakes.' And he drove off.

"The first policeman took a notebook from his pocket and said, 'You'll need to give me your names, gentlemen. It's only because you're witnesses.' And then, with agonizing slowness, he wrote down our names, one after the other, in his notebook; probably his fingers were numb, but we poor bastards were frozen stiff by the time he finished. When I got back to my room it was only eleven twenty-five, so the whole spectacle hadn't lasted more than ten minutes.

"I suspect that Mr. Taussig here will think there's nothing particularly unusual about this affair. But you know, Mr. Taussig, in a respectable little street like ours, something like this is a very big deal. The streets right next to ours are still basking in reflected glory and telling everybody that it happened just around the corner. The streets a bit farther off pretend it's a matter of complete indifference to them, but you can chalk that up to pure spite and envy because it didn't happen there. A few streets away in the other direction, they simply dismiss the whole thing and say, 'Supposedly somebody took a pot shot or something at somebody there, but who knows if there's anything to it.' Petty grumbling is what I call it.

"You can imagine how all of us on our street made a dash for the newspapers the next day. For one thing we wanted to learn more about our murder, and for another we were really rather pleased to think there'd be something in the newspapers about our street and what had happened to us. It's a well-known fact that what people like to read about most of all in the papers is something they themselves have seen, something to which they were, as they say, eyewitnesses. Let's say a horse falls down in Ujezd Street, thereby holding up the traffic for ten minutes. If there's nothing about it in the newspaper, the people who saw it happen get angry at the paper and slam it down on the table, swearing that there's nothing worth reading in it. They're insulted nearly to the point of libel that the paper didn't consider it important enough to mention the accident that they are, so to speak, co-owners of. If you ask me, the only reason papers publish local news items is because if they didn't, the eyewitnesses would have such a fit they'd stop buying newspapers altogether.

"Let me tell you, we were flabbergasted when not one newspaper carried a single word about our murder. Scandals of every kind you'd want to name, and blasted politics, they've got plenty of articles about those, we grumbled, they've even got a story about a streetcar colliding with a pushcart, but not one mention of the murder anywhere; these newspapers are rotten, they're corrupt! But then it occurred to the stamp-collector that maybe the police had asked the papers not to write anything about the matter for the moment, in the interests of their investigation. Well, that satisfied us, but it also heightened our curiosity. We were proud to think that we lived on such an important street and that we might even be called as witnesses in what was evidently a very secret affair. But the next day, again, there was nothing in the papers and nobody from the police turned up to ask questions. And what struck us as strangest of all was that nobody had come to Mrs. Janska's to conduct a search or to at least seal off the Russian's room. That's when we started getting alarmed; the zitherist said that maybe the police wanted to hush it up, because who knows what might be behind it. And when on the third day there was still no mention of our murder, our street began protesting that we weren't going to let the matter drop, that the Russian had been one of us and we were damn well going to get to the bottom of it; that anyhow, our street had been brazenly and shamefully ignored; we had bad paving and bad lighting, and no doubt things would look very different if a member of parliament or someone from the newspapers lived here. But the problem was, our respectable little street had no one to plead its case. In short, spontaneous dissatisfaction ballooned, and the neighbors prevailed on me, as an older and more or less unaffiliated resident, to go down to the police station and point out just how improperly this murder was being handled.

"So off I went to see Captain Bartosek. I know him slightly, he's a glum sort of man; they say it's because he's suffering from an unhappy love affair and that's why he joined the police. 'Captain, sir,' I said to him, 'the reason I'm here is to ask you what's being done about that murder on Krucembursky Street. We're beginning to think it's being kept under wraps.'

" 'What murder?' asked the captain. 'No murder's been reported there, and it's in our precinct.'

" 'The one that happened just the other day,' I explained to him, 'when that Russian Kopytenko or Kovalenko was shot in the middle of the street. Two policemen came, and one of them wrote down our names as witnesses and the other drove off with the Russian to the hospital.'

" 'That's not possible,' said the captain. 'Nothing's been reported. There must be some mistake.'

" 'But, Captain,' I said, beginning to lose my temper, 'there were at least fifty people who saw it, and we can all testify to what happened! We're all good, honest citizens, sir. If you tell us to keep our mouths shut about the murder, we'll do our best to keep them shut, even if we don't know why. But just allowing someone to get shot, that's too much. We'll give the story to the newspapers.'

" 'Now wait a minute,' said Bartosek, and his look was so grim it frightened me. 'I want you to tell me, if you please, in a nice orderly way, exactly what happened.'

"So I told him, in a nice orderly way, exactly what had happened; and if you can believe it, his face turned purple, as if something inside were coming to a full boil. But when I got to the place where the first policeman told the other one: Look, old buddy, you go with him and I'll get the names of the witnesses — when I told him that, his pent-up breath exploded and he roared, 'Those weren't our men, thank God! In the name of heaven, why didn't you call the police on those police? Your common sense should have told you that uniformed police never call each other Old Buddy! Maybe plainclothesmen do, but uniformed officers, never in all their born days! You damned civilian, you Old Buddy, you should have had those two hauled into custody at once!'

" 'But why?' I faltered, feeling miserable.

" 'Because *they* shot the Russian,' the captain bellowed. 'Or at any rate, they had a hand in it! How long have you been living in Krucembursky Street?'

" 'Nine years,' I said.

" 'Then you ought to know that at eleven fifteen, the nearest patrol officer is down at the market hall, and the nearest one after that is at the corner of Slezka and Perun Streets, and the third one's walking his beat according to the duty roster for Officer number 1388 and so forth, right on down the line. That corner where your policeman came running from, *our* policeman would have come running from there at either ten forty-eight or else twenty-three minutes after midnight, but not at any other time, because he's not there at any other time! Every crook in town knows that, for God's sake, everybody but the people who live there! You probably think there's a policeman on every corner, don't you? Look, if one of our uniformed men had appeared around that goddamned corner of yours at the time you say, that would be a terrible thing, first of all because at that exact time, according to the duty roster, he's supposed to be walking his beat at the market hall, and second, because he didn't report the murder. That would be an extremely serious matter indeed.'

" 'But sir,' I said, 'what about the murder?'

"The captain was obviously calmer now, and he said, 'That's another matter entirely, and I think we'll find it's pretty ugly business, Mr. Houdek. There's a clever brain behind this and a lot more than meets the eye. Those scoundrels had it all worked out! First of all they knew what time the Russian came home, in the second place they knew our people's appointed rounds, and in the third place they needed the two days or more it would take for the police to hear anything about the murder — no doubt they wanted time to get away or cover their tracks. Now do you understand?'

" 'Well, not exactly,' I said.

" 'Well, look,' the captain explained patiently. 'They dressed up two of their men as policemen, and the two of them were waiting just around the corner, either to shoot the Russian or to wait until some third person had picked him off. You were delighted, of course, to see how quickly our praiseworthy police arrived on the scene. By the way,' he suddenly remembered, 'when the first policeman blew his whistle, what kind of sound did it make?'

" 'Fairly weak,' I said, 'but I thought he probably had a sore throat.'

" 'Aha,' the captain said with satisfaction. 'Obviously they wanted to make sure you didn't report the murder to the police, to give them time to get out of the country, see? And you can bet that cab driver was one of the gang, too. You don't happen to remember the license number of the cab, do you?'

"'We didn't notice the number,' I said, crestfallen.

"'Never mind,' said the captain, 'it was most likely a fake anyway; but that's how they got rid of the Russian's body. As a matter of fact, he wasn't a Russian at all, but a Macedonian named Protasov. I'm grateful to you, sir, but I'd be even more grateful if you kept this whole thing quiet — in the interests of our investigation, you know. No doubt politics are mixed up in this somehow. But there must be a damned clever person behind it, because as a rule, Mr. Houdek, these political assassinations are handled pretty clumsily. Politics, that's not even an honest crime; it's nothing but a vulgar, sordid brawl,' the captain said with disgust.

"Later on, a few inquiries were made. They never did find out the motive behind the murder, but they did get the names of the men who did it, only they'd long since left the country. And so it happened that our street lost out completely on its murder. It's just as if somebody had torn out the most glorious page of its history. If some stranger, someone living in Foch Street, say, or someone from the wilds of Vrsovice should happen to pass our way, he'd probably say to himself, 'What a dull little street this is!' And nobody believes us when we brag about the mysterious crime that was committed there. The fact is, though, those other streets still begrudge us our murder."

The Case Involving the Baby

"As long as we're talking about Captain Bartosek," said Mr. Kratochvil, "I recall one case that never went public: it was a case involving a baby. What happened was, one day this young woman came running up to Bartosek at the police station, she was the wife of an estate manager, name of Landa, and she was crying so hard she couldn't even catch her breath. Bartosek felt sorry for her, with her swollen nose and her face all splotchy from all those heartrending sobs, so he tried to calm her down, well, to the extent that an old bachelor can, anyway, and as much as a cop knows how. 'Jesus, young lady,' he told her, 'cut it out, he's not going to bite your head off, you know; go home and get a good night's sleep and then you'll be just fine. And if he's going to make a big stink about it, well, Hochman here will come with you and read him the riot act. But you, little lady, don't give your man any cause for jealousy.' That's pretty much how it went — What I mean is, that's pretty much how the police deal with most of these domestic tragedies.

"But this woman only shook her head and cried so much, it was an awful sight to see.

"So then Mr. Bartosek took a different tack: 'So he ran out on you, did he? The dirty, no-good rat. But look, he'll be back again; a bum like that's not worth making a fuss over!'

" 'S-sir,' the young woman wailed, 'you don't understand. Th-they snatched my little baby right out on the street!'

" 'Go on,' the captain said in total disbelief, 'why would anyone do that? It could have run away on its own.'

" 'How could she run away?' moaned the unhappy mama. 'Ruzenka's only three months old!'

" 'Aha,' said Mr. Bartosek, who didn't have a clue as to

when a kid learns to walk. 'And how, if you please, did they manage to snatch it away from you?'

"Slowly it was dragged out of her, but not before he'd sworn by every oath in the book that he would find the baby without fail, in the hopes of pacifying the poor woman. Here's what had happened: Mr. Landa had gone off to his office, and Mrs. Landova had made up her mind to embroider a nice little bib for Ruzenka. And while she was in the fabric shop, picking out embroidery thread, she left the buggy, and Ruzenka, sitting outside. And when Mrs. Landova went back out again, Ruzenka was gone and so was the buggy. That was all he could get out of the weeping mama after a good half-hour's questioning.

" 'Well then, Mrs. Landova,' Captain Bartosek finally said, 'that's not so bad. Look, who'd swipe a baby? It's more likely that a little brat gets mislaid someplace or other; I had a case like that once. If you ask me, a tiny tot like that wouldn't be worth much, I doubt if you could get much of a price for it. But the buggy'd be worth something, and the blankets — you had blankets in it, right? — well, they'd be worth something, too; something like that would be worth stealing. I think somebody just stole the buggy and those blankets. I'd say it was a woman, because probably a man with a buggy would look a little conspicuous. So this woman tossed the baby somewhere,' Bartosek said soothingly, 'because I ask you, what else would she do with it? I bet we have the little nipper back to you before the day is out. It'll turn up somewhere.'

" 'But Ruzenka's going to be so hungry,' the little mother bawled; 'she's already due for a feeding!'

" 'We'll get her something to drink,' the captain promised. 'You go back home now.' And he telephoned for a plainclothes officer to take the poor lady home.

"That afternoon the captain himself rang the doorbell of the young woman's house. 'Well, Mrs. Landova,' he reported, 'we've got the buggy; now the only thing missing is the baby. We found the buggy, empty, in the hallway of a house where there aren't any babies. Some woman had come there and told the apartment manager she only wanted to feed her baby, and after that she left. — Damnedest thing,' he went on, shaking his head, 'it turns out this person wanted to swipe the kidlet and nothing else. What I think, dear lady, is that since this person was so concerned about the little shrimp, there's no way she'd hurt it or take a bite out of it or anything. In short, you can stop worrying now, and that's that.'

" 'But I want my Ruzenka back,' Mrs. Landova screamed in desperation.

" 'Then you'll have to give us some photographs, missus, or a description of the baby,' the captain said authoritatively.

" 'But Captain, sir,' the young woman sobbed, 'you know that babies who aren't even a year old yet shouldn't be photographed! It's supposed to be bad for them, they say it stunts a child's growth — '

" 'Hm,' the captain said, 'then at least tell us what the little jigger looks like.'

"With this the young mama complied copiously. 'Everybody says my Ruzenka has such pretty hair, and this cute little nose, and such beautiful little eyes, and she weighs nine pounds, fourteen point three ounces, and she has this beautiful little bottom, and little folds on her chubby little legs — '

" 'What sort of folds?' the captain asked.

" 'You just want to kiss them,' the mama wept, 'and you should see her sweet little fingers and the way she smiles at her mommy — '

" 'Jesus, lady,' Mr. Bartosek roared, 'we can't possibly recognize her on the basis of that! Doesn't she have any identifying marks?'

" 'She has little pink ribbons on her bonnet,' the young woman sobbed. 'All baby girls have little pink ribbons! For the love of God, sir, find my Ruzenka for me!'

" 'What about her teeth?' Mr. Bartosek asked.

" 'She doesn't have any, she isn't even three months old! If you could only see how she smiled at her mommy!' Mrs.

Landova fell to her knees: 'Captain, sir, tell me that you'll find her for me!'

" 'There there, we'll be on the lookout,' mumbled Mr. Bartosek, totally perplexed. 'Please, get up! Look, the question is why this person stole her. Can you tell me what purpose a little sprout like that might serve?'

"Mrs. Landova's eyes stared at him in alarm. 'It is the most beautiful in the world,' she explained. 'Sir, have you no maternal feelings at all?'

"Mr. Bartosek, not wishing to acknowledge his insufficiencies, quickly said, 'I think that the only person who'd snatch a little bugger like that is a mother who's lost her own and wants another one. You know how it is when somebody takes your hat in a tavern: you just pick up another one and leave. So here's what I've arranged: I'm to be notified of any place in Prague where a three-month-old kiddie has died, and our people will go there and check it out, understand? Except that, given your description, we won't know how to identify her.'

" 'But *I'll* know her,' Mrs. Landa sobbed.

"The captain shrugged his shoulders. 'Even so,' he said, mulling it over, 'I'd be willing to bet that woman stole the little half-pint for a financial gain of some kind. Very little's stolen on account of love, dear lady; usually it's for money. My God, don't cry like that! We're doing all we can.'

"When Mr. Bartosek returned to the station, he said to his people, 'Listen, which one of you's got a three-month-old brat? Go bring it in here.' So the wife of one of the officers brings in her youngest. The captain has it unwrapped, and he says, 'Well, it's definitely wet. Anyway, look, it's got hair on its head and it's got wrinkles, too — this'll be its nose, right? — and it doesn't have any teeth, either — Tell me, young lady, please, can a little kid be identified on the basis of that?'

"The officer's wife hugged her youngest to her bosom. 'It's definitely my very own Manicka,' she said proudly. 'Can't you see, Captain, sir, that she's the very image of her father?'

"The captain, sir, stared at Officer Hochman, who was

simpering over the undeniable fuzziness and small, puckered snout of his heir and going 'cootchy-coo' with his fat finger and saying 'kee kee kitty-cat' — 'Well, I don't know,' the captain muttered, 'the nose looks a little different to me, but probably it's still growing. Hang on a minute, I'm going over to the park and see what some other of these small fry look like. What I mean is, any one of us can spot pickpockets and muggers right off, but little sprigs in blankets, we just don't have anything to do with them.'

"After an hour Bartosek returned, defeated. 'Listen, Hochman,' he said, 'it's a nightmare. All those babies look alike! How am I ever going to put together a description? We're looking for a three-month-old infant, female sex, with hair, a small nose, small eyes, and a wrinkled bottom; vital statistics: weighs nine pounds, fourteen point three ounces. Think that'll do it?'

" 'Captain, sir,' Officer Hochman said earnestly, 'I wouldn't put much faith in those ounces. Those little fellers weigh more one time and less the next, depending on how much they dump in their diapers.'

" 'Jesus Christ,' the captain groaned, 'how am I supposed to know that? A kid who can't talk isn't going to give us much of a statement! Listen,' he suddenly said with relief, 'suppose we dump this case on somebody else, maybe the Society for the Protection of Mothers and Infants!'

" 'Except we've got it down as a theft,' the officer objected.

" 'That's true,' the captain murmured. 'My God, if it was stolen watches or stolen anything else that's reasonable, I'd know how to deal with it. But I don't have the least idea how to go about looking for a stolen baby!'

"At that moment the door opened and a policeman came in, leading the weeping Mrs. Landova. 'Captain, sir,' he announced, 'this lady was trying to wrench a baby right out of the arms of some woman on the street, and she was creating a disturbance and making this huge racket the whole time. So I pulled her in.'

" 'For Christ's sake, Mrs. Landova,' the captain spluttered, 'what are you doing to us?'

" 'But that was my Ruzenka,' the young woman wailed.

" 'That wasn't any Ruzenka,' said the policeman. 'That woman was Mrs. Roubalova from Budecsky Street and that baby is her three-month-old boy.'

" 'Look here, you wretched creature,' Mr. Bartosek thundered. 'You get yourself mixed up in police business one more time and we quit the case cold, understand? — Wait,' he remembered suddenly, 'what sort of name does your baby answer to?'

" 'We call her Ruzenka,' sobbed her mother, 'Ruzenka Dudenka, deedle-deedle dee, ducky-poo, scooter, tiny pockets, angel baby, Daddy's little sweetheart, Mommy's girl, funny face, kissy missy, Her Wetness, baby bug, darling birdie, precious — '

" 'And she answers to all of those?' the captain asked, astounded.

" 'She understands all of them,' the little mama asssured him through her tears. 'And the way she smiles when you say hafhaf, bububu, tiddlymiddly, or teeteetee — '

" 'That's not going to help us very much,' the captain remarked. 'Unfortunately, Mrs. Landova, I have to tell you that, frankly, we're stymied. In those families where a child's death has been registered, your Ruzenka didn't show up. Our people have already checked out everything.'

"Mrs. Landova stood motionless, staring straight ahead. 'Captain,' she cried out in a sudden flash of hope, 'I will give ten thousand to whoever finds Ruzenka for me! Write down the amount: whoever tracks down my child for you will receive ten thousand!'

" 'I wouldn't do that, dear lady,' Mr. Bartosek said doubtfully.

" 'You haven't any feelings,' the young woman cried. 'I would give the whole world for my Ruzenka!'

" 'Well, if that's what you want,' Mr. Bartosek grumbled, thoroughly fed up, 'I'll announce it, but only if you'll for God's sake stop interfering with our work!'

" 'This is one tough case,' he sighed, the moment the door closed behind her. 'But wait, I know exactly what's going to happen next.'

"And that's exactly what happened. The next day, three plainclothes officers each brought in a screaming, three-month-old baby girl, and one of the men, it was that same Pistora, even stuck his head in the door with his toothy smile and said, 'Captain, sir, couldn't it have been a baby boy? I could get you a baby boy cheap!'

" 'That's what comes of having a reward,' Mr. Bartosek railed. 'Any minute now, it'll look like a foundling home in here. Damned case!'

" 'Damned case,' he said to himself in exasperation when finally he left for his bachelor's abode. 'I'd like to know how we're going to find that tyke now.'

"When he arrived home, he found that his cleaning woman, an outspoken, irreverent old scold, was glowing with rapture. 'Get over here, Captain,' she told him by way of a greeting, 'and take a look at your Baryna!'

"I should mention that a judge had given Mr. Bartosek this thoroughbred boxer bitch, Baryna, who'd been seduced by a certain German shepherd. You know, given all the different breeds there are, it's a wonder that dogs ever recognize other dogs as dogs. I just don't understand how a borzoi knows that a dachshund is a dog, too. We people differ only in language or religion, so it's easy for us to sniff each other out. Anyway, Baryna the boxer had nine puppies with this German shepherd, and now she was all curled up with them, wagging her tail and grinning away like crazy.

" 'Just look at her,' the cleaning woman blared, 'see how proud she is of those puppies? She's bragging about 'em, the sinful bitch! Bragging just like any mama!'

"Mr. Bartosek thought for a moment, and then he asked, 'Is that a fact? Is that what mamas do?'

" 'Course it is,' the cleaning woman trumpeted, 'why wouldn't they? Give it a try yourself, flatter any mama's baby!'

" 'This is interesting,' Mr. Bartosek muttered. 'All right, I'll give it a try myself.'

"One day later, every mother in greater Prague was in pure ecstasy. No sooner would they go out with their babies, in their arms or in buggies, but a uniformed cop or some plainclothesman in a bowler was right there next to them, making foo-foo faces at their darling kiddies and chucking them under the chin. 'That's a fine baby you've got there, lady,' they'd say, friendly as can be, 'how old is it? — ' In a nutshell, it was a day of pride and pleasure for each and every mama.

"And sure enough, at eleven o'clock in the morning, one of the plainclothesmen came to see Captain Bartosek with this pale, shaking woman. 'We've got her, sir,' the man announced obsequiously. 'I came across her pushing a buggy, and when I said to her, say, that's a fine baby you've got there, how old is it? — I'm telling you, she flashed me this evil look and stowed her baby right out of sight. So I told her, come with me, lady, and don't give me any trouble.'

" 'Fetch Mrs. Landova,' the captain said. 'And you, woman, tell me for God's sake why you stole that baby!'

"The woman didn't even try to deny it for very long, just reeled off her story straightaway. It turned out she was a single girl who had a baby by this man. Then not long ago the baby got a little sick to her stomach and cried for two nights. The third night this woman nursed her in bed and then dozed off afterwards; and when she woke up the next morning, it seems the baby was blue and dead. I don't know if that's possible," Mr. Kratochvil added with a degree of uncertainty.

"It's possible," Dr. Vitasek interrupted him to say. "In the first place, the mother wouldn't have had any sleep; second, the child probably had catarrh and had rejected the breast for a couple of days. Therefore the breast was too hard, and when the mother nursed her, the baby's nose slid down and she died from suffocation. That must have been what happened. Go on."

"Maybe that's how it was," Mr. Kratochvil continued. "When in the morning the woman saw that her baby was dead, she went out to tell a priest. But on the way she saw Mrs. Landova's buggy and that's when she got the idea that, if she could get hold of another baby, then this man would keep on making payments to her. Besides," Mr. Kratochvil said in embarrassment, turning red, "they say that the pressure from the milk can be really awful."

Dr. Vitasek nodded. "That's also true," he said.

"You realize," Mr. Kratochvil countered, "that I'm not knowledgeable about these matters. Anyway, that's why she stole the baby and the buggy and later left the buggy in the hallway of somebody else's house. And then she carried this Ruzenka home to take the place of her Zdenicka. But she had to be some kind of crackbrain or eccentric, because meanwhile she'd put her own dead baby in the fridge. They say she wanted to bury her or set her out somewhere during the night, but she couldn't get up the nerve to do it.

"Meanwhile, Mrs. Landova had arrived. 'Well, young lady,' Mr. Bartosek told her, 'here's your little nipper.'

"Tears spurted from Mrs. Landova's eyes. 'But that's not my Ruzenka,' she choked, 'Ruzenka was wearing a different cap!'

" 'The hell you say,' the captain shouted, 'unwrap it!' And since it was lying on his desk, he picked it up by the feet and said, 'Look, it's got folds on its rear!' But Mrs. Landova had already fallen to the floor on her knees and was kissing the piglet's tiny hands and feet. 'You're my own Ruzenka,' she cried through her tears, 'my tweety bird, deedle-deedle dee, funny face, baby-buns, you're my precious — '

" 'Please, lady,' Mr. Bartosek said, fuming, 'knock it off or I swear to God I'll get married myself. And as for that ten thousand, give it to an unmarried mother, understand?'

" 'Captain, sir,' Mrs. Landova said solemnly, 'hold my child and give it your blessing!'

" 'Do I have to?' grumbled Mr. Bartosek. 'How are you supposed to hold onto it? Oh, right. But it's starting to blubber! Take it back, lady, and get out of here — now!'

"And that's how it ended, the case involving the baby."

The Little Countess

"These crazy women," said Mr. Polgar, "sometimes they get up to things a person wouldn't believe. It was in the year nineteen or twenty, at any rate in those years when things were smoldering everywhere in this blessed central Europe of ours; people were just waiting for a scuffle to break out on one side or the other. This place was swarming with spies then, you can't imagine. I was in charge of contraband and counterfeit money in those days, and from time to time the army called on me to provide them with certain kinds of information. And that's when this business with that silly little countess occurred . . . let's call her Countess Mihalyova.

"One day, I don't remember exactly when, but anyway, the army received an anonymous letter telling them to keep an eye on correspondence sent to W. Manasses in care of General Delivery, Zurich. Later they intercepted just such a letter. Believe it or not, it was in cipher, in our Code Number 11, and in it was military information to the effect that a regiment from the 28th Infantry was garrisoned in Prague, that there was a rifle range in Milovice, and that our forces were armed with not only rifles but also bayonets: in short, silly information. But you know, the army is very strict about that sort of thing. If you let it leak to some foreign power that our infantry wears calico leggings manufactured by the Oberlander Company, you'd be brought before a military court and get at least a year for espionage. But that's all part of military prestige.

"Well, the army showed me this coded letter and also the anonymous tip. Listen, I'm no graphologist, but at first glance I said to myself, maybe I'm crazy, but both of these letters were written by the same hand. The anonymous tip is written in pencil, true — most anonymous letters are written in pencil, mind you. But it was obvious that this spy and this informer were one and the same person. 'You know what?' I told those soldiers, 'drop it, it's not worth your time; this spy is some sort of amateur; those military secrets of his are known to everyone who picks up a newspaper.' So much for that.

"About a month later, this captain from counterintelligence came to me, a slim, handsome fellow. 'Mr. Polgar,' he said, 'the strangest thing has happened. Not long ago I went dancing with this beautiful, dark-haired countess. She didn't speak Czech, but she danced divinely. And then today I received a very emotional letter from her. I mean, people don't do that sort of thing.'

" 'Be glad, young man,' I told him. 'Sounds to me like you're just lucky with women.'

" 'But, Mr. Polgar,' the captain said in despair, 'this letter is written in the same handwriting, with the same ink, and on the same paper as those intelligence reports to Zurich! I don't know what to do. Imagine what it's like for a fellow to have to inform on a woman who . . . hm, who is, to him . . . I mean,' he blurted out in agitation, 'well, she's a lady.'

" 'Indeed, Captain,' I said to him, 'those are chivalrous feelings. You will have to take this woman into custody and, given the seriousness of this matter, we'll have to condemn her to death; and you will have the honor of giving the command to the twelve soldiers: Fire! You know, life is so romantic. But unfortunately there is one obstacle: no W. Manasses exists in Zurich, and to date fourteen coded letters are waiting in his name at General Delivery in the Zurich post office. Just forget it, young man, and go dancing again with your dark-haired countess while you're still young.'

"For three days the captain suffered from a remorseful conscience to the point of losing weight, and only then did he go to his superior. Well, six soldiers left in a car and they arrested Countess Mihalyova and rummaged through her papers. They found the code there and all kinds of letters from foreign agents, the contents of which were, as they say, highly treasonable. Nevertheless, the countess refused to answer any questions at all, and her sister, a tadpole of sixteen, sat on a table with her knees to her chin so that everything showed, smoking cigarettes, flirting with the officers, and laughing like an idiot.

"When I heard they'd hauled in the little Mihalyova, I hurried down to military headquarters and I told them, 'For heaven's sake, let the silly girl go, nothing but trouble's going to come of this.' But they told me, 'Mr. Polgar, the Countess Mihalyova confessed to us that she is in the service of a foreign spy ring. This is a serious matter.' 'Well, the woman's lying,' I yelled. 'Mr. Polgar,' the colonel told me sternly, 'remember that you're speaking of a lady. Countess Mihalyova speaks the truth.' — You see how that woman had them bewitched? 'Damn you,' I swore, 'you'll get her the death sentence with your gallantry! The hell with your chivalrous sentiment! Can't you see that this woman put you on the trail of her treasonable activities herself and on purpose? The whole thing's a fake, don't believe a word she says!' But the soldiers only shrugged their shoulders in tragic regret.

"Naturally, the newspapers were full of the affair, even the foreign press. The aristocracy the world over got on their high horses and signed petitions, diplomats made formal protests, public opinion was indignant even as far away as England. But justice, you know, is unflinching. In short, the little countess of noble birth, due to the state of martial law, was brought before a military court. I went one last time to the army — by now I already had all the information I needed — and I told them, 'Turn her over to me and I'll see that she's punished.' No use, they wouldn't even hear me out. But I must say it was a beautiful trial. I sat there as moved as if I were watching a performance of *Camille*. The foolish little countess, slender as an arrow and dark as a Bedouin, admitted her guilt. 'I am proud,' she said, 'that I could serve the enemies of this land.' The judges were torn between gallantry and sense of duty, but it was no use. There were those treasonous letters and all the other foolishness, and the court, in view of the extraordinary extenuating and aggravat-

ing circumstances, could do nothing else but sentence Countess
Mihalyova to a year in prison. As I say, I've never seen such a
beautiful trial in my life. At its close the countess rose and in a
clear voice declared, 'Your Honor, I consider it my duty to state
that, in the course of my interrogation and arrest, all Czechoslovak officers behaved like true gentlemen.' By then I was nearly
blubbering out loud.

"But there you have it: when a man knows the truth, it
tickles his tongue and the truth must out. I don't think people
lie out of spite or stupidity, but from some kind of need or
irresistible urge. Imagine this Mihalyova, then, striking up an
acquaintance somewhere in Vienna with the famous Major
Westermann and falling head over heels in love. You know, of
course, who this Westermann is. He's the fellow who practices
heroism as a trade, and he's clanking with medals: the Maria
Theresa, the Leopold, the Iron Cross, the Turkish Star with
diamonds, and I don't know what all he collected during the war.
This Westermann, then, is a ringleader in every illegal monar-
chistic putsch, plot, and conspiracy imaginable. So the silly little
countess fell in love with this professional hero and most likely
wanted to win her knightly spurs in order to be worthy of him.
In short, for love of him she faked being a spy and then gave
herself away, all so she could look like a martyr for the glorious
cause. Only a woman would do such a thing.

"So I went to the prison where she was sitting out her
sentence, and I asked to talk with her. 'Madam,' I said to her,
'look: sitting in prison a whole year is a bore. They will grant you
a new trial if you would only confess how your so-called espionage came about.'

" 'Sir, I have already confessed,' the little countess told me
icily, 'and I have nothing more to say.'

" 'Jesus Christ,' I burst out, 'stop this foolishness. Major
Westermann has been married for fifteen years and he's got three
children.'

"The countess turned pale as ashes; to this day I've never
seen a woman grow ugly so suddenly. 'What . . . what is that to

me?' she finally said, but she had to force it out through clenched teeth.

" 'And it should also interest you,' I added, 'that your Major Westermann's real name is Vaclav Malek and he's a baker from Prostejov, do you understand me? Here's an old snapshot of him; you recognize him, don't you? For Christ's sake, Countess, why would you go to jail for a fraud like him?'

"The little Mihalyova sat there stiff as wood. All at once I saw that, in reality, she was an aging woman whose lifelong dream had suddenly collapsed. I felt so sorry for her and also somewhat ashamed. 'Madam,' I said quickly, 'let's at least agree that I'll send for your lawyer and you'll tell him — '

"The little Mihalyova rose, pale but taut as a bow. 'No,' she whispered, 'that is not necessary. I have nothing more to say.' And she left. But right outside the door she fell; they had to force her fingers apart, she had clamped them together so tightly.

"I bit my lips. Well, it's all out in the open now, I told myself; truth has been served. But what, in heaven's name, is the whole truth of the matter? All these disclosures and disillusionments, these bitter truths, disappointments, and painful experiences, these are only a pinch of the truth. The whole truth is greater. The whole truth is that love, pride, passion, and ambition are such great and foolish things, that every victim is heroic, and that human creatures in love are something beautiful and astonishing. This is the other and greater side of truth; but you would have to be a poet to see and tell about it."

*   *   *

"That's right," said police officer Horalek, "it always depends on how the truth is told. Last year we picked up an embezzler and took him to the lab to be fingerprinted. And let me tell you, that fellow leaped smack out of the second-floor window into the street and took off running. Our fingerprinter may be an old man, but at that moment he forgot it, leaped right out the window after him, and broke his foot. That got us good and mad, the way it always does when something happens to one of our men, and after we picked up that fellow we brought him back and roughed him up a little.

"Then when we were called as witnesses at the trial, this fellow's lawyer told us, 'Gentlemen, I don't want to ask you any inconvenient questions, and if you find them disagreeable you don't have to answer' — you know, that lawyer was smooth as a bottle of poison — 'but when my client tried to escape, you beat him up, didn't you?'

" 'Not at all,' I said, 'we only wanted to find out if he'd injured himself when he jumped, and when we saw he hadn't, well, we reproved him.'

" 'That must have been quite a reproof,' the lawyer said with a real polite smile. 'According to the police doctor's report, my client, as a result of that reproof, had three broken ribs as well as eight hundred square inches of bloody bruises, most of which were on his back.'

"All I did was shrug. 'He must have taken the reproof to heart,' I said; and it was just as well. The truth can be many things, you know, but you need to find the right words when you're telling it."

The Orchestra Conductor's Story

"Sometimes," said Mr. Dobes, "a bloody bruise or contusion like that can hurt more than a fracture; but only when the bruise is close to the bone. I know that; I'm an old soccer player and I've broken a rib, my collarbone, and a thumb. They just don't play it with the same fire these days, not like they did in my time. Anyway, last year I played one more game; us older gents wanted to show these modern youths what kind of tacticians we used to be. I was playing fullback again, just like fifteen or twenty years ago. But when I blocked the ball with my belly, my own goalie kicked me right in the — well, what's called the coccyx or *cauda equina*. What with all the fuss and bustle, I just swore for a second or two and then forgot about it. It didn't start to hurt until that night, and by the next morning I couldn't even move. No kidding, it hurt so bad I couldn't even lift my arm or sneeze — it's odd how everything in the human body's connected. So I just lay there on my back like a dead bug. I couldn't shift over on my side or even wiggle my big toe, nothing. All I could do was wheeze and moan about how terrible the pain was.

"I lay there in that sorry state the whole day and the next night, too. I couldn't sleep even for a second. It's curious how slowly time drags by when you can't move; it must be really hard, for instance, for someone who's dead and buried. I did some calculations in my head and then did some harder ones, I prayed, I even called to mind a few poems to make the time pass, but the night wouldn't end — All of a sudden, it must have been about two in the morning, I heard somebody running down the street as fast as his feet could take him; and then a whole bunch of people came charging after this somebody and you could hear maybe half-a-dozen voices yelling, 'Stop, I'm going to tear your guts out,' 'You rotten scoundrel,' 'You bastard,' and things like that. They caught him right under my window, and you wouldn't believe the free-for-all that started up, with some six pairs of legs, grunting and swearing, dull thuds like when somebody's whacking a head with a stick, panting, muttering, but not a single scream. Listen, that's not fair at all, six against one and pounding on him like a punching bag. I tried to get up out of bed and tell them it was just plain unsportsmanlike, but I was howling with pain; dammit, I couldn't move! Helplessness like that is appalling. I gritted my teeth and whimpered with rage like an animal. And then suddenly it was like a dam broke inside me and I leaped out of bed, grabbed a walking stick, and tore down the stairs. When I burst out on the street I was completely blind. I crashed into one fellow and, believe it or not, I started clobbering him with the stick; the rest ran off in all directions, but I've never in my life thrashed anybody like I did that dolt. Only later did I realize that tears of pain had been pouring down my face the whole time, and afterwards it took me a whole hour to make my way back upstairs to bed. But the very next morning I was walking again. I want to tell you, it was nothing short of a miracle. I'd like to know, though," added Mr. Dobes reflectively, "which one of them I clobbered like that; whether it was one of that lopsided gang or the one getting beat up by the others. But one on one, at least that's fair."

"Helplessness is indeed appalling," said Kalina, the conductor and composer, shaking his head. "I had an experience like that once, in Liverpool; I'd been invited to conduct a concert with their orchestra. You know, I can't speak a word of English; but we musicians can communicate among ourselves without a lot of talk, especially when we have a baton in hand. You just give it a tap, shout something, roll your eyes and wave your arms, and then start all over again. Even the most delicate feelings can be expressed that way: for example, when I do *this* with my arms, everyone knows that it means a mystical soaring and redemption-from-the-burdens-and-sorrows-of-life sort of thing. Well, when I arrived in Liverpool these English people were waiting for me at the station, and they took me off to a hotel so that I could rest. But after I'd had a bath, I went out by myself to have a look at the city. And while I was wandering around I got lost.

"Whenever I go someplace new, the first thing I do is to look for a river; a river gives you a sense of what I would call the orchestration of the city. On one side you have all the hubbub of the streets, the drums and tympani, the woodwinds and brasses, and on the other side of the river are the strings, a *pianissimo* of violins and harps; that way you hear the entire city at once. But that river in Liverpool, I don't know its name, but it's all yellow and nasty; and let me tell you, that river booms and thunders, roars, bellows and clatters, rumbles and hoots with steamships, tugboats, packetboats, warehouses, shipyards, and cranes. You know, I have an immense love of ships, whether it's a black potbellied tug or a red-painted freighter or those white trans-atlantic liners. So I said to myself, well then, the ocean's bound to be just around the corner somewhere, I'll go take a look at it. And I started walking downstream along the bank of the river. I trotted along for a good two hours, past nothing but warehouses and pilings and docks; every once in a while I would catch sight of a ship as tall as a cathedral, or three fat, slanting funnels. There was a stench of fish, horse sweat, jute, rum, wheat, coal, iron —

Liverpool

I don't know whether you know this, but a huge pile of iron has an overwhelming, unmistakably iron-like smell. I was absolutely delighted. But by that time night was already falling, and I had come to a sort of sandy bank, a lighthouse was shining opposite me and tiny lights were drifting to and fro — it could well have been the ocean. I sat there on a stack of planks and felt so wonderfully alone and lost, listening to the lap and murmur of the water, I could have bayed with blissful longing. Then two people approached, a man and a woman, but they didn't see me. They sat down with their backs to me and started conversing in low tones — if I'd understood English, I would have coughed to let them know I could hear. But since I didn't know a word of English other than 'hotel' and 'shilling,' I kept quiet.

"At first, their talk was rather *staccato*. Then the man began to explain something slowly and quietly, as if he were reluctant to let the words escape, and finally his words came pouring out in a rush. The woman cried out in horror and said something to him with great agitation; but he gripped her hand until she whimpered, and then he began to urge her, forcing the sounds out between his teeth. Believe me, this was not an amorous conversation, a musician can recognize that. A lover's attempts at persuasion have quite a different cadence and don't sound so tense — a conversation between lovers is a deep cello, but this was a high-pitched double bass, played in *presto rubato*, in a single key, as if the man were repeating the same phrase over and over again. I began to feel rather alarmed: whatever the man was proposing was something evil.

"The woman began to weep softly, and several times she cried out in protest, as if she were trying to restrain him. Her voice was a bit like a clarinet, with a woody resonance that didn't sound overly young. But the man's voice became harsher and more sibilant, as if he were threatening or commanding her. The woman's voice began to plead desperately and she gasped with horror, the way a person gasps when you apply an ice-cold compress, and I could hear her teeth chattering. Then the man's voice began to murmur in a very deep, pure bass, almost loving in tone. The woman's weeping faded into short, passive sobs, which indicated that her resistance had broken. But then the amorous sound of the bass rose again and disjointedly, deliberately, insistently, piled on phrase after phrase. At this the woman's voice just sobbed and wailed helplessly, and there was no longer any resistance in it, only a frantic fear — not fear of the man, but a tremulous, anticipatory dread of something to come. And then the man's voice sank down again to a consoling murmur, laced with gentle threats. The woman's weeping changed to dispirited, defenseless sighs; and in a cold whisper the man asked some questions to which she apparently replied with a nod, for he was no longer insistent.

"Then the two of them got up and left, each in a different direction.

"I must tell you that I don't believe in hunches, but I do believe in music. When I listened to those two voices that night, I knew with absolute certainty that the bass was persuading the clarinet to take part in some appalling act. I knew that the clarinet would return home utterly subdued and would do whatever the bass had ordered her to do. I had heard it, and hearing words is better than understanding them. I knew that preparations had been made for a crime of some sort, and I knew what sort of crime it was. I could tell by the horror those two voices conveyed: it was in the timbre of those voices, in the cadence, the tempo, the intervals, the rests — you see, music is precise,

more precise than speech. The clarinet was too simple, too uncomplicated to carry anything out by itself; it could only assist, it could only hand over a key or open a door. The harsh, deep bass would perform the actual deed, while the clarinet stood by, choking with terror. I ran back to the city, convinced that something terrible was going to happen and that I had to do something to prevent it. It's a dreadful feeling, when you're afraid you'll arrive too late.

"At last I saw a policeman on a street corner, and I rushed up to him, sweating and completely out of breath. 'Officer,' I gasped, 'any moment now, right in this city, there's going to be a murder!'

"The policeman shrugged his shoulders and said something to me that I couldn't comprehend. Damn, I suddenly remembered, he can't understand a word I'm saying!

" 'Murder,' I yelled at him, as if he were deaf, 'don't you understand? They're going to kill some woman who's living alone! The maid or housekeeper is part of the plot — Good Lord,' I roared, 'do something!'

"The policeman only shook his head and said something that sounded like 'yurvay.'

" 'Officer,' I tried to explain in desperation, and I was shaking with rage and horror the entire time, 'that wretched woman's going to let her lover into the building, you can bet your life on it! You *can't* let it happen! Search for her!' Just then I realized that I didn't even know what the woman looked like; but even if I did, of course, I couldn't have told him. 'Jesus Christ,' I shouted, 'it's absolutely inhuman to let this happen!'

"The English policeman looked me over carefully and tried to soothe me. I clutched my head in my hands. 'You fool,' I screamed, beside myself with desperation, 'I'll find her myself!'

"I know, it was sheer madness, but look, you have to do *something* when someone's life is at stake. I ran all over Liverpool that night, to see if I couldn't spy somebody, somewhere, trying to sneak into a house. It's such a strange city, so appallingly dead at night . . . Towards morning I sat down on a curb and sobbed with fatigue. That's where a policeman found me, said 'yurvay,' and took me back to my hotel.

"I don't know how I conducted the rehearsal that morning. But when I finally threw the baton to the floor and dashed out to the street, the newsboys were shouting the evening papers' headlines. I bought one — across the top, in huge letters, was the word MURDER, and underneath it was a photograph of some white-haired woman. Evidently 'murder' is the English word for what I was trying to say."

The Death of Baron Gandara

"Listen," Mr. Mensik told them, "those cops in Liverpool were bound to catch that murderer; it was a professional job, and they usually do just fine with those. What they do is round up all the notorious bad guys that are running around loose, and then it's, all right, boys, let's hear what kind of alibi you have this time. And when somebody hasn't got one, he's it. What the police don't like is dealing with unknown entities. I'd say they make a point of hauling in well-known or notorious big-time criminals. Once they get somebody like that in their hands, they get his vital statistics and take his fingerprints, and then he's their man; from that time on, they can turn to him in confidence whenever something happens. They can go to him as an old acquaintance, the same way a man goes to his barber or his tobacconist. It's worse when some amateur or greenhorn, let's say you or me, commits a crime; it's that much harder for the police to get their hands on him.

"I've got a relative down at police headquarters, his name is Pitr and he's my wife's uncle. And what Uncle Pitr says is, if it's a robbery, then some kind of professional did it; but if it's a murder, then it's bound to be someone in the family. He has a very fixed point of view, does Uncle Pitr. For instance, he claims that a man hardly ever murders a stranger, because it's not that easy. The opportunity to do it's much more likely to be found among people he already knows; and in his own house, the opportunity's right in the palm of his hand. When they assign a murder case to Uncle Pitr, he finds out who could have done it with the least bother, and that's who he goes after. 'Look, Mensik,' he says, 'I don't have a scrap of imagination or inventiveness. Anyone at headquarters can tell you I'm the biggest bonehead there. The thing is, you see, I'm simple-minded the same way a murderer is. Whatever I think of is just as ordinary, everyday, and stupid as his motive, scheme, and deed. And by and large, that's exactly how I catch him out.'

"I don't know if any of you recalls the murder of that foreigner, Baron Gandara. He was a sort of mysterious soldier of fortune. He had hair black as a crow's and was handsome as the devil. He lived in one of those nice houses in Grabovka, and some of the things that used to go on there you wouldn't .want to know about. Anyway, one morning these two pistol shots were heard, some sort of alarm went off, and later they found the baron in the garden, shot to death. His wallet was gone, but otherwise there weren't any clues to speak of; in short, a mystifying case of the first order. They assigned the murder to Uncle Pitr because he wasn't working on much of anything else, but the chief also told him, 'Admittedly, Lieutenant, this case isn't your usual style, but see to it that you prove you aren't yet ripe for a pension.' So Uncle Pitr grumbled that he would see to it and took off for the scene of the crime. Needless to say, he found nothing, swore at the detectives, and went back to sit at his desk again so he could light his pipe. Anyone seeing him there in that stinking cloud of smoke would suppose that Lieutenant Pitr was deep in thought about the case, but that would be a big mistake. Uncle Pitr wouldn't have been deep in thought, because he's basically opposed to thinking. A murderer doesn't think either, he says; either something occurs to him or it doesn't.

"Everyone else at headquarters felt sorry for Uncle Pitr. It isn't his type of case, they said, it's a shame to waste beautiful material like that on Pitr; Pitr does old women who kill off their nephews or their maids' skirt-chasing boyfriends. One colleague, Dr. Mejzlik, strolled over to Uncle Pitr as if by chance, sat down by his desk, and said, 'What's up, Lieutenant, anything new with the Gandara case?'

" 'It's got to be a nephew or something,' said Uncle Pitr.

" 'Lieutenant,' said Dr. Mejzlik, wanting to be helpful, 'this case might be a bit different. I want to remind you that Baron

Gandara was an international spy; who knows what kinds of strange things are going on here? — It puzzles me that his wallet was missing. If I were in your place, I'd take care to — '

"Uncle Pitr shook his head. 'Mejzlik,' he said, 'we've each got our own methods. The first thing is to find out if there are any relatives who could inherit anything.'

" 'For another thing,' said Dr. Mejzlik, 'we know that Baron Gandara was a high-stakes gambler who took a lot of chances. You don't want to get mixed up with that crowd, Lieutenant, you don't have the background for it; all you play is dominoes with Mensik. If you want, I can ask around to see who played with him most recently — you know, maybe what we have here is some kind of debt of honor — '

"Uncle Pitr frowned. 'Listen,' he said, 'that means nothing to me. I never had any dealings with those high-class circles, and at my age I'm not going to start now. Forget about debts of honor, I never had a case like that in my life. If it isn't a family murder, it'll be robbery and murder; and somebody from the household had to have done it. That's pretty much how it happens. Maybe the cook has a nephew or something.'

" 'Or Gandara's chauffeur,' Mejzlik offered, to needle Uncle.

"Uncle Pitr shook his head. 'Chauffeurs,' he said, 'never had a part in any of my cases. I can't ever remember a chauffeur pulling off a robbery and murder. Chauffeurs booze it up and steal gas; but as for murdering somebody, that I've yet to see. Look, Mejzlik, I stick by what I know. When you get as old as I am — '

"Dr. Mejzlik was losing his patience. 'Lieutenant,' he blurted out, 'there's still a third possibility here. Baron Gandara had an intimate relationship with a married woman, the most beautiful woman in Prague. It's possible that this is a crime of passion.'

" 'It happens,' Uncle Pitr agreed. 'I've had five murders like that. And what does the little lady's husband do?'

" 'Big businessman,' Dr. Mejzlik replied. 'Huge company.'

"Uncle Peter turned this over in his mind. 'Then that

doesn't get us anywhere either,' he said. 'I've never had a case where a big businessman shot somebody. Swindling, that's what they do; but crimes of passion, that's done in other circles. You're wrong there, friend.'

" 'Lieutenant,' Dr. Mejzlik continued, 'you know how Baron Gandara made his living? Blackmail. Believe me, that man knew horrible things about — well, about a whole lot of very wealthy people. It's worth considering, the number of people who might have an interest in — hm, in clearing him out of the way.'

" 'Sure,' Uncle Pitr said, 'I had a case like that once, but we couldn't prove it; it was a total washout and a disgrace to the force. I'm not getting my fingers burned a second time with a case like that, not on your life. Your ordinary robbery and murder suits me just fine. I don't like sensation and scandal. When I was your age, I too thought that someday I'd crack some fabulous criminal case, ambition and all that. It passes with the passing years, son. Later on, you realize that most cases turn out to be pretty ordinary — '

" 'Baron Gandara is no ordinary case,' Dr. Mejzlik objected. 'I know him: a gentleman rogue, dark as a gypsy — the best-looking scoundrel I ever saw. A mystery man. A demon. A cardsharp. A fake baron. Listen, a man like that doesn't die in any ordinary way; not because of any ordinary murder, either. Something else is going on here. A lot of mysterious things.'

" 'Then they shouldn't have given the case to me,' Uncle Pitr muttered in disgust. 'I don't have a head for mysterious things. I like plain, ordinary murders, like a tobacconist's murder. Look, I'm not about to learn new methods. Since they gave the case to me, I'm going to handle it my way; and as far as I'm concerned it's an ordinary robbery and murder. If they'd given it to you, it would have turned into some kind of crime sensation, a torrid romance, or a political scandal — You've got a flair for romance, Mejzlik. You'd have worked up a wonderful case with the material we've got here. Too bad they didn't give it to you.'

" 'Listen,' Dr. Mejzlik burst out, 'you wouldn't have any objection, would you, if I . . . strictly on my own . . . pursued this case? The thing is, I have a lot of contacts who know a great deal about this Gandara — Naturally I'd put any information they gave me at your disposal,' Mejzlik added quickly. 'It would still be your case — how about it?'

"Uncle Pitr snorted in irritation. 'Thank you kindly,' he said, 'but it wouldn't work. Your style's different from mine; you'd go about it in an entirely different way than me. Best not to mix things up. What would I do with your spies, gamblers, fancy ladies, and all those bigwigs? That's no use to me, my young friend. If I'm the one that has to do this, then it's going to be my own grubby little run-of-the-mill case . . . People do what they know how to do.'

"At that moment there was a knock and a detective entered. 'Lieutenant,' he reported, 'what we found out is that the caretaker at Gandara's house has a twenty-year-old unemployed nephew living at 1451 Vrsovice, but he often stayed at the caretaker's. And the maid at the house has a boyfriend who's a soldier, but right now he's on maneuvers.'

" 'Good,' said Uncle Pitr. 'Run over and have a look at the caretaker's nephew, search the place, and bring him back here.'

"Two hours later, Uncle Pitr had Gandara's wallet in his hand, which they'd found under the young man's bed. That night they caught the lad out on a drinking spree, and in the morning he confessed that he'd shot Gandara so that he could steal the wallet; there was more than fifty thousand in it.

" 'You see, Mensik,' Uncle Pitr told me afterwards, 'it's just like the case with that old lady on Kremencova Street; the caretaker's nephew was the killer there, too. But damn it, son, when I think what might have happened if they'd given that case to Mejzlik, what he would've done with that material! I just don't have the imagination for it, that's all.'

The Breach-of-Promise Man

"To tell you the truth," Detective Holub said and then coughed politely, "we policemen don't much care for unusual, out-of-the-ordinary cases, and we don't much care for beginners, either. An old, accomplished crook, though, that's a different story. In the first place, we know right away he's the one who did it, because it's his specialty; in the second place, we know where to find him; and in the third place, he doesn't kick up a fuss and try to deny it, because he already knows it won't do him any good. I tell you, friends, it's a pleasure to work with an experienced man like that. And I can tell you too that, even in jail, the old, skilled practitioners are the most popular and trustworthy. It's the rookies and the random lawbreakers that're the worst grumblers and whiners, and nothing's ever good enough for them. But an old-timer knows that prison's just one of the risks of the trade, so there's no point in being a nuisance either to himself or to anybody else. But that's getting away from the story.

"About five years ago, we started getting reports from here, there, and everywhere that an unknown breach-of-promise man was raising hell all over the Bohemian countryside. According to descriptions, he was an older man, stout and bald, with five gold teeth. He went by the names of Muller, Prochazka, Simek, Sebek, Sinderka, Bilek, Hromadka, Pivoda, Bergr, Bejcek, Stoces, and who knows how many others. Well, dammit, the description didn't check out with any of the breach-of-promise con men we knew, so it had to be someone new to the business. Our captain sent for me and said: 'Holub, you're on train duty, so wherever you go, I want you to be on the lookout for a fellow with five gold teeth.' Fair enough, I began to look at people's teeth on trains, and in two weeks' time I bagged three fellows with five gold teeth. They had to show me their I.D., of course, and damned if one of them wasn't a school inspector and another a member of parliament. Friends, don't even ask about the chewing-out I got, first from them and then from the boss. It made me mad as hell, and I decided then and there that I was going to get my hands on the rascal. True, it wasn't really my case, but my heart was set on revenge.

"So I went off on my own to see all those hoodwinked orphans and widows who'd been bilked out of their money by this gold-toothed crook with his promises of marriage. You wouldn't believe the amount of gabbling and sniveling those poor, abused orphans and widows were capable of. But at least they all agreed that he was a solid, well-spoken gentleman and that he had gold teeth and that he showed a fit and proper enthusiasm for family life. But not a one of them had even taken his fingerprints — it's shocking, really, how naive and trusting these females are. The eleventh victim — that was at Kamenice — told me in tears that the gentleman had been to see her three times. He always arrived by train about ten-thirty in the morning, and when he'd left for the last time, with her money in his pocket, he'd looked at the numbers on her little house and said in surprise: 'Why, look at that, Miss Marenka, it must be God's own will that we're going to get married. Your house number is 618, and I always take the 6:18 train when I come to see you. Isn't that a good sign?' — When I heard that, I said, 'Miss, it's a very good sign indeed.' And I immediately pulled out the timetable and looked for the station where a train leaving at 6:18 connected with the train that got into Kamenice at 10:35. When I'd checked everything out and matched it all up, I saw that most likely he'd taken the train from Bystrice-Novoves. A railway detective, you know, has to be up to speed on trains.

"Needless to say, on my next day off I went to Bystrice-Novoves and asked if there might be a stout gentleman with a lot of gold in his mouth that traveled from that station often enough for them to notice. 'There is,' said the stationmaster, 'and it's Mr. Lacina, a commercial traveler who lives down that street. He came back here from somewhere only yesterday evening.' So off I went to find this Mr. Lacina. A tidy, spick-and-span little woman came to the door, and I asked her, 'Does Mr. Lacina live here?' 'That's my husband,' she said, 'but he's taking a nap after lunch right now.' 'No matter,' I said, and in I went. On the sofa lay a man in his shirt sleeves, and when he saw me he said, 'Well, if it isn't Mr. Holub. Give him a chair, Ma.'

"At that moment all my anger vanished. Why, it was Plichta, the old sweepstakes grifter, you know, the one who pulled off all those lottery scams. He'd already been behind bars at least ten times. 'Greetings, Plichta,' I said, 'given up on lotteries, have you?'

" 'You bet,' said Plichta, and he sat up on the sofa. 'The thing is, Mr. Holub, there's a whole lot of running around involved, and I'm not a young man anymore. Fifty-two years, a man likes to sit in one place. No more of this going from house to house for me.'

" 'And that's how come you're trying your hand at the old breach-of-promise game, you old phony,' I said to him.

"Plichta just sighed. 'Mr. Holub,' he said, 'A man's got to do something. You know, the last time I was inside, my teeth rotted on me; I think it was all those beans that did it. So I had to get 'em fixed, see. Mr. Holub, you wouldn't believe the benefits a man derives from gold teeth. It builds your confidence, see, and your digestion picks up and you start putting on weight. The point is, see, folks like us have to work with what we've got.'

" 'And where's the money?' I asked him. 'I've got you down for eleven separate scams, for a net profit of two hundred and sixteen thousand. Where is it?'

" 'But, Mr. Holub,' said Plichta, 'all that belongs to my wife, see. Business is business. I've got nothing except what's on me: that's six hundred and fifty in bills, a gold watch, and my gold teeth. Ma, I'll be going off to Prague with Mr. Holub. Mr. Holub, I have some installments to pay on those teeth, in the amount of three hundred. I'll just leave it here.'

" 'And you owe your tailor a hundred and fifty,' his wife reminded him.

" 'So I do,' said Plichta. 'Mr. Holub, I'm a real stickler when it comes to accuracy. There's nothing like having everything shipshape, see. Keep things shipshape and know what you owe. Once you're all paid up, you can look people straight in the eye. It's all part of the racket, Mr. Holub. Ma, give my overcoat a quick lick with the brush, so I can do you proud in Prague. All right, Mr. Holub, we can leave now.'

"As it turned out, Plichta got five months. Most of those women, if you please, swore to the jury that they'd given him the money of their own free will and that they'd forgiven him for what he'd done. There was only one old lady who wouldn't let bygones be bygones, and she was a rich widow he took for only five thousand.

"Six months later I heard that two more breach-of-promise swindles had been pulled off. That'll be Plichta, I said to myself, but I didn't bother doing anything about it, because I was headed for the train station in Pardubice at the time. They had a trunk-man operating out of there, you know, one of those fellows that steals luggage from the platform. And since my family was at a summer cottage in a village about an hour or so from Pardubice, I'd packed a little bag for them with some sausages and other kinds of smoked meat; it's hard to get things like that in a village, you know. And on my way to get the connection at Pardubice, I walked on through the train out of habit. And in one of the compartments who should I see but Plichta, sitting with an elderly lady and explaining something or other about what a corrupt place this world is.

" 'Hello, Plichta,' I said, 'promising marriage to somebody again?'

"Plichta turned red and straightaway asked the lady to excuse him, because he had some business to talk over with the gentleman. And when he joined me out in the corridor, he said reproachfully, 'Mr. Holub, you shouldn't of done that to me in front of strangers. All you had to do was wink and I'd of come on out. What do you want me for?'

" 'We've got a couple more cases on our hands, Plichta,' I told him. 'But I've got something else to do today, so I'll hand you over to the federal agents when we get to Pardubice.'

" 'Look, Mr. Holub, don't do that to me. I'm used to you by now, and you know me, too — I'd rather come with you. Come on, Mr. Holub, just for old times' sake.'

" 'Can't be done,' I said. 'I'm off to see my family, and that's a good hour from Pardubice. What would I do with you in the meantime?'

" 'I'll go with you, Mr. Holub,' Plichta offered. 'At least that'll help pass the time for you on the way.'

"Well, that's what happened. Plichta came with me, and after we'd left Pardubice he said, 'Say, Mr. Holub, I'll carry that little bag for you. Look here, Mr. Holub, I'm older than you are, and when you talk to me in front of other folks in a policeman-like way, it gives the wrong impression.'

So I introduced him to my wife and sister-in-law as my old friend Mr. Plichta. Listen, my sister-in-law is a good-looking girl of twenty-five, and Plichta talked so nice and respectfully and gave the children candy — well, to cut a long story short, after we'd had some coffee Mr. Plichta proposed that he go for a stroll with the young lady and the children; and he winked at me as if to say that we men understand each other and I'd probably want some time alone with my missus. That's the sort of gentlemanly person he was. And when they got back an hour later, the children were hanging on to Mr. Plichta's hands, my sister-in-law was blushing like a rose, and when we left she squeezed his hand for quite a while.

" 'Listen, Plichta,' I said to him afterwards, 'what kind of ideas were you putting into Manicka's head?'

" 'It always happens like that, Mr. Holub,' Plichta said almost sadly. 'I can't help it. It's the teeth that do it. They're always getting me in trouble, and that's a fact. I never flirt with the ladies, it wouldn't do for a man of my age; but that, you see, just attracts them all the more. Sometimes I think the ladies don't like me so much for myself as for the possible pickings, because they take me for a man of means.'

"When we got back to the station at Pardubice, I said to him, 'Plichta, I'm going to turn you over to the federal agents now, because I have to investigate a theft.'

" 'Mr. Holub,' Plichta begged me, 'why don't I just sit here in the restaurant while you go investigate? I'll have a cup of tea and read the newspaper — here's my money, fourteen thousand and a bit of change. And I can't run away without money — why, I couldn't even pay my bill.'

"So I let him take a seat in the station restaurant and went off to do my job. An hour later I glanced through the window. He was sitting where I'd left him, reading a newspaper with a gold pince-nez on his nose. Maybe half an hour after that I was ready, and I went to fetch him. By then he was sitting at the next table with a strikingly buxom blonde, scolding the waiter in a very dignified manner for putting spoiled milk in her coffee. When he saw me, he took his leave of the woman and came over to where I was waiting. 'Mr. Holub,' he said, 'couldn't you give me, say, a week before you run me in? There's some business here I'd like to take care of.'

" 'Very rich?' I asked him.

"Plichta gestured with his hand. 'Mr. Holub,' he whispered, 'she's got a factory; and she badly needs an experienced man to advise her now and then. Right now she has to pay for some kind of new machinery.'

" 'Fancy that,' says I. 'Come on, then, I'll introduce you.' And I went over to where she was sitting. 'Hello there, Lojzicka,' I said, 'still chasing older gentlemen, I see.'

"The blonde turned red to her roots and said, 'Heaven help me, Mr. Holub, I didn't know this gentleman was a friend of yours.'

" 'Better make yourself scarce,' I told her. 'There's a certain Mr. Dundr who'd like a word with you. He calls what you're up to fraud, you know.'

"Plichta looked miserable. 'Mr. Holub,' he said, 'I'd never in my born days have believed that she was a swindler, too!'

" 'She is,' I told him, 'and on top of that, she's no better than she ought to be. You might as well know, she finagles elderly gents out of their money with false promises of marriage.'

"Plichta paled instantly. 'Downright disgusting,' he spat, 'that's what it is. Catch me trusting women after this! Mr. Holub, that's the absolute limit!'

" 'So wait here,' I told him, 'and I'll get you a ticket to Prague. Second or third class?'

" 'Mr. Holub,' Plichta protested, 'that's a waste of money. Being as I'm in custody, I get to ride for free, right? Then let the government pay for it. A man in my position has to watch every penny.'

"Plichta cursed that woman all the way to Prague; it's the deepest moral indignation I've ever come across. When we got off at Prague, Plichta said, 'Mr. Holub, I know it'll be seven months this time, and prison food don't agree with me. Look, what I'd really like is one last proper meal. That fourteen thousand you took was all I got from my last job — so let me have at least one good dinner out of it. And I'd like to square accounts for the coffee at your place.'

"So off we went together to one of the better restaurants. Plichta ordered pot roast and drank five beers, and I paid for it out of his stash, while he checked the bill three times to make sure our waiter hadn't cheated us.

" 'That's it, and now off to the station,' I said.

" 'Just a moment, Mr. Holub,' said Plichta. 'I had a lot of overhead in connection with that last job. There were four trips there and back at forty-eight apiece, which comes to three hundred eighty-four.' Then he put on his pince-nez and did some calculations on a piece of paper. 'Then there's out-of-pocket expenses, say thirty per day — I have to keep up appearances, Mr. Holub, it's all part of my stock in trade. That's a hundred and twenty. Then I gave the young lady a bunch of flowers for thirty-five, that's just common courtesy, you know.

The engagement ring cost two hundred and forty — it was just gold-plated, Mr. Holub. If I wasn't an honest man, I'd say it was gold and chalk it up at six hundred, wouldn't I? Then I bought her a fancy cake for thirty; after which we have the postage for five letters, at one each for a total of five, and the ad by which I got acquainted with her cost me eighty. That comes to a grand total of eight hundred and ninety-four, Mr. Holub. What you really ought to do is deduct that amount from the total, and I'll leave the money with you for the time being. I like to keep everything shipshape, Mr. Holub; at the very least we have to cover expenses. All right, that's it. We can go now."

"But when we were in the entryway to police headquarters, Plichta suddenly thought of something else: 'Mr. Holub, I gave the young lady a bottle of perfume, too. So that's another twenty to my credit.'

"Then he blew his nose fastidiously and, his mind at ease, let them take him away."

The Ballad of Juraj Cup

"It really can happen, gentlemen," said Captain Havelka of the regional police, "I mean that, sometimes, criminals turn out to be surprisingly honest and conscientious. I could tell you about a number of cases that prove the point, but the strangest is the Juraj Cup case. It happened when I was stationed way out east in Jasina, in Ruthenia.

"One night in January we were drinking it up at the Jew's place; there was a district manager, a railroad superintendent, and similar sorts of higher-ups taking care of government business in those remote parts; and, of course, gypsies. Listen, these gypsies, I don't know what stock they come from, but I think it's the tribe of Ham. When a gypsy plays the fiddle, coming closer and closer, playing softer and softer, those wretched devils, when they work their magic on your ears that way, it's . . . it's like . . . it's like they're dragging your soul right out of your body. I'm telling you, that music of theirs, it's unearthly, it's depraved. And when they got right up next to me I blubbered, I bellowed like a stag, I rammed my bayonet through the table, I smashed glasses, I sang and banged my head against the wall, I wanted to kill someone or make love — gentlemen, that's the kind of hell-raising a man gets up to when gypsies cast a spell on him. And right when I was at my wildest, up comes the Jew innkeeper to say that some Ruthenian was waiting for me out in front of the tavern.

" 'Let him wait or let him come back tomorrow,' I shouted, 'I'm weeping for my youth and burying my dreams. I'm making love to a lady, a noble, beautiful lady — play, you gypsy thieves, play on and drive the sorrow from my soul' — Well, that's the way I was carrying on; you know, it all goes with the music, the suffering, and that awesome drinking. About an hour later the innkeeper comes back again and says the Ruthenian's still outside there in the freezing cold, waiting. But I was still weeping for my youth and hadn't finished drowning my sorrows in Tokay. So I just waved my hand like Genghis Khan, as much as to say, it makes no difference to me, just play on, gypsies. And what happened after that, believe me, I don't know, but when I left the tavern at dawn it was so cold out that the snow squeaked and tinkled like glass, and there in front of the place stood the Ruthenian in white bast shoes, white britches, and white sheepskin. When he saw me, he bowed to the waist and said something in a hoarse voice.

" 'What do you want, shepherd,' I say to him, 'waste my time and I'll crack your jaw.'

" 'Your lordship,' says the Ruthenian, 'the mayor of Volova Lehota sent me here. Marina Matejova's been killed.'

"That sobered me up a bit. Volova Lehota, that was a village, or rather a lonely little clump of thirty huts, fifteen miles or so back up in the mountains; in other words, no pleasure jaunt in winter. 'For God's sake,' I yelled, 'who killed her?'

" 'I did, your lordship,' the Ruthenian said humbly. 'My name is Juraj Cup, son of Dmitri Cup.'

" 'And you're here to give yourself up?' I fired at him.

" 'The mayor told me to,' Juraj Cup said resignedly. 'Juraj, he said, go tell the police you killed Marina Matejova.'

" 'And why did you kill her?' I yelled.

" 'God told me to,' said Juraj, as if it were the most natural thing in the world. 'The Lord commanded: kill Marina Matejova, your beloved sister, by an evil spirit possessed.'

" 'Damn you,' I said, 'how did you get here from Volova Lehota?'

" 'With God's help,' Juraj Cup said devoutly. 'The Lord protected me so I would not perish in the snow. Praise be to His name.'

"Listen, if you knew what a blizzard's like in the Carpathians; if you knew what it's like when there's a good six feet of snow on the ground; if you could have seen that poor, puny little fellow Juraj Cup and how he'd waited for six hours in front of the tavern in that terrible cold to turn himself in for murdering Marina Matejova, God's unworthy handmaiden, I don't know what you would have done. But what I did was cross myself, and Juraj Cup crossed himself, and then I arrested him. The next thing I did was wash my face in the snow and strap on my skis and, along with an officer named Kroupa, I set off into the mountains for Volova Lehota. And if the commander-in-chief of the regional police himself had stopped me and said: Havelka, you're crazy, you won't get anywhere, you're putting your life in jeopardy in weather like this, I'd have saluted him and said: With all due respect, sir, the Lord commanded it. And I'd have gone. And Kroupa would've, too, because he's from Zizkov; and I never met a man from Zizkov who didn't want to jump right in when there's some kind of grandstanding or harebrained caper afoot. So we left.

"I'm not going to describe that trip of ours. I'll only tell you that, by the end of it, Kroupa was sobbing like a child with fear and exhaustion, and that twenty times we told ourselves we were done for and couldn't last a minute longer. And that it took us eleven hours, from one night to the next, to go those fifteen miles. I'm only saying this so you'll get an idea of how it was. A policeman's got the constitution of a horse, gentlemen, but when he falls down in the snow and whimpers that he can't go on, well, it simply means there's no way to describe what it was like. But I kept on walking as if in a dream, and kept on telling myself that Juraj Cup had made it, Juraj Cup, a little pocketknife of a man, and on top of that he'd waited six hours in front of the tavern in the freezing cold, because the mayor had told him to — Juraj Cup in his wet bast shoes, Juraj Cup in the blizzard, Juraj Cup in God's hands. Listen, if you saw a stone falling up instead of down, you'd call it a miracle. But that journey Juraj Cup made to give himself up, nobody calls that a miracle; and yet it was a bigger phenomenon, and a more fearsome power at work, than a stone that's falling up. Wait, let me speak. What

I'm saying is, if you want to see miracles, keep your eye on people, not stones.

"Well, when we got to Volova Lehota we were staggering like shadows, more dead than alive. We banged on the mayor's door, but everyone was asleep. Then the mayor, a bearded giant of a man, crept out with a rifle in his hands, and when he saw us he knelt down and unfastened our skis, but he never uttered a word. When I think back on what happened, it's as if I'm looking at a series of strange paintings, simple and solemn images: the mayor leading us without a word into one of the huts; two candles burning in the room, a woman in black kneeling before an ikon, on a bed the body of Marina Matejova in a white shift, her throat cut clear to the bone — it was a horrible and yet such an oddly clean stroke, like when a butcher splits a suckling pig in two. And the face was such an eerie white, the white you only see in people who've been drained of their last drop of blood.

"Then, still without a word, the mayor led us back to his place. By now, eleven men in fleece coats were waiting there — I don't know if you have any idea how those sheepskins smell: there's something sort of stifling and Old Testament-like about them. The mayor sat us down at the table, cleared his throat, bowed, and said, 'In God's name, we bring an accusation before you in the death of His servant Marina Matejova. May the Lord have mercy on her!'

"'Amen,' the eleven countrymen said, and they crossed themselves.

"And then the mayor began: Two nights ago he had heard someone scratching outside, scratching softly at the door. He thought it was a fox, and he took his gun and went to open the door. On the doorstep lay a woman. It was Marina Matejova with her throat slit. Because her vocal cords were cut, she was dumb.

"The mayor carried Marina into his hut and laid her on the bed. Then he ordered a shepherd to blow his horn and summon all the peasants of Volova Lehota. When they had gathered, he turned to Marina and said, 'Marina Matejova, before you die, bear witness to who killed you. Marina Matejova, did I kill you?'

"Marina could not shake her head; but she closed her eyes.

"'Marina, was it this man here, your neighbor Vlaho, son of Vasil?'

"Marina closed her anguished eyes.

"'Marina Matejova, was it this shepherd here, Kohut, known as Vanka? Was it this one here, who is Martin Dudas, your neighbor? — Marina, was it this one, Baran, known as Sandor? — Marina, was it the one who is standing here, Andrej Vorobec? — Marina Matejova, was it Klimko Bezuchy, who is standing before you? Marina, was it this man, Stepan Bobot? — Marina, was the one who killed you Tatka, the gamekeeper, son of Mihal Tatka? Marina — '

"At that moment the door opened and in came Juraj Cup, the brother of Marina Matejova. Marina shuddered and her eyes grew wild with fright.

"'Marina,' the mayor persisted, 'who killed you? Was it this one here, Fodor, whose name is Terentik?'

"But Marina no longer responded. 'Pray,' said Juraj Cup, and all the peasants fell to their knees. At length the mayor arose and said, 'Let the women in!'

"'Not yet,' said old Dudas. 'Marina Matejova, the servant

of God, now no more, in the name of God give a sign: did Duro the shepherd kill you?'

"There was silence.

" 'Marina Matejova, whose soul is with the Lord, did Toth Ivan, son of Ivan, kill you?'

"No one breathed.

" 'Marina Matejova, in the name of God, then it was your own brother who killed you, Juraj Cup?'

" 'I killed her,' said Juraj Cup. 'The Lord commanded me: kill Marina, by an evil spirit possessed.'

" 'Close her eyes,' ordered the mayor. 'Juraj, you will go now to Jasina and present yourself before the police. You will tell them: I killed Marina Matejova. Until that time neither will you sit nor will you eat. Go, Juraj!' — Then he opened the door and let the women into the hut to lament for the dead.

"Listen, I don't know whether it was those sheepskins or fatigue or because there was such strange beauty or dignity in what I had seen and heard, but I had to go outside, into the bitter cold, because my head was in a whirl. It's the truth, something rose up inside me as if telling me to stand up and say: God's people, God's people! We will judge Juraj Cup in accordance with earthly codes, but within you is the law of God. — And I would have bowed from the waist before them. But that's not fitting for a policeman, and that's why I went outside and stayed there, swearing, all alone, until I recovered my policeman's soul again.

"You know, police work is a rough, hard business. In the morning I ransacked Juraj Cup's hut and found the dollar bills that the dead Marina's husband had been sending her from America. Of course I had to report it, and those lawyers ran with it and made a case for robbery and murder. Juraj Cup got the rope; but nobody can convince me that he made that journey on human strength alone. I know a lot about human strength, you know. But I think I know a bit about God's judgment, too."

The Tale of the Missing Leg

"A lot of people," Mr. Tymich said in response, "wouldn't believe what a person will put up with at times. Let me tell you about something that happened during the war, when I was serving with the Thirty-fifth. We had one soldier there named Dynda or Otahal or Peterka or something, but I'll call him Pepek. He was a good man otherwise, but such a simpleton you could cry. Anyway, as long as they had us running around in drill formation he was fine, he took it like a lamb. But when they sent us up to the front, it was at Cracow then, they picked some damfool spot the Russian artillery was targeting that very moment. Pepek just gaped, that's all. But when he came to this horse with its belly ripped open and the horse still snorting and trying to get up, Pepek turned white, slammed down his cap, said a few unkind things about His Majesty, threw his rifle and rucksack on the ground, and headed for home.

"How he made it over those three hundred or so miles, I couldn't tell you to save my soul. But one night there he was, knocking on the door of his little farmhouse and saying to his wife, 'It's me, Ma, and I'm not going back there, so it looks like I'm done for. I'm a deserter.' After they had a good cry together, his wife says, 'Pepek, I'm not going to bawl you out, I'm going to hide you in the dung heap. Nobody'll look for you there.' So she buries him in the manure pile and covers it over with boards, and Pepek sat in that stinkpit for five months. Let me tell you, not even a martyr to the faith could've stood something like that. Then some old biddy of a neighbor tipped off the authorities after a quarrel over a hen, and they came to haul Pepek out of the dung. Listen, they had to buy about thirty feet of rope so they wouldn't have to smell him when they brought him into town all trussed up.

"After Pepek had aired out a little, they took him before a military court. The hearing officer was a man named Dillinger. Some say he was a fine man and others that he was a dirty dog, but how that man could swear — well, there's no denying it, under the Austrians we all learned how to swear! It got to be kind of an old tradition. These days nobody can do a decent job of cussing out; insulting, though, we're sure good at that. Anyway, this hearing officer, Dillinger, stood Pepek out in the courtyard and tried his case from the window; he wouldn't let him come any closer. Well, things were looking bad for Pepek: an army deserter, you know; you can get the firing squad for that, and not even God Himself can help you. And this Dillinger wasn't going to waste his precious time on anybody — I guess he was just a dirty dog after all. But when he was ready to pronounce sentence, Dillinger yelled from the window, 'So what about it, Pepek, all that time you were buried there, didn't you get a good night's sleep now and then with your old lady?'

"Pepek shifted from one leg to the other in embarrassment and then suddenly burst out, his face all red: "Respectfully reporting, sir, now and then, sure. Elsewise I couldn't have done it.'

"At that Dillinger shut the window and said, 'Jesus!' After a moment he just shook his head and quick-stepped around the room till he'd recovered, and then he said, 'They can pension me off, but I'm not sentencing this fellow to death. For his wife's sake alone, I just can't do it. Ugh and phew! There's married love for you!' And somehow or other he got the sentence knocked down to three years' imprisonment.

"Pepek's prison assignment was to tend the warden's garden, and afterwards the warden said that never in his life did he have such big, beautiful vegetables as when Pepek was cultivating the crop. 'The devil only knows,' the warden said, 'how he got them to grow so good.'"

* * *

"Well," said Mr. Kral, "all kinds of strange things happened during the war, you know. And if you made a collection of everything that people did so they wouldn't have to fight for Austria, you'd get more books out of it than the Jesuits came up with for the *Acta Sanctorum*. I've got a nephew, Lojzik, who has a bakery in Radlice, and when they took him away in the war he said to me, 'Uncle, I can tell you straight off, they're not sending me to the front. I'd chop off my leg before I'd give them a hand, those German bastards.'

"Well, Lojzik was a clever lad, and all the while those rookies were drilling with their rifles, he was nearly bending backwards with enthusiasm, so much so that his superiors saw him as a future hero, or at any rate the next to get his corporal's stripes. But when he got wind they were going to be sent to the front in a couple of days, he faked a fever, grabbed the right side of his belly, and started moaning something awful. So they took him off to the hospital and yanked out his appendix. Lojzik made sure the incision took a long time to close, but after about six weeks it healed up fairly well no matter what he did to it, and still the war wasn't over. That's when I visited him in the hospital. 'Uncle,' says Lojzik, 'not even my drill sergeant can get me out of this one. I'm just waiting any minute now for them to muster me out of here.'

"The medical chief-of-staff at the time was the infamous Dr. Oberhuber. It turned out later that the fellow was a complete lunatic. But you know, the army's the army, and if you stuck gold stars on a warthog, he'd be a general. As you can imagine, they were all scared of Oberhuber, because all he ever did was run around to the hospitals screaming, 'Off to the front!' at everybody, even if the soldier had a certified case of TB or bullet holes in his spine, and no one could answer back. He wouldn't even look at the chart over a sick man's bed, just peer at him from a distance and scream, 'Frontdiensttauglich! Sofort einrucken!' And all the saints in heaven couldn't help you then.

"So one day this Oberhuber came to inspect the hospital where Lojzik was waiting for the inevitable. The moment they heard the storm brewing down at the gate, all the patients except the ones who were already dead had to stand at attention by their beds to receive his High-and-Mightiness in the proper manner. The thing is, the waiting went on for quite a while. So Lojzik, just to get more comfortable, bent one leg, rested his knee on the hospital bed, and stood there on his other leg. At that very moment Oberhuber pushed his way into the ward, purple with rage, and yelled right from the door, 'Off to the front! That man, too! Tauglich!' — Then he took a look at Lojzik and how he was standing there on one leg, and he got even more purple in the face. 'Einbeinig!' he screamed. 'Sofort send him home! Himmel, why do you keep here a one-legged man? Is this a pigsty for cripples? Get him out of here! You slackers, for that I send you all to the front!' The noncoms, ghostly pale, stammered that steps would be taken at once; but Oberhuber was already screaming at the next bed, 'Sofort to the front!' to a new recruit who'd just been operated on the day before.

"Within the hour, Lojzik, his release papers personally signed by Oberhuber himself, was discharged from the hospital and sent home as a one-legged disabled veteran. Well, Lojzik was a very practical young man. He immediately put in a request that, as a permanent cripple, he be struck from the roll of military conscripts and granted a disability pension, because as a baker he needed both legs — even if, as they say about bakers, their legs're crooked. In other words, with only one officially-certified leg he couldn't practice his trade. After the appropriate official delay, he received notice that he was being discharged as forty-five-percent disabled, in consequence of which he was eligible to draw thus-and-so-much money in disability pay per month. So far so good, but this is where the story of the missing leg really begins.

"From that time on, Lojzik drew his disability pay, helped his dad in the bakery, and even got married. Only sometimes he noticed that he was limping or hobbling just a bit on the leg that

Oberhuber had officially certified as missing; but he was glad that at least it made him look like he might have an artificial leg. Then the war ended and the Republic came along; but Lojzik, being so orderly and thorough, went right on drawing his disability pay.

"Then one day he came to see me, and it was pretty clear that he had some sort of worry on his mind. 'Uncle,' he bursts out after a minute, 'it seems to me this leg of mine is getting shorter or shriveled up somehow.' And he pulled up his pants leg and showed me his leg. It was thin as a stick. 'Uncle,' he says, 'I'm scared I'm going to lose this leg after all.'

" 'So take it to the doctor, you blockhead,' I tell him.

" 'Uncle,' sighs Lojzik, 'I don't think it's some kind of disease. I think maybe it's because I'm not supposed to have this leg. I mean, I've got it written down in black and white that my right leg up to the knee is gone — don't you think that's why it's shriveling up on me?'

"After a time he came to see me again — by then he was already leaning on a cane. 'Uncle,' he says in agony, 'I'm a cripple. I can't even put any weight on this leg anymore. Doctor says it's atrophy of the muscles and it's probably something to do with nerves, so he's sending me off to the mineral baths, but it seems to me he doesn't really believe it'll help. Uncle, feel how my leg's all cold, just like it was dead. Doctor says it's bad circulation — don't you think that what it's doing is just rotting away?'

" 'Listen, Lojzik,' I tell him, 'I'm going to give you some good advice: report your leg to the authorities and ask them to cross you off the list as a one-legged man. Then I think your leg'll get better.'

" 'But, Uncle,' Lojzik objects, 'then they'll say I took that disability pay under false pretenses and that I cheated the state out of a whole pile of money. I'll have to pay it all back for sure!'

" 'Then keep the money, you cheapskate baker,' I tell him, 'but you'll lose your leg. Just don't come whining to me afterwards.'

"A week later he was back at my place again. 'Uncle,' he rattles off straight from the doorway, 'they don't want to officially recognize my leg at all. They say it's all shriveled up, so it's no good anyway. Now what do I do?'

"You wouldn't believe the amount of running around it took before they officially recognized that Lojzik had two legs. And you can bet he had to settle accounts afterwards for cheating the state over the disability pay; they even prosecuted him for dodging his military obligations. Poor Lojzik was racing around from office to office, but the whole time his leg was getting stronger and stronger. Maybe it was because of all the running around he had to do, but my guess is it's because he finally got official recognition. After all, an official ruling like that conveys a ton of authority. But what I really think is that his leg shriveled up on him because what he did was wrong. He wasn't playing fair, and you pay for that. I'm telling you, a clear conscience is the best health care there is. And if people were fair and honest, maybe they wouldn't even have to die."

Vertigo

"Conscience," said Mr. Lacina, "is a word that's no longer used; nowadays it's called repression, but it's six of one and half-a-dozen of the other. I don't know if any of you recall that case involving Gierke, the industrialist. He was extremely rich and a very high-class person, tall and strong as a column. They said he was a widower, but other than that, nobody knew anything about him, he had such a reserved nature. Anyway, when he was well over forty he fell in love with the prettiest young thing, she was seventeen years old and so beautiful it made you catch your breath; real beauty like that somehow squeezes your heart with compassion or tenderness or something. And Gierke married the girl, because he was the great and wealthy Gierke.

"They went to Italy for their honeymoon, and here's what happened while they were there: They climbed up the famous campanile in Venice, and when Gierke looked down — they say it's a very fine view — he grew pale, turned toward his young wife, and collapsed like a felled tree. From that time on he became more reserved than ever. He tried very hard to make it seem that nothing was wrong with him, but there was this anxious, desperate look in his eyes. His wife was terribly frightened, as you can imagine, and she took him back home. They had a beautiful house overlooking the public gardens, and that's where Gierke's eccentricity came to light; he'd go from window to window, making sure they were tightly locked, and he'd hardly sit down before jumping up again to make sure some other window was locked. He'd even get up during the night and wander over the whole house — in reply to questions, he'd only mutter that he had this damned vertigo and that he wanted to shut the windows so he wouldn't fall out of them. So then his wife had gratings fastened over all the windows, to relieve him from this ceaseless anxiety. This served the purpose for a few days and Gierke calmed down a bit, but then he began running from window to window again, shaking the gratings to make sure they were firmly in place. Then steel shutters were added, and they lived behind them like shut-ins. This quieted Gierke some-what, but then the vertigo appeared again when he had to use the stairs. They had to guide him up and down the stairs and hold onto him as if he were lame, and meanwhile he'd be trembling like a leaf, all drenched with sweat. Sometimes, in fact, he had to sit down in the middle of the staircase and he'd burst into a fit of sobbing — that's how badly frightened he was.

"Of course, they'd begun consulting every doctor they could find and, as is often the case, one sawbones said that the attacks were due to overwork, a second that it was some kind of inner-ear disorder of the labyrinth, a third that the problem was caused by constipation, and a fourth that it resulted from a lack of blood in the brain. Listen, it's my observation that as soon as someone becomes a prominent expert, the first thing that springs forth from him, on account of some sort of internal process, is a point of view. Then what a specialist like that says is, 'My dear colleague, from my point of view, it is of course thus-and-such.' And another specialist objects, 'Yes, my dear colleague, but from my point of view the situation is diametrically opposite.' What I think is, points of view ought to be left at the door, like hats and walking sticks. As soon as you turn a man with a point of view loose anywhere, he's bound to get up to some kind of mischief or at the very least disagree with everybody else. But to get back to Gierke, every month he was tortured and treated by some other prominent specialist according to some totally different method. Gierke was a huge mountain of a man and he could take it. But the time came when he couldn't get up out of his arm-chair, because he'd have an attack of vertigo as soon as he looked down at the ground, and so he just stared into the darkness, without speaking or moving, and sometimes he'd shake all over — when he was sobbing.

"Then some new doctor, a neurologist named Spitz, began working miracles. This Dr. Spitz had set himself up as someone who treated repression. What I mean is, he said that almost all of us, deep in our subconscious, have all kinds of horrible thoughts or memories or cravings that we repress because we're scared of them; and these repressions create a lot of turmoil and confusion inside us and what you'd call nervous breakdowns. And when a doctor who knows what he's doing pokes around and drags this repression right out into God's own daylight, the patient feels relieved and is all right again. This sort of psycho-analytical quack has to gain the complete confidence of the patient in question and haul everything imaginable out of his brain: what he dreams about at night, what he remembers about his childhood, and things like that. And afterwards, when it's all over, he tells him: Well, my good man, years ago you had such-and-such an experience (usually it's something pretty awful) and it's been pressing on your subconscious — it's what we call a psychical trauma; now it's out in the open, abracadabra, phoney-baloney, and you're cured. That's the sort of sorcery it is.

"I'm telling you, this Dr. Spitz really worked magic. You wouldn't believe how many repressions rich people have; poor people as a rule don't worry that much about them. In short, Dr. Spitz had a fabulous clientele. So after all the other medical gurus in turn had done what they could for Gierke, Dr. Spitz was called in. And Dr. Spitz declared that the vertigo attacks were neurotic in origin and that he, Hugo Spitz, guaranteed that he'd rid the patient of them forever. Well and good. But the only thing was that Gierke, to put it mildly, was not exactly talkative. No matter what Dr. Spitz asked him about, Gierke would barely mumble in reply, after which he'd fall completely silent and, eventually, show Spitz the door. Dr. Spitz was in despair; with an important patient like that, you know, it's a question of prestige. Besides which, it was a particularly attractive and diffi-cult case of nervous breakdown. And on top of that, Gierke's wife, Irma, was a very beautiful and unhappy woman. As a result, Dr. Spitz put everything else aside. Either I track down Gierke's repression, he growled, or I drop medicine and get a job at Lobl's as a salesclerk.

"What he did was turn to a new psychoanalytical method. First of all, he identified all of Gierke's aunts, cousins, brothers-in-law, and other elderly kin, both near and distant, who were still alive; then he set out to gain their confidence — the main thing this kind of doctor has to learn is how to listen patiently. These relatives were thrilled to meet such a charming and attentive gentleman as Dr. Spitz. But in the long run, Spitz got seriously down to business and turned to a certain private investigating firm, which sent out two reliable people somewhere or other. When the two of them returned, Dr. Spitz paid them for their trouble and went straight to Mr. Gierke. Gierke was sitting in semi-darkness in his armchair, now barely capable of moving.

" 'Mr. Gierke,' said Dr. Spitz, 'I'm not going to impose on you; you don't have to say a single word. I won't ask you about anything. All I want to do is to release you from what is causing your vertigo. You have pushed it down into your subconscious, but this repression is so strong that it produces serious disorders — '

" 'I didn't send for you, Doctor,' Gierke interrupted him hoarsely, and he reached out his hand toward the bell.

" 'I know,' said Dr. Spitz, 'but wait just a moment. When you first had that attack of vertigo on the campanile at Venice, try to remember, sir, just try to remember what you felt at the time.'

"Gierke sat there rigidly with his finger on the bell.

" 'What you felt,' continued Dr. Spitz, 'what you felt was a terrifying, maniacal urge to hurl your beautiful young wife from the bell tower. But because you loved her beyond measure, a conflict raged within you and vented itself in the form of psychical shock. You collapsed with vertigo — '

"There was silence, but the hand stretched toward the bell suddenly dropped to one side.

" 'From that moment on,' said Dr. Spitz, 'this vertigo, this dreadful fear of the abyss, has never left you. From that moment on, you have locked the windows and been unable to look down from heights, because inside you there was always the horrifying thought that you might push your wife, Irma, into the depths below — '

"From Gierke's armchair came an inhuman groan.

" 'Yes,' continued Dr. Spitz, 'but now, sir, there is the question of where this obsessive tendency came from. Mr. Gierke, you were first married eighteen years ago. Mr. Gierke, your first wife died on a walking tour of the Alps. She fell from a precipice while climbing the Hohe Wand, and you inherited her estate.'

"The only sound that could be heard was Gierke's harsh, rapid breathing.

" 'Gierke,' cried Dr. Spitz, 'you murdered your first wife. You pushed her over the precipice. And that is why, listen to me, that is why you believe that you will kill your second wife as well, the one you truly love. That is why you're afraid of heights; that is why you suffer from vertigo — '

" 'Doctor,' howled the man in the armchair, 'doctor, what am I to do? What can I possibly do about it?'

"Dr. Spitz grew immensely sad. 'Sir,' he said, 'if I were a religious man, I would advise you to take your punishment, so that God may have mercy on your soul. But we doctors don't ordinarily believe in God. You yourself will have to decide what to do; but from a medical point of view, it's obvious that you've recovered. Stand up, Mr. Gierke!'

"Gierke stood, white as a sheet.

" 'Tell me,' asked Dr. Spitz, 'do you feel dizzy?'

"Gierke shook his head.

" 'There you have it,' said Dr. Spitz, catching his breath in relief. 'Now the other symptoms will disappear, too. That vertigo was only from your subconsciously repressed thoughts. Now, since we have released them, all will be well. Can you look out the window? Excellent! It's as if all your worries had vanished, isn't it? Not a hint of vertigo, right? Mr. Gierke, you are the finest case I've ever had!' Dr. Spitz rubbed his hands together with delight. 'Completely cured! May I call Mrs. Gierke? No? Aha, you want to surprise her yourself — good heavens, won't she be pleased when she sees you walking! — So you see, Mr. Gierke, what miracles science can perform!' In his sheer joy at his success he could have babbled on for another two hours, but he saw that Gierke needed rest; therefore he wrote out a prescription for a sedative and took his leave.

" 'I'll escort you, doctor,' said Gierke politely, and he accompanied the doctor to the head of the stairs. 'That's strange,' he said, 'not a trace of vertigo, not a trace — '

" 'Wonderful,' Dr. Spitz cried out enthusiastically. 'So you feel quite well, do you?'

" 'Completely well,' Gierke said softly, and he watched the doctor descend. And after the front door had slammed behind Dr. Spitz, there was another heavy thud. A moment later they found Gierke's body at the bottom of the stairs. He was dead, his body broken in several places from having struck the banisters of the staircase as he fell.

"When they notified Dr. Spitz, he whistled and a very odd expression crossed his face. Then he took the book in which he logged the names of his patients, and opposite Gierke's name he merely wrote the date and a single word: *Suicidium*. And as you know, Mr. Taussig, that means suicide."

The Confession

"Repression," mused Father Voves, the priest at St. Matthew's. "Listen, treating repression is one of the oldest human experiences; except that our Holy Church calls the medicine *sacramentum sanctae confessionis*. When something is pressing on your soul, when there's something you're ashamed of, go, wretched sinner, to holy confession and rid yourself of the filth you're carrying around inside! Only we don't call it treating nervous breakdowns, we call it contrition, repentance, and the absolution of sins.

"I'll tell you something that happened a number of years ago. It was a brutally hot summer day, and so I'd stayed inside my little church — you know, it's always seemed to me that these Evangelicals could only have got their start in the northern countries, where you can't get warm even in the summertime. In a church like ours, the Catholic Church, you've got something going on all the livelong day — mass, devotions, vespers or, if nothing else, the paintings and statues; you can drop by anytime you like, cool off, and meditate — but it helps when it's hot as an oven outside. That's why you have the dissenters in the cold and inhospitable regions and us Catholics in the warmer climes; it's probably the shade and coolness in God's holy cathedrals that does it. Well, as I was saying, it was a broiling hot day; when I entered the church, I felt something beautiful and peaceful wafting gently toward me. And then the sacristan came up and told me that a man had been waiting there for more than an hour for someone to hear his confession.

"Well, of course, that happens often enough; so I fetched my surplice from the sacristy and sat myself down in the confessional. The sacristan brought the penitent over — he was an older, rather well-dressed man, he looked like a salesman or a real estate agent, and his face was pale and somewhat swollen. He knelt at the confessional and remained silent.

"'Now then,' I said to encourage him, 'say after me: I, a miserable sinner, do confess and acknowledge unto Almighty God — '

"'No,' the man blurted out, 'I say it differently. Let me do it my way. I have to do it differently.' Suddenly his chin began to tremble and sweat broke out on his forehead. And like a bolt out of the blue I had this peculiar and revolting feeling of disgust — Only once before had I ever been shaken like that, and that was at the exhumation of a corpse which was . . . which was in a state of decomposition; I'm not going to tell you, gentlemen, what that was like.

"'For heaven's sake, what's wrong?' I called out, thoroughly frightened.

"'Just a moment — just a moment,' the man shuddered. He gave a deep sigh, blew his nose loudly, and said, 'It's all right now. I'm ready to begin, Father. It was twelve years ago — '

"I won't tell you what I heard. To begin with, of course, there's the seal of confession; and in the second place, the act was so ghastly, so sickening and bestial, that — well, it simply cannot be said aloud. And that man spurted it all out in such gruesome detail — and he left nothing to the imagination, nothing what-soever! I thought I'd have to run out of the confessional, that I'd have to stop up my ears or I don't know what. I crammed my surplice into my mouth to keep from crying out in horror.

"'There, it's out now,' the man said with satisfaction, and he blew his nose with relief. 'My thanks, Father.'

"'Wait,' I cried, 'what about repentance?'

"'Not on your life,' said the man, and he looked at me through the little window almost confidentially. 'Father, I don't believe in anything at all. I only came here to get this off my chest. You know, when I haven't talked about . . . about that business for a while . . . then I see right there in front of me . . . everything . . . and I can't sleep, I can't even close my eyes —

— And when that happens, it has to come out, I have to tell someone about it. And that's what you're here for, that's your job and you can't tell anyone else because it's under the seal of confession. As for absolution, I don't give a rap about that; it doesn't mean a thing when you're not a believer. Many thanks, Father. Best regards.' — And before I could recover from the shock, he drifted jauntily out of the church.

"About a year later he turned up again. He buttonholed me in front of the church, looking pale and extremely humble. 'Father,' he stammered, 'may I confess to you?'

" 'Look,' I told him, 'without repentance it can't be done, and that's all there is to it. If you can't repent, we can't do business.'

" 'My God,' the man sighed miserably, 'that's what every priest tells me now! Not a one of them will hear my confession, and I need it so badly — Look, Your Reverence, what difference does it make to you if I — if just once more I could — '

"With that his lips began to tremble as before. 'Nothing doing,' I shouted, 'unless you tell me in the presence of a layman!'

" 'Sure,' wailed the man, 'and then the layman would turn me in! The hell with you,' he yelled, painfully offended, and then he ran off. And it's a funny thing, but even from the back you could see how desperate he was —

"Since that time I've never laid eyes on him again."

"Your Reverence," said Dr. Baum, the lawyer, "your story isn't over yet. One day — it's been a few years now — a fellow with a pale and swollen face came to my office — to tell the truth, I didn't much like the looks of him. When I'd seated him and asked what had brought him there, the man started off like this: 'Look, sir, if a client consults you in confidence and reveals to you that he's, say, committed some offense, then — '

" ' — then obviously,' I told him, 'I wouldn't be allowed to use it against him. If I did, there'd be a serious disciplinary hearing, if not worse.'

" 'Good,' the man said with a sigh of relief. 'There's something I have to tell you. Fourteen years ago — ' and then, Your Reverence, I must have heard the same thing you did then."

"Don't say it," Father Voves interrupted him.

"It never occurred to me," muttered Dr. Baum. "You know, it was a thoroughly ugly affair. And that fellow just went on spewing it out as if he were choking; sweat pouring off of him, livid, his eyes closed. . . . It seemed as if he were vomiting, psychologically speaking. Then he paused and wiped his lips with his handkerchief.

" 'For God's sake,' I told him, 'there's nothing I can do about this! But if you want my most sincere advice — '

" 'No,' the odd creature gasped, 'I don't want any advice. I only came here to tell you what I did. But remember,' he added almost savagely, 'you can't use it against me!' Then he stood up and said, quite calmly, 'So how much do I owe you, sir?'

" 'Fifty,' I said, feeling miserable; and he took out a fifty, said good day, and left.

"I'd like to know how many lawyers in Prague he called on like that, but he never paid me a second visit."

"That's still not the end of the story," remarked Dr. Vitasek. "Some years ago, when I was a doing my residency, they brought in a man with that same kind of pale and swollen face; his legs were bloated like tubs, he was having convulsions, and he had difficulty breathing. In short, a classic case of kidney failure, straight out of a medical text. Needless to say, there was no help for him. One night the nurse notified me that the patient with kidney failure in ward seven was starting to have convulsions again. So I go to him, and I see the poor man gasping for breath, sweating like the devil, his eyes panicky with terror — the death agonies in kidney failure are appalling.

" 'Look, old fellow,' I said, 'I'll give you an injection and you'll feel better again.'

"The patient shook his head. 'Doctor,' he managed to say, 'I . . . there's something I have to tell you . . . But send that woman away!'

"I'd rather have given him an injection of morphine, but when I saw those eyes of his, I sent the nurse on her way. 'Out with it then, my good fellow,' I said, 'but afterwards you need to get some sleep.'

" 'Doctor,' the man groaned, and there was such insane fear in his eyes that I can't describe it, 'Doctor, I can't — I keep seeing this — I can't sleep, I have to tell you — '

"And then, amidst gasps and convulsions, it all came out. I tell you, I have never to this day heard anything like it."

"Hm, hm," coughed the lawyer Baum.

"Don't worry," said Dr. Vitasek, "I'm not going to tell it; that's privileged information between doctor and patient. Afterwards he lay there like a wet rag, utterly exhausted. You know, I couldn't give him absolution, Your Reverence, or any kind of wise counsel. But I did give him two shots of morphine, and when he woke up, another, and then once again, until he didn't wake up anymore. You might say I gave him a helping hand."

"Amen," said Father Voves, and he thought for a moment. "That was kind of you," he added softly; "at least he's no longer suffering."

A Lyrical Thief

"Sometimes it happens the other way around," Mr. Zach, the editor, broke in after an appropriate silence. "Sometimes you really don't know if it's a bad conscience or nothing but bragging and showing off. No doubt a lot of these crooks would quit the business if they couldn't boast now and then about what they've pulled off. I think crooks would become extinct if society simply ignored them; being singled out for public attention is very gratifying to professional wrongdoers, and it gives them a great deal of pleasure. I'm not saying that people rob and steal just for the glory of it; they do it for money or from muddleheadedness or the influence of the wrong kinds of friends, but once they get a whiff of *aura popularis*, a sort of megalomania begins stirring in them — it's the same with politicians and other people in the public eye.

"Let me tell you about a case from a number of years ago, when I was the editor for our excellent regional weekly, the *Eastern Herald*. True, I'm from the western part of the country, but you'd never believe how fervently I fought for the regional interests of eastern Czechs. It's temperate, hilly country, the kind you'd paint with plum trees and peaceful streams lining the roads. But every week, in print, I roused 'our rugged highland people, struggling mightily for their daily bread with inhospitable nature and an unsympathetic government' — gentlemen, what can I say except that it was beautifully written and straight from the heart. I only worked there for two years, but during those two years I stamped on the minds of the people there the conviction that they were rugged mountaineers, that their lives were heroic and demanding, that their region was deprived, however somberly beautiful and mountainous — I think there's nothing

better a newspaperman can do for eastern Bohemia than trans-
form its image into some sort of Norway. That gives you an idea
of the great tasks of which the press is capable.

"A regional editor, you know, should concern himself
mainly with local events. One day the local police captain
stopped me on the street and said, 'Last night some good-for-
nothing scoundrel broke into Mr. Vasata's grocery store. What
would you say if I told you the rascal wrote a poem and left it
lying on the counter? That takes a lot of nerve, doesn't it?'

" 'Show me this poem,' I said immediately, 'I can use it in
the *Herald*. You'll see how, with the help of the press, we'll catch
this joker. Besides, just think what a sensation it will be for our
town and for the entire region!'

"In short, after much talking, I got the poem and ran it in
the *Eastern Herald*. I'll recite it for you, to the extent that I still
remember it. It went something like this:

> One, two, three, four, five, six, seven,
> Eight, nine, ten, and then eleven,
> And now the hour of twelve is pealing,
> It's the the hour when burglars do their stealing.
> While I was jimmying your lock,
> Someone was coming down the block,
> But if I was scared, I wouldn't be a thief,
> And the footsteps passed, to my relief,
> If you listened in the dark for some kind of sound,
> All you would hear is my heart pound,
> The heart is an orphan and I am, too,
> My mother would weep if she only knew,
> For some life is nothing but bad luck and worrying,
> There's only me here, and a mouse that's scurrying,
> The mouse and I, each a thief and a sinner,
> That's why I crumbled some bread for its dinner,
> But where it's hiding it won't tell,
> Because a thief has to fear other thieves as well.

And it went on like that until, at the end, came:

> I could keep writing on and on,
> But I can't because now my candle's gone.

"Well, I ran the poem with an extensive, soul-searching and

esthetic analysis; I stressed its balladic elements and pointed eloquently to subtle strains in the criminal soul. It was, in its own way, a sensation. The papers from other political parties and towns claimed that it was a spurious, outright forgery; our eastern Czech competitors protested that it was plagiarism, a clumsy translation from the English and what have you. But when I was right in the thick of the controversy over our local poet-thief, the police captain came to me and said, 'So that was supposed to put an end to it, to this damned thief of yours. Let me tell you, sir, he's already robbed another store and two apartments this week, and every single time he's left a long poem behind him at the scene of the crime!'

" 'I'm happy to hear it,' I said. 'We'll print them!'

" 'That would be taking quite a gamble,' grumbled the captain. 'That's abetting criminals, sir! Now the fellow's only stealing from some sort of newly-roused literary ambition! You've got to stop him somehow, and right now, understand? Write that the poems are worthless, that they're lacking form or spirit or anything you want. Then I think this scoundrel will stop stealing.'

" 'Hm,' I said, 'we can't write that when we've already praised him. But I'll tell you what, we won't print any more of his poems, and that's that.'

"So far so good. During the next two weeks five new burglaries were committed, complete with poetry, but the *Eastern Herald* was silent as a clam about the poems. I was just afraid that our thief would move to Turnov or Tabor out of offended author's vanity and bring his stuff to the attention of the regional press there. Imagine how those old duffers would look down their noses at us! — The silence evidently confused our thief somewhat. At any rate there was peace for three weeks, but then the burglaries started up again, only with this difference, that the poems in question were mailed directly to the editor of the *Eastern Herald*. But the *Herald* was adamant, partly because it didn't want to mess things up for the local authorities, and partly because the poems got worse and worse. The author began

repeating himself and coming up with all kinds of crazy, roman-
ticized notions and nonsense. In short, he started behaving like a
real writer.

"One night I came home from the tavern, whistling like a
starling, and struck a match to light a kerosene lamp. At that
very moment somebody blew at the match from behind me and
snuffed it out.

" 'Don't light another one,' said a gloomy voice. 'It's me.'

" 'Ah,' I said, 'and what would you be wanting?'

" 'I'm here to ask you,' said the gloomy voice, 'what's
happening with the poems.'

" 'Look,' I said — I still didn't understand what was going
on — 'these aren't exactly office hours, you know. Come see me
tomorrow at eleven.'

" 'So you can turn me in?' the voice said resentfully. 'Forget
it. Why aren't you printing my poems anymore?'

"Not until then did it dawn on me that this was our thief.
'That's a long story,' I told him. 'Take a seat, young man. If you
really want to know, I'm not printing your poems because they're
not worth a damn. So there.'

" 'I didn't think,' the voice said painfully, 'they were . . .
they were any worse than that first one.'

" 'That first one wasn't bad,' I said sternly. 'There was
sincere feeling in it, understand? It had an intuitive freshness, it
had the immediacy and intensity of experience, it had all of that.
But those later ones, those were dogs.'

" 'But look,' the voice pressed on, 'look, I wrote them just
like I wrote the first one!'

" 'That's the whole point,' I said harshly. 'You're just repeating yourself. You always hear footsteps outside — '

" 'But I really heard them,' the voice said defensively. 'Mr.
Editor, when I'm stealing, I have to keep my ears pricked up in
case there's somebody walking around out there!'

" 'And there's always that same business about a mouse,' I
continued.

" 'About a mouse,' the voice said despondently. 'But there's always a mouse there every single time! I only wrote about a mouse in three of them — '

" 'To be brief,' I interrupted him, 'your verses have become empty and routine literary efforts. Without originality, without inspiration, without emotional innovation. My well-meaning friend, it won't do. Poets mustn't repeat themselves.'

"The voice fell silent for a while. 'But Mr. Editor,' it said after a moment, 'it's always the same, see. You try stealing, and you'll see one job's just like another. It's hard work.'

" 'It is,' I said. 'You ought to switch subjects.'

" 'Maybe I could rob a church,' the voice suggested. 'Or a graveyard.'

"I shook my head vigorously. 'That's neither here nor there,' I said. 'It isn't the topic that matters so much as the experience. In my view, what's lacking in your poetry is any kind of conflict. There's never anything in your poems but a superficial description of some ordinary burglary — You should explore an internal theme of some sort. Conscience, for instance.'

"The voice thought it over for a bit. 'You think like maybe twinges of conscience?' it said hesitantly. 'You think the poems would be better then?'

" 'Of course they would,' I exclaimed. 'My young friend, give them psychological depth and passion!'

" 'I'll give it a try,' the voice said reflectively. 'Only I don't know if I'll get much stealing done. You can lose your self-confidence, you know? And if you don't have self-confidence, they'll nab you for sure.'

" 'So what?' I cried. 'Dear boy, it doesn't matter if you're caught! Can't you imagine the poetry you'd write *in carcere et catenis*? I could show you one poem from prison that'll make you gasp!'

" 'Was it in the newspaper?' the voice asked eagerly.

" 'Friend of my heart,' I said, 'it is one of the most famous poems in the world. Light the lamp, and I'll read it to you.'

"My visitor struck a match and the lamp flared. It showed a pale, somewhat pimply young man, as thieves and poets tend to be. 'Wait a minute,' I said, 'I'll find it for you right off.' And I dug up a translation of Wilde's "The Ballad of Reading Gaol." It was all the rage in those days, you know.

"Never in my life have I recited anything with such feeling as I did that ballad, you know, the line: Yet each man kills the thing he loves — My guest couldn't take his eyes off me. And when I got to the part about how the man goes off to the gallows, he covered his face and sobbed.

"When I finished reading, we both were silent. I didn't want to mar the fullness of the moment. I opened the window and said, 'The shortest way out is over the fence. Good night.' And I blew out the lamp.

" 'Good night,' the trembling voice said in the darkness, 'I'll give it a try. Thanks very much.' And then he vanished quietly as a bat; after all, he was an accomplished thief.

"Two days later they caught him inside a store he'd broken into. He was sitting at the counter over a piece of paper, biting the end of a pencil. On the paper was written only:

Each man swipes the thing he loves —

and nothing more. No doubt it was meant to be a variation on "The Ballad of Reading Gaol."

"And so our thief got eighteen months in prison for a string of break-ins. Several months later I received a whole notebook of poems from him. They were awful: nothing but dank underground cells, small stone windows, iron bars, clanking shackles on legs, musty bread, the walk to the gallows and what not. I was thoroughly shocked by the dreadful conditions prevailing at said prison. But, as you may know, an editor like me can worm his way in anywhere. So I finagled an invitation from the warden for a tour of the place. What can I tell you but that it was an entirely humane, presentable, and well-cared-for prison. And I met up with my thief, just as he was finishing a meal of canned beans.

" 'So tell me,' I said, 'just where are those clanking shackles you wrote about?'

"Our thief turned red and shot a disconcerted look at the

warden. 'Well, as to that, Mr. Editor,' he faltered, 'the thing is, there's nothing to write any poems about here! It's hard work, and that's a fact.'

" 'So you're fairly comfortable?' I asked him.

" 'Except for that I would be,' he mumbled in embarrassment. 'There's nothing to write about here.'

"From that day on I never came across him again. Not in the crime reports column, and not in the poetry section either."

Mr. Havlena's Verdict

"Since Mr. Zach's brought up the subject of newspapers," said Mr. Beran, "let me tell you something: the first thing most readers do when they open their newspapers is turn straight to the crime reports. Nobody knows if they read the reports so assiduously for their moral and legal edification or out of latent criminality, but what's certain is that they read them with a passion. That's why newspapers have to publish some sort of crime report every day. Say there's a government holiday, for example, and the courts aren't in session; no matter, the paper still has to run its 'From the Courtroom' column. And lots of times there isn't a single interesting case in any of the courts. Well, the reporters still need an interesting case, wherever they can get their hands on one. At times like that, crime reporters simply have to dream up interesting cases on their own. Consequently, they've got a regular market among themselves for bogus cases, which they buy, borrow, or swap for twenty cigarettes or so per case. I know all about it, because I used to room with one of those reporters; he was a hard drinker and lazy to boot, but apart from that he was a talented although poorly-paid young man.

"Well, one day a very odd, bloated-looking fellow, all grimy and down-at-heel, turned up at the tavern where the crime reporters used to gather. His name was Havlena and he'd studied law, but he never got his degree and his life had gone downhill ever since. Nobody, not even he himself, knew exactly how he made a living, but I have to tell you, that Havlena, that loafer, was a whiz on criminal and legal matters both. When this reporter friend of mine would give him a cigar and a beer, he'd close his eyes, take a few puffs, and begin telling him the most colorful and outlandish criminal cases you could possibly imagine. Then he'd start in on the main points of the defense and the prosecutor's rebuttal, after which he'd pronounce sentence in the name of the Republic. And then he'd open his eyes as if coming out of a trance and mutter, 'Loan me a five.' Once they put him to the test and he cooked up twenty-one criminal cases at one sitting, each one better than the one before. But when he got to the twenty-second he stopped short and said, 'Wait a minute, this isn't a case for a JP or even a district court. This one would have to go before a jury, and I don't do juries.' He was against juries in principle, you see. But to be fair to him, I must say that his rulings, though severe, were models of their kind from a legal point of view. He was especially proud of that.

"When the reporters discovered Havlena and saw that the cases he could supply them with weren't as humdrum and routine as those that actually came before the courts, they formed a kind of cartel. For every case he thought up, Havlena got what they called his court fee, meaning a set rate of ten crowns and a cigar, plus two crowns extra for every month of imprisonment he imposed. The heavier the sentence, you understand, the more interesting and complex the case. Never have newspaper readers been so mesmerized by the crime reports as they were when Havlena was churning out his fictitious cases. It's been ages since newspapers were as good as they were in his day. Now they're filled with nothing but politics and libel suits against the press — I don't know who on earth can read that stuff.

"One day Havlena thought up a case — not nearly one of his best, but up to then none of them had got him into any trouble. This time, though, it all came crashing down. Briefly, the case went like this: an old bachelor had a falling-out with a respectable widow who lived across the courtyard from him, so he got a parrot and trained it so that every time the neighbor lady came out on her balcony, the parrot screeched at the top of its voice, 'You slut!' The widow sued him for defamation of character. The district court said that the defendant, by means of his parrot, had made the plaintiff a public laughingstock, and they sentenced him in the name of the Republic to fourteen days in jail and court costs. Havlena wrapped up his account with, 'That'll be eleven crowns and a cigar.'

"Now, this particular case of Havlena's appeared in about six newspapers, subject to very different literary treatments, of course. In one paper the headline was, In a Quiet Building. In another, Landlord and Poor Widow. A third paper had, Parrot Charged, and so on. But no sooner did the stories appear than each of these papers received an official communication from the Ministry of Justice, to the effect that said Ministry wished to know the particulars of the defamation-of-character case tried in district court, as reported in issue number so-and-so of your esteemed journal. The letters stated that the verdict and sentence in the aforementioned trial were confused and contrary to law, in that the incriminating remarks had been uttered not by the defendant, but by the parrot; that the evidence offered in the trial could not be regarded as proof that the words uttered by said parrot applied solely and specifically to the plaintiff; and, hence, that the remarks in question could not be considered defamation of character but at the very most as disorderly conduct or disturbing the peace, which could have been dealt with quickly by a reprimand from the police, by duly imposing a fine, or by issuing a warrant to remove the bird in question from the premises. Accordingly, the Ministry of Justice desired to know which district court had handled the case, in order that it might initiate appropriate inquiries and so forth. In short, it was a regular judicial scandal.

" 'God, Havlena,' the reporters railed at their supplier, 'you've done it to us now. Look, it says here that your ruling against the parrot is confused and contrary to law!'

"Havlena turned white as a pillowcase. 'What,' he screamed, 'they're saying that *my* verdict is contrary to law? The Ministry of Justice has the nerve to tell *me* that? Me, Havlena? Unbelievable!' The reporters said they'd never seen a man so outraged and offended. 'I'll fix them,' Havlena roared, beside himself with fury. 'They'll see if my ruling's contrary to law or not! I'm not going to take this lying down!' In his anger and excitement, he proceeded to get drunk on the spot, and then he took a sheet of paper and, for the benefit of the Ministry of Justice, drew up an extensively-detailed legal disquisition in vindication of said verdict. He wrote that the defendant, by teaching his parrot to insult the lady, had manifested deliberate intent to insult and disparage her; that consequently this was a clear case of malicious intent; that the parrot was not the perpetrator of, but rather the instrument for, the offense in question, and so forth. In truth, it was the most brilliant and sophisticated legal analysis those reporters had ever seen. After which he signed his full name, Vaclav Havlena, Candidate for Doctor of Laws, and sent it to the Ministry of Justice. 'That's that,' he said, 'and until this matter's taken care of, I'm not handing out any more verdicts. I intend to receive satisfaction first.'

"As you can imagine, the Ministry of Justice took no notice whatsoever of Havlena's letter. For a while, Havlena went about disgruntled and embittered, looking even seedier and getting even thinner than before. When he realized that no response from the ministry would be forthcoming, he would only scowl and spit in silence or say treasonous things, until at last he declared, 'You just wait, I'll show them who's in the right!'

"For two months nobody saw him at all. Then one day he turned up again, beaming and smirking, and announced, 'Well, I've finally got my lawsuit! Damn the old woman, I had a devil of a time trying to talk her into it. You wouldn't believe an old girl like that could be so unflappable. She made me sign all these papers saying that no matter how it turned out, I'd foot the bill. Anyhow, boys, now the whole thing's going to be settled in court.'

" 'What thing?' the reporters asked.

" 'That business with the parrot,' said Havlena. 'What else? I told you I wasn't going to take it lying down. I bought a parrot, see, and taught it to say, You slut! You wicked old bag! Believe me, boys, it took a hell of a lot of hard work. I didn't set foot out of the house for six weeks, and the only words I said the

whole time were, You slut! Anyway, now the parrot says it
beautifully. The only thing is, the stupid bird squawks it all day
long. It simply can't get in the habit of squawking only at that
old woman across the courtyard. She's an old girl from one of the
better families, and she gives music lessons, a very decent person,
actually; but there aren't any other women in our apartment
building, so I had to pick on her for the defamation of character.
Listen, it's easy enough thinking up an offense like that, but
when it comes to pulling it off, God knows that's something else
again. I just couldn't teach that wretched parrot to swear at her
and nobody else. It swears at absolutely everyone. If you ask me,
it does it out of sheer cussedness.'

"Havlena took a deep swig and went on. 'So I took a
different tack. Whenever the old lady showed her face at the
window or out in the yard, I'd pop open the window so the
parrot could screech: You slut! You wicked old bag! And would
you believe it, the old girl would just laugh and call over to me:
Oh, Mr. Havlena, what a cute little bird! Damn that woman,'
growled Havlena, 'I had to keep after her for two weeks before I
could get her to sue me, but I've got witnesses from every apartment in the building. So now it's going to be settled in court,'
gloated Havlena, rubbing his hands. 'They'll have to convict me
for defamation of character, no two ways about it! Those
red-tape tyrants from the ministry will get no mercy from me!'

"Havlena got very restless and impatient, and he drank like
a Dutchman right up to the day of the trial. Once in court,
however, he was legal respectability itself. He gave a scathing
indictment of his own wrongdoing, cited in evidence the testimony of all the other apartment-dwellers that the offense was
flagrant and disgraceful, and demanded the severest punishment
possible. The judge, a very prudent old fellow, scratched his
beard and said he'd like to hear from the parrot. So he adjourned
the hearing with instructions that, when the court reconvened,
the defendant was to bring the bird with him as an exhibit or, if
need be, as a witness.

"Havlena arrived at the next hearing with the parrot in its

cage. The parrot goggled its eyes at the startled lady clerk and began squawking at the top of its voice: You slut! You wicked old bag!

" 'That's enough,' said the judge. 'From the evidence provided by the parrot, it is clear that its remarks could not have been directed solely and specifically at the plaintiff.'

"The parrot fastened its eyes on him and shrieked: You slut!

" 'It is equally clear,' continued His Honor, 'that it employs the remarks in question toward all persons, irrespective of gender. Accordingly, Mr. Havlena, there is an absence of malicious intent.'

"Havlena leaped up as if he'd been stung. 'Your Honor,' he protested in great agitation, 'malicious intent is established by the fact that I opened the window, thereby giving access to the plaintiff for the sole purpose of her vilification by the parrot!'

" 'That's a moot point,' said His Honor. 'The opening of the window may possibly indicate some degree of intent, but it is not in itself a malicious act. I cannot sentence you for opening the window from time to time. And you, Mr. Havlena, cannot prove that your parrot had the plaintiff in mind.'

" 'But *I* had her in mind,' Havlena cried in rebuttal.

" 'We have no evidence to that effect,' the judge objected. 'No one heard you utter the incriminating remarks. It's no use, Mr. Havlena, I shall have to acquit you.' Whereupon he pronounced the defendant not guilty.

" 'And I hereby announce my intent to appeal the acquittal,' Havlena burst out, and he grabbed the cage containing the parrot and swept out of court, nearly weeping with rage.

"Afterwards they would come across him here and there, drunk and disconsolate. 'Tell me, boys,' he would sob, 'do you call that justice? Is there no justice anywhere in this world? But I'm not giving up! I'm taking it to the highest court! They'll vindicate me for this grievous wrong, even if I have to spend the rest of my life in litigation. I'm not fighting on my behalf alone, I'm fighting for justice!'

"I don't know exactly what went on in the court of appeals, but I do know that Havlena's motion to overturn his acquittal was dismissed. After that, Havlena seemed to vanish into thin air, although there are people who say they've spied him wandering around the streets like a lost soul, muttering something or other to himself. I've also heard that to this very day the Ministry of Justice still receives, several times a year, an extensive and fiery petition headed: Defamation of Character Committed by a Parrot. But Havlena stopped supplying court cases to reporters once and for all, no doubt because his faith in the justice system and the law had been badly shaken."

The Needle

"I've never had anything to do with the courts myself," said Mr. Kostelecky, "but I can tell you that what I really like about them is how incredibly painstaking they are, and all the speechifying and formalities they tend to go in for, even if it's only over some little nitpicking thing. It really gives you a lot of confidence in the justice system. If Justice has a set of scales in her hand, they must be truthful as a druggist's, and if she's holding a sword, it must be sharp as a razor. That reminds me of an incident that took place once on our street.

"This concierge, a Mrs. Maskova, bought some rolls at the corner grocery, and while she was munching away on one of them, something suddenly jabbed her in the roof of the mouth. So she reached around inside and pulled out a needle. It wasn't until a little later that she got scared and thought, 'My goodness, I could've swallowed that needle and it could've punctured my stomach! It's a matter of life and death, and I'm not letting it drop! They're going to have to find out who the louse was that snuck the needle in that roll.' So she took the needle and what was left of the roll and went to the police.

"The police questioned the grocer who'd sold the roll, and they questioned the baker who'd baked it, but of course both of them claimed they knew nothing about the needle. So then the police turned it over to the courts, because, you see, it was just a case of minor bodily injury. The examining magistrate, who performed his official duties very thoroughly and conscientiously, questioned the grocer and the baker again; both of them solemnly swore that the needle couldn't have got inside the roll while it was at either of their establishments. The magistrate went to check out the grocery store and satisfied himself that there weren't any needles there. Then he went to check out the bakery and see how rolls are baked. He sat all night in the bakery kitchen and watched how the dough was mixed, how they let it rise, how they lit the fire, and how they shaped the rolls and put them in the oven until they were baked to a golden brown. In that way he satisfied himself that indeed no needles are used in the baking of rolls.

"You wouldn't believe what fine work it is to bake rolls, and especially to bake bread. My grandfather, bless his soul, had a bakery, so I know what it's like. The thing is, you see, there are two or three great, you could almost say holy, secrets in making bread. The first secret is how you prepare the yeast: you let it sit in the kneading trough, and then this mysterious transformation takes place under the lid, and you have to wait until the flour and water become fermented. Then the dough is worked up and mixed with a wooden paddle; it looks like a religious dance or something when you're doing it. After that you cover the dough with a piece of canvas and let it rise, and that's the second mysterious transformation, the way the dough rises so gloriously and plumps itself up — but don't you dare give in to curiosity and lift the cloth to peek underneath. I tell you, it's as strange and beautiful as a pregnancy; I've always had the feeling there was something very feminine about that trough. And the third secret is the actual baking and what happens to that soft, pale dough in the oven. Good glory, when you take out that loaf, all crisp and golden, it smells more delicious than a baby, it's a miracle — I think they ought to ring a bell in bakeries when those three transformations take place, just like they do in church at the elevation of the Host.

"But what I started out to say is that, at this point, the examining magistrate was stumped — but he didn't let the matter drop, not at all. What he did was send the needle to the Institute of Chemistry, to see if they could figure out whether the needle got into the roll before it was baked or afterwards; I should mention that this magistrate was very particular about getting expert opinions. The head of the Institute at the time was a certain Professor Uher, a very scholarly man with lots of whiskers. Well, when Professor Uher got the needle in the mail, he started swearing something awful about everything these courts were always wanting him to do, and that only the other day they'd sent him some entrails that were in such a state of decomposition that even the head of the dissection lab couldn't bear it, and what business did the Institute of Chemistry have with needles, anyway? But then, for some reason or other, he started having second thoughts, and the question began to interest him, from a scientific point of view, of course. 'I wonder,' he said to himself, 'if maybe needles really do undergo some kind of change when they come into contact with dough or when they're baked inside it. Maybe acids of some kind are formed when the dough is fermenting, or again during the baking process, and that could erode or, to put it differently, corrode the surface of the needle somewhat. In that case, it would show up under a microscope.' So he set to work.

"First of all he bought several hundred needles, some spotlessly clean and others more or less rusty, and then he began baking rolls at the Institute of Chemistry. For the first experiment, he put the needles directly into the yeast to find out what effect the process of fermentation had on them. For the second experiment, he put them into the freshly mixed dough. For the third, into the rising dough. Then he inserted them immediately prior to baking. Then during the baking. After that he pushed the needles into the rolls while they were still warm and, finally, when they were done. Then he conducted the entire series of experiments one more time, as a control. In fact, for two weeks they did nothing else at the Institute but bake rolls with needles inside. Day after day, the professor, the associate professor, four researchers, and a lab assistant kneaded dough, baked rolls, and pulled them out of the oven, whereupon they examined the various needles under a microscope and compared the results. This meant an additional week's work, but in the end they established beyond any possibility of doubt that the needle in question had been inserted into the roll after it had been baked, because, microscopically, it corresponded exactly to the experimental needles that had been stuck into the rolls when they were done.

"On the strength of this expert opinion, the magistrate determined that the needle must have got into the roll either at the grocer's or on the way to the grocer's from the baker's. That's when the baker suddenly remembered, 'By thunder, that's the same day I sacked that apprentice, the boy who used to deliver my rolls in a basket!' So they summoned the boy, and he confessed that he'd stuck the needle in the roll because he wanted to get even with the baker. The boy, who was underage, only got a reprimand. The baker was fined, because he was responsible for his employees' actions, but the sentence was suspended. So there you have an example of how precise and thorough the justice system is.

"But there's another side to the story. I don't know what it is about us men that makes us so all-fired ambitious or mulish or whatever, but once they started baking experimental rolls at the Institute, those chemists got it into their heads that they had to do it right. When they first started out, the rolls were a real hodgepodge, they didn't rise properly and they were pretty short on looks; but the more of them the chemists baked, the better they got. Then they started sprinkling poppy seeds, caraway seeds, and salt on top, and they shaped the rolls so nicely that even looking at them was a pleasure. In the end, those chemists were boasting that there was no place in all Prague where the rolls were as crunchy, tasty, and beautiful as the ones they baked at the Institute of Chemistry."

"You may call it mulishness, Mr. Kostelecky," said Mr. Lelek, "but if you ask me, it's more like the sporting instinct. You know, the desire to perform at one-hundred percent of your best. A fellow isn't thorough and methodical only for the sake of the results, which may not even be worth the trouble; he does it because it's a sort of game, an exciting challenge he takes on of his own free will. I can explain what I mean with a single example, even if you do think it's a lot of foolishness and beside the point anyway.

"When I used to be with our bookkeeping department and did the twice-yearly closing of the accounts, it sometimes happened that I couldn't get the figures to tally. Once, for instance, we were exactly three cents short. Of course, it would have been the easiest thing in the world for me to make up the three cents out of my own pocket, but that wouldn't have been playing the game; from an accountant's point of view, you see, that would have been unsportsmanlike. The thing to do was to find out in which of the fourteen thousand or so entries the error lay. And I have to confess that I always looked forward in advance to the possibility that some such error would crop up.

"When it did, I'd stay all night in the office, if need be, pile the whole stack of ledgers in front of me, and get to work. It may seem strange to you, but I always thought of those columns of figures not as numbers, but as things. Sometimes I'd pretend that I was climbing up those rows of figures as if they were a steep cliff, or that I was lowering myself down on them into a pit, as if they were a ladder. Sometimes I felt like a hunter squeezing his way through brambles of figures to catch a rare and timid beast — those three cents were the beast. Or I'd fancy myself a detective, lying in wait around the corner in the dark; thousands of figures pass by me, but I'm waiting to get my hands on that rascal, that culprit, that tiny error in the accounts. At other times it seemed to me that I was sitting on the bank of a river with a rod, angling for a fish; suddenly I jerk the line, and now I've got you, you little devil! But more often than not, I imagined myself to be a hunter, splashing up and down through wet thickets of berrybushes, and I got such pleasure and excitement from the activity, such a curious sense of freedom and power, it was as if I were actually living the adventure. Believe me, I could spend the whole night chasing down those three cents. And when I'd caught them, it would never occur to me that it was only three piddling little coins; it was nothing short of a trophy, and I'd go home in such high and triumphant spirits

that it's a wonder I didn't fall into bed with my boots on. That's
what I wanted to tell you."

The Telegram

"You call them trifles," mused Mr. Dolezal. "It's my observation that, for the most part, people behave naturally and normally only in trifling, everyday matters. But as soon as they find themselves in unusual and highly emotional situations, it's as if a completely new person got into them. They start talking in a different, I'd say dramatic voice, and they use different kinds of words, different kinds of arguments, even experience different kinds of feelings than they normally do. Nine times out of ten, they burst out in bravery, nobility, self-sacrifice and other such heroic and high-principled traits. It's as if they'd inhaled some sort of ozone that impels them to make grand gestures; or maybe they gain some kind of secret satisfaction from extraordinary or catastrophic situations, and it's somehow pleasing to them and puffs them up. The thing is, they start behaving like heroes on stage. Later, when the dramatic moment is over and done with, they revert to their normal size. But afterwards they feel just a touch embarrassed, as if they'd been disillusioned or let down.

"I've got a cousin named Kalous, a decent and respectable bureaucrat, citizen, and paterfamilias, a bit of a fence-sitter and a stuffed shirt, the way we older men tend to be. Mrs. Kalousova is a fine, deserving woman, a model mother hen, a meek homebody, a so-called doormat and so forth. Then there's a daughter, a really pretty girl named Vera, who was off in France at the time, so she could learn French and pass her exams in case she didn't get married. Finally there's a son, a strapping high-school lad called Tonda, a good soccer forward, but pretty weak in his studies. In short, a good, typical, normal family from what's called the better middle class.

"Well, one day the Kalouses were seated at lunch when somebody rang their doorbell. Mrs. Kalousova reappears in the doorway, wiping her hands on her apron and saying all in a dither, her face flushed, 'Oh my goodness, Dad, some kind of telegram's arrived.' You know how women get alarmed when a telegram arrives; it's due to their internal functioning, no doubt, that they're always expecting some kind of fateful blow.

" 'Come, come, Mother,' Mr. Kalous grumbled, 'try to get hold of yourself, no matter who sent it.' But his hand trembled when he opened the telegram. Everyone, even the maid in the doorway, stared breathlessly at the head of the family.

" 'It's from Vera,' Kalous finally said in a voice not quite his own. 'But I'm damned if I can understand a word of it.'

" 'Let me see it,' Mrs. Kalousova burst out.

" 'Wait,' said Kalous sternly. 'It's all garbled up. It says, Gadete un ucjarc peuige bellevue grenoble vera.'

" 'How can it say that?' gasped Mrs. Kalousova.

" 'Look at it yourself, then,' Kalous said spitefully, 'if you think you can understand it any better than I can! Well, now you've seen it, what's in it?'

"Mrs. Kalousova's eyes flooded with tears over the ill-omened telegram. 'Something's happened to Vera,' she whispered. 'Otherwise she wouldn't have sent us a telegram!'

" 'You think I don't know that?' shouted Kalous, and he put on his coat; obviously, it would be bad form in so grave a situation to stand there without a coat. 'Go to the kitchen, Andula,' he ordered the maid; after which he announced, tragically, 'the telegram is from Grenoble. I think Vera's eloped with somebody.'

" 'With who?' exclaimed Mrs. Kalousova, shocked at the thought.

" 'How the hell should I know?' Mr. Kalous roared. 'He's bound to be some kind of scoundrel or artist! *This* is what female independence gets you! I expected something like this! I didn't want to let her go there, to that damned Paris! But you, you were always taking her side — '

" 'You think I wanted it? Me?' seethed Mrs. Kalousova.

'*You're* the one who was always preaching to her about how she was supposed to study something, how she was supposed to earn a living for herself!' At which point she broke into sobs and crumpled into a chair, 'Dear Jesus, poor Vera! Maybe something did happen to her — Maybe she's lying there sick — '

"Mr. Kalous, all worked up, began to pace about the room. 'Sick?' he cried. 'Why would she be sick? Let's just hope it wasn't some kind of suicide attempt! Probably that fellow kidnapped her — and then he ran out on her — '

"Mrs. Kalousova began to tear off her apron. 'I'm going after her,' she declared with a moan. 'I'm not leaving her there — I — '

" 'You're not going anywhere,' bellowed Kalous.

"Mrs. Kalousova rose; never before had they seen her display such dignity. 'I am a *mother*, Kalous,' she said. 'I know my duty.' Whereupon she withdrew with a certain grandeur.

"The two men, that is, father Kalous and the boy Tonda, remained alone. 'We must be prepared for the worst,' said Kalous darkly. 'Maybe Vera was kidnapped — Don't say anything in front of your mother. I'll go to Grenoble myself.'

" 'Father,' said Tonda in his deepest voice — at all other times he said Dad, 'let me do it. I'll go there. I know a little French, you know — '

" 'They'd be scared to death of a boy like you,' jeered father Kalous. 'I'm rescuing my child! I'm taking the next train out — Let's just hope it's not too late!'

" 'Train!' scoffed Tonda. 'You might as well go there by foot! If *I* were going, I'd take a *plane* to Strasbourg — '

" 'You think I'm *afraid* to fly?' yelled father Kalous. 'For your information, I'm flying! As for that scoundrel,' he threatened belligerently, shaking his fists, 'I'll p-p-pulverize him! Poor child!'

"Tonda laid his hand on his father's shoulder; it was wonderful how all at once that lout had turned into a man. 'Father,' he said soothingly, 'this isn't for you; you're too old for it. You can rely on me. You know I'll do everything humanly possible for my sister.' Until that moment, of course, like younger brothers in general, he had regarded his sister with nothing but heartfelt masculine contempt.

"Kalous shook his head. 'No,' he said solemnly, 'this is *my* affair. A child can't rely on anyone like she can on her father. I'm going there, Tonda. Meanwhile, you must be Mother's support. These women, you know — '

"Just then Mrs. Kalousova entered, dressed to go out. Oddly enough, she did not look in the least like someone in need of support.

" 'And where, if you please, are you off to?' sputtered Kalous.

" 'To the bank,' said the courageous woman, utterly aloof. 'To get *my* money. So I can go to *my* daughter in that foreign country.'

" 'That's nonsense!' exploded Kalous.

" 'It's not,' said Mrs. Kalousova, cool as ice. 'I know what I'm doing. And I know why I'm doing it.'

" 'Woman,' said Kalous decisively, 'just so you know, I'm going after Vera myself.'

" 'You?' said Mrs. Kalous with something approaching disdain. 'What use would *you* be in France? Not that you'd ever drag yourself away from your comforts here,' she added crushingly.

"Father Kalous tensed and turned red. 'Don't you worry,' he said sharply, 'about what use I'd be in France. I've already figured out *exactly* what needs to be done. I am prepared for everything. Just tell the maid to pack my overnight bag, all right?'

" 'I know you,' declared Mrs. Kalousova. 'If your boss doesn't give you the time off, you won't be going anywhere.'

" 'The hell with my boss!' Kalous yelled. 'The hell with the office! Let them fire me! I'll make a living somehow! I've sacrificed my whole life for my family up to now and I'll sacrifice the rest of it, too, understand?'

"Mrs. Kalousova dropped down on the edge of a chair. 'Man,' she said through clenched teeth, 'get through your head what's going on here! I'm the one who's going to go take care of her! I have a feeling that Vera is hovering between life and death! I have to be with her — '

" 'And I have a feeling,' declared Kalous, 'that she's in the clutches of some scoundrel. If we only knew what that telegram meant, we could prepare — '

" ' — for the worst!' wailed Mrs. Kalousova.

" 'Maybe,' Kalous said gloomily. 'I'm just afraid to think what that telegram actually says.'

" 'Listen,' Mrs. Kalousova offered uncertainly, 'maybe we could ask Mr. Horvat about it.'

" 'About what?' said Kalous, taken aback.

" 'About what's in that telegram. After all, Mr. Horvat works out codes and things — '

" 'He does for a fact,' Mr. Kalous breathed in relief. 'He could figure this out! Andula,' he bawled, 'run up to the fifth floor and ask Mr. Horvat to please come down here!'

"I should tell you that Mr. Horvat is with our intelligence service, and his work is mainly involved with deciphering secret codes. They say he's a genius, this Horvat; give him enough time and he can break any code. But it's horrendously painstaking work, and anyone who does it gets a little unhinged.

"Anyway, it wasn't long before Mr. Horvat arrived at the door; he's such a fussy little shrimp and he gives off this awful smell of peppermint.

" 'Mr. Horvat,' Kalous began, 'I received this completely unintelligible telegram, and we thought that maybe you could kindly — '

" 'Let me have a look,' said Mr. Horvat. He read it through and remained seated with his eyes half closed. There was a deathly silence.

" 'Yes indeed,' said Mr. Horvat, breaking the silence by and by, 'and who is the telegram from?'

" 'From our daughter, Vera,' explained Kalous. 'She's study-ing in France.'

" 'Aha,' said Mr. Horvat, and he rose. 'You're supposed to

wire two hundred francs to her at the Hotel Bellevue in Grenoble, that's all.'

" 'You figured out what was in the telegram?' Kalous burst out.

" 'Of course I did,' grumbled Mr. Horvat. 'This is no code, it's only garbled words. But I ask you, why else would a young girl like that send a telegram? Probably she lost her purse with her money in it, that's all. That's what's happened.'

" 'And there couldn't be . . . there couldn't possibly be something worse in the telegram?' Kalous asked uncertainly.

" 'Why would there be anything worse in it?' Mr. Horvat wondered. 'Look, more often than not it's always something ordinary that happens. Women's purses aren't worth a darn.'

" 'We are grateful to you, sir,' said Kalous frigidly.

" 'Don't mention it,' grumbled Mr. Horvat, and he left.

"There was silence for a brief moment at the Kalouses'. 'Listen,' broke in Kalous, embarrassed, 'I don't care for that man at all. He's a . . . well, he's a boor.'

"Mrs. Kalousova began to unbutton her coat. 'A bore,' she said. 'Are you going to send Vera the money?'

" 'Of course I'm sending it,' Kalous muttered peevishly. 'Silly goose, she had to go and lose her purse! Does she think money grows on trees? She deserves a couple of good — '

" 'I scrimp like crazy,' Mrs. Kalousova added bitterly, 'and she, Miss Spendthrift, can't even keep an eye on her purse! That's what's wrong with these children — '

" 'And quit gawking and go do your homework, you lazy brat,' Kalous snapped at Tonda, and then he straggled off to the post office. Never in his life had Kalous been so irritated as at that moment. And from that time on he considered Horvat a rather rude, cynical, almost indecent man, as if Horvat had offended him somehow."

The Man Who Couldn't Sleep

"When Mr. Dolezal here was talking about deciphering," Mr. Kavka said, "it reminded me of something I once pulled on my colleague Musil. Musil is an unusually well-educated and sophisticated man, but he's the type of intellectual who sees a problem in everything and has to cast around for his point of view on it. For example, he even has a point of view on his own wife: Musil isn't a partner in the state of matrimony, he's a partner in the problem of matrimony. He thinks in terms of the social problem, the sexual question, the problem of the subconscious, the problem of education, the crisis of contemporary culture, and a whole range of other problems. These people who see problems in everything are just as insufferable as people who have principles. I don't like problems. To me, an egg is an egg, and if somebody starts telling me about the problem of the egg, well, I start worrying that the egg is rotten. I'm telling you this so you'll know what Musil is like.

"Once, just before Christmas, he took it into his head to go skiing up in the Krkonose Mountains. And because he still had a few things to pick up, he announced that he'd stop by the office later to say goodbye. Right after he left, Dr. Mandel came in looking for him — you know, the famous columnist and a very strange character — and said he had to speak with Musil at once. 'Musil isn't here,' I told him, 'but he'll probably drop by before he leaves. Why don't you wait for him?' Mandel frowned. 'I can't wait,' he said, 'but I'll write him a note telling him why I wanted to see him.' Then he sat down at a desk and began to write.

"I don't know if any of you can imagine handwriting more illegible than Dr. Mandel's. It looks like a seismograph reading

— a sort of long, jerky, horizontal line that twitches from time to time or leaps up and down, zigzag fashion . . . I knew his handwriting well, so I just watched the way his hand rode around on the paper. Suddenly Mandel scowled, crumpled up the paper impatiently, flung it into the wastebasket, and jumped up. 'Takes too long,' he muttered, and then he was gone, just like that.

"The day before Christmas, you know, a man doesn't want to do any serious work. So I sat at my desk and began making seismograph lines on a piece of paper: a long, shaky stroke, bouncing up and down every so often, whatever happened to strike me. I amused myself with it for a while, and then I put the paper, covered with my scrawls, on Musil's desk. Just then Musil showed up at the door, all decked out for the mountains, with skis and ski poles over his shoulder. 'I'm off,' he blared cheerfully from the doorway.

" 'Someone was here looking for you,' I said cautiously. 'He left you a note; apparently it's important.'

" 'Show it to me,' said Musil with zest. 'What's this?' he said, somewhat taken aback by that product of mine. 'It's from Dr. Mandel,' he remarked. 'I wonder what he wants with me.'

" 'I don't know,' I mumbled brusquely, 'he was in a hurry. But I'd hate to have to figure out his handwriting.'

" 'I can read his scribbling,' Musil declared recklessly, and he propped up his skis and poles and sat down at the desk. 'Hm,' he said after a moment, and then he began concentrating in earnest. There was half an hour of dead silence. Then Musil fetched a sigh of relief and stood up. 'There, I think I've got the first two words. They're: Dear Sir. But now I have to dash to the station. I'll take the note with me, and if I can't solve it on the train ride, then the devil himself must have written it!'

"After New Year's he returned from his expedition to the mountains. 'So how was your vacation, friend Musil?' I asked. 'It's beautiful in the mountains now, isn't it?'

"Musil merely waved his hand. 'I have no idea,' he said. 'I must confess I spent the entire time in my hotel room. I didn't even poke my nose out the door, but everyone there said it was magnificent.'

"'What happened?' I asked sympathetically, 'Were you sick?'

"'Not at all,' Musil answered with feigned modesty. 'I spent the whole time deciphering Mandel's note. And I want you to know that I BROKE THE CODE,' he declared in triumph. 'There were only two or three words I couldn't make out. I sat up all night over them — but I'd made up my mind that I was going to break it, and I did.'

"I hadn't the courage to tell him that the note was only my chicken-scratches. 'And was the message that important?' I asked with concern. 'Was it at least worth your efforts?'

"'That doesn't matter,' Musil replied imperiously. 'To *me*, it was more interesting as a graphological problem. In the note, Dr. Mandel asked me if, within the next couple of weeks, I would write an article for his journal — about what, I can't exactly make out. And then he wishes me happy holidays and a pleasant stay in the mountains. Altogether it isn't much; but the deciphering, Dolezal, that was truly a hard nut to crack — there's nothing like it for improving the mind. It was well worth the couple of days and nights I spent on it.'"

"You shouldn't have done that to him," Mr. Paulus said reproachfully. "The hell with the 'couple of days,' but those nights without sleep — there's the harm. Sleep, my friend, isn't only for resting the body; sleep is more like a purification and forgiveness for the day just ended. Sleep is a divine gift, and for the first few minutes after a good sleep, the soul is pure and innocent as a child.

"I know this, because at one time I suffered from loss of sleep. Perhaps it was the consequence of a misspent life, or perhaps there was something physically wrong with me, I don't know. But hardly had I gotten into bed and sensed that first prickle of drowsiness in my eyes than a sort of tingling would begin, and then I would lie for hours and hours staring into the darkness until it began to grow light. And this went on for an entire year, a year without sleep.

"When a man can't fall asleep, he first of all tries not to think about anything. That's why he counts things, or prays. Suddenly the thought comes to him: Oh no, I forgot to do such-and-such yesterday! And then it strikes him that they probably overcharged him at the store. Next he remembers that, just the other day, his wife or his friend answered him in such an odd way. Later on, a piece of furniture creaks, and he thinks it's a burglar and begins to feel the heat of fear and shame. And then, once he's thoroughly alarmed, he starts to examine the condition of his body and, sweating in terror, tries to remember everything he's ever heard about Bright's disease or cancer. Then, from out of nowhere, some embarrassing nonsense from twenty years ago pops into his mind, and even now it makes his sweat run cold. Step by step he's confronted with his alien, persistent, unredeemed self; with his weaknesses, his crude and loathsome ways, the misbehavior, idiocies, and ridicule, how he made a fool of himself, slights and suffering from the long-ago past. Everything awkward and painful and humiliating comes back to him, just as when he first lived through it. Nothing is spared the man who cannot sleep. His whole world is distorted and his perspective is increasingly tormented. Things you forgot long ago smirk at you as if they were saying, 'You clown, you conducted yourself nicely that time, didn't you? And remember, when you were fourteen, how your first love didn't show up for that date? You know she was kissing somebody else, don't you, your friend Vojta, and they were laughing at you! You fool, fool, fool!' — You writhe in your burning bed and try to persuade yourself that, damn it, it's nothing to me now! What happened happened, and that's that! — You should know how untrue that is. Everything that was, is. Even what you're unaware of exists. And I am convinced that memory exists even after death.

"Look, you know me pretty well. You know I'm not a sorehead or a hypochondriac or some other kind of crank. I'm

not a whiner, not quarrelsome or touchy, not a crybaby, bore, or
pessimist. I love life and people and also myself, I barge right
into the middle of things like a fool, I love to grapple with life.
In short, I'm just a rough-edged, ordinary kind of fellow, the way
any man should be. Even during that time when I couldn't sleep,
I spent my days rushing about, I took on whatever came my way
and went from one task to the next. I comforted myself with the
myth of the blessedly active man. But the moment I crept into
bed and began my sleepless night, my life fell apart. On the one
hand, there was the life of a busy, successful, self-satisfied, and
healthy man, who prospers in everything, thanks to energy,
know-how, and shameless good luck. But in bed lay a man
exhausted, a man who realized with horror the failures, the
shame, the sordidness and humiliations of his entire life. I was
living two lives which had almost no connection with each other
and which were frighteningly dissimilar: one, by day, consisting
of activity, accomplishment, personal contact and trust, the
enjoyment of challenges and the ordinary sort of getting by — a
life with which I was, in my own way, happy and content. But
during the night a second life unfolded, woven from pain and
confusion: the life of a man who has met only with failure; a man
who was betrayed by everyone and who was false and mean-
spirited to everyone in return; a tragic, clumsy fool whom everyone hated and deceived; a weakling, a loser who reeled from one
dishonorable defeat to the next. Each of these lives was consis-
tent, coherent, and entire in itself. When I was in the midst of
living one of them, it seemed to me that the other belonged to
somebody else, that it had nothing to do with me or that it was
only make-believe; that it was self-deception, a pathological
illusion. In the daytime I loved; at night I suspected and hated.
In the daytime I lived in our world; at night I lived in mine.
Whoever thinks only of himself loses the world.

"And so it seems to me that sleep is like dark, deep water;
and in it, everything we do not and should not know drifts away.
These odd impurities that deposit themselves in us rise to the
surface and flow into the unconscious, where there are no shores.

Our wickedness and cowardice, all our painful, everyday transgressions, our humbling follies and failures, the fleeting look of dislike and deceit in the eyes of those we love, everything of which we ourselves are guilty, even that of which others are guilty towards us, everything wanders silently away somewhere beyond the reach of awareness. Sleep is boundlessly merciful. It forgives both us and those who trespass against us.

"And I'll tell you something else. That which we call our life is not at all everything that we have experienced, it is only a selection. That which we are experiencing now is too much, more than we are capable of understanding. That's why we choose only this or that, whatever suits us or is convenient, and from it we somehow knit the simple plot, the fabrication we call our 'life.' But at the same time, what rubbish we leave behind, what strange and terrible things we unconsciously omit. My God, if we only realized what it is we do! But we are capable only of living one simple life. More than that would be more than we could bear. We wouldn't have the strength to endure life if we could not discard the larger part of it along the way."

The Stamp Collection

"It's the holy truth," said old Mr. Karas. "If a man rummaged around in his past, he'd find enough material in it for several different lives. At some point . . . whether by mistake or inclination . . . he chooses only one of them and lives it through to the end. But the worst of it is that those other, those possible lives, aren't entirely dead. And sometimes you can feel pain from them, just as one does from an amputated leg.

"When I was a boy of about ten, I began collecting stamps. My dad wasn't at all happy about it, because he thought it would interfere with my schoolwork. But I had a pal, Lojzik Cepelka, and together we indulged in our passion for stamps. Lojzik was an organ-grinder's son, a grubby, freckled lad, scruffy as a sparrow, and I loved him as only kids can love their buddies. Listen, I'm an old man; I've had a wife and children, but I'm telling you there's no human emotion as beautiful as friendship. You're only capable of it when you're young, however; later on you get crusty somehow, and selfish. The kind of friendship I'm talking about springs up from pure enthusiasm and admiration, from an overflow of vitality, from exuberance and an abundance of emotion — you have so much of it that you just have to give it away to someone. My dad was a lawyer, head man among the local notables, a terribly dignified and demanding gentleman — and I'd taken up with Lojzik, the friend of my heart, whose father was a drunken organ-grinder and mother a work-worn laundress. And yet I worshiped and idolized Lojzik, because he was more handy and resourceful than I, because he was self-sufficient and brave as a rat, and because he had freckles on his nose and could throw stones left-handed — I can't even remember now what all I loved him for, but it was undoubtedly the greatest love of my life.

"And so Lojzik was my beloved, trusty pal when I began collecting stamps. Somebody once said that only men have a flair for collecting. It's true: I think it's an instinct or a holdover from the times when every male collected his enemies' heads, stolen weapons, bearskins, stags' antlers and, on the whole, anything he could capture. But a stamp collection, it isn't merely a possession, it's a nonstop adventure. It's as if somehow, trembling with excitement, you're touching a bit of some faraway land, Bhutan, say, or Bolivia, or the Cape of Good Hope. To put it simply, it's like having a personal and intimate connection with all those foreign countries. There's something about stamp-collecting that makes you think of travel and voyages and the whole wide world of manly adventures in general. It's a lot like the Crusades.

"As I was saying, my father didn't like the idea at all. Fathers as a rule don't like it when their sons do something different from what they do themselves; look, I was the the same way with my own sons. By and large, this business of being a father is a matter of mixed emotions: there's a great deal of love involved, but there's also a certain preoccupation, mistrust, hostility or whatever you want to call it. The more you love your children, the more this other emotion enters in. Anyway, I had to hide my stamp collection in the attic so my dad wouldn't catch me with it. There was an old chest in the attic, one of those old-fashioned flour bins, and we used to crawl into it like a couple of mice and look over each other's stamps: Look, this one's a Netherlands, this one's an Egypt, here's one from Sverige — that's Sweden. And because we had to hide out like that with our treasures, there was something almost deliciously sinful about it. The way I got hold of those stamps was adventurous, too. I'd go around to different households, whether we knew the families there or not, and beg them to let me soak the stamps off their old letters. Every so often people would have drawers crammed with old papers in their attics or desks; those were my most blissful hours, sitting on the floor and sorting through those dusty piles of junk paper, looking for stamps I didn't already have — in other words, fool that I was, I didn't collect duplicates. When I'd find an old Lombardy or one of those tiny German states or free cities, the joy I felt was perfectly agonizing — every vast happiness carries its own sweet pain, you know. Meanwhile, Lojzik would be waiting for me outside, and when I'd finally come out, I'd whisper right from the doorway: Lojzik, Lojzik, there was a Hanover in there! — Got it? — Yes! — And off we'd run with our plunder, home to our treasure chest.

"We had some textile factories in our town that made all kinds of shoddy stuff: jute, calico, cheap prints, and other third-rate cotton goods; in other words, the kind of worthless trash we churn out specially for colored people all over the globe. Anyway, they used to let me ransack their wastepaper baskets, and that was my richest hunting ground. That's where I found stamps from Siam and South Africa, China, Liberia, Afghanistan, Borneo, Brazil, New Zealand, India, the Congo — I don't know about you, but to me even the very names ring with mystery and fill me with a kind of longing. Great heaven, the joy, the savage joy I felt when I'd come across a stamp from, say, the Straits Settlements — or Korea! Nepal! New Guinea! Sierra Leone! Madagascar! Listen, it's a rapture that only a hunter or a treasure-seeker can understand, or an archaeologist on a dig. To seek and to find, that's the greatest thrill, the greatest satisfaction life can offer. Everyone should search for something; if not stamps, then truth, or golden ferns, or at least stone arrowheads and ashtrays.

"Well, those were the happiest years of my life, my friendship with Lojzik and the stamp collection. Then I had scarlet fever and they wouldn't let Lojzik come and see me, but he'd stand in our hallway and whistle so I could hear him. One day they weren't paying that much attention to me or something; anyway, I slipped out of bed and headed lickety-split for the attic to have a look at my stamps. I was so weak I could hardly raise the lid of the chest. But the chest was empty. The box with the stamps was gone.

"There's no way I can possibly describe my heartache and horror. I think I must have stood there as if I'd been turned to stone, and I couldn't even cry, there was such a lump in my throat. To begin with, it was horrifying that my stamps, my greatest joy, were gone. But what was even more horrifying was that Lojzik, my only friend, must have stolen them while I was sick in bed. Dismay, disillusionment, grief, despair — believe me, it's astonishing what someone who's only a child can suffer. How I got out of that attic, I have no idea. But afterwards I lay in bed once again with a high fever, and in my clearer moments I remembered and grieved. I never said anything about it to my father or my aunt — I didn't have a mother. I knew they simply wouldn't understand me, and because of that I became more or less alienated from them. From that time on I no longer felt any close attachment to them, the way children normally do. As for Lojzik's betrayal, it was very nearly a mortal wound; it was my first and greatest disillusionment in my fellow human beings. Beggar, I said to myself, Lojzik's a beggar, and that's why he steals; it serves me right for being best friends with a beggar. And it hardened my heart. From then on I began to make distinctions among people — I lost my state of societal innocence. But I didn't realize, then, how deep a shock it had been to me and how much damage it had done.

"When I got over my fever, I also got over my pain at the loss of my stamp collection. Except that my heart still ached when I saw that, in the meantime, Lojzik had found new pals. But when he came running up to me, a little embarassed because it had been such a long time, I said to him in a blunt, grown-up way, 'Shove off, I'm not talking to you.' Lojzik turned red, and after a moment he said, 'Suits me, too.' And from that time on he hated me with stubborn, working-class scorn.

"Well, that was the incident that determined the course of my life, my choice of life, as Mr. Paulus would say. What I would say is that my world had been desecrated. I lost my faith in people. I learned to hate and despise. I never had a close friend again. And when I grew up, I even began to take pride in the fact that I was alone, that I didn't need anyone and didn't yield an inch to anybody. Later I discovered that nobody liked me. I told myself it was because I had nothing but contempt for love and didn't give a damn for sentiment. And so I became a proud and ambitious man, self-centered, exacting, altogether correct in every particular. I was harsh and heavy-handed with my subordinates; I made a loveless marriage and brought up my children to fear and obey me; and, thanks to my diligence and industry, I gained a well-deserved reputation. That was my life, my whole life. I attended only to that which I considered my duty. When I go to meet my Maker, no doubt the newspapers will say that I was a leader in my field and a man of exemplary character and principle. But if people knew of the loneliness in all that, the mistrust and the callousness —

"Three years ago my wife died. I never admitted it to myself or to anyone else, but I was deeply saddened. And in my grief I rummaged through all kinds of family keepsakes that had been left by my father and mother: photographs, letters, my old notebooks from school — my throat constricted when I saw how carefully my stern father had saved them and stored them away; I think he must have loved me after all. The cabinet in the attic was filled with things like that, and at the bottom of one of the drawers was a box which had been sealed with my father's seals. When I opened it, I discovered the stamp collection that I had put together fifty years before.

"I'm not going to keep anything back from you; I burst into a flood of tears, and I carried that box into my room as if it were a treasure. So *that's* what happened, I suddenly realized: while I was confined in bed, somebody had found my stamp collection and my father had confiscated it so that I wouldn't neglect my studies! He shouldn't have done it, but it was because of his strict love and concern for me. I'm not sure why, but I began to feel pity for him, and for myself, too —

"And then it came to me: This meant that Lojzik hadn't stolen my stamps! Great heaven, how I had wronged him! — Again I saw the freckled, scruffy urchin before me — God knows what had become of him or even whether he was still alive! I can't tell you the pain and shame I felt when I thought back on it all. Because of one false suspicion I lost my only friend; because of that I lost my childhood. Because of that I began to despise the poor and their verminous brats; because of that I became puffed up with self-importance. Because of that I never again formed a close attachment to anyone. Because of that I could never in my entire life look at a postage stamp without resentment and disgust. Because of that I never wrote to my wife, either before or during our marriage, and I disguised it by pretending that such outbursts of sentimentality were beneath me; and it hurt my wife deeply. Because of that I was harsh and aloof. Because of that, only because of that, did I rise so high in my profession and fulfill my obligations in such an exemplary manner —

"I saw my whole life afresh. All at once it seemed empty and meaningless to me. Why, I might have lived my life in an entirely different way, I suddenly realized. If that hadn't happened — there was so much enthusiasm and love of adventure in me, so much affection, imagination, and confidence, so much that was singular and passionate — my God, I might have been someone else altogether, an explorer or an actor or a soldier! Why, I might have loved people, drunk with them, understood them, who knows what I might have done! It was just as if ice were thawing inside me. I turned over stamp after stamp; they were all there, Lombardy, Cuba, Siam, Hanover, Nicaragua, the Philippines, all the lands I had wanted to travel to and now would never see. Every stamp embraced a small piece of something that might have been and never was. I sat there through the entire night, going over the stamps and taking stock of my life. I saw that it had been someone else's life, artificial and impersonal, and that, in reality, my true life had never come into being." Mr. Karas gestured with his hand. "When I think of all that I might have been — and how I wronged Lojzik — "

Upon hearing these words, Father Voves frowned and looked extremely unhappy; most likely he had remembered something in his own life. "Mr. Karas," he said, much moved, "don't think about it now. What would be the use, you can't rectify it now, you can't make a fresh start — "

"No," sighed Mr. Karas, and then he flushed slightly. "But you know, at least — at least I've started collecting stamps again!"

An Ordinary Murder

"I've often wondered," said Mr. Hanak, "why injustice seems worse to us than almost anything else that could happen to a person. For instance, if we saw a single innocent man sent to prison, we'd be more upset and bothered by that than by thousands of people living in poverty and pain. I've seen misery so horrifying that any prison is sheer luxury by comparison; and yet the worst possible misery doesn't offend us as much as injustice. I think we must have some kind of inherent instinct for justice, and that our feelings about guilt and innocence, fairness and right are just as primitive, awesome, and deeply instinctive as love and hunger.

"Take this example: I was at the front for four years, just as many of you were. We won't tell each other what we saw there, but you'll agree with me that the likes of us got accustomed to pretty much anything — to dead bodies, for instance. I've seen the corpses of hundreds and hundreds of young men, sometimes unbelievably grisly corpses, as you well know; and I don't mind telling you that, after a time, they meant no more to me than if they were so many bundles of old rags, as long as they didn't stink. All I said to myself was, if you get out of this bestial mess alive and whole, nothing's going to shake you for the rest of your life.

"About six months after the war, after I was back home in Slatina, somebody banged on my window one morning and called, 'Mr. Hanak, better come have a look. Mrs. Turkova's been killed!' This Mrs. Turkova had a tiny shop that sold stationery and thread. Nobody ever paid much attention to her, except that now and then someone would come into her shop for a spool of thread or some Christmas cards. At the back of the shop there was a glass-paneled door leading into a small kitchen, which is where she slept; curtains hung over the door, and when the bell at the shop door jingled Mrs. Turkova would peep through the curtains to see who it was, wipe her hands on her apron, and step into the shop. 'Yes? What do you want?' she'd ask suspiciously. The customer would feel like an intruder there and try to get out again as quickly as possible. It was the same as when you lift up a stone and there underneath, in a damp little hole, is this solitary, startled beetle scurrying about; so you put the stone back, to let the disagreeable creature calm down again.

"Well, when I heard the news, I ran to have a look, I suppose just out of common curiosity. People were swarming like bees in front of Mrs. Turkova's shop, but the local policeman let me go inside because he regarded me as an educated man. The bell jingled and broke the silence just the way it always had, but now its bright, lively peal made me shiver; it struck me as being out of place there. Mrs. Turkova lay in the doorway between the shop and the kitchen with her face to the floor, and under her head was a pool of blood which by now had turned nearly black; the gray hair at the nape of her neck was matted and stained with more dark blood. And at that moment I suddenly became aware of a feeling I had never experienced during the war: horror over the body of a dead human being.

"It's strange, but I've almost forgotten about the war; in fact, everybody's gradually forgetting about it, and maybe that's why, sooner or later, there'll have to be another. But I will never forget that murdered old woman who, essentially, was of little use or interest to anyone at all, that old woman with her tiny shop who couldn't even sell a postcard properly. A murdered person isn't the same as a dead person, because there's a kind of terrible secret about it. I simply couldn't understand why Mrs. Turkova of all people had been murdered, that ordinary, unremarkable, faded old lady to whom no one had ever given a second thought, or how she came to be lying there so pathetically with a policeman bending over her, while outside, all those people were pushing to take a look. Believe me, the poor thing had never attracted as much attention as she did then, lying there with her face in that dark pool of blood. It was as if she'd suddenly acquired a strange and horrifying importance. Never in my life had I taken any notice of how she was dressed or what she really looked like, but now it seemed as if I were looking at her through a glass in which everything was vastly and grotesquely magnified. There was a carpet slipper on one foot; the other slipper had been removed and you could see where the stocking had been mended at the heel — I could see every stitch, and there was something dreadful about it, I thought, as if even that poor, frayed stocking had been murdered, too. One hand was clutching at the floor; it looked as wizened and fragile as a bird's claw. But most horrifying of all was that twist of gray hair at the nape of the murdered woman's neck, because it was so painstakingly braided and it shone like old pewter among the congealed rivulets of blood. I felt as if I'd never seen anything more heartrending than that stained and spattered little coil. One ribbon of blood had dried behind her ear; a small silver earring with a tiny blue stone glistened above it. I couldn't stand the sight any longer, my legs were shaking. 'Jesus Christ,' I said.

"The policeman, who was in the kitchen looking for something on the floor, got to his feet and looked at me. He was pale, as if he were on the verge of fainting.

" 'Oh,' I blurted, 'were you at the front, too?'

" 'I was,' the policeman said in a husky voice. 'But this — this is different. Look at that,' he added suddenly, and he pointed to the curtains on the door. They were crumpled and smeared with blood; evidently the murderer had wiped his hands on them. 'Good God,' I gasped. I don't know what was so unbearably harrowing about it — whether it was the image of hands sticky with blood, or the idea that the curtains, those clean and tidy curtains, had also become a victim of the crime — I simply don't know. But at that moment a canary in that little kitchen began warbling and then burst into a lengthy trill. Well, that was really more than I could stand. I bolted out of the shop in sheer horror — I think I must have been even paler than the policeman.

"I sat down on the shaft of a wagon in our yard and tried to collect my thoughts. 'You fool,' I said to myself, 'you coward, it's just an ordinary murder! Haven't you ever seen blood before? Haven't you been splashed with your own blood, like a pig with mud? Haven't you shouted to your men to hurry up and dig a pit for a hundred-and-thirty dead bodies? A hundred-and-thirty corpses side by side, that's one long line, even if you lay them out as close together as shingles on a roof. You'd walked alongside them, smoked cigarettes, and yelled at the troops, 'All right, get moving, get moving, we haven't got all night.' You've seen so many dead people, so many dead —

" 'Yes,' I said to myself, 'that's it. I've seen so many dead, but I never saw one single, lone Dead Human Being. I've never knelt down beside it to look into its face and touch its hair. A dead human being is horribly silent; you need to be alone with it . . . and not even breathe . . . if you want to understand it. Every one of those hundred-and-thirty would have tried his best to say to you: Lieutenant, sir, they've killed me; but look at my hands, they're the hands of a man! — But we all turned our backs on the dead. We had a war to fight, we couldn't stop and listen to the ones who'd fallen. By God, maybe what's needed is for people — boys, women, and children — to swarm like bees around every man who fell, so that they could see at least some small part of him, at least a foot in its army boot or a lock of blood-stained hair. Then maybe these things wouldn't happen; then they *couldn't* happen.

"And I had buried my mother. She looked so solemn, so peaceful and dignified in her coffin. She looked strange to me, but not terrifying. But this, this was something other than death. The murdered are not dead; the murdered lament as if they were screaming with the most extreme and unbearable pain. We knew that, the policeman and I, and we knew that the shop was haunted. And then something began to dawn on me. I don't know whether we have souls or not; but there are immortal things within us, and one of them is this instinctive desire for justice. I'm no better than anyone else, but there is something within me that isn't only mine, that doesn't belong only to me — the notion of a more exacting and more powerful order. I know I'm saying this badly, but at that moment I understood what crime is and what is meant by an offense against God. You see, a person who's been murdered is like a holy place that's been violated and defiled."

"But what about the man who killed that old woman?" Mr. Dobes asked after a moment's silence. "Did they catch him?"

"They caught him," continued Mr. Hanak, "and I saw him two days later, when the police were taking him out of the shop; they'd been cross-examining him at the scene of the crime, as it's called. I don't suppose I saw him for more than five seconds, but once again I seemed to be looking through some sort of lens that magnified things to a monstrous size. He was a young farm hand of some sort; they'd handcuffed him, and he was barreling along at such a pace that the policemen could hardly keep up with him.

His nose was sweaty and his bulging eyes were blinking with fear — he looked as scared and horrified as a rabbit undergoing vivisection. I'll never forget that face as long as I live. That encounter was very painful for me, and it left me feeling sick. Now they'll prosecute him, I thought; they'll drag him through the courts for a couple of months and then they'll sentence him to death. In the end, I realized that I truly felt sorry for him, and that I would almost have been relieved if, somehow or other, he'd gotten off scot-free. Not that his face was sympathetic, rather the opposite; but I'd seen him at too close quarters — I'd seen those eyes, blinking in agony. Damn it all, I'm not some bleeding-heart sentimentalist. But at such close range he wasn't a murderer, he was just a man. Look, I don't understand it myself; and frankly, I don't know what I would have done if I'd been the judge. But the whole thing left me feeling as sorrowful as if it were my own soul that needed saving."

The Juror

"I had to judge once," Mr. Firbas said, clearing his throat, "because I was called up as a juror. That's when the case of Lujza Kadanikova came before the court, that woman who murdered her husband. There were eight of us men on the jury, and four women. Well, we men agreed beforehand, more or less without saying a word, that those four females would see to it that the woman went free! And so we steeled ourselves against this Lujza in advance.

"By and large, it was an ordinary enough case of an unhappy marriage. Kadanik was a public surveyor who'd married a wife some twenty years younger than he. Lujza was just a young girl when she married, and a witness was found who testified that on the day after her wedding she was already crying, white as chalk and trembling in protest whenever her new husband tried to touch her. I've often thought that it must be an appalling experience sometimes, what an innocent and inexperienced girl goes through after her wedding; her husband's probably accustomed to girls, you see, and treats her accordingly. My guess is, a man can't begin to imagine what it's like. — But the state prosecutor, in turn, ferreted out other witnesses who said that this Lujza had already had something going with some student or other prior to her marriage and that she corresponded with him even after the wedding. In short, it was shown that no sooner was the wedding over than the marriage had already turned sour. Lujza made her physical disgust for her husband clear; after a year she had a miscarriage, and from that time on she had some kind of female disorder. Kadanik went looking elsewhere to compensate for his marriage turning sour, and at home he made a fuss over every cent. On the unhappy day they had another scene, this time on account of a silk blouse, and Kadanik began giving her a piece of his mind about how he wasn't going to be badgered in his own home. That's when Lujza approached him from behind and shot him with a revolver in the base of his skull. Then she bolted down the corridor and banged on the neighbors' door, telling them to go to her husband, that she had killed him and was going to go turn herself in; but she toppled over on the steps, in convulsions. That's the whole case.

"Well, we sat in judgment for twenty days. They say that Lujza used to be a pretty thing, but custody, you know, doesn't do much for female beauty; she looked bloated, with only these angry and hateful eyes blazing out from her pale face. The presiding judge was enthroned up above like justice personified, terribly dignified and almost priest-like in his black robe. Counsel for the prosecution was the best-looking lawyer I've ever seen: strong as a bull, tense and aggressive as a well-fed tiger; you could tell with just what kind of greedy intensity and skill he'd swoop down on his prey sitting there below, hating him so fervently with those burning eyes. Counsel for the defense leaped up irritably every other minute and quarreled with counsel for the prosecution. It was distressing for us jurors, because it seemed like the quarreling wasn't about the trial of the murderous woman, but about some sort of dispute between the prosecution and the defense.

"Well, we were judges representing the people; we'd come there to judge in accordance with the consciences of ordinary people. But even with the best will in the world, we were mostly bored to despair by the lawyers' bickering and the courtroom formalities. The audience pushed their way forward and gloated over the case of Lujza Kadanikova; whenever she was silent from nervous strain and exhaustion, you could hear those people almost grunting with pleasure." Mr. Firbas wiped his forehead, as if he were sweating. "I can tell you, in those moments it was as if I weren't a judge drawn by lot but a man on the rack — as if I myself were compelled to leap up and say, I confess to everything, do with me as you will.

"After that came the witnesses, each of them giving their statements with great significance, inflated with self-importance just because they knew something. And from their testimony you got the impression of a whole town there, a scrap heap of spite, gossip, favoritism, speculation, envy, intrigue, politicking, and boredom. According to the witnesses, the deceased was an honorable and forthright man and a decent citizen, enjoying the finest of reputations; furthermore, he was a womanizer and a tightwad, a brute, a pervert, and an animal; in short, take your pick. Lujza came out worse: they said she was a vain and flirtatious little minx, she wore silk underwear, she didn't give two hoots for housework, she ran up debts —

"Counsel for the prosecution leaned over with an icy smile: 'Defendant, you had an intimate relationship with a certain man even after you were married?'

"The defendant said nothing, but a dull red flush spread across her cheeks.

"Counsel for the defense pounced: 'Might the court hear from so-and-so, whom Kadanik took advantage of when she was a maid in his household? He had a child by her — '

"The presiding judge frowned; you could tell that he was thinking, my God, will this trial never end? — Meanwhile, the painful domestic affairs dragged on without end: which of the two was responsible for initiating the marital strife, how much Lujza received for household expenses, whether her husband had any cause for jealousy. Throughout the hours and hours of this, it sometimes seemed to me that they weren't talking about the dead Kadanik and his marriage, but about me or some other juror or, for all I knew, any one of us. Good Lord, what they were saying about the dead man I've done, too; I suppose everyone everywhere does such things, so why talk about it? It seemed to me as if, one by one, they were stripping down all of us there, men and women both; as if they were washing our private squabbles in public, airing our dirty little intimacies, dredging up the secrets of our beds and habits. Believe me, it was just as if they were describing our own personal lives there, but somehow so cruelly and relentlessly that it seemed like hell. This Kadanik wasn't, as a matter of fact, the worst of men. He was a bit on the rough side, he flew off the handle at his wife and humiliated her; he was heavy-handed and stingy, because he didn't make that much. He was a randy bastard: he seduced the household help and was having an affair with a widow — but maybe it was out of spite and injured male vanity, because Lujza hated him as if he were some kind of disgusting insect. And I can tell you that when one of the defense witnesses testified against the murdered man, about how he was cantankerous and small-minded, a brutal, sexually crude, and domineering man, something akin to dislike and solidarity stirred in us male jurors. Stop right there! we thought, if we could be shot for no worse than *this* — And again, when another witness made things worse for Lujza, saying that she was a featherbrain, a flashy dresser and all those kinds of things, we men in the jury box felt something almost like generosity, something like wanting to take her under our wing, while the four women amongst us pressed their lips together tightly and stared at her with unforgiving eyes.

"For hours and days this conjugal hell dragged on, as seen through the eyes of maids and doctors, neighbors and gossips: the discord and the debts, the illnesses, the household scenes, every nasty, irrational, and agonizing experience that a human couple undergoes. It was like having human entrails hung out on display in all their wretched ugliness. Listen, I have a decent and loving wife; but in those moments I saw not Lujza Kadanikova there below me, but my own wife, my Lida, accused of shooting her husband Firbas in the back of the skull. I felt the terrible, biting pain of that bullet in my head. I saw Lida, pale and swollen, compressing her lips and raking me with eyes frantic with terror, disgust, and humiliation. It was Lida whom they were stripping and eviscerating here; it was my wife, my bedroom, my secrets, my sorrows, my crudeness. I all but wept and said, 'Oh, Lida, see what you have brought us to!' I closed my eyes so that I could drive away those terrible delusions, but the witnesses' statements were even more tormenting in the dark.

And when my eyes stared down in horror at Lujza, my heart constricted: My God, Lida, how you've changed!

"And when I got back home from jury duty that day, Lida was waiting for me impatiently with the question, 'Well, will she be convicted?' — In its own way, the trial was a sensation, attracting the interest mainly of married women — 'I,' my wife announced with agitation and urgent concern, 'I would convict her!'

" 'It's absolutely no business of yours,' I shouted at her; it was harrowing for me to talk about it with her. The final night before the verdict, anxiety closed in on me. I wandered from room to room, contemplating: Suppose we let Lujza go; what use would those four women on the jury be? One more vote *against* conviction, and she'll go free. So what, then, will my vote be? — I found no answer to that; then from out of nowhere the uneasy thought struck me: *I* have a loaded revolver in the bedside table — it's a habit from the army; how easily it might happen that someday it would come in handy for my wife, Lida! I seized the revolver in my hand — couldn't I hide it or just get rid of it altogether? Not yet, I thought wryly, not until I see how things turn out for Lujza! — And then I began torturing myself again: Yes, how will things turn out — and what in heaven's name will I do, what will my vote be?

"On the last day counsel for the prosecution spoke, forcefully and well. I don't know what made him think he had the right, but he made use of every word in the book about the value of family relationships. I listened as if from a distance to how he put such heavy, special emphasis on the words family, domestic life, marriage, husband and wife, the role and obligations of women — they say it was one of the most brilliant speeches ever given before the court. Then Lujza's lawyer took the stand and did a horrible thing: he based his defense on an analysis of sexual pathology. He tried to establish the kind of disgust that a sexually cold or, as they say, frigid woman must feel for the sexual organs of a crude, insensitive man; how her physical disgust grows into hatred; how a woman like that, surrendering to the will and lusts of a ruthless sexual tyrant, becomes a tragic victim. — In that moment you could sense how the entire jury changed course and hardened their hearts against Lujza, how a subconscious disgust broke out among the jurors against these abnormal things that somehow upset and threatened the rules of society or whatever. The four women on the jury were ashen-faced, and their icy hostility bore down on the woman who had violated such things as obligation. And that idiot lawyer went on fervently spreading his sexual theories.

"The presiding judge patiently eyed the shocked faces of the jury and in his summation did his best to salvage the situation. He spoke about neither the family nor sexual serfdom, but about the murdered man, and that made it easier for us jurors. Frankly, from that point of view the case became more digestible for us somehow, more simple and very nearly bearable.

"Up to the final moment I didn't know how I would vote on the question of guilt. But when they put the question before us: Is Lujza Kadanikova guilty of shooting her husband, Jan Kadanik, with intent to kill? — I, whose turn came first, said yes without thinking twice, because in truth she had intended to murder him, and she did.

"After that there was a puzzled silence. I looked over at the four women on our jury. Their expressions were stern and almost ceremonial, as if they were prepared to do battle on behalf of the family.

"When I returned home, my wife Lida burst out, pale with excitement, 'Well, how did it turn out?'

" 'You mean for Lujza,' I said mechanically. 'Twelve votes for conviction. She was sentenced to death by hanging.'

" 'That's awful,' Lida gasped with naive cruelty, 'but she deserves it!'

"Suddenly the tension or whatever it was inside me broke. 'Yes,' I shouted at Lida with an irritability that I myself could not comprehend, 'she deserved it because she was a fool! Just keep in mind, Lida, that if she'd shot him in the temple instead of in the base of his skull, she could claim that he committed suicide. Do you understand, Lida? Then she would have gone free. — Remember that: in the temple!'

"I banged the door shut behind me; I needed desperately to be alone. In case you're wondering, my revolver is still in that unlocked drawer. I never got rid of it."

The Last Things of Man

"Being sentenced to death is a horrible experience," Mr. Kukla said. "I know this, because I once experienced my last moments of life not long before my execution. Needless to say, it happened in a dream; but dreams are as much a part of our lives as anything else, even if they're only on the margin. You won't find much on the margin that speaks to your better qualities, nothing in your life that you go around bragging about; what's out there are sex, fear, vanity, and several other things that we're more or less ashamed of. Maybe these are the last things of man.

"One afternoon I came home exhausted as a pack horse, I'd been working so hard. So I lay down on the floor, and in no time I was sleeping like a log. And then, for no reason at all, I dreamed that the door opened, and there in the doorway stood an utterly unfamiliar man with two soldiers behind him, holding bayonets at the ready; I don't know why, but the soldiers were wearing Cossack uniforms. 'Get up,' the stranger said harshly, 'and get ready. Tomorrow morning we carry out your death sentence. Did you hear me?'

" 'I heard you,' I said, 'but I don't understand why — '

" 'That's not our affair,' the man snapped. 'We're here to serve the order for your execution.' And he banged the door shut behind him.

"Afterwards I stood there, alone, and thought it over. But I don't really know: when a man thinks in a dream, is he really thinking or does he only dream that he's thinking? Were they *my* thoughts, or were they only thoughts that I dreamed, the way we dream of faces? All I know is that I was thinking fast and furiously, and yet at the same time I was marveling at my

thoughts. At first I concentrated, with a certain malicious satisfaction, on the idea that it was all a mistake, that I would be
executed tomorrow morning because of some official blunder and
that *they* would be disgraced and discredited by it. But along with
that a terrible distress arose in me: that I really would be
executed and that my wife and child would be left behind; what
would happen to them, what in God's name would they do — I
can tell you that the pain was genuine, as if my heart were truly
bleeding, and yet at the same time I found it rather pleasant and
gratifying for me to think so solicitously of my wife and children.
Well, well, I said to myself, so these are the last thoughts of a
man who is going to his death! It cheered me up, somehow, that
I was indulging in such overwhelming paternal grief; it struck me
as being rather noble and uplifting. I basked in the idea of telling
my wife about it.

"But then a shock ran through me: I remembered that
executions usually take place in the wee hours around daybreak,
at four or five in the morning, and that I would have to rise up
early in order to be executed. The fact is, I hate getting up in the
morning; and now the image of those soldiers rousing me at
dawn blotted out everything else; my heart plummeted and I
nearly wept with sorrow over my fate. It was so terrifying that it
woke me up, and I could only lie there, gasping with relief. And
I never did tell my wife about that dream."

"The last things of man," said Mr. Skrivanek, and his face
grew red with embarrassment. "I could tell you something about
that, but maybe it would sound silly to you."

"It wouldn't," Mr. Taussig assured him. "Just spit it out!"

"I just don't know," Mr. Skrivanek said uncertainly. "What
I mean is, I once wanted to shoot myself, and so — since Mr.
Kukla here was talking about the margin of life — That's out
there on the margin of life, too: when a man wants to kill
himself."

"Go on," said Mr. Karas, "why did you want to do it?"

"It was out of weakness," said Mr. Skrivanek, turning still redder. "What I mean is, I . . . I'm no good at tolerating pain. And at the time I had inflammation of the trigeminal nerve — The doctors say it can be one of the worst pains that a person can — I just don't know."

"That's true," muttered Dr. Vitasek. "I commiserate with you. Does it keep recurring?"

"It does," Mr. Skrivanek blushed again, "but I no longer want to . . . That is, what I was going to tell you — "

"Then please, tell us," Mr. Dolezal encouraged him.

"It's hard to put it into words," Mr. Skrivanek resisted shyly. "As a matter of fact . . . that pain . . . "

"Would have a man screaming like an animal," remarked Dr. Vitasek.

"Yes. And when it was worst of all . . . the third night . . . I set my revolver on the nightstand. One more hour, I thought, I can't endure it any longer than that. Why me, why is it that I'm the one who has to suffer so much? I kept thinking that a terrible injustice was being done to me. Why me, why is this happening to me — "

"You had medicine to take," growled Dr. Vitasek. "Trigemin or veramon, adalin, algokratin, migradon — "

"I took them," protested Mr. Skrivanek. "Listen, I'd gulped so many pills that . . . that they stopped working. What I mean is . . . those pills put *me* to sleep, but the pain never slept, do you understand? The pain remained, but it was no longer *my* pain, because I was . . . so drugged that I was completely outside myself. I was no longer aware of me, but I was aware of the pain; and it began to seem that the pain was someone else's. I could hear that other being . . . He was howling and moaning so quietly, and I felt so terribly sorry for him . . . I was weeping tears of sorrow. I could feel the pain growing and growing — my God, I thought, what this person is enduring! Perhaps . . . perhaps if I shot him, he wouldn't have to suffer so! But at the same time I was horrified at the thought . . . no, it's not possible, I can't do it! I don't know; suddenly I felt a curious respect for his life, simply because he was undergoing such incredible pain — "

Mr. Skrivanek rubbed his forehead in bewilderment. "I don't know how to describe it to you. Perhaps it was delirium from all those pills, but at the same time it was so incredibly clear to me . . . dazzlingly clear. I had a vision of that being, that other who was suffering and groaning, as humankind . . . as Man himself. And I was only a witness to its torment . . . a night watchman at the bedside of pain. If I hadn't been there beside it, I thought, the pain would have been in vain. It would have been a kind of great achievement, an act of greatness that no one would have known anything about. I mean, earlier . . . when it was *my* pain . . . I'd felt as wretched and pitiful as a worm . . . and every bit as insignificant. But now . . . now that the pain had transcended me . . . I felt almost with a sense of terror how great life truly is. I felt that . . . " Mr. Skrivanek was sweating with embarrassment. "Don't laugh at me. I felt that the pain was a . . . a kind of offering, a sacrifice. That's why, you see, that's why each religion . . . places pain on the altar of its god. That's why there were bloody sacrifices . . . and martyrs . . . and Christ on the cross. I understood that . . . that . . . that a kind of mysterious blessing flows from the pain of Man. That's why we have to suffer, so that life can be sanctified. No joy is strong or great enough . . . And I felt that if I came through this, I would be carrying something like a sacrament inside me."

"And are you?" Father Voves asked with interest.

Mr. Skrivanek blushed violently. "Oh, no," he replied hurriedly, "that's something a person wouldn't know anything about. But ever since that time . . . I've had such respect, such a reverence in me; everything seems more important to me now . . . each little thing and each human being, do you understand? Everything has enormous value. Whenever I see a sunset, I tell myself it was worth that incredible pain. And people, their work, their ordinary lives . . . all of it has value because of that pain. And I know it's a terrible and unspeakable price to pay — But I truly believe that it isn't some evil or punishment; it's only pain, and it serves to . . . to give life this enormous worth — " Mr. Skrivanek stopped, not knowing how to go on. "You've been so kind to me," he suddenly blurted out and, much moved, he blew his nose to hide his burning face.

Acknowledgments

Whereas Čapek knew a great deal about a great many subjects, this translator did not. Thanks for filling those knowledge gaps are due to experts on the criminal justice system and the law, as might be expected, but also to many others who shared their expertise in such varied and fascinating fields as cacti, fortunetelling, Oriental carpets, billiards, orchestra conducting, psychiatry, and the shotput. Among the principal informants: Thomas Bascom, M.D., Frank Drysdale, Ladislav Filip, Sr., Cleve Hadnott, Luboš Hubata-Vacek, Vera and Henry Langer, Claudia Leone, Father Fred Lucci, O.P., Marsha Mabrey, Regina McGlothlin, M.D., Scott Meisner, Hal Misner, Lida O'Donnell, Peg Spaete, Reyn Staffel, Father Augustine Thompson, O.P., L'udovít Treindl, Zdenka Tripp, and Johnny B. and the guys at Luckeys Club Cigar Store. All gave generously of their time and knowledge, and this acknowledgment is offered in return.

Leopold Pospíšil, JUDr. not only instigated my interest in Čapek, but also co-translated "The Last Judgment" with me long ago. That version appeared in *The Realm of Fiction: 61 Short Stories* (McGraw-Hill, 1965), whose editor, James B. Hall, kindly gave permission for its reprinting (in another version) herein. Paul Selver, the first, British translator of half the Pocket Tales in 1931, deserves credit for introducing Čapek to English-language readers in the first place and for finding, on occasion, the precise and perfect word in our sometimes-shared language.

My gratitude also to the Oregon Council for the Humanities for the award of a 1992 Summer Research Fellowship, which provided support for studying how, why, and under what circumstances the Pocket Tales were written. Interviews with B. R. Bradbrook, William E. Harkins, and Josef Škvorecký were a memorable component of the research; and the University of Oregon Knight Library's interlibrary loan department cheerfully tracked down hard-to-find material for me.

Wholehearted thanks in particular to Peter Kussi, who advised me of translation errors with enviable grace and humor. The list of "without whom it couldn't have been done" ends with Catbird publisher Rob Wechsler, who not only made superb editing recommendations, but also suggested a fresh, complete translation of the Pocket Tales in the first place. Responsibility for any remaining errors and for all of the choices that accompany the act of translation remains my own.

Norma (Bean) Comrada has translated a wide range of works by Karel Čapek, and has published articles and given talks on his life and work based on research and interviews conducted in Prague, London, Paris, and the United States. Besides this volume, she has translated Čapek's *Apocryphal Tales* and *Wayside Tales* (consisting of the story collections *Wayside Crosses* and *Painful Tales*), and she did the plurality of the translations included in *Toward the Radical Center: A Karel Čapek Reader*. She lives in Eugene, Oregon.

Garrigue Books is Catbird's imprint for Czech literature in translation. Its name is meant to honor the American most involved in Czech history and culture: Charlotte Garrigue Masaryk, the Brooklyn born-and-bred first first lady of Czechoslovakia.